Blood Ties

A David Danjou Thriller

Steevan Glover

Copyright © 2015 Steevan Glover

The author asserts the right under the Copyright, Designs and Patents Act 1988 to be identified as the author of this work.

All characters in this book are fictitious and any resemblance to actual persons, living or dead, is purely coincidental.

All rights reserved.

Published by Biglove Books 2015 – First Edition

ISBN: 1493504665

ISBN-13: 978-1493504664

Blood Ties

For Hieronymus

Steevan Glover was born in the Seychelles, but lived with his family in Malawi before they eventually settled in Bedfordshire, England. A former drama student and rugby player Steevan is a brand and marketing specialist that lives with his family in a village near Windsor.

Also by the author

The frog and the scorpion

Mighty like a Rose

Find out more about the author and his work at:

www.steevanglover.com

@steevglover

Prologue

He tried not to think about her. He wanted to avoid the thoughts that dwelled on what might have been, what he had missed and the life that could have been. He wanted to stay awake, but he knew sleep would engulf him and with it came the faces and ghosts of his life. At first he had tried to fight them but the demons rose each night to taunt him into making amends, to pay his penance. He knew there could be no escape, it was hopeless, and he would have to live with them for the rest of his days.

With each sleep the demons arrived and with each sleep he understood that he had to look into the very face of hell. Forever a penitent man.

WEDNESDAY

The wheels of the old lorry skidded to a halt on the gravel. The cabin door opened and the rotund driver clambered down, his breathless half-run to the lorry's rear indicating his near cardiac arrest level of physical fitness. He turned his head and scanned the vast isolated lay-by. A steep cliff rose up and hemmed the road in on the far side, while the wooded road and valley side shielded it on the other.

The half-light of the early morning had begun creeping through the valley below; it would take some time to penetrate the secluded and heavily shaded spot. He paused, shifting his melon-like head from left to right looking and listening for his contact. He'd never been late, not once in the many similar trips he'd made. But he always worried that he may end up at one of these meeting points in the middle of France and no one would come. He heard the crunch of the gravel before the voice.

"You have a new lorry?" The voice measured and accented, East European, as always. The driver had never asked where from, but he always assumed Russia.

"Yeah well – this was what was available." He avoided eye contact and finished with the door.

"You got my money?" His voice wavering as he tried to look unthreatened. The man stepped forward, his stylish dress a contrast to the rugged nature of the location. He nodded towards the doors, his large muscled frame defined by the velvet lapelled tailored coat. The aura of a retired heavyweight fighter lingered around him. The cropped grey-flecked, blonde hair framed a stoic, stone carved face.

The door swung open without so much as a creak, the dim interior now illuminated by the slowly rising sun. The big man moved forward, hands clasped together and peered in. Not a flicker of emotion passed across his face at the sight that greeted him.

Deep within the lorry's trailer a cluster of blinking eyes peered back at the open door. They belonged to a huddled group of thirty dishevelled women and children, the youngest child a babe in arms and the youngest woman somewhere in her sixties. All the women had the lines and sags of those that had lived tough lives.

"It is a small load today?" His voice remained placid and unemotional. It was more a statement than a question. The lorry driver shifted from one foot to the other, wanting to unload and move on. "I deliver what I'm given. Don't ask questions and I don't want answers."

The big man turned and looked at him; his usually bright blue eyes looked grey and lifeless as they met the driver's. He said nothing and just held his gaze. The driver gulped and recoiled a touch when, with an efficient sweep, the big man's hand moved into his inside pocket and removed a crisp white envelope. The driver held his hand like an expectant toddler. He knew not to grab for the envelope, not to look desperate; it would come to him soon enough and they always paid for a job well done.

"Do you want to ask a question?" The big man still hadn't blinked.

The lorry driver shook his head.

"You can. Today is special day - you can ask one question... I'll let you?"

The driver swallowed hard. He always had questions, like, why did he never make deliveries on the same day, why did he go from different UK ports to different places all over France and why was he paid in pounds and not Euros for a cash delivery to France? But he understood how this shit worked, he didn't need further information. Not knowing felt safer.

"Don't be scared little man... if you have question, ask it." The voice and expression remained unchanged. The driver struggled to hide is irritation and with an idiotic sense of bravado he spoke.

"I got a question, yeah?"

"So ask it." The big man kept his eyes fixed on the lorry driver. The driver flicked his tongue across his lips, and looked around him.

"Well, I've done a lot of these trips... maybe twelve now."

The big man nodded. "That many?" And then carried on, "But that was not a question."

"No... I know...well on all those trips," he stumbled over his words. "On all those trips there hasn't been a single young woman or man...all of them have been, giffers, old hags... loadsa kids and old women. How come?"

The big man's face cracked into a small smile. The driver mimicked it warily. "That is very good question...

my little friend. A very good question."

The driver's smile broadened and he nodded with simple enthusiasm, eager for the answer. The big man let out a little laugh, patted him forcefully on the shoulder and dropped the envelope into the driver's hands before facing the open lorry. He beckoned the contents to come out, a friendly but firm gesture. They hesitated, reluctant at first, but one by one they edged towards the door, as they slowly emerged several transit style vans drove out of the shadows of the lay-by and encircled the lorry. Their rear doors swished open like giant mouths waiting to be fed.

"Ssshhhhh," the big man whispered at the women and children, his finger pressed to his lips. The tattered group filed out, meekly obeying the silent gestures of the van drivers and clambering out of the truck and into the awaiting vans.

The lorry driver watched as the last of the sorry looking cargo left his lorry, still hoping for his answer. The big man turned, nodded his thanks and held out his hand, inviting the lorry driver to return to his cab and take his vehicle back to England. The driver opened his mouth to speak, but a sense of self-preservation prevented the words forming and he closed the doors and trotted back to the cab.

The driver watched him in his side mirror; the Russian stood stock still as the lorry and vans chugged into life, belching fumes, and pulled away from the giant lay-by and onto the deserted road.

The big man stood alone in the lay-by and smiled at the question the lorry driver had posed. He noted the organisation should not use him for these trips again.

David Danjou sipped the red wine from the sturdy scarred glass tumbler. The deep flavours of the Dordogne countryside and hot French sun sang across his tongue. The wine while unrefined had a simple beautiful taste. And it was cheap. It only cost three or four Euros a bottle in the local hyper Marché, you certainly couldn't get it in England, and David doubted you'd even be able to get it outside of the region. Produced by a small local vineyard, a throwback to a less commercial time and producing no more than ten thousand bottles a year. He gazed happily at the unlabelled bottle that sat on the cheap white plastic table alongside his half-full tumbler. He'd had several glasses since his release from the labours at the vines. The sun had just begun its slow late summer dive into night; he'd have plenty of time to enjoy the remaining wine and admire the sunset in solitude.

He leant forward, shielded his eyes from the bright setting sun and peered out along the dusty track stretching from the vineyard and winery towards the village of Sainte-Innocence, which sat with Gallic élan in the valley below. A car rolled along the narrow uneven road towards him; it had the air of something lost. It moved as if it had never been here before and that it wasn't even sure where here was.

David ducked his head back into the shadow of the tattered awning, leaving only his black-clothed body exposed to the last rays of the sun. His tanned skin had that natural, working-the-land hue. His fair hair and skin prevented him from achieving true Mediterranean deep brown tan levels, but he had a rich golden honey brown glow that spoke of health and vigour.

He tore off another hunk of near stale baguette, dunked it in the wine and then popped it into his mouth. A gooey lump of unpasteurised Brie followed. He chewed the food like a person with no one to impress, mouth open and lips smacking. David preferred eating alone. He hadn't done so for sixteen years of his life, genuine privacy is one of the simple pleasures others take for granted, but he embraced being alone and celebrated solitude.

He sat at the furthest table from the narrow door that led to a makeshift bar of planks on up-turned barrels. It served only the vineyard's red wine in unlabelled old bottles. His table afforded the best views of the lush sun-kissed valley and rolling countryside as it spread toward the famous old town of Bergerac.

He usually sat here. Always alone.

A scattering of men, chatted and played cards in threes and fours around the other tables. One or two worked at the winery with him, but the older ones had strolled out from the village to play petanque in the cool of the late afternoon before enjoying a bottle of the vineyard's finest, accompanied by copious cigarettes and impassioned debate. They knew David now. They left him alone to enjoy his wine and the setting sun, they'd all had a tough day in the vines, but at least, they mused to themselves, 'you don't have to go home to my wife'.

The vehicle crunched along the road, eased itself through the tired stone gateposts and pulled up in front of the nest of tables, blocking David's view. A cloud of fine white dust kicked and swirled before settling in a delicate blanket on the unimpressed occupants of the bar's chairs. The nondescript silver hire car had the tell-tale caked-on dust patches of a vehicle that had been up and down many tracks like this one. The air-conditioner whirred, draining the power of the inadequate engine that whined a feeble protest. A tourist's car, it had no right to be here. The Sales Office sat on the other side of the vineyard, signposted via obvious painted barrels, along another road on the southern side of the village. Only workers and locals came down this road; neither of which drove hire cars with air-con.

David's grey-blue eyes fixed on the driver. The car's door burst open and the driver clambered out, his joints stiff from sitting for a long time. His crinkled cream cotton suit looked untidy and like it should be on a younger fitter man. The white cotton shirt that sat under the scruffy jacket may have once looked good on the mannequin, but now it had lost its fight to contain the man's mid-life, easy-living gut and as he stretched the drive out of his tired limbs David saw more of the man's pallid hairy belly than he needed to. His dirty 'Man from Del-Monte' attire came topped with a cheap service station style straw Fedora, which he popped onto his head with a self-conscious shuffle.

The little moment of theatre was lost on the old men to David's left, who remained captivated with their cards and debating the merits of the France of the past. David noticed him. He watched his every move; his life and training had made him observant and cautious. Not that you could ever tell by his outward demeanour.

"Hello....*BONJOUR*....er parlay vooze Anglay," the man managed in his best butchering of a French accent.

David hoped one of the locals would pick up the offering and deal with the stranger. In true French style, they ignored him.

"Missyerr, Parlay vooze Anglay…please?"

David accepted his fate.

"Oui," he replied, as if a native. "Un peu."

"I'm sorry?" the man moved around the front of the car and towards David's table. "What was that?"

"I speak Engleesh…a leetal," David repeated in deliberately broken English accent. One of the old men looked across at him and let out a smoke-filled cackle.

"I'm looking for someone," Dirty Del Monte said. David nodded, his face the same placid mask. The intruder rubbed his unshaved chins.

"An Englishman… he might be living down here?" he removed his hat and wafted it airily towards the open vista. "Might be passing through, may have been and gone."

David nodded again, but remained silent. If the man had come to the vineyard then someone in the village would have told him an Englishman worked there. He'd had a brief moment of small town celebrity when he first arrived, a novelty Englishman that spoke French like a native and could spend time in the sun without going a blotchy pink. He had no desire to move on, not just yet anyway.

"Do you know of any Englishmen working here?" Del

Monte pushed on.

"Zis man av err name?" David asked.

"Yeah, he used to go by the name of David Edwards…You heard that name, Mr…er?"

David narrowed his eyes and searched the man's tired old face, the bloated and veined nose indicated a penchant for alcohol, the bags under the eyes betrayed that this man did not sleep well. Fat, tired and greying he may be, but he didn't appear to be stupid. Nor did he look like he represented any kind of legitimate authority. David appreciated that and felt a little reassured.

"Danjou…ma name iz Daveed Danjou." David emphasised the French pronunciation of his first name. He didn't offer his hand to be shaken, rather sipped his wine instead. "Non monsieur - I av not heard zis name." David hadn't heard the name David Edwards spoken for several years. It was an unwelcome signpost to his past.

"I have a picture as well… it's a little old." The old man tugged a dog-eared snapshot from his jacket side pocket. It looked like it had been liberated from a family album. David took the photo and examined it.

His mother had taken the photo.

He could recall the day clearly.

His final day in England.

The last time he'd seen his mother and sister. The sun had shined that day; Windsor castle stood resplendent in the background, but he remembered that as the shutter had clicked, he had known he would be unlikely to see her for a long time and maybe never again. The creased piece of cellulose caused a wave of memory induced emotion to run through him. He knew he was the man in the photo, but others might not see the likeness. The young man in the photo looked athletic rather than slim and his downbeat ashen face was partially hidden under an unruly mop of sandy hair. The features appeared symmetrical and proportioned; nothing too prominent or noticeable. A world and almost a lifetime away from the powerful, tanned and heavily muscled figure that sat looking at the photo. David had added at least two stone to his six foot frame since the picture had been taken. The young man of the photo, with his sad hopeless expression, had become a well-worn veteran. A cautious iron-hard, bulldog tough man confident of his place in the order of things.

"It iz an old fertow monsieur." He handed it back; he'd looked at it for too long. David took a slug of his wine emptying the tumbler; he pushed his hand through his habitually short, militaristic grey-flecked fair hair, resting his arm behind his head.

"Yeah it is… he's been away from home a long time. Picture was taken a while ago." He never took his eyes off David. He didn't need to look at the picture to make a comparison. He'd looked at it way too many times already. David met the man's gaze and both men held the stare, sizing each other out, seeking a truth.

"Peepal zay change monsieur," David interrupted.

The scrape of a plastic chair across gravel and the noticeable drop in background chatter caught his attention. He flicked only his eyes in the direction of the disturbance.

"Est-ce que tout est bien? Que ce clown veut-il?"

Marcel, a gnarled figure from the group near the bar moved towards them; but halted halfway when he caught David's eye.

"Il veut trouver l'Anglais qui travaille ici," David said, informing the inquisitive old man.

"Aucun Anglais ici, ils ne sont pas bienvenue." The old man said it with as much venom as he could muster. David smiled appreciating the sentiment.

"What did he say?" Mr Del Monte looked to David for translation.

"He said 'No Anglais here' monsieur."

"And before that?"

"He wanted to know what ze clown wanted."

David let the insult sink in.

"I told him you iz looking for zis English man." He waved at Del Monte's pocket that housed the battered photograph.

The old man pushed his hand, palm down, back and forth and at the foreigner, as if trying to move him along by thought and gesture alone.

"Peut-être cette personne ne veut pas être trouvée," he added.

David didn't wait for the question. He translated while at the same time using his hand to placate the old man back into his seat.

"He said maybe zis person don't want te be found?"

Mr Del Monte looked from the old man to David and

considered the passionate exchange as is if weighing up what he knew with what he suspected.

"He may not. But I've been hired to find him and deliver a message. So if you know the man I'd be grateful of an introduction."

David shrugged his reply.

"You joost want to geev a mess-arge?"

"Nothing more." Del Monte had opened his arms out in a placatory gesture of goodwill and attempted a charming smile.

"Is the wine good here?" he asked pointing at the bottle.

"Zis is France monsieur - C'est bien."

Without being asked Del Monte pulled out a chair and sat down at David's table and mopped his brow with a crumpled handkerchief before replacing his silly hat.

"May I?" he said pointing at the bottle.

David shrugged an indifferent Gallic reply. Reaching over to a neighbouring table Del Monte scooped up an unused tumbler and poured himself a glass. He slurped it up and swallowed the wine hard. The sun began setting fast now and shadows across the courtyard had lengthened. The old men began the sedate collection of their things and started their goodbyes.

"I'm staying in the village tonight, at the little hotel on the square."

David nodded, he knew it well. The best bar in town. Very local. Saint-Innocence had nothing to offer the average tourist, it had no day destination appeal; the only visitors being the renters of gites and apartments in the surrounding valley who came in to town to stock up on supplies and cheap wine.

"If you are in town, come in, I'll gladly buy you a drink."

"What is the mess-arge for the zee man… if I see Im I'll give it to heem."

Del Monte stood up and drained his glass. He hitched his trousers and smiled. "Thanks, if you see him, tell him where I am. I want to give him the message personally."

"Who shood I zay is askeeng for him?"

"Tell him James Thomas is looking for him… he won't know me."

"And ooh should I say yoo are?"

"I'm a private investigator from London, tell him that he has a message from Eve Du Pisanie and that it's for his ears only."

David felt him watching him, looking for what he thought would be the inevitable response to the woman's name. He got nothing, nothing more than the same stone cold face he'd seen since he arrived.

David gritted his teeth and sat motionless as James Thomas, PI, returned to his car and flopped back in to the seat with the grace of a wallowing hog. He fired up the engine and thrashed the car out through the gates and back down the lane – scattering the homeward bound old men as it sped past.

Eve Du Pisanie. A name dredged from his grim past. At its mention a shot of adrenalin pulsated through his veins and reverberated through his heart. Hearing it should have left a warm contented feeling in the pit of his stomach, but David didn't work like that anymore. Instead he had an empty, aching butterfly feeling of anxiety.

He just asked himself, 'why now'?

Eve Du Pisanie flicked open the local newspaper and scanned the inside cover headlines. Her eyes tracked top left to top right across the double page, she found what she had expected to see halfway down the left page. As always the picture took up more space than the actual article and, as had become tradition with the Slough Express and their coverage of her, they'd used a full length picture. She winced at the headline, she detested the 'Crusading Civil Rights' angle that they had decided to label her with. Eve's moral driving force had always been, justice, the helping of those without a voice. She turned over the front cover and looked for the date, the paper came out two days earlier and she mentally rebuked herself for having failed to read the article before, not that it had been worth reading. They had managed to skip any real detail or even the salient point that Eve and her team had more evidence of organised crime running more brothels in the Windsor and Slough area. Instead the article rehashed some elements from the bigger story of four months ago when she and her partner had first exposed the sheer scale of immigrant prostitution in the area and the seeming indifference and tolerance of it by the local authorities.

Eve had hoped the paper would follow that up with a piece on how the situation hadn't changed and in fact had appeared to get worse. Instead, this new article appeared too simply portray her as a moaning woman on the same doomed crusade that had already failed to make a difference. A figure strode by the frosted glass wall of the office, the movement caused Eve to look up and she recognised the scrunchy tied pony tail of her friend and sometime business partner Jacqui Edwards. "JACQUI!" she called out and watched as the head turned and searched for the shout before finding Eve. She pushed into the office without pause and flopped with a confidence of a comfortable acquaintance into the chair opposite.

"What ho Evie?"

"Jacqui... late start this morning I see," Eve teased.

"I am indeed. Late night fun and frolics can play havoc with your working week... you should try it."

"What, coming in to work late?"

"No... having fun the night before and yes even on a work night!" Jacqui pushed her hand to her mouth in faux shock and then smiled at her friend. They ribbed each other like this regularly and those that saw it and weren't in on the joke could mistake the banter for malice. Eve stuck out her tongue in response to the jibe while Jacqui scanned the desk, she didn't need her police training to assess the situation.

"Collecting your press clippings?"

"I have only just got round to reading it. It's shit isn't

it?"

"Utter bollocks, but then what had you expected?"

"Something better than this." Eve said with a genuine disgust.

"As soon as they sent that spotted numpty with an aversion to deodorant you knew it could never be an award winning piece of journalism, even by local paper standards,"

"True enough... but Jacs... it didn't even mention how the police have done nothing since our last investigation. It just paints me as some mad crusader who isn't making a difference!" Eve folded her arms in a genuine huff.

"Good picture though, full length. You may well have become the Slough Express's answer to the Sun page three girl."

"Stop it..."

"Seriously Eve... you do look hot, you and your leg revealing suits do make for good photos and oh look, yes they mention it again, former model, there it is in the last line."

Eve clutched the paper off her friend and folded it shut. "I wasn't a model!" She had been told often enough by drunken idiots that she looked 'gorgeous' and while she didn't resent it she knew, even in these more enlightened times, that people made assumptions based on her looks.

Jacqui stayed quiet for a moment, knowing Eve had few genuine sensitive issues but her looks had proved to be one. Jacqui appreciated her friend's grace and style and had never tried to compete with it and had as a result never been jealous of it. While no knock-em dead stunner herself, she liked her look and it proved alluring in its own way. Eve didn't speak and the silence rolled on. They looked at each other and then finally Jacqui spoke about what had been at the back of both their minds in the last few days. "I had another letter yesterday," she said.

"Right... same as a last time?" Eve said.

"More or less. It seemed to be in response to the Radio Berkshire interview we did. Standard cut out letter format and short. Implicit though. *'Stop interfering or we will have to take action'*. Nothing illegal or legally threatening."

Eve sighed. "I'll probably get one in the next day or so as well then."

They stayed silent for a moment, contemplating that this would make it the third letter each that they had received in the last few months, they had immediately reported it to the police and had been given little help or sympathy. Frankly there had been a lack of interest. Even Jacqui's ex-force status had failed to garner much of a response. But then Jacqui had decided that for her private security incarnation she'd adopt her mother's maiden name, Evards, and had dropped the Edwards except for private use. As a private investigator she had now jumped sides and her links to Eve hadn't endeared her to anyone in the police

"Peter rang me last night, he'd read the article," Eve said.

"Oh the missing man, what did my brother want this time? Embarrassing him again are we?" Jacqui sniped.

"Basically... yes. He called me irresponsible and said I was a headline chasing harpy!"

"I see the charm school lessons are working well then?" Jacqui had little respect for her older brother and hadn't seen him for some time. "Ignore him Eve, he's been so distant recently, frankly he's been horrid to Mum and well he's so wrapped up in himself and his 'new job' that he thinks he's the centre of the universe." Jacqui said it with a tinge of sadness in her voice.

"Is he coming to the funeral?" Eve asked.

"Yeah... he'll be there. Not many others will be."

"Is it worse than you thought?"

"A little, it's sad and I feel bad for mum. We knew he wasn't captain popularity but I figured more would come when it came to it." Jacqui played with her fingernail as she spoke. Eve didn't say anything else, she just reached out her hand and covered her friend's and gave it a reassuring squeeze. "Anything new on David?" She asked. Jacqui shook her head. "He's the best you have Jacqui, give him a little more time." Jacqui shrugged.

The little town of Saint-Innocence came to life around 9.00 p.m.; and that life drank, talked, sang and danced into the small hours. The narrow streets all appeared to lead, maze-like, to the central square. A cobbled market area that by day thronged with stalls and their purveyors of local produce. The market happened on a daily basis and remained the hub of food shopping in this tiny corner of France. If you wanted the delights of the air-conditioned hypermarché then you had to head thirty kilometres North towards Bergerac. Now as 9.00 p.m. approached, the cafes and restaurants that ringed the square had spilled their contents and tables into it, filling it with chatter and the sound of people relaxing.

David stood at the top of the small rise of Rue De Gaulle, one of the larger streets in the town and surveyed the scene. He had changed into a fresh pair of baggy black linen trousers and fitted black cotton t-shirt and then slouched into a cotton artisan style jacket. His sockless feet tucked into the black ankle boot style trainers he always wore. He referred to it as his everyman attire, neither smart nor scruffy, but acceptable to all, no matter the occasion. He focused on the hotel bar on the far side of the square; enthusiastic drinkers obscured the bar itself, while the cluster of tables, inside and out, had people squashed around them. A normal, summer's Friday night. It didn't take long for him to visually sift through the mêlée of people and find James Thomas.

He sat alone, in the same clothes as earlier, at an inside table at the back of the hotel's narrow bar. He sipped a glass of red wine. The slow measured rise and fall of his drinking hand indicated he had been there since he left David several hours ago.

As a rule, David didn't really talk to people. He remained polite, as he detested rudeness, but he tried wherever possible to keep conversations within the realms of small talk. He aspired to be unremarkable, a shadow that moved through people's lives without causing concern. Badly dressed investigators were not, therefore, high on his list of potential candidates to chat with.

Training and discipline induce habit and that habit required him to scope out and recce the ground ahead before advancing. Saint-Innocence didn't have many visitors; anyone new stuck out. James Thomas looked as conspicuous as a warning flare, and although he won the worst dressed 'out-of-towner' award he did have company. A smattering of tourists sat at the tables of various bars; they looked starched and uncomfortable.

David began the slow descent down the tame incline. House owners sat in folding chairs outside the doors of their white washed houses, he nodded occasional recognition and greetings as he moved towards the square. He paused just before moving from the street to the square and reviewed the terrain once more. The perspective changed; angles differed. He recalculated, adjusted his assumptions and took in the scene again. David usually mooched to the café on the right hand side of the square. He liked Marcel, the owner; a roly-poly man with a jowly face and bushy moustache. As comically French as a man could be. David looked to make his apologies that he would be going to a competitor when he noticed the two men.

Not tourists.

Not local.

They sat comfortably upright, with an air of self-assurance, their tanned and toned skin wrapped in black shirts and black chino style trousers. Solid, with broad shoulders and short hair, the men could have been brothers. The rigidity of their backs and the serious look on their faces told David they weren't out for a night of fun.

He weaved through the lithe teenagers that draped themselves over their scooters in the middle of the square. They squabbled and all talked at once in that hyper way only the young can, ignoring the soft striding "L'homme en noir". Only one girl looked up and took notice, admiring David's profile as he moved, pantheresque, through their ranks.

He paused at the hotel's exterior tables and peered into the bar from the makeshift perimeter. James Thomas, face flushed with a red wine blusher, sat in the back right corner and lazily ran his eyes over the derrières of the female patrons slouched at the bar. David watched as his gaze fell upon the round backside of a brunette. James Thomas let an appreciative smile play across his lips. David worked his way around the tables and up into the bar, the room held the heat and smell of the day, lacking the cooling breeze that had descended on the square. The smell of cigarette smoke hung heavily in the air, spirals of it dancing in the turbulence created by the ineffectual ceiling fan. Sacha Distel's dulcet tones reverberated around the bar. Francine, proprietor and Distel devotee, refused to play anyone else since the crooner's demise some years before. Now the music had become as integral to the bar as the furniture and fixtures.

David moved down the length of the bar, he cut across James' gaze as he passed the much admired backside. Once at the back of the room, he leaned casually against the far wall, blocking the corridor leading to the lavatory and looked down at the dishevelled man. He waited for several beats, surprised but unconcerned that the so-called private investigator hadn't noticed his arrival. However, his needle of concern jumped as he cast his gaze back across the square towards Marcel's café. The two mystery men remained unmoved, their backs rigid and their eyes focused on the hotel bar. David downloaded the information. Coincidences and surprise visitors made him uncomfortable.

"Why does Eve Du Pisanie want to get a message to David Edwards?" David ensured his words came through strong and clear. His voice cut through the hububb of the bar and the warblings of the late Mr Distel, his phoney accent cast aside.

James Thomas looked up, surprised by the voice from above. It took a beat or two for him to place the face, once he had, a little grin followed the blank expression.

"Are you David Edwards or are you David Danjou?" he said with a chortle.

"I'm David Danjou… like I said before," he replied.

"My message is for Mr Edwards." He sipped his wine by way of emphasising his point. David shot a glance over at the two men at Marcel's, their focus now trained on the investigator and him.

"David Edwards doesn't exist anymore."

"He's dead?" asked Thomas.

"No the name doesn't exist anymore. It and the man that was David Edwards ceased to be years ago." David wanted to keep it simple. "So…why does Eve Du Pisanie want to get a message to David Edwards?" he asked again.

"Mine is not to reason why, young man. It is but to do… I have been tasked with passing on a message. I am not privy as to the thought processes behind it." He wasn't looking at David, his eyes were back on the now dancing buttocks at the bar.

"You should be aware that when an identity is no longer relevant to a person and it's discarded, they tend to be wary of those investigating it… they have moved on and want others to leave them be." David affected his most reasoned tone.

"I concur… Monsieur Danjou, really I do. The part I struggle with, is caring." His eyes moved up to look at David's. "You see - I know you're David Edwards, now I know you're David Danjou, formerly David Edwards. But I don't care. Do you understand?"

David nodded.

"I don't care who you are or who you were, or what you did. Frankly, finding you has been a complete pain in the arse, and I fucking well hate France." He let out a sarcastic smile.

David nodded again, he focused on the 'what you did'– clearly the old man had investigated and knew about David Edwards' past. He cast an eye out of the window. The two men had left their table, Marcel stood over the table collecting the bill and payment. David did a quick scan, but could not spot the figures in the bustling square. Maybe he was wrong about them.

"So listen up sunshine – I'm back to England tomorrow and my final report will be that I found you, that you're now called David Danjou and that you didn't want to hear the message. Alright by you?"

The old man's belligerence grated. His wine

consumption had been enough for him to affect pompous buffoonery, and David wanted to be away from him as quickly as possible.

"Tell them what you want… but remember one thing. You didn't find David Edwards. David Edwards is dead."

David didn't wait for a reply, he swooped down the corridor past the lavatory and into the cramped and deserted kitchen. Francine didn't bother competing with the restaurants in town. David stepped out of the disused kitchen and into the cool dark of the alley at the hotel's rear. It didn't matter who wanted to find him or why. He lived only for the present and the future; he'd made that bargain with himself a long time ago. David knew that there are few second chances in life and even fewer people prepared to offer them to people like him. Saint-Innocence had been a pleasant interlude, but tomorrow he'd move on, maybe head east and the Ardeche.

David stood in the courtyard behind the hotel and focused on the starlit sky and tried to contain his frustration at Mr Del Monte's irascible nose poking into his life. He moved with languid ease round the corner and onto a small alley that led to a larger street, which in turn would run back to the square. He'd settle at his customary table at Marcel's café, maybe have a beer and some Moules before snaffling several brandies.

He patted his pockets as he walked, hoping that some cigarettes and a lighter would magically appear in them. He shouldn't smoke, but maybe Marcel would have a filtered cigarette. The point of living your life for you is to do what you feel, when you feel like it. The alley had no street lights and what little ambient light there was escaped from the buildings on either side. No car could fit down it; this was no major thorough-fare. Clad head-to-toe in his habitual black, David proved hard to spot and as he pondered the varied merits of smoking. He saw, up ahead, the bright glowing end of a cigarette as a figure sucked heavily on it. The man stood a hundred yards ahead and as David's eyes adjusted to the light he could see the man stood with his back to him, at the very exit of the alley into the main street. David watched him flit a furtive glance round the corner and down towards the square, and then back the other way. He did it again and then once more in quick succession. David cocked his head and listened hard. The low murmurings of the town square frivolities obscured most other noise; the sound rose over the buildings and sounded as if a neighbour had their TV on too loud. David pressed himself a little more into the wall and eased forward, his eyes never leaving the dark figure. He recognised a man waiting in hiding when he saw one, and with the day's occurrences already unsettling him, David decided to proceed with a little more caution.

He'd cut the distance to fifty yards, when he recognised the figure, clad in black, with cropped hair. Unmistakeably, one of the men from Marcel's Café. One of the men that had been watching him and the old PI a few moments ago.

David crouched, his limbs almost moving of their own free will, his combat senses on full alert. He moved forward and then halted, too close now to make any more direct progress. The man's manner and posture betrayed that he stood in wait for someone to come up the street from the square. Ambush.

David nodded agreement to himself that the man's

position, head forward, shoulders against the wall and legs braced showed his focus was forward and that he had no idea that someone had taken up position behind him. David wanted to move back down the alley and loop round in to the square via another route. He wanted to forget the man. He wanted to ignore the fact he was waiting in ambush for someone. But David knew they had been watching him, one person had turned up today uninvited looking for him, why not two more? Coincidences don't exist.

David shut his eyes and breathed in and out slowly, calming his heart rate and controlling the adrenalin now bubbling through him. Trouble imminent, David would deal with it. It's what he knew best.

Where was the man's partner?

The dull calm of the alley suddenly reverberated with the booming voice of a drunk Englishman. "Fucking phone… fucking France… shithole… no reception crapola. Jesus…" The man slurred, his irritation underlined by the stream of beeps his phone emitted as he punched at the buttons with his chubby finger.

The voice belonged to James Thomas. Pomposity personified.

The man ahead of David tensed, he bent at the knee and readied himself. The voice drew nearer, less aggressive, now no more than a mutter. Behind it came another sound, the faster rhythmic tapping of well-heeled shoes on cobbles. David skipped forward, taking advantage of the distraction, cutting the distance to just twenty yards behind the man. James Thomas moved into view, bumbling along the cobbled avenue, oblivious to the alley and the existence of his would-be attacker. He stuttered a step and then came to a teetering halt, his mobile phone held out in front him. He appeared to be inspecting it, admiring the aesthetic; David recognised the action of a man searching for a signal. The footsteps sped up and a streak of black moved in behind the drunk old man.

The hidden man's partner from the café.

He moved at pace, his actions measured, rehearsed even. He took hold of the PI's limp right arm and wrenched it round and behind his back while marching him forward. The force of the attack raised the victim on to his toes and he careered towards the alley wall. The hidden man sprang forth and the duo passed over the threshold of the alley and into the hidden shadows away from the avenue. He grabbed the other arm and put it into an elbow lock, the mobile dropped from the PI's hand and the second attacker caught it. James collided, face first, with the alley wall. The sound of flesh smacking hard surfaces has a familiar sound, David acknowledged the force used and surmised that the old man would be sporting a broken nose and bloodied mouth at the least. He'd be groggy but he doubted if he would have been knocked out. The forehead is a tough bone to crack.

David adjusted his position, he crouched and edged forward along the wall, keeping his hands on the ground and remaining in the darkest shadows. He waited for the moment to move forward, attack fast becoming his only option.

The first attacker, the taller of the two, spun Thomas around to face him. The old man wobbled but held his balance. His grubby white cotton shirt had blood splatters down the front. The second attacker rose to his feet with the phone in his hand. His fingers flicked across the buttons as he searched the contents.

David edged closer, eager to determine the reason for the assault. He didn't much care what happened, but if he might be involved then he wanted to know.

James Thomas moved his groggy gaze from one to the other. "Wha' do you two fuckers want?" It came as more of a demand than a question. The shorter of the two jabbed his arm forward and rammed his fist into his hardened gut. A short, well trained and precise punch, David hardly saw the arm move. Thomas absorbed the full force of the blow, he fell back against the wall and clutched his stomach.

"Cheeky wankers." He managed to splutter out.

"Be quiet fat man". The taller attacker's voice had the familiar clipped tones and heavy accent of an East European. David noted it, Russian he judged.

"You are big pain in ass… making us come way down here… you know that. My friend – he does not like France." The man's tone stayed monotonous and unemotional.

"Me neither," murmured the old man through a mouth full of blood. "Full of fucking French."

The Russian looked blankly back, then said, "You should not be working down here fat man."

"You the tourist board?" he replied.

"What?"

"Cut to the chase comrade... can't you see I've got bleeding to do?"

David half smiled. He admired the old fella's metal. He certainly had balls. David couldn't see the Russian's face but he'd bet he wasn't smiling.

He'd have lost the bet.

The big Russian did smile. A sick, patronising smile that showed his nicotine stained teeth. His colleague, without prompting, took hold of Thomas's left hand and violently wrenched the little finger with an audible snap. The old man gasped for breath as the pain shot through his arm, He stuttered and panted out groans of agony.

David waited.

"I am a messenger. That is first message." The big Russian said.

"The second message is easier... I tell. You nod you understand. You understand?"

Thomas nodded.

David crept closer. He pressed himself further against the wall, no more than thirty yards from the trio on the other side of the alley, hidden in the shadows. He primed his limbs and readied himself with a deep breath.

"Message you need to understand... what you do for a living is dangerous. Pushing your nose into people's business is dangerous. Understand?" He prodded the old man in the gut.

Thomas nodded he understood. No clever comeback.

"Good. We make progress. Stay away from France,

don't investigate here don't investigate in Slough." The smaller Russian showed his colleague the phone. He glanced at the screen before curtly nodding his approval.

"Now fat man... you send this message. You send it to the bitch lawyer that hired you." His face lost what remnant of joviality it had. David noticed the two men stiffen as they handed the phone over.

James Thomas read the text on the screen, the little square of green light spotlighted his features and the damage done to his face. He nodded in defeat, taking the phone and fiddling with buttons before turning the phone to face the Russians.

"Well done," the Russian offered.

Then David saw the knife. The flash of steel caught the moonlight as the smaller Russian dropped the blade down his coat sleeve and into his palm. Nothing big or frightening, but a practical weapon and in the right hands it could easily kill a man. David knew the time had come.

David shot to his feet in one movement.

Now less than twenty yards to cover. His leap up had taken care of the first five. Two big softly landed strides and he had less than five to go. He rose into the air, aiming for the nearest Russian, the one with the blade. His leg stretched out, he flexed at the knee, horizontal to the floor, perpendicular to his upright torso and planted his heel squarely into the ribs, behind the Russian's arm.

He had taken less than two seconds to reach them.

He'd made almost no sound.

The first the Russian knew of David was when his

ribcage caved in upon the impact of David's foot. The air rushed from his lungs as the ribs snapped and ripped inwards puncturing his left lung. The force of the strike blasted him off his feet and into the second bigger Russian. The force of his colleague barrelling into him barged him sideways back out into the street, but he stayed upright.

David landed on the balls of his feet. His eyes scanned the revised scenario and he sidestepped the gasping prostrate Russian and moved towards the foe still upright. The big Russian had done well to remain standing, David admired that, but he still hadn't computed what had happened. His eyes flicked to his colleague, then to the prostrate old man, who had not been as stable, he too had slumped back against the wall and down to the floor.

David skipped two steps sideways and then pivoted, forcing one leg up. The side-on kick hit the Russian in the throat and the foot rose up under the chin. The force shattered the lower jaw, but not before the powerful blow had crushed his larynx and windpipe. The Russian flew back and landed in a strangulated heap in the lit avenue. David considered the damage and frowned. Too much force. The Russian would be dead within a minute. Not ideal, he'd meant to only take him down, not out. Collateral damage.

David spun to meet the potential retaliation of the remaining Russian. David needn't have worried. Now on his knees the man wheezed and groaned, his eyes wide with agonised terror. Bile, blood and drool leaked from his mouth. His lungs filling with blood. He would be dead within minutes as well, but he'd drown in his own bodily fluids. '*Shit,*' thought David. Two dead. Careless. He would need to rethink his trip to the Ardeche. He scooped up the knife. A neat razor-sharp K-bar hunting knife with a four-inch blade now covered in blood.

He'd been quick, but not quick enough.

David looked at the slumped figure of the old PI and the telltale dark wet patch that spread over his middle. The Russian had hit him hard and the knife had pierced the liver. The old man let out a slow gurgle.

Three dead any moment now, he thought.

David moved to cradle the dying man.

His head lolled into David's arms and the dimming eyes focused on his face one last time.

"You?" he said, confused.

"Me… taking the air. I thought I might help?"

"Shame you didn't get here a bit quicker."

David stayed silent.. "Who were they?" he finally asked.

"A couple a wankers." James croaked.

"Seriously... who were they?"

The old man coughed and blood filled his mouth. "Wannabe gangsters. Russians from Slough is my guess."

"What did they want with you?"

Thomas shook his head, "My trip was nothing to do with them... nothing. It was about you!" David could see the man's life draining away. Despite the half-light his skin had lost the pinky tones and had begun to look grey. He had precious few moments left to live.

"I best give you that message... no point pissing about now. Can't get fired, can I?"

David smiled.

"I was to tell you that you can come home, your father has died."

Then, so did he.

David's eye's narrowed and his face went blank. He kept his eyes on the old man. He had just killed two men, a third had now died in his arms telling him his father had passed away. Death is never routine, but the more you see of it the more numb to it you become.

David had seen a lot of death.

All of it needless. All of it avoidable.

He'd deal with the consequences of his actions tonight when alone in the dark, it always came the same way. He'd discovered early on that the taking of a life wasn't the problem. Living with it was.

He picked up the mobile phone, a bulky and unfashionable model. The scuffs and scratches testament to its hard short life. He looked at the screen and then flicked through the menu and located 'messages sent'. He opened the last one sent. It read:

"I have been convinced to retire. Maybe you should too. Staying here. A very clear message coming soon."

He scrolled on and found the recipient's details. The screen blinked and the name appeared.

Eve Du Pisanie. He couldn't hide any longer.

THURSDAY

Wladimir Povetkin rubbed a calloused hand over the grey stubble on his prominent chin. He had time to finish his tea, shave and dress before the meeting. He didn't like to rush his mid-morning break.

The glass cup sat in its ornate silver holder, the hot sweet milk-free tea enveloped a single slice of lemon. Wladimir believed in habit; habit defined a person, he had faith in the concept of reason and action. When a man breaks his habit it causes ripples and vibrations, surges, in the natural balance of things. Wladimir liked to be able to recognise the blips in the natural balance of the people around him. Habit often proved the ideal signpost.

No matter the day, or where he was, at 11.00am. Wladimir took tea. As he had aged, he found that savouring the steamy aroma of the tea, the ceremony of the moment, mattered as much as the actual drinking of it.

He took an inelegant sniff.

He sat back from the table and lounged on the velveteen cushions that adorned the circular booth where he sat. As one of eight booths that sat on the raised upper circle of the restaurant it spectated on the central, round polished maple dance floor that in turn was surrounded by dining tables and chairs. A deep blood maroon colour with matching carpet, and cushions contrasted against the white table clothes and gold Doric columns that supported the narrow viewing gallery and faux stained glass domed ceiling above. One of the bulbs that skulked behind the glass and created the illusion of natural light had blown.

Now the remaining bulb worked alone, casting unnatural shadows across the room.

The Cossack Dacha is an ostentatious, yet comfortable restaurant. Some might describe it as sumptuous and luxurious; but while not tatty or tired, the décor remained a pastiche, a theatrical representation of Tsarist Russian opulence. The building had been a small theatre and cabaret bar for much of its life, but as with many of its contemporary's it failed to survive the Second World War. Wladimir's Uncle Boris, a decorated freedom fighter who was commonly mistaken for Polish, wandered into a post war Windsor and saw the sad building overlooking the river. He often told the tale of how he heard the building singing to him, telling him about its once glorious past. Uncle Boris always told the story with tears in his eyes; he claimed it to be love at first sight. True or otherwise, he worked hard to breathe life into the decaying old building and build himself a home and business. His efforts subsequently began the uplift of the properties nearby and eventually the whole street.

The post war Russian and Ukrainian community embraced London and its surrounding towns, patrons came to see what the eccentric Cossack had created, attracted by the proprietor's genuine roots, heroic war tales and the restaurant's cabaret style. It proved to be a refined cultural separation from the ogre that the cold war 1960's Soviet Union had become. For the Povetkin clan, which proved extensive, it was a conduit out of the Ukraine and to a better life.

The tea had cooled and the old man felt ready to take a sip. He held the cup, pinkie raised and let the golden liquid roll down his throat. A satisfied smack of the lips followed. His admiration of his family's legacy was interrupted by the appearance of Yuri. The thirty-something man strode through the kitchen's swing door and across the polished dance floor towards his master; his steel heel caps tapped out the monotonous tune of an eager, if unaccomplished, employee on the wooden dance floor.

He stopped twenty yards from Wladimir and indicated the old man had a call by wafting the mobile phone. The old man made no effort to retrieve the phone, but replied with a resigned nod. Yuri spoke efficiently into the phone, he conducted a few moments of conversation with the person on the end and then clicked the sliding phone shut. He mixed Russian with accent-free English happily.

Wladimir raised his eyebrows.

"Valentyn reports all is well with the deliveries. But he says there are too few. He was surprised that a shipment with so few was sent."

"How many were on the shipment?" Wladimir's face the perfect balance between inquisition and annoyance.

"Thirty-three Uncle." Wladimir was no blood relative of Yuri's, uncle had become the de-facto term of respect. Honour. The old man pushed his hand at Yuri, who turned on his heels and exited as he had arrived. The old man muttered under his breath and shut his eyes. He pushed the tea to one side and rose to his feet, his right hip silently complaining about the workload. He rubbed it out of habit and moved towards the large, roped off, staircase at the back of the restaurant. He eyed the stairs accusingly and then barked up them just like a man calling his pets.

"Masha... Zenovia... Come. NOW!"

He turned and walked back to his seat with a half limp. His jaw tensed and he clenched his teeth together. His beloved mother had told him to mind his temper and now as he aged and longed for a slower paced life he found himself counting to ten a lot more than he used to.

Wladimir never called or repeated himself twice. Anyone that made him do so usually ended up in a position to never make the same mistake again. No exceptions. Not even his daughters. The stairs rumbled with their impending arrival; neither moved with grace or charm. Wladimir had resigned himself to their lack of etiquette, he knew from birth that neither would blossom into a beauty. But then with their mother, that shouldn't have come as a surprise.

Zenovia arrived first, the taller but younger of the two by three years. She had delusions, believing herself the archetypal Slavic beauty. Certainly she had high cheek bones, and strong angular features, but they nestled, camouflaged under a layer of excessive 'puppy fat'. She had the chance of just being a plain girl if she lost some weight, but that was another of the girl's many delusions. At twenty-seven she had lived a protected and spoilt life, but her childlike tantrums looked as absurd on a girl, that stood over 5'10, as the Ugg boots she seemingly refused to ever take off.

Masha bustled past her sister; determined, despite being slower, wider and shorter to get ahead of her. Masha had none of the delusions of her sister, but nor did she have any of her childlike sweetness. Her goal, her single-minded ambition, was to become the head of the family once her father stepped down.

Wladimir waited for the sisters to settle and for the heavy breathing to subside. He eyed Zenovia's denim miniskirt with distaste, the podgy orange peel skin of her thighs seemed to be erupting from underneath it, and she lacked the guidance of a mother. Masha looked as she always did. Hefty. She had inherited his broad shoulders and prominent nose, but both had their mother's coal-black hair, their best feature.

"Ya called Papa?" Neither girl had any hint of a Russian accent but Zenovia had adopted a peculiar version of a mockney accent since her early teens.

"What is it Papa?" Masha chimed in a more acceptable 'Estuary' twang.

The old man refused to be hurried; he concluded his appreciation of his offspring's failings, once more making a mental note that he could strike nothing from the list. Progress nil.

"The van arrived safely in France… Valentyn is on his way home." The news came as neither a surprise or of any great interest to the girls. "Valentyn expressed disappointment that the shipment contained only thirty-three units?" The girls exchanged a hurried glance.

"I'm surprised… I was led to believe that it would be a full shipment… what, after all, would be the point of sending only thirty-three units?" His voice didn't rise or fall in pitch, the light accent emphasised the tempered ferocity. Wladimir never played poker, he knew he would lose, his poker face didn't exist. His face creased with lines of cautious wisdom and he looked every one of his seventy-five years.

"So, daughters, explain to me why we paid for the lorry, the transits and ran all those risks for just thirty-three units?"

Masha smiled and made an attempt to bat her eyelids. "But Papa, we simply loaded the shipment with the available cargo."

Wladimir nodded, his lips pursed together.

"Ok... all the cargo that could go, went. So I ask another question, why was there so little cargo available?" He circled his sturdy forefinger on the desk, his eyes focused on the table and not his daughters.

"Well Papa, we were given the list by the 'librarian' and we identified the cargo...Valentyn told us we had to get it resolved quickly... so we did." Zenovia tried to deflect the inevitable onslaught.

"So it was the librarian's fault – he only furnished you with thirty-three names..."

"And Valentyn said send the shipment... so we sent the shipment." Masha interrupted. The old man stayed silent a moment, letting the indiscretion sink in. Then he looked up from his fidgeting fingers and held the girls gaze.

"So Valentyn forced you to send a shipment of only thirty-three people, he knew how many it was before he went over to France to check the process and arrangements?"

The girls' heads dropped and their shoulders slumped. They had no idea Valentyn would be on a fact finding mission and checking the work.

"So Valentyn phoned me and pretended he was surprised, he made it up… is that what you are telling me?"

Zenovia shrugged heavily and shot a glance at her sister, but Masha had her bowed and had abandoned her sister. "Mebbe Papa?" she whimpered.

"Maybe Papa," he mimicked, genuine anger flashing across his face. "… Maybe Valentyn lied to me. Yes I should consider that. I should consider that a man that has never lied to me, not ever, a man who has bled for me, who protects me, protects you, protects the business. I should accept that after maybe twenty-five shipments, he lies to me about this one?" The words hung in the close confines of the restaurant.

"There is a first time for everything Papa..." Masha squeaked the words out, as unconvinced by them as her father would be.

"Why did god bless me with you…? I ask precious little of you, I expect even less. If your Great Uncle Boris could see how you disrespect his legacy… he would turn and rattle around in his grave."

No one of course knew where Great Uncle Boris had been buried, or if indeed he had a grave at all. When the Soviet Union broke up he had decided to go home to Kiev… and hasn't been heard of since. There had been talk of a feud with the Cossacks, others said he got drunk in a brothel and fell from a window. Either way, Wladmir, the eldest of his nephews, wasted no time in reinforcing his position as the head of the family. He wanted to ensure his daughters had a legacy and an empire to run when he was dead and gone.

"I give you time and money and I help you. Yet you still disappoint me… and what scares me is you have no concern for the security of your actions."

This time the girls offered no reply, heads still bowed they waited for the storm to blow over. They'd retreat together and lick their wounds in private. The old man thumped his hand down hard on the booth table. The vibrations shook through the floor.

"It isn't good enough. We cannot ship so few, we have commitments and obligations… people expect. I want Valentyn to speak to the Librarian… he needs to have a fucking good reason why he processed only thirty-three units. Do you know the reason?"

The girls said nothing. He thumped his other fist down hard again. Yuri's face appeared at the circular window of the kitchen door, he could always be found near the old man's side. A little smile played across his face as he saw the old man chastise the two "*shlakov*". Maybe Zenovia would call him and take her frustrations out on his body again.

"Get out of my sight. I don't need your shit today."

The girls trooped off and made their way back

across the dance floor to the stairs that lead into the luxurious isolation of the apartments above. The old man muttered and cursed under his breath. He didn't need hold-ups and problems, not now. He pulled his hand across his chin. He felt the stubble and cursed again. He flicked his wrist over and stared at the Rolex, wishing the hands had not moved as far round the clock face.

"YURI… my suit and bring me a tie, blue."

He rose with unrestricted haste and the hip complained again, he made for the kitchen door. He still had time, just, to shave and dress for the meeting. He had missed his tea though.

FRIDAY

David stood in line and waited. It's a myth that only the English queue. It's just they do it better than anyone else. It had been over seven years since he had set foot in England. The world had become a global village, city dwellers and scholars talked of overcrowding and mourned the loss of a less technologically linked society. The internet had 'ruined society', they wailed. David marvelled at the naivety of it all. People herded together, a giant flock of the scared and the desperate is how he summed up the cities of the world. If you wanted a simple life, you just had to pursue it, make the decisions to remove yourself from the grid, seek out the empty spaces on earth and revel in the fact that few have the courage to do likewise.

He heard people say every major city was the same, that the world had lost its identity. *'Rubbish'*, thought David. Sure, super brands permeated everything, they had created a common neon landscape, but why had that surprised people? MacDonald's and Starbucks spread like cancerous growths across the USA, when the borders of that vast country shrank under brand recognition, surely the logical pattern of growth would be from USA to North

America, Europe and then to the world… that's how capitalism works. Isn't it?

London is nothing like Paris. They share a development process; as any ancient organic cities might. Growth is through necessity not design. Disaster and war rendered large chunks of each city inoperable. Then the planners and architects moved in, creating sweeping boulevards, parks and epitaphs to their own egos. The similarities are structural, nothing more. London is nothing like Paris. It's cleaner for one thing. David had spent a long time in train stations all over Europe. The lines leading to them cut through the rough and decayed parts of the city. The lines run behind the architects' carefully planned façade; as you travelled you had a window seat looking right into the soul of the city, however depraved, rancid or dishevelled it may be. The routes into Paris are more depressing than the ones into London, but then Paris had the advantage of being French, the perception is that being French rates higher than being English. David had done his own survey and the ladies of the world he'd met preferred his French self.

Cities breathe and live, they have a vibe, an urgency that their inhabitants create, move to and unconsciously endorse. As David stood in the line waiting for his coffee, the London vibe felt very different to Paris. Maybe he'd lost touch with the city, but to him, it felt urgent, hurried and stressed.

On arrival he used his French Citizen card; when he had left all those years ago he had been British. Back then he had gone from London to Paris via Eurostar. Today it was Paris to London, but arriving at King's Cross and not

Waterloo. How the French must have loved arriving in the UK at the memorial to their grandest and final defeat by "les rosbifs".

Times change. The shit service didn't.

He still had a British passport. He couldn't let it go. He looked at the picture on the back page of the passport and he felt that pang of nostalgia. The image had not been taken around the same time as the picture the detective had shown him. The face looked the same but he had nothing else in common with man in the image. Not anymore.

He always used his French Citizen card for travel now.

David Edwards left. David Danjou returns.

He didn't know why, but he felt odd doing that. He'd never formerly eradicated his David Edwards identity, just cast it aside. Granted; a decision not entirely his own.

He returned with his head held high. No shame. No fear.

Finally the mix of tourists and crumpled suited workers cleared a path at the coffee counter. He ordered an Americano with a dash of cold milk. He had to repeat the order. When it came he needed to ask for the milk again.

He knew it would taste awful but he needed the caffeine hit. The early morning Eurostar had been crammed with super commuters, sleeping executives and too many people who felt the need to shout into mobile phones. David had never owned a mobile phone. He'd cut a strange figure; a tanned and casually dressed interloper, army issue kit bag at his feet, in a sea of corporate stress bunnies. David had slept for an hour on the Eurostar but not on the late train from Bergerac to Paris, the old charabanc had rattled and rolled at what seemed a snail's pace through the French countryside. Going without sleep, travelling light had become the accepted norms of his life. So had leaving bodies behind.

David didn't relish the dark, sleep is when you are at your most alone and when old faces haunt your mind's eye. He used to see his father, his family and sometimes Eve. For so long he hated seeing them, had wished them gone and tried hard to banish them from his thoughts. Now, he couldn't conjure the friendly faces up. They couldn't fight past the grimaces, anguish and contortions of the new ones that inhabited his consciousness. They came with screams, with pleading and the guilt of responsibility for life. Six years in the French Foreign Legion does that and much more to a man.

For so long he hadn't been able to own things, possessions became nothing more than an inconvenience. Anything of value was merely a target for the greed of others and sentimental items triggered doubt and reliance and dulled the instinctive process. David had witnessed a man beat another near to death over the theft of a photo in his barracks. A picture of the man's girlfriend, his most prized possession, and something worthless but still prepared to kill over.

Despite leaving that life behind, the habits die hard, David carried three identical changes of clothes, some shorts, his artisan jacket and a wash bag. Nothing else. He'd tried to live without any luggage, buying what he needed as he went, throwing away clothes as if disposable and travelling in nothing but what he stood up in and a toothbrush. That proved just silly, impractical and the laundry and personal hygiene issues alone made it unworkable.

He knew if he stayed for too long he'd need to modify his uniform for the English climate. David, the worn green duffle style kit bag draped over his shoulder, mooched in to the internet café. He paid his £1 and sat at a machine near the window. From memory he logged into his online bank account and reviewed his funds. He'd been living on cash alone since arriving at the vineyard and hadn't checked the balance for several months. The monthly war veteran stipend from the French government and his Legion pension had been paid in each month.

Nothing substantial, but it met his lifestyle needs.

He carried only a bank-branded Mastercard credit card, the balance paid in full each month. His postal address had long been a Legion Veterans Charity in Corsica and that satisfied curious banks and governments. Everything else he did, he did online. Transactions complete, he switched sites to Google. A life on the road had taught him how valuable a tool the internet could be. While it seemed too many to be one huge social playground for David it was the perfect place to hide from the world but still see what everyone was doing. He typed in Eve Du Pisanie and searched UK only.

It took just 0.34 seconds for Google to return 2,564 results. The first identified Elvis Du Pisanie, South Africa's leading 'King Impersonator', who would be on a UK tour soon. The next for a man called Ken, he liked rabbits, a lot, apparently. There appeared to be several local paper articles with Eve's name as well, but on the second page of results he found what he wanted.

The headline read, "Partner Biographies. Eve Du Pisanie." The website was listed as www.PAC&C.co.uk, solicitors at law. He clicked on the link; the machine whirred and the loading symbol rotated. The website had a utilitarian design, very much standard information only. Simple navigation across the top and solid blocks of colour filled the page. A two hundred word career summary sat alongside a picture of Eve. The full length picture showed her sat perched on the table, dressed in a cream designer suit. The skirt cut just above the knees. She always did have good legs. In a moment of pure pleasure butterflies skipped around his stomach.

She looked wonderful.

She hadn't aged, just matured. The biog had her listed as thirty-four. He did a rough calculation, it was a year old. She had always been elegant and statuesque, as a teenager she'd been lithe, maybe gawky. Uncomfortable about her height, self-conscious of her looks. Her mother's Croatian heritage had ensured she retained the angular cheek bones, ink-black hair and classic good looks of the Mediterranean, but her father had given her his green eyes. Her rough and ready South African father had thankfully offered no other physical input into his daughter's DNA. He took pride in the eyes though; he told anyone who would listen that his stunning daughter inherited her green gems from him. The description proved accurate, not just a biased father's rambling pride. Gems that sparkled out from what could be an austere face and radiated simple beauty. They sucked you in, they drew you from afar, like Sirens on the rocks, they had enough power to convince a man to talk to her face and not just her chest.

Eve understood her effect, if her looks had been traffic stopping at eighteen, heart stopping at twenty-eight, then now, they are simply mind blowing thought David.

Storm, the model agency had signed her. She lasted just a matter of months; it proved a waste of her true talents. She could have and should have been the next big thing. But Eve wanted to be a lawyer. She'd always rallied to a cause, hated injustice, campaigned and been active in every cause available. She had been one of the few to stand by him.

The office address was Slough.

No doubt still a shit hole mused David.

The biog was CV style rhetoric and brief. She had been made partner several years before. Now the P in PAC&C. Clearly she'd done well. He noted no rings on her hands and wondered, maybe even hoped a little. He memorised the office number and the address for PAC&C and shut the machine down. He had to go somewhere else first. He rose silently, careful not to scrape the chair or bang his bag on the furniture.

He needed to get across London to Waterloo station to catch the slow suburban train out to Windsor. The tube would be the most efficient way, Taxi the most comfortable. David had already decided to walk. He'd been away from the capital for a long time. He needed to walk its streets, look around and maybe take in the sights.

He'd never done that. A friend, now gone, advised him that in any big old city people forget the basic rule – look up. They walk head down or never raising their eyes above head height. Seeing only the true of height of buildings in the distance, failing to take in their detail and beauty close up.

David strode out of the main station doors, passed the ever present Big Issue seller and dishevelled beggars and headed for the crossroads. Before his much-needed departure, London's former mayor Ken Livingston had made sure the city was criss-crossed by brown heritage signs. David had looked at the map of the city on the train and he'd taken in some key reference points. He wouldn't need any more than that; his mental map taking over.

He followed the sign for Farringdon and then cut across to Leicester Square. That would lead to Covent Garden. Then he'd stroll to St. Paul's Cathedral; nip over the Millennium Bridge, maybe test to see if it still wobbles; go up the river past the Tate Modern and check out the Globe and the National Theatre and then continue onto the London Eye. A mixture of the old and the new, sights remembered and sights built since he'd left.

It would be circuitous but worth it. He'd feel the vibe of the city, he'd remember how to be English again, remember how to be David Edwards.

He had time; the funeral didn't start until 3.00p.m.

Masha twisted on the uncomfortable aluminium chair. The breeze had picked up and now blew through the Windsor Central station concourse causing untended napkins and tissues to fly from tables. Goose bumps rose on Masha's bare legs in response and she cupped her Latte in both hands as she sipped it. Her sister was late.

The Windsor Central station used to be the personal railway station of monarch when in residence at Windsor castle, now it was a public space packed with coffee shops, a market, restaurants and art shops. The wrought iron and glass roof providing a perfect alfresco dining cafe culture space for the innumerable tourists and locals alike.

Masha cast her eye around the concourse and took in the view, it was before 11.00am, so the coaches and trains had yet to regurgitate their tourist groups. At this time the locals bustled into town and did what they needed to do before vacating the space. Long term residents knew that the town centre became gridlocked with tourist groups and anorak wearing foreigners feasting on the Royal history of the town. She liked Windsor; she had been here all her life and had always defended it when people put it down. Culturally her and sister where Russian, raised with a strong sense of the home land and what that meant, but despite being able to speak the language her real family was the gang land landscape their father ran. They had known nothing different, to school friends and acquaintances her father had made money from oil and gas in the old country and now invested in property and businesses within the town. It was a convenient stereotype.

Wladimir had despaired that his daughters had embraced a more 'English' persona when away from him and the confines of the gang. Masha had tried to explain to her father that it simply formed part of creating an identity for themselves and that they already felt 'isolated' by the secrets they carried each day. Their mother dying young hadn't helped either. While a stern woman she offered love unconditionally and had no agenda about ensuring they were ready for the life they would inhabit once an adult. Wladimir had always been preoccupied with preparing them, toughening them up for the business. He had no hesitation in including them in the family business in some form once they were old enough.

Masha knew she lacked the looks or the natural charm of others, genetics hadn't blessed her with a head start so she relied on her wits and cunning to get what she wanted. For the most part it worked, though her father was immune and the growing sense that he simply didn't respect her or her ideas now overtook all other concerns. She knew the limit of his patience was fast approaching, if she and Zenovia didn't step up and show him they could handle the business then they would be overlooked and be destined to play a bit part and nothing more.

Masha's musings were interrupted by the appearance of her sister. Although still at the other end of the concourse she was immediately noticeable. Her long hair swishing back and forth as she adopted what she supposed was the gait of the beautiful and glamorous. Her short skirt had ridden up to reveal excessive mottled flesh and the low cut, striped, top revealed so much cleavage it appeared as if two bald men were fighting to get out of her top. She pushed through the discarded chairs from other tables and flumped into the chair beside her sister her mouth working overtime on a piece of chewing gum.

"Did Papa see you leave dressed like that?" Masha asked in a conspiratorial whisper.

Zenovia didn't remove her enormous sunglasses but still fixed her gaze on her older sister and arched an eyebrow at her. "Course he didn't. The top alone would have sent him over the edge... I'm not an idiot you know." Zenovia's mockney accent grated even Masha's patience, but she understood why her sister had adopted it. Fitting in is always important, no matter how strong a personality you are.

"But I'll bet Yuri or the others saw you leave..."

"Probably... It's no biggie."

"They are loyal to Papa. He'll ask them how you were dressed and how you behaved he always does."

Zenovia waved her hand at her sister as if pushing the complaints aside. "So what, ever since he began this whole people smuggling deal he's been well grumpy and demanding. I'm not a child Masha. I'll wear what I want!" As she said it she shifted in her seat and pulled her skirt down and then jostled her breasts back into a comfortable position before finally removing her sunglasses.

Masha motioned to the waiter, who came over but never really engaged her with eye contact. The young man had been transfixed by her sister's cavernous cleavage. "Two Americanos. Cold milk on the side. Bring a Blueberry muffin too." She said. The waiter turned his face and nodded to her before snatching one last leer at Zenovia.

"We'll be lucky if he gets that simple order right." Masha moaned.

Zenovia removed the chewing gum and dumped it

unwrapped in to the ash tray on the table. "Why?"

"Because... sweet little sister, he spent more time staring at your tits than listening to me."

"Well he's just a man..." Zenovia replied with a flourish of pride. Masha knew her sister believed herself a genuine beauty and a literal honey-pot for all men. While Masha conceded she was more attractive than herself she recoiled at her sisters clothing choices and sluttish antics.

"Well as long as you're happy sis."

"What's that supposed to mean? The skirt is D&G, the top is Armani..."

"Wonderful, but it would have helped if you had bought the right size!" Masha snapped back.

"Oh fucking 'ell Mash... leave it will you. I can't dress like some repressed school teacher like you do. Dad aint gonna hand the business to us no matter what we do or how we dress." The oft repeated spat was curtailed by the arrival of the Blueberry muffin. A different waiter bought it over but the cleavage had the same eye grabbing appeal as before.

Masha let out an exaggerated sigh when she saw him do it. "Oh Jesus... Look Zenny, the first waiter told him about the tits at table 12 and he's come to check them out... look he's laughing about it with him now." Masha pointed out the two waiters seemingly sharing a joke and the hand gestures seemed to imply something of size. Zenovia looked over and stretched an unconvincing smile across her face.

"Look Mashi – Dad didn't listen to us about the

shipments. We told him the spreadsheets weren't being updated properly, we told him the guys at the warehouse didn't listen to us... and what did he do?"

Masha tore a hunk of blueberry muffin off, "Nothing. He said we had to earn respect." She popped the piece into her mouth. "But he is holding us responsible for them not being right..."

"And what can we do if the hired fucking 'elp don't listen? He shouts and tells us we're useless all the time. He does it when Valentyn, Yuri and soldiers can here. He's the boss and the way he treats us is the benchmark for the others. They try to hide it from us because they still shit themselves at the thought we can hav'em killed."

Masha ate another piece of Muffin. "I think we can still make him see sense and understand that we can run this... he forgets that the restaurants and the bar are doing well under us. He needs to remember the good things and not just the bad! It's our job to remind him..."

Zenovia put her head in her hands, "Jesus Mashi – give it up. He loves us and dotes on us, in his fucked up way, but he aint ever gonna give us power over the business."

Masha shrugged but Zenovia pressed on. "He 'finks the restaurants do ok coz Yuri manages them... and nowt to do with us. You know I'm right." She raised her head in time to let the waiter deliver the coffees. Both she and Masha ignored the leer at her cleavage.

"So we just give it up? We let Valentyn and the others disrespect us?" Masha pushed the remnants of her muffin away. Zenovia watched and resisted the urge to snaffle what remained. "Zenny, I know we aint proper close, but if we work together then I reckon we can make things work for us."

Zenovia smiled a fake smile. They hadn't ever really got on. They weren't raised to be make-up and shopping buddies, more like competitive brothers seeking the adulation of their father before the inevitable crowning of a winner. "Papa always plays us against each other, he 'finks it's good for us to argue and fight to the top. It's getting boring now."

"Maybe we should use that... maybe we can make that work in our favour?" Masha said.

"Make what work... being competitive? How's that gonna work?" She furrowed her brow in genuine confusion.

"Papa wants you to look after one part of the business and me the other – he wants to see who will run it best, right?" Masha said. Zenovia nodded. "So... we know that Valentyn has to run the soldiers and is trusted completely by Papa and that Yuri is his confidante. But... they don't like each other."

Zenovia smiled. "Na! They don't like each other at all. You 'fink we can use them to help us to get Papa to see that we can do things and can manage business."

"Yes... but it's important that Papa realises we are responsible for what works well and that others – say Yuri and Valentyn get the blame for the stuff that is a cock up." Masha smiled at her sister.

"I'll work with Yuri – he and I get on already. Anyway Valentyn always liked you more than me." Zenovia said.

"Fine... You're welcome to Yuri. He gives me the creeps!"

"Aah Yuri's alright... ambitious little fucker mind. I can handle him." Zenovia said it with a twinkle in her eye. Masha noted it.

"Sure you can sis. But remember, it's ok for Yuri and Valentyn to think we don't get along. Let's keep the rivalry fired up as if it's Yuri versus Valentyn. This can work sis... we can make them all see us in a different way."

Zenovia shrugged. "Fine." She said. "But this is it, the last time I'm trying to win over Papa. If he don't want us to run the business then fine, I'll go do summit else."

Masha bit back an acidic response. "Ok... then we better give this a real good go sis. The money in this new plan is huge. I want to be at the top of that." Masha said.

Valentyn climbed out of the back seat of the gun-metal Range Rover. He eyed his surroundings and made no attempt to hide his disgust. He pulled down the pristine white cuffs of his shirt and straightened his jacket before leaning back into the car to talk to the driver. "Stay with the car Gregor, keep the engine running and don't let any one of the little fuckers scratch it this time!" He slammed the door shut before a reply could come back.

"No welcome committee..." Valentyn mused, neither addressing his accomplice nor encouraging a reply. "I hate it here Oleg. Let's be quick, see the facilities and get away again. If I stay too long I'm going need another shower."

The squat, powerful man to his left just nodded; he

made no attempt to join in or make conversation. Valentyn had come straight from a trip across the channel and hadn't looked pleased about it. He led the way as the pair picked a path across the pot-holed concrete road surface, stepping around the occasional abandoned child's bike and the odd cluster of piled-up and rotting furniture. They rounded the corner and the full array of caravans, trucks, vans and mobile homes greeted them. One stood out; a large mobile home with a white picket fence surround and mock Doric columns supporting an inept porch over the main door. A small huddle of men, everyone in some kind of vest, sat around a wooden picnic bench to the side of the home. They noticed and ignored the pair at the same time, carrying on with their conversation and occasional burst of laughter.

Valentyn had grown used to the Gypsies' ways. He neither respected them nor liked them, but their involvement in the process had been a means to an end. While they were needed he'd tolerate them. He stopped some ten metres short of the group and said nothing, waiting for them to acknowledge him. He paid them. He could stop paying them anytime he wanted. For all their bravado they still knew who was master and who was dog.

It took another thirty seconds before the Gypsies turned to him. Patrick rose from the table and hitched his jeans under his rounded paunch and then spat forcibly on the ground before stepping over the picket fence towards them. "Yerz here... didn't see ya big man."

Valentyn smiled.

"Did we agree a meet terday?" Patrick's accent hovered between an Irish brogue and country yokel – he had never sported the traditionally favoured mullet, opting for a more unruly, curly mop-head look. His off-white t-shirt had several undefined stains competing with the sweat patches. Valentyn sneered.

"Don't act like a cock. I've had complaints; show me the storage facility. As agreed."

Patrick raised his hands in placatory gesture, "Easy now Valentino... c'mon and have a look for yerz'lf."

Valentyn rested a giant hand on the man's chest. A strong and forceful gesture that the Gypsy tried to walk through and couldn't. "Do not call me such names."

"Ok then," said Patrick, trying to look irritated but unconcerned.

"Be respectful... do your job, get paid and stay alive."

Patrick just nodded.

"Show me." Valentyn pointed towards the patchwork of badly built brick and wooden sheds and out-buildings at the far end of the site. "Show me all of them."

As they walked down the avenue of caravans and vehicles Patrick pulled out a bunch of keys. "We shipped da last of it yesterday... so we iz not cleaned up or nuttin."

They reached their goal and Valentyn waited as Patrick opened the main padlocked door on the left. He pushed it open and then removed two bricks at the back wall and pulled open the disguised hinged plywood door that had masqueraded as a wall. It revealed a long narrow room, maybe ten feet wide and some fifty feet long. From the front it looked like a terrace of small storage units, the large room behind unseen to the casual observer.

Valentyn peered in and reared back a little at the smell. "Dat's the bins," Patrick said. "We use the space at the front to store the rubbish like. It stops any fucker being nosy."

The room contained about ten single mattresses lying end to end down one side, no covers and no blankets. No sanitation or washing facilities... no windows.

"How many do you keep in here?" Valentyn asked.

"We can store up to fifty in here."

"It's disgusting, I understand why when they come to us they are filthy, smelly and terrified." Valentyn made no effort to hide his derision. "It makes them hard to handle," he added.

Patrick nodded, then he spat on the floor once more, "So what? The deal was we get the feckers, store'em a week while you do ya thing and then ship'em back. Suppose yerz expect me to feed the bastards as well!"

"You don't feed them?" Valentyn's fury had begun to bubble within, the veins in his neck bulged and he clenched his fist. Patrick sensed what was coming and tried head off the confrontation.

"You and the fat bitch came here and promised us a-towsand units a week... I get what, mebbe three-hundred is all. We spread them around the camps, we incur costs. It aint what we agreed."

Valentyn's rage bubbled over, he shot his hand out and grabbed the smaller man by the throat and began to lift. Patrick panicked, his hands shot up to the massive paw that had began a slow and measured squeeze of the life out of him. His eyes bulged as his feet lifted off the floor.

"You will get the units when you can prove you are fit to handle them and not before. You will make sure they have access to water and sanitation in each camp and you will feed them a meal a day... understand?" Patrick tried to nod, his face transitioning from red to purple. Valentyn dropped him into a heap on the floor and the Gypsy gasped for breath.

"Understand me you cunt of a man, do as I say, make it happen or you will cost me time and money. If you cost me time and money then you should be scared... very, very scared. Do you know why?" Patrick shook his head still gasping in breath.

"Because if you do cost me time and money I will gather everyone in this camp, all women, men and children and hack off one leg each. Then I'll lock you all in this shit hole you call storage and burn you all alive."

Patrick sneered at the image and swallowed hard at the sincerity in Valentyn's eyes.

The tree provided two serviceable functions. It sat atop a small rise and afforded David a comfortable place to lean while he spectated, at a distance, on the burial. Secondly, it provided shade from the surprising heat of the afternoon sun. Datchet when viewed for the first time looked English postcard picturesque, with giant oaks and shaded greens, a village pub, a cluster of shops and the Thames river and Windsor Castle as a backdrop. St. Mary's church sat on the outskirts of the small town, on the Eton road. The graveyard sprawled through aged trees towards the

M4 motorway. What may have once been a secluded spot now had the permanent accompanying hum of motorway traffic, a trundle of a local train and the regular engine blast of planes rising into the air from the nearby Heathrow airport. Datchet: the very heart of commuter Berkshire.

He could hear some of the Vicar's words before the cacophony got the better of him, but David didn't mind. He had arrived in plenty of time but avoided the church service. Preferring to have a cold pint of Stella in the local pub. It wouldn't be right to upset people by attending the service. He had no time for the pious vitriol of a village sermon. He had taken up his position by the tree well before the funeral party exited the church. He counted just twelve mourners.

His mother looked fragile, old and tired. She hadn't seemed old when he left. But over seven years had passed and time clearly refused to be kind. She moved with careful purpose, flanked by Peter, his razor thin brother and beloved sister Jacqui. She didn't cry; no one cried. Not even as the coffin began its short drop into the grave. Eve, the divine Eve, stood at the back, designer sunglasses strapped over her eyes, her head held high above the other wizened mourners. He hadn't expected her to be here, but now he thought about it seemed logical for her to attend. David couldn't be certain, but he felt sure she was looking at him. None of the other mourners looked familiar, maybe one of the old men was a relative. His parents had been only children, so it could be a cousin of his father's. David didn't know or care. His father hadn't been old, mid-sixties, too young for all his peers to be dead but too old for a mass turn out. No matter, David didn't ponder for long on why more hadn't come.

The vicar, his white robes billowing in the gentle breeze scratched his scraggy beard before he closed his bible and said something else David couldn't hear. The bowed heads popped back up and the familiar listless shuffling of a group without a leader or clear direction began. Jacqui worked the graveside. She shook hands and looked people in the eye with earnest intent. David imagined the words.

"Please do come back to the house... nothing grand, but some food is laid on." Polite, understated reassurances that someone had thought beyond just the burial.

She looked good, the black trouser suit and hairstyle suited her. The frizz issue she had when an angst-ridden teenager must have passed. She had put on weight, but it was more a case of matured aging, not fat. No bloated rings, no muffin-top. Yet still unmarried. He'd find it all out soon.

David watched as the group of people moved back towards the cemetery gate. An older man supporting his mother down the path and out through the gate. He saw Eve take Jacqui's arm and nod towards him. His sister looked up and clasped a hand to her mouth. Before she could move a long arm draped itself over her shoulders. Peter, his brother held her back and hugged her. It looked forced and neither appeared comfortable, they exchanged words and Jacqui raised her hands and then dropped them to her side with an exasperated sigh.

Peter moved away from her and Eve and headed towards David.

David straightened up, as if coming to attention. His brother stood several inches taller at 6' 4 and whole lot leaner than him; he didn't seem to have changed much. David remembered him as a whinging, geeky, uncoordinated teenager and then a bitter, boring young man. He'd been sixteen at the time of the fight, loathing his older brother already. So it had been no hardship for him to follow their father's stance and disown David. Neither of them turned up to support him at the trial. They hadn't spoken or communicated in any way for over seventeen years.

Peter's over striding gait looked more unsteady and peculiar than he remembered as he weaved around and across the plethora of unkempt ancient graves. He halted more than ten feet away, his arms folded across his chest.

"You shouldn't be here." No pre-amble, no small talk, the voice deeper and more authoritative than he recalled.

"Tough," David replied.

"You're not welcome…" He tried to be stern.

"Tough," David repeated.

Peter had always been meek, easily intimidated. The years since their last meeting had shown him the need to develop a backbone, but he would never be a physical match for his elder brother.

"Dad wouldn't have wanted you here…" he stammered.

"Tough," David said again.

"That's disrespectful."

"Mmmm maybe," he said, "but he's in no position to care or complain, is he?"

Peter unfolded his arms and shook his head.

"Dad will have his judgement..." he said, eyes cast to the heavens. "Go away David, no one wants you here."

David stared hard at his brother, he doubted the religious streak to be genuine. "I'm here for mum and for Jacqui. I couldn't care less about you Peter. If my being here is an issue, then tough. You're a big boy now, you'll get over it."

The words hovered between them like a challenge waiting to be met. Peter said nothing. But hearing his brother's loathing out loud upset David more than he thought it would.

"I don't care what you have to say on the matter. I gave up that notion when I was eighteen years old." David added with venom.

"So you didn't come for Dad, for the funeral?"

"No."

Peter stared at him, his angular face thrust forward with amazement.

"I didn't like the man. His death is a release, nothing more."

"A release?" Peter asked a contrived look of disgust on his face.

David relaxed a little, as if an invisible Sergeant had shouted '*at ease*'.

"I came so that I could see and speak to Mum in person, without her being worried about his reaction."

"She's managed this long without speaking to you. Jacqui too. They can continue if they want."

"Well that's the point isn't it – *if they want.*" David looked beyond his brother and saw Jacqui by the grave watching their altercation. Eve stood a few feet to her right, offering silent support and friendship, ever the diplomat.

"I know they don't want your type back in their life… who would?" Peter noticed his brother's alternate gaze and stepped across it to block the view. Both men knew it was childish and Peter looked a little ashamed the moment he did it.

"My type?" David's attention snapped back to Peter. "You have no idea who I am Peter. You never have and you probably never will." A little more venom sneaked into his words than he planned, but he knew how to control his anger. His arms and shoulders remained relaxed, the tension he felt not registering on his face.

"I know you're a murderer…what else do I need to know?"

David's lips broke into a wry smile. Technically he wasn't wrong.

"Manslaughter."

"What?"

"I was convicted of manslaughter, not murder."

Peter scoffed, "Right. A technicality. You murdered someone Peter and it destroyed dad's life, mum's, all of our lives…"

The smile evaporated. But he held his head high, his eyes had little reason to sparkle these days and the cold look of despair returned to them.

"I did it Peter. I've never tried to pretend otherwise, have I?"

"Do you want some kind of prize, maybe I should applaud?" His voice rose in volume. Jacqui moved towards them, circumventing the open grave.

David could hear his father in Peter's shrill words. The sarcasm and the vitriol that his brother spouted felt like needles against his skin. He'd left England to avoid ever hearing it again, to escape the judgement and misplaced notion of respectability. Seventeen years later his brother seemed to be happily taking up the mantle where his father left off. David the untouchable, the outcast and undesirable who should be publically shunned. *'I have just one son'* – the words still wounded, no matter his bravado. Peter didn't seem to be in the mood to forgive or forget. Blood isn't always thicker than water.

"That's enough Peter." Jacqui came up behind him. Unsteady on the long grass and soft ground in her heeled shoes. Flecks of cooch grass pollen clung to her trouser suit.

"Stop it both of you. Today is bad enough without you trying to play the heavy handed brother." Her voice came across flat and strong, a voice of authority.

"Hello Sis." David said.

"Hello Dooby," she replied.

They moved together, ignoring the now inert Peter.

She opened her arms wide and David moved into the welcoming embrace. Despite the width of his shoulders and the height difference she bear hugged him and they rocked from side to side.

"It's so good to see you Dooby," she said into his shoulder. He smiled, his face over her right shoulder, his eyes clamped shut. 'Dooby'. He hadn't been called that for so long. He'd almost forgotten she had used it. His little sister, just fifteen when he was convicted of the murder and twenty five on his release from prison. That was the last time he had seen her.

"You look great Sis… really great." He smiled a smile he hadn't shown or felt since before his time in prison. His heart pounded, he had no idea he would feel like this. Wave after wave of happiness, regret and loss washed over him, alone for so long, isolated by choice, now the barriers had crashed and splintered. He felt as if his very soul lay open, vulnerable to attack.

"Let's go see mum," she said.

"Does she know I'm here?"

"Of course, she's the one who recognised you. She told Eve she had seen you before we went into the church. She saw you in the village by the butcher's."

They uncurled from the embrace, she took his hand in hers and kissed it, before leading him back towards the grave and Eve.

"Remember this face?" Jacqui asked.

David took in all of Eve's beauty in one giant gulp. She removed the sunglasses and flashed him a nervous, glamorous smile. Her eyes danced and the sun seemed to shine just a little brighter.

"Who could forget it?" he said.

Valentyn Maskaev hung his overcoat on a sturdy wooden hanger and deposited it into the Cossask Dacha's cloakroom. He smoothed down the velvet lapels and ensured the collar had been turned down correctly. Then he brushed the imagined or real detritus from the Gypsy camp off the whole jacket. He hadn't really needed it in France, but it was a new acquisition and he liked the way it made him look. Then he checked the hang of his suit jacket, pulling at the lapels, and admired his reflection in the full-length mirror.

He cocked his head to one side, searching for imperfections that needed addressing. He noticed a small scuff on his patent leather shoes. He dropped to one knee and lightly dabbed the offending mark with his finger; then removed his handkerchief from his top pocket, apologetically spat onto the end and then dabbed at the mark again. Content the scuff had been polished away he rose to his feet once more and repeated the inspection, this time he passed.

Valentyn strode through the empty restaurant like a man on a stroll in a park and made straight for the kitchen, extending his arm ramrod straight to open the swing door. The early hour ensured it lacked the usual bustle and noise of a commercial kitchen, but the lights blazed. Sitting at the far end, Wladimir Povetkin, his boss, perched on a high stool at the end of a steel work top. A cup of tea steamed away in front of him.

"Uncle," Valentyn said.

"My boy," replied the old man.

"How was France?" he asked.

"Frustrating Uncle…but a trip is never wasted. The process is working well, but we may need to review the driver."

The old man scratched his chin, the bristles had returned. "Does he want more money?"

Valentyn shook his head. "No, he notices things, thinks about them; maybe he thinks too much." The old man nodded and took a slim sip of the hot tea. He shifted on the stool and straightened his hunched back.

"Small numbers," Wladimir said.

"Yes. Too small. It is not good business; the cost of the shipment will not be met by the fees paid."

The old man snorted, a bullish shrug of the shoulders accompanied it.

"My daughters…" he left the sentence hanging.

"Da!" Valentyn understood.

"Lazy and foolish. Lazy and foolish like their mother."

"Da!" Valentyn said it with less conviction. He knew better than to criticise the old man's family. Family is everything as important as he is to the business he'll never be family.

"You need to meet with the Librarian. We have to be sure we can process the numbers."

Valentyn nodded his approval and agreement deciding to keep his last meeting with the Gypsies to himself. "Did you meet the heads of the families?"

The old man nodded and sucked in his cheeks and then blew out his breath in one slow continuous breath. "I did. They were happy with the trial runs. They think all five thousand units have been re-located. They will begin the big shipments in one month. September 1st."

"How many?"

"Five thousand."

"A month?" Valentyn queried.

The old man looked up and shook his head. "A week."

Valentyn's eyes flared in surprise, he fought to keep the response under control. He didn't hide it well. The old man nodded his appreciation of Valentyn's shock. He drank some tea, a bigger glug this time.

"They have decided to shift stock from further afield than originally planned. They have faith in the plan. Can we manage that many?"

"Maybe. Not all of them need to pass through the same process place perhaps. We will need weekly convoys now. Security worries me."

"Weekly, monthly, daily - it doesn't matter. They never check what leaves the country." Wladimir waved his hand as if dismissing it as a minor concern.

Valentyn took note, "We will need to vary the European ports. It can be managed." Valentyn did the mental calculation, five thousand units a week meant twenty thousand a month, two hundred and forty thousand a year. He could get maybe two hundred into a truck, he would need twenty-five trucks a week, plus spares... and drivers.

"How much are we to be paid per unit?" he asked.

"They wanted a discount, because of the bulk shipments," the old man said.

"How much?" Valentyn persisted.

"£100. Women and child same."

Valentyn did the maths again. "£500,000 a week, is ok."

The old man pursed his lips and nodded his head. "Maybe. We need to look at costs. Trucks and drivers will be expensive."

"Storage too, we will need to spread them out more."

"Do we have the space?"

Valentyn shook his head, "Maybe, if we expand the Gypsies' process."

Wladimir smirked and then shrugged, he didn't trust the Gypsies. They had been useful for small jobs, hiding shipments here and there. Their camps never got raided and the public treated them as if they were invisible. "Maybe..."

"I'll find an answer Uncle." He stepped forward and put a hand on the old man's shoulder. It was greeted with a smile, and he placed his own soft hand on top of it and patted.

Blood Ties

"I know you will. You always do Valentyn."

David avoided conversation with the other mourners; he spent most of the afternoon in the meticulously manicured garden. His mother had simply kissed him and held him when they finally met. She held him as if she planned to never let him go; by English standards it was a long hug. David felt as if perhaps they both wanted to make up for all the lost hugs and loving touches they had missed. Then she had cupped his face and said she would be out to chat in a few minutes, before resuming her duties with the mourners.

David didn't mind. He could wait a few minutes more.

He sat on the lichen-covered bench at the far end of the garden and watched the comings and goings of people through the patio doors. The apple tree shaded him from the sun and he savoured the heavy scent of the herb garden that wafted over on the light breeze.

Peter came to the patio doors every few minutes and scowled. He had the appearance of a nosy neighbour checking up on the hired help. To his credit he stayed inside, maybe revelling in his role as grieving host and son. A pang of guilt shot through David. He was the elder brother, and it should be him. But it would be false and ridiculous if he tried to do it. His father had disowned him and he had done so right back. David had refused to rationalise his feelings for his father, preferring to think of him as already dead all these years. Jacqui never left her mother's side, an emotional and physical crutch, as she urged the visitors to eat and listened to their condolences for a man they really didn't know.

Eve glided through the diminishing crowd, paused at the buffet table and loaded a plate with nibbles and neat triangular sandwiches. David watched as her long legs carried her through into the kitchen and to the back door. It opened and she stepped into the garden. She took short even strides, their length restricted by her skirt. A smile broke on her face as she neared.

"I thought you would be hungry." She pushed the plate ahead of her like a peace offering.

"I am. Thank you." He took the plate from her and nudged along the bench to allow her to sit down. She did so in that elegant feminine way.

"My man found you then?" She said, a proud smile forming on her lips.

David thought back to James Thomas, to how he had been annoyed at being located and then to the alleyway and the dead men. He blinked as if caught in a strobe, the flash memories stunning him for a second. A moment of darkness washed over his face.

"You ok?" she asked. "You went a little blank."

"Remembering Del Monte…"

"Who?"

"We need to talk about your Mr Thomas," he said.

"He hasn't returned from France yet…I'm worried about him." Her eyes never left David's face, he looked away and down at the plate of buffet treats.

"Had he worked for you for long?" He asked.

"Several years, a former Met police officer. CID."

"He looked the type." David shuffled his feet, thought a moment and then continued, "Did he work solely for you?" he asked.

"He was a contractor rather than full-time staff, but yeah he worked for me mostly. Why?"

"He was followed, in France. When he found me there were two men watching him. Serious men. Not the sort you'd like to meet in a dark alley."

Eve eyed him with a suspicious narrowing of the eyes.

"You're sure they were after him and not you?"

"Yes. No one knows who I am anymore. After I left your man in a bar, I saw them follow him, he was trying to get a signal on his mobile phone." David took a bite of a corned beef sandwich, a long-forgotten taste danced across his tongue and ended in predictable disappointment.

"So you followed him being followed?" She smiled as she said it.

David swallowed, and moved a savoury mini egg around the plate with his finger.

"Did you get his last text message?" he asked.

"How do you know about that?" She sat back a little as she spoke, creating an unnatural distance between them.

"He didn't send it. The two men that followed him attacked him. An ambush."

"Jesus! Is he alright?" Her hand had moved to her mouth in shock, her back straightened with the surprise.

"They roughed him up, then entered that text message in his phone and made him send it. When I went through his phone afterwards I saw it had been sent to you. What are you involved with Eve?" He still didn't look at her, the mini egg kept moving around the plate.

"Hold on – let's take a step back a minute, what were you doing going through my investigator's phone?" She stood up and took a strong defiant stance. Like you'd see on an assertiveness training course, hands on hips, demanding an explanation. "What happened to him David?"

David looked up at her from his hunched position. Despite his size and physical self-confidence, David felt nervous in one-to-one conversations with everyone, especially women. His life had made him suspicious of others and their motives. Being guarded and wary had become second nature.

"He died on the street in Saint-Innocence." He looked at his plate wishing this didn't have to be his first conversation with her and realising his interpersonal skills had ballsed it up again.

"Jesus Fucking Christ. James is dead!" Her hands left her hips and became clasped by her face.

"One of his attackers stabbed him before I could… intervene," he said.

"Fuck David, what did you do?" He shrugged, reluctant under interrogation to give any more information. "David, what did you do?"

"I dealt with it." He bit into the mini Scotch egg.

Another long-forgotten taste.

"I don't know what that means."

He took a deep breath, first day back and David the 'murderer' had to confess all over again. "I killed them... I hadn't intended to, just injure them. But..."

Eve's hand shot to her mouth and she stared at him, the look of the appalled. "How many died?"

"Two. I think they were Russian, maybe Ukrainian." David swallowed and prodded a mini sausage as if inspecting it prior to eating it.

"You killed two men... how?" Her hands came down from her face, a veil of incredulous understanding replaced them.

"Kicks, I think. I don't recall exactly how. It's not important."

"You killed two men in the street in France of course it's important…what about the police?" Her hands back on her hips the defiant stance restored.

"What about them?" David looked up, surprised at the question.

"You left the scene of a crime, after you killed two men… Jesus David!"

She turned her head as if to see if anyone else had heard.

"Eve, I've been a soldier for a long time. One thing I can be pretty sure of, they died like they lived."

"You the judge, jury and executioner now?" her

indignation plastered across her face. Frustrated at not being able to scream or shout her anger she hit out, catching David across the face and shoulder with a half-hearted slap.

"Eve. They killed your man... I got involved trying to help him."

"What world is that David?" She spat the words at him.

"A world where life is cheap. They had no intention of warning your man off. They wanted to deliver a message. Not just a cryptic text message about retirement." He paused, wanting to be sure he had her full attention. "Killing him was the message." He looked at her fuming face as the realisation of the situation dawned on her.

"Did James die instantly?"

"Not quite... he was alive for a while afterwards. A tough old boy." David said. "His last words, it was your message for me, about dad. He said his trip to France had nothing to do with Russian gangsters. What's going on?"

Eve put her hand to her temple and shut her eyes. David watched as the face crumpled into a grimace and she began to weep. Small, controlled sobs that accompanied a trickle of tears that collected on her chin. David stood and dithered, he wanted to comfort her, but didn't know how best to proceed. He settled for putting a hand on her shoulder. She didn't look at him, just shrugged it off.

David put the hand by his side and felt awkward. He left it another moment before he spoke again. "Someone serious is upset with you Eve... can I help?"

"I'm not sure I want your kind of help David." She wiped the tears away, her head held up looking at the sky

"Eve, don't be like that." But the words fell on deaf ears; Eve had already turned and begun a slow walk back to the house.

"The police will come to me eventually I suppose, he was working for me after all." Eve didn't turn round. "What do I tell them about you? Nothing I suppose?"

"Tell them what you want...but until I came back you had no idea I'd been found, so tell them the truth about why he was there. I don't expect you to lie for me."

Eve sighed and moved towards the kitchen door, she passed Jacqui on route; who paused to see why she was upset. Eve didn't slow, just waved off the enquiry and went back into the house. Jacqui moved towards David and turned her palms up in the form of a query.

"She seems upset?" she said to David, who had sat back down.

"It's been an emotional day," he replied.

"True," she said, plonking herself beside him and resting a manicured hand on his thigh. She let her head drop back, shut her eyes and slumped down on the seat. David turned and looked at her, taking in all that was different from his muddled memories. The mousey blonde hair mirrored his, but she had their mother's features. The nose, while not big, seemed a little large for the face and her chin receded a touch. The face had the symmetry of good bone structure and full round eyes, all together pretty rather than beautiful. She wouldn't stop traffic like Eve, but David thought her still a damn good catch for the right man.

"Are you staring at me?" she said, her eyes still closed.

"Just getting to know your face."

"You had pictures."

"Nothing for a long time."

"Really?" She sat up and looked at him.

"In front of Windsor Castle. You me and mum. That's the last photo I had of you."

"Jesus, that was, what, seven years ago. Christ what was my hair like?" She sat forward, to look at him back.

"Long. Frizzy. You had your application for the police accepted a few days before. You were really chuffed"

"A double celebration. Your release and my acceptance. Ironic."

"You were off to make sure the police got it right next time…"

The pair sat in silence for a few seconds, the nature of decisions and their effect on lives weighing heavily on their memories.

"Why could we never write to you David?"

"It was better that way. I knew how Dad and Peter felt. I figured if I just left, then that would be simpler for all. I moved around a lot as well."

"I'm not saying the cards weren't great, but we really needed more. Mum especially." She looked down at her feet, uncomfortable to be chastising him.

"I know. Sorry. I wanted to write more. Came close a few times. I just needed to be away from it all. I needed to start again. A new life. "

She nodded as if she understood.

"Where did you go?"

David bristled. He hadn't explained himself or his life to anyone. For seven years no one had asked or cared what had gone before. He was a new man, un-judged and free from the sneers of others. Returning today had opened old wounds and bought the sense of guilt and feeling of being ashamed back to the forefront of his mind. His Pandora's Box of bittersweet emotions.

"I travelled the world. Changed my name. Lost all the trappings of a normal life. I don't want them back either."

"No home?"

"No home, no possessions and no responsibilities."

"You must own something?"

"What I'm wearing and that green kit bag."

"That's a military bag isn't it?"

"It is."

"Dad checked, I checked too. We found no record of you in the armed services?"

"British Armed Services?" he asked.

"Yeah and others in the Commonwealth."

"Dad checked? Was he hoping I didn't join his old regiment? He'd never have been able to handle the shame."

Jacqui just let out a little laugh, the notion was too close to the truth.

"I joined the French Foreign Legion."

He knew the admission would have an impact, it always did. People had this absurd Beau Geste notion of the Legion. A ragtag bunch of petty criminals and murderers in blue tunics and white trousers marching through the dessert to fight hordes of marauding Berber tribesmen.

"Fucking hell David – the Foreign Legion, bit dramatic isn't it? Couldn't you have gone to Corfu and 'found' yourself?" She let out a big grin as she mocked him.

"Maybe," he said, "not really me though."

"No... not sure I'd know what was 'you'." she said. "But the Foreign Legion, they're proper mentalists?"

He laughed this time.

"Some of them are, yeah. It was tough, very tough."

"Why?" It was more of a plea than a question.

David sighed, blew the air from his cheeks and rubbed his hand over his head.

"It's a cliché, but I went to forget. When you join you're forced to change your name, even if you don't need to. They make you leave everything at the gate. They strip you of everything and give you all you'll need. Literally, they strip you naked and let you start again. That's what I needed."

Jacqui looked hard at him as he spoke, he faced forward looking at the house.

"It's a five year contract and then I signed up for another term when that was done."

"When did you join?" She followed his eyes and saw they were tracking their mother as she moved around with the last of the funeral guests.

"Just after I left here, not long after we took that photo at the castle, but I was invalided out a year or so ago."

"You were wounded? Where?"

"I took a hefty chunk of shrapnel in the arse and back of my right leg."

Jacqui chuckled. "I meant where were you serving?"

"Oh right." He looked at her for a moment and smiled.

"Did it do a lot of damage?"

"Well I won't be running in the Olympics, put it that way. Nothing permanent, beyond some ugly scars. It got infected and side-lined me for a long time. I was serving in Afghanistan. Special liaison with the British SAS."

Jacqui's mouth dropped with exaggerated surprise. She saluted him.

"How come you got to work with the SAS?"

"The Legion has become the fighting force called on to do the UN's dirty work. France hires them out at will. We had a parachute battalion in Helmand Province, I spoke English so got the job of combat liaison. Nothing special."

"Jesus my brother the legionnaire." She said it as if her brother were the must have socialite accessory. "Peter will spit fire when he finds out."

"Still a bit of a cock is he?"

"Colossal. As uptight as a homophobe in a gay men's choir. But he's ok David. He'll struggle with your return the most."

David nodded. Little brothers and big brothers; complicated. Peter was the middle child as well. He had it all stacked against him, or so he'd think.

"Why will he spit fire?" he asked.

"Well he'd convinced himself you were dead or a vagrant or something. He liked the idea of being the only successful older brother."

"You never let on to him that I was in contact?"

"No, not worth the grief; he'd just go off on one like dad could."

David nodded again. "Fair point – he should still feel good about all he's accomplished. Whatever it is. What other people do doesn't detract from that," he said.

"True. But that's not Peter. He's always tried to impress, to seek praise."

"Especially from dad," David interrupted.

"Yeah especially from dad. He's not a bad guy, just a bit of a cock. A bit highly strung for sure, but he's ok. You might like him if you get to know him." She patted him on the back as she said it. "He works for the government, senior civil servant or something. He's in tax or finance or similar... we don't see him much," she said.

David shovelled a crab paste sandwich into his mouth and chewed. Peter working for the government and dealing in tax. He and his brother couldn't be more different.

"So what name did you have to use in the Legion?"

He shifted on the bench and pulled out his wallet. He removed his French ID card and handed it to her. She took it, intrigued, and studied the details.

"Daveed Donjooo," she exaggerated. "Why?"

"He's a real person from the Legion's past – a real hero. They said I should keep David as I was familiar with it but change my surname to something French. They all laughed, prattled on in French and kept calling me "hero" in English. They just wrote that name down, no debate."

"Why'd they do it?"

"For a laugh. See how long it took for me give up and leave probably. I had no idea who the real David Danjou was or how important to the Legion he is…I found out pretty quickly. I've had the piss taken out of me ever since."

"Were you picked on? Bless." She dug an elbow into his ribs to emphasise the point.

"Mmmm a bit." His mind momentarily flashed to another time, to darkness, pain and utter fear. He blinked it away, "It wasn't like school bullying. I had to prove I was worthy of the name all the time." He frowned as he said it.

She had heard about stories of brutality in the Legion, 'beasting' it was called.

"Nasty stuff?"

"Yeah, very. But ten years in prison pretty much prepares you for anything."

Jacqui sat back on the bench, silent and reflective. She had changed her professional name from Edwards to Evards to get away from her past life. But it didn't really compare. She had often thought of David and what he might be doing. But she buried the prison years deep within her memory. Not wanting to think about the realities of prison life or how her brother coped. She saw him only a handful of times after he was released, then he disappeared. Jail visits aren't the time to ask loved ones what their day to day routine is like and whether they were being bullied. She had no idea of the truth of his life. The memories remained, just buried. Now, she realised that David had spent seventeen in prison or in the army, almost as many as he had living at home.

"So the cards with all the foreign post marks, they came from where you were serving?"

"That's right." He swallowed down another mini sausage.

"Did you see combat?"

"A lot. Plenty of wars going on, lots of people wanting to kill other people."

"Where?"

"Er... all over. I did service in Somalia, Iraq and Afghanistan of course." He flicked at some lichen on the bench and sighed a little at the memories. "I was in Liberia for a while, Chad too. I spent time stationed in Djbouti, no fighting there though."

"The French are fighting in lots of places aren't they? I had no idea. Do you mind talking about it?" She shook her head in genuine amazement.

"I don't mind, not with you anyway. I might be vague on the details."

"Official secrets act?" She said it with a smile in her voice.

He shook his head. "Hah! No let's just say some things are best left unsaid."

Jacqui took the hint. Her father had always been proud of his service record but if anyone asked him for details or probed too far he clammed up and developed the same stare David had now. She wanted to understand what her brother had seen and experienced but that would be for another time.

"But you have a French ID card? Are you a French citizen then?"

"Now I am, yeah. The French have a rather noble principle, *Francais per le sang verse*. It means, if you spill blood defending France you have the right to be a citizen. It's like a reward."

"Was the injury serious?"

"Enough to get me out with an injury pension. I have some metal floating about in my arse, the hamstring got pretty torn up – took a long time to convalesce. No way of getting back into the front line after the injury. They don't give desk jobs to non-French."

"So you left last year. What ya been doing?"

"Travelling, working and resting. Learning to live life without rules."

"What just roaming about?"

"Yep, exactly that. I wake up and head off, no plans and no worries. If I want to stay I do, if I don't I go."

"A proper hobo?"

"Kinda. I've been all over Europe, but travel costs, so recently I have been walking around France a lot. I get buses, trains sometimes. All free with my veteran status. The French take their former soldiers to their heart."

"And money?"

"Still got the interrogation skills from the force I see?" he said.

"Sorry – just fascinated Dooby, I don't get how you live?"

"I take casual jobs if I need extra money. I have an injury stipend and pension from the Legion and a lot of my salary saved up. It's enough… just. I like being on my own."

"Really?"

"You have to remember I spent ten years sharing a cell and was never alone in the Legion, except sometimes in a hole in some African shit hole. I like the solitude."

Jacqui rocked back and forth as she absorbed the information, coming to the realisation that she had no real idea who her brother was. He had never denied killing the man in the fight. He'd always pleaded self-defence, but the police and jury saw it otherwise. She knew he had killed, but as she sat here now and heard about his lonely life she realised he must have killed a lot more since.

"It must have taken a lot to come here today."

"More than you know Jacqui… enough about me. What about you?"

"Me, what's to tell?"

"Everything."

"Not married, single - maybe getting desperate. Run my own business. Use the name Evards rather than Edwards for business."

"Really? So no longer in the police?"

"I did nearly six years, started to hate it. Too much red tape and bollocks."

"So what did you do?"

"I started a corporate fraud investigations company."

"A what?"

"We specialise in technical frauds, embezzlement. Following the money trail. As well as some corporate espionage and employee and citizen fraud work."

"Explain?"

"You know when staff or the public sue their companies for injuries received in accidents or such like. We follow them and investigate the legitimacy of the claims – that's the day-to-day shit but we also investigate businesses and employees that might be dodgy or corporate theft, that kinda thing."

"Is business good?"

"Sadly it's booming. We also do other pro bono work for Eve as well."

"Eve? You do investigations for Eve's firm?"

"Absolutely, about 30% of our work comes via Eve. She's the one that persuaded me to start up on my own, we share office space with her firm."

David mulled over the news, digested the information and tried to avoid jumping to conclusions.

"You do some free stuff for her?"

"You know Eve, always got a cause. She represents illegal and migrant workers that get chewed up and spat out by the system. My lot do some undercover work from time to time."

"James Thomas, was he one of them?"

"He's a contractor we used for some stuff, Eve too. You met him then?"

"He found me."

"He's very good…still on holiday in France I think."

David didn't correct the tense. He stared at the house and the patio doors. Beyond the reflection of the garden he could see shapes and shadows moving about. The tall slender shape of Eve floated back and forth.

"What was he working on before being sent to find me?"

Jacqui shrugged, "Something to do with illegal immigrants. Eve's convinced there is a smuggling ring based in Slough…"

"Russian…" he interrupted.

Jacqui stopped and turned to look at him.

"Yes…Ukrainian and Russian is her theory. How did you know?"

David turned and smiled. A half smile that didn't show any teeth and his eyes didn't back it up. The reason James Thomas died had nothing to do with looking for him and everything to do with what he'd been investigating for Eve. "Just a stab in the dark."

Valentyn didn't like to be to be unprepared. Having all the information at your fingertips when Wladimir wanted it proved to be one of the many reasons he had become invaluable to the business. At this moment though he didn't have the answers, he too had been left in the dark and would need to find the answers to the questions Wladimir wouldn't yet know he wanted to ask.

Yuri hovered nearby, Valentyn tried to ignore him. Neither Sascha nor Demitry had answered their phones for more than three days now. The message had been received, the old man had not returned to England, all as planned, but his two soldiers remained missing.

"Yuri!" he barked, knowing Yuri would always be within earshot.

"Yes…" Yuri half bowed as he answered and moved towards Valentyn. It had the look and intention of a faux gesture of subservience.

"The import shipments arrived safely – correct?"

"Da!"

"How many ports did they use this time?" Valentyn knew the answer but he wanted to hear the confirmation out loud.

"Three. The biggest import yet boss, three lorries arrived at each a minimum of 100 units per lorry." Yuri had been elevated to more than just a gofer, but still not a soldier. He loitered in a servile domain between the old man, the daughters and Valentyn. Neither respected the other. Valentyn thought for a moment, this near one thousand strong import would be the largest so far but in a matter of weeks they would be dealing with up to five times the amount.

"Which lorry was Sascha and Demitry escorting?"

Yuri smirked a little and then turned it into cough, "You don't know?"

Valentyn stiffened and gave the little man a stare, his cheeks tightened as he gritted his teeth, not for the first time he imagined snapping the little fool's neck.

"I ask and you tell. Let us keep it simple, like you."

"No neither Sascha nor Demitry were on any of the shipments, their teammates that came from Folkestone were moaning when they unloaded at the warehouse."

Valentyn nodded, it confirmed what he suspected. "Maybe," Yuri continued, "they stayed in France to take a holiday?" Yuri didn't lack bravery and had ambitions all his own, but he wouldn't be daft enough to poke the bear that is Valentyn and not expect to get mauled. His reputation wasn't hearsay, so Yuri conceded he'd managed to land some smart-arse body blows to the ice cool exterior of the old man's enforcer and that now would be a good time to get out of the way of the likely backlash to Sascha and Demitry's fuck up.

"Is that all Valentyn? I need to sort out the party details for Uncle and it is a big job."

He rose to his full 5'11 and tried to puff out his chest in pride. Valentyn simply waved him off. As Yuri moved away, Valentyn returned to his neck-snapping day dream. Yuri might be solidly built but Valentyn remained confident he could still do it with one hand. Sascha and Demitry going missing proved both odd and unprofessional. He had recruited them and trained them, both ex-military, tough and seasoned, he chose them for the job because they would deliver. Valentyn wasn't a man easily overcome by foolish pride, he knew something serious must have happened. He took out his iPhone and opened the web browser. He searched for 'headline, Saint-Innocence' and waited.

'*3 deaths in a small French town*' ran a headline on the BBC website, some French websites were listed with more detail, but Valentyn spoke no French. The short story focused on the death of a former British policeman on holiday in France. Valentyn scanned the story and saw the story had been published that same day and the French police had confirmed that the two other men found dead at the scene had not been identified, though witnesses had said they could have been East-European.

Valentyn pondered the likelihood of the fat PI killing his two soldiers and doubted it. He read to the end, then he got worried. "French police are looking for a French man seen talking to James Thomas in a cafe shortly before his body was discovered."

Valentyn made the calculation and considered the scenario. Someone else had to be involved, someone good - very good, to have taken out his soldiers. The knife that killed the PI had been found at the scene, a standard issue weapon amongst his men. His men had trailed the old man for several days. Valentyn wanted to be sure they found out what the old man knew about their business and how far his investigations went. His men hadn't reported anybody like a bodyguard and his movements in France had not indicated he knew anything about the depth of their dealings in France. No, Valentyn dismissed the notion of a bodyguard and that left him with a problem. Who had come and helped the old man, why had he helped and what did he know?

Wladimir would need to know some, but not all, of the details.

David settled onto the sofa, he tried to relax. The last of the mourners and triumphant aged survivors had left a while ago, but David patiently waited until Jacqui beckoned him towards the house. He'd reached the tired conservatory door just in time to hear his brother shout his disgust and disagreement. Doors slammed and David felt the pang of time travelling memories, he half-expected his brother to yell "it's not fair, I hate you." He manoeuvred through the chintz and floral patterns of the conservatory to settle down on the sofa, he cast his eye around the room, taking in the vista of knick-knacks, pleasant Turner prints, the oblong mirror and unfilled vases.

No family portraits, no sentimental pictures of husband and wife or children graced the walls. He assumed that was normal and not some act of benevolence to spare his feelings. David thought it odd that Jacqui and Peter hadn't been celebrated, as for much for their successes as for simply not being him. His curiosity halted with a slow clunk and creak of the door handle, instinctively he rose to his feet in expectation of a superior. His mother entered the room, still in her funeral attire, but accessorised with slippers and plain blue apron. She stared silently, a small smile came upon her lips, partially catching the pair of them by surprise. A tear rolled down her cheek and she raised her arms for an embrace.

David hesitated and then stooped and wrapped his arms around her, strong shoulders and muscular arms dwarfing the petite woman. He squeezed and she responded, they swayed momentarily and David gently lifted his mother off the floor with the weight of his hug.

"I want to look at you; I need to see my boy without all the others and their silliness." She reluctantly pushed away from his embrace and stepped back to take in her son, a man she hadn't seen for seven years.

"Fit and healthy I see."

"I try Mum."

"Handsome, no model, but you don't have any issues in the lady department do you?"

"Mum..." It was David's turn to feel like an embarrassed teenager.

"A mother is a woman all the same David. You've

changed more than I could have imagined, you seem so solid, strong. Physically you remind me of your father."

The mention of the deceased caused a momentary stop in the pleasure at seeing each other, the grim realisation of the reason for their meeting intruding on the private joy of their reunion.

"The Foreign Legion hey?"

"Yes Mum."

"Your father said you'd head for the Army. He was terrified you'd use his name and try to join his old regiment." She said it without a hint of opinion.

"I wanted to forget, not seek out memories and comparison at every turn. The Legion seemed like a romantic as well as pragmatic option." He stood to attention and saluted.

"Impressive" she said. "Your father may have even approved. Not that we'll ever know."

David lowered his hand and looked down, "Sorry about dad..." he mumbled.

"Don't be. Your father had the ability to be an utter fool, he kept you from me for years David. He kept you from your family. I could never forgive him for that."

David nodded. His mother moved forward and stroked fluff from his shoulder, "He never gave you credit for much, always criticising. Putting you down, he thought he would toughen you up. Get you ready for the world."

David looked down at his mother, her auburn hair now liberally peppered with grey, she looked all of her sixty-two years. "Maybe he did. Dad was dad, he couldn't change."

"No" she replied, "I suppose not. But maybe he could have believed you."

David turned away and picked up a knick-knack from the mantel piece. It was a sterling silver antique match holder, he flicked it open and twisted it over and round with his fingers. He'd found it in a shop in Olney, Buckinghamshire, and bought it for his mother, a symbol of her giving up smoking.

"Your father always assumed I bought that," she said. It survived his purge of all memories of you." David placed it back down on the mantel piece. "Are you back for good?"

"I doubt it Mum... but at least I can visit now."

"I'm so sorry, baby boy, I'm so sorry." She moved forward with feverish zeal and grabbed him round the waist and pulled tight. "I should have been stronger, I should never have let him drive you out of our lives, I'm so sorry."

David wrapped his arms around her again and kissed the top of her head. "I know Mum, but I left remember. I walked away too. I couldn't be around him. We shared the same disgust for each other. I'll never know why he never believed it was self-defence. I have tried to reason it through, he just assumed I was lying and nothing I said or did altered his view."

His mother squeezed again, "He should have supported you. It's what families do."

David didn't reply, he had nothing he could offer in

way of a platitude. The Legion had been his surrogate dysfunctional family and he knew he could count on the men he had served with to be there for him if needed.

"Had a little barnie with Peter I hear," his mother turned her head but left it resting on his chest as she spoke. "He tried to tell you weren't welcome I hear?"

"Well technically I doubt dad wanted me there, so Peter thought he was doing the right thing."

"Hmmm, not sure that boy knows what the right thing is anymore."

"Peter just followed dad's lead mum. I knew I wasn't wanted here, ten years in prison hadn't softened his views, he couldn't care less that I lost ten years of my life due to the lies of others." David shook his head as if to hold back the rising anger. "Peter could only see a murderer, nothing less."

"I believed you. Jacqui believed you. Eve believed you." she said.

"I know." He did know it as well, but hearing it again eased some of the feeling of abandonment. "its water under the bridge mum, new times new life."

She looked up at him and planted a big mum style kiss on his cheek.

"Yes. I'll not miss your father David - sorry that I'm saying this to you, but Jacqui and Peter had some semblance of a relationship with him, so can't hear it. But I need to vent some spleen too. I'm almost glad he's dead, that's horrid I know, but I have sat here today and listened to idiot after idiot talk utter rubbish about the man.

Eulogising about how the golf club will miss him, how the pub quiz team won't be the same without him." She wrung her hands and sneered, "All the time I wanted to shout – please all of you just SOD OFF – my son is here."

David smiled at the spirit he knew had always existed in his mother. He saw the same spark of mischief when his mother used to allow Saturday morning TV whenever his father went to play golf or the fact that she never took them to church if his dad was away. "We don't need any of that sanctimonious drivel today do we..." she would say. It was that very spirit that seemed to desert her when David got his freedom and needed her to be strong. David wondered if maybe he'd drained it from her.

"Come on you." She took him by the hand and pulled him towards the kitchen. "You can help tidy up, Jacqui's washing and Eve is no doubt doing something clever with emails on her phone."

She stopped at the door and turned to him. "Give Peter a chance... I know in your mind he doesn't deserve one, but he's not a clone of your father. He's hurting very badly right now. He may not realise it, but he needs his older brother now more than ever."

David nodded. "I'll try Mum, promise."

"Good boy, spend a couple of days with me, let me spoil you, allow me to be a mum ok?"

David smiled, "Sounds great."

MONDAY

Peter Edwards eased his lanky frame into his office chair, the high-backed ergonomic contraption looked more wheelchair than office furniture but it kept his 6"3" frame aligned and him free from back pain. He spent a lot of time at his desk, he was neither 'in tax' or an accountant as his family members and many friends so often failed to grasp. He did indeed work for the government, in a quango-esque fashion and remained proud of his civil servant status. Peter understood that he came across as a dorky pen-pusher and that despite his height he remained unimposing, almost limp in stature. No matter how he dressed or wore his hair he couldn't shake off the look of a man never in fashion and never quite with the times. Resignation to this state of affairs had empowered Peter with a dismissive disinterest in others and their perception of himself. He came across as unashamedly pompous.

He didn't care. He was good at his job, he was professionally respected and liked by his peers. He had always kept a professional separation of social and work life, certainly he attended all the 'team' and office functions, but he had never popped to the pub for a beer or attended any softball games on a Sunday. He had long ceased to be included in the invites as well. Peter tapped in the passwords and codes that gave him access to the various work networks he had permission for. He opened several tabs and viewed his calendar. Before he could get underway with his days' work a beach ball masquerading as a woman galumphed into the room.

"Peter Perfect!" Barbara Filsom crowed. Peter shuddered momentarily.

"Barbara!" he replied with rehearsed glee.

"Petey, in early I see, readying for the rigours of the day. What wonders does the world of procurement hold for you today?"

Peter smiled unconvincingly. "What can I do for you, I have a 9.00 o'clock and need to prepare." He kept his riposte on the right side of succinct without being rude.

"Well, I'm being chased by the Quilter Group, they are ever so keen to know if they have won the contract for the immigration centre upgrades and ..."

"The committee sits tomorrow, "Peter interrupted her, "They will ratify who is awarded the contract then. You know that Barbara."

Barbara shuffled a little, "Of course, but everyone knows they automatically approve your recommendations, tis just a rubber stamp job... go on Peter give me a clue would you. Counsellor Dawes is keen to find out as well."

Peter sighed. Barbara's enquiry would be one of several he'd get this week. While no official part of procurement, which is rightly viewed as a tedious and officious role, but sadly a necessary one when dealing with government contracts Peter's role as an IT and software specialist meant his recommendations carried significant weight. He saw his input as not one of denying money or opportunity but of ensuring contracts and cash was spent well. No doubt the counsellor had made promises or had a financial interest in who won the deal, maybe Barbara did too. She loved her golf and the Quilter Group had membership at Wentworth. Peter didn't judge, that was the world, back scratching and favours made life a little easier and he could never claim to be whiter than white in his governmental contracting days any case.

"I doubt Barbara that the Quilter Group will fail to land the business, objectively, any recommendation would look very favourably on their good record in development of government property and their long history in affordable housing."

He used his tame, tried and tested diplomatic answer. Quilter Group would get the contract, they were cheap enough and just about exceeded the acceptable quality standard. They were a safe option for risk averse management who preferred minimal scrutiny of their decisions. Not that Peter cared if they were a risk, on no piece of paper, email or otherwise would anyone find an actual endorsement or recommendation by Peter Edwards. If anyone would be blamed for a future cock up he always ensured it wouldn't be him.

Peter tapped his pen across his teeth and leant back in his chair. He pondered the weekend that had just finished. His colleagues and superiors had no idea his father had passed away, they couldn't know he'd just had the funeral and the brother he had never told any of them existed had returned to the family fold.

Peter didn't hate his brother, he didn't know his brother well enough to have a defined emotional response. When his name or the notion of him was mentioned in the past he simply felt the presence of an invisible irritation, like a random humming. No, Peter resented his brother and the expectation and importance his father placed on David's successes or failures. Like a true middle child he never grasped the responsibility the eldest child absorbs on behalf of his siblings, nor he did realise how much not having his father's focus would be a blessing.

He pulled out his iPad and powered it up, he swivelled round towards the window and rested it on his knees, from here he picked up a reasonably strong signal for the free Wi-Fi hot-spot from the cafe in the square. Ultimately these were probably unnecessary precautions, but Peter preferred a cautious approach to most aspects of his personal life. He entered the password and then opened up his remote server logins, alternate emails and online bookmaker apps. Then he launched the browser and the 'incognito' window before typing in the additional security details and from memory tapped in the url to the network where he did his 'bonus work'.

Zenovia grunted and snorted, her rise and fall matched the laboured heavy breathing. She rode her victim, pushing all her weight down onto her partner's groin, he floundered under a tide of cellulite and large limbs. She grabbed at his hands and pulled them up her doughnut rings of flesh and forced them to cup her wallowing breasts. "Squeeze my nipples..." she demanded, the hands reached a little further forward and did as commanded. She arched her back in reaction and let out a contented snort of pleasure. The shift of her weight had 'Richter' like consequences, the man squirmed in discomfort and let out a slow release of breath and groaned with flattened submission. Mistaking this for an enthusiastic response, Zenovia repeated the shift, rising and falling with ever more vigorous intent, the figure beneath seemingly sinking further into the bed and being consumed by her acres of flesh.

The bed pitched and lurched in time with the writhing until finally Zenovia grabbed the hands away from her nipples. Squeezing them in a vice like grip, she orgasmed, with all the shuddering mystique of a Caterpillar earth mover; rising one final time she let out a near childlike squeak of pleasure and then pitched forward, with no consideration for whom would break her fall. Her pendulous breasts and fat-rippled torso smothering the face of her sexual saddle.

She panted for several moments, sweat glistening off her back, waiting to catch her breath, pushing herself onto her forearms she looked down at her partner for the first time since she sat astride him.

Yuri turned over and arched his back into a long stretch, Joints clicking in response. He looked at Zenovia and a smile played across his lips. "Top job Yuri." She said mirroring his smile. She executed an exaggerated roll manoeuvre and sat up in the bed. She examined her nails and occasionally picked out some detritus from under one and flicked it across the room. In many ways she was a distinctly unpleasant person, in both manners and personality, but Yuri could see the attractive girl under the cloak of a spoilt child. She did have fine features; just the consumption to excess had laid a fat camouflage over her body and rendered her too big to be voluptuous. Yuri made no pretence of not being shallow, her looks and shape ensured that he wouldn't publically date the girl by choice; his ego couldn't take that... No her status within the 'gang' community made her an attractive opportunity. She was certainly better looking than her sister Masha.

"Your sister, she keeps messing things up with your father doesn't she?" He ventured. Zenovia shrugged and offered a half-nod of consensus. "This business with the half-full shipments, is your father blaming her for it?"

"We both got the blame for that one. The lorries were always gonna be light for that trip, the process for managing the people is rubbish... we didn't set it up remember."

Yuri did know. Her father had given his daughters various responsibilities in the people shipments but hadn't involved them in the planning. Whenever they came back with suggestions or had wanted to change something they had received the dismissive wave of the hand that Wladimir had become so adept at.

"Papa only listens to Valentyn these days. And that big lump finks we're stupid. Aint easy to get Papa to listen to stuff that might make his star soldier look bad." She said it with a resigned tone and remained focused on the nails and her limited excavations.

"I understand that... Valentyn isn't my biggest fan either. He thinks I'm just a Gofer, he forgets that I hear a lot that he doesn't in those heads of family meetings. I know things."

"Wadda you know Yuri? Serious… wadda you really know beyond what you're allowed to know?" She shifted her gaze down to the man lying by her side. He offered no real response but tried to look like he had secrets he couldn't divulge with others.

"My father treats everyone like they're an idiot... until they prove they aint. He finks his daughters are worthless to the business, that we can't run anything. He's wrong, he forgets no fucker knows the business straight away and that you gotta have time to learn..."

Yuri let out a little chuckle that stopped her mid-sentence and she stared at him, eyebrows raised seeking an explanation. "What? I laugh because I know you have ideas and can do better, but Masha? Please..."

Zenovia turned to face him, "Careful Yuri. My sister can be a right bitch, I know more than most, but she's my big sister. Right?"

"Right." Yuri murmured.

"Did you cum?" she said.

"Na... not yet. Sorry." Yuri shifted his weight under the duvet and knew it was not what she wanted to hear. He had no issue with Zenovia using him, if anything he preferred to be useful, but her insistence that he not only came every time but also wilfully conceded it was the best sex he'd ever had, proved to be both impossible and exhausting.

"Fuckin'ell when I ride a man like that, he should come like a fountain..."

Yuri shifted his hand under to duvet toward his groin in preparation for what was likely to happen. "I was enjoying it too much to cum just yet" he lied.

"You've gotta cum," she ordered, "Its only right, c'mon I'll give you a wank..."

Yuri smiled to himself. "Don't be silly – you can have an orgasm without me, its fine it's my duty to make you happy." Zenovia nodded her agreement.

"I know its fine, but if I tell you to cum then you cum... understand?"

Yuri smiled again, "Of course." He knew the futility of arguing, and had long given up understanding the insecurities that led to her needing to order men to have sex with her and then demanding they physically demonstrate their enjoyment. Yuri, had however begun to use it in his favour, convincing her that to climax with her he could only do so in one particular way. "You know how it works best for me," he offered.

She didn't answer, but simply flopped off the bed on to her knees. Yuri swung his legs over and stood in front of her, a few gentle tugs and the notion of the true subjugation of his boss's daughter were enough for the fatigued old chap to rise to the occasion once more. Yuri began to masturbate.

Masha steadied herself at the door and leaned in once more. The talking had stopped and the grunting and thumping had ceased. Masha desperately wanted to know what her sister was doing to Yuri now. She wanted to laugh at her sister and poke fun that Yuri was the best she could get and how very sad that was. But in truth she had no high horse from which from she could crow. Papa didn't hate his daughters, she knew that, but he didn't trust them with the business. Masha's attempts to get Valentyn had proved unsuccessful and despite the obvious sense in a match up the big ape simply wasn't interested in her. Time was running out to impress her father into handing the reigns of the business to her. Yuri didn't command the same respect as Valentyn for sure, but he had become close with her father and that gave her sister a head start.

A muffled moan of anguished relief emanated from behind the locked door, Masha leant back and furrowed her brow in confusion.

"Listening at doors again Masha?" The deep strong voice startled her into the look of the caught red-handed, she swung to see who had said it and there was a pregnant pause as she evaluated the situation. Valentyn noted her lack of composure and the time it took for her to regain her unearned air of superiority.

"It is best to know what *should* be being said, rather than listening at a door to find out what *is* being said." Valentyn maintained a respectful tone.

"Did my father teach you that?"

"No." Valentyn held her gaze and loomed a little over her. "My father taught me that. If you are reduced to hovering at doorways trying to hear something important then you are a long way from where you need to be."

He took hold of her forearm and gently guided her away from the bedroom door and back towards the stairway. Masha resisted a tiny amount and then capitulated, happy to be escorted. Only Valentyn cast his eyes back towards the door.

"Zenovia doesn't take the business seriously Valentyn."

"And you do of course."

"I do. More seriously than her," she protested.

Valentyn let out a little laugh. "That is not too hard to achieve and not much of a claim."

Blood Ties

Masha allowed herself to be led back to the ground floor and into the back offices of the restaurant. Valentyn had a small area he could, but didn't, call his office. It had a second door that opened to a narrow service corridor which in turn led to a back door and onto the alleyway behind the restaurant, an alleyway that had to be kept clean and obstacle free at all times.

Valentyn poured a shot of vodka into two glasses and handed one to her. She looked at it with raised eyebrows.

"It's genuine – you know I love Stolchinaya."

"I do... about me being at the door..."

Valentyn raised a hand to halt her confession, "Your sister rides Yuri two or three times a week Masha, he is stupid, he thinks no one knows."

"How long have you known about it?"

"Since it began, it's my job to know all that goes on here."

Masha slugged back the vodka and then watched as Valentyn sipped his and sat down. "Does my father know about it?"

Valentyn, shook his head and took another sip. "Not yet, but he will do soon if they keep being so stupid."

"I should be the one to tell my father"

"Why?" Valentyn looked through his glass and admired the pure spirit. "Think about what you know, consider what your father needs to know and consider how having such information is of benefit to you."

Masha couldn't help but show her confusion, she wore

her base emotions like vulgar jewellery. "Your father hates things happening behind his back – but he realises a lot happens without him. He trusts people to share what he needs to know, to run the business."

Masha nodded.

"You need to realise that your father will be angry and see it as a betrayal by Yuri, the touching of his daughter – but if you run and tell tales on your sister the crime seems less important, a sisterly squabble, maybe your father will think your are jealous."

Masha snorted her derision. "Maybe your father will think more of Yuri because both of his daughters argue over him," he continued.

"Yuri is a pig and he has his head stuck so far up papa's arse he burps shit."

Valentyn almost tasted the metaphor, and it showed on his face. "Yes he does, but your father likes him and he can be useful. Stupid men with ambition can be dangerous if left uncontrolled."

"You need to control Yuri?"

"*We* need to have control of Yuri's ambition, ensure his ambition serves the future of the family business and not just his own greed."

"I understand," Masha said. He doubted this to be true. While Masha had proved smarter than her sister she still lacked the true understanding of the value of keeping friends and enemies close.

"We, *you*, should use Yuri to do some business for you, something vital. It would make you look good to your father. If Yuri does well, you present it as your good management and not your sister's. Yuri loves glory and looking good in front of your father so he will be indebted to you. If he fails then your father will be impressed you tried and Yuri's failure can be put down to something else... maybe his mind not being on the job."

He hoped Masha would finish the little tale. She didn't.

"Yuri will have fucked up because he was too busy fucking your sister... do you see?"

Masha nodded and Valentyn smiled.

"We have a situation developing, nothing big, but something it is best we resolve quietly. There is a woman here in Windsor, she has been working with the lawyer woman who is asking a lot of questions about immigrants and illegal benefit claims. He claims he knows this woman. He boasts to the soldiers about it but denies it to me."

"He's good with the ladies I hear, has many internet 'honies'..." Masha said.

"Apparently," said Valentyn, "Yuri is almost not Russian at all – if he truely does know this woman then I'd like to know why he thinks he can get away with not helping me deal with the situation?"

Masha didn't say anything.

"Yuri doesn't like taking orders from me, but if you talk to him, have him report to you about this lady and get him to reveal what she knows." He stopped to let the idea take hold. "It would show your father that you're being clever, that you're using Yuri properly – your father will be impressed."

Masha said nothing more and just nodded, a vague look of expectation on her face, Valentyn couldn't be sure if she wanted more vodka or simply to hear him explain it better. He offered neither. Valentyn knew the time was coming when the old man would have to hand the business over – this new deal, the size and scale of it eclipsed all that had gone before, it pushed the family into the limelight and could make them huge amounts of money and with that came greater threats. Valentyn's role had always been to protect and serve, he had built his forces quietly and steadily, away from the old man's direct control. He had secured his own position, which had been priority number one, now he needed to focus on ensuring the 'family' remained strong. One of the old man's stupid daughters had to be brought into the greater understanding. Masha had more potential than her sister; her desperation to be of value to her father could easily be manipulated. Her clumsy attempts at seducing Valentyn in the past at least demonstrated her willingness to create a partnership that would be of future mutual value. Touching the old man's daughters would be idiotic and career limiting, no matter how much he said he hated them. Valentyn could never inherit the business, but he could run it and expand it. War was coming, it had been a long time since the last one and the Romanies in Slough had grown in confidence, eating into the Poles' territory and drawing too much attention to the benefits scams. They would need to be stopped and they only understood one way.

War always had casualties and it always brought change.

Blood Ties

Peter Edwards tapped his computer keys with a lightness of touch-typing that any 60's secretary would have been rightly proud. He spent a lot of time on PCs and his life revolved around the internet; he made no apology for this fact. Making friends and socialising wasn't something that he was naturally gifted at. That said, he had a full social life and not all of it was confined to chat rooms and darkened rooms with a wad of loo roll to hand.

Under conventional thought he could legitimately say he had at least three girlfriends, granted one he had never seen let alone touched, she was Brazilian and Peter had no illusions about her final objectives. Either way she made for an interesting diversion. He had met and slept with the other two; both had come via different dating websites and both relationships the product of very different personal profiling techniques. He liked to experiment with what worked best and what moves to take. It had been a frustrating process at first, women are outnumbered ten-to-one on dating sites and standing out from the crowd isn't easy.

He stuck to simple rules, he always travelled to them until confident he wanted them to see his life up close. He always maintained that the first few meetings should be daytime and neutral territory and that anything further must be controlled or dictated by the lady. Not lying, being polite and considerate and not a moron seemed to have yielded his best results. Today however, he'd managed only a few minutes on IM and had made no progress with Siobhan in Ross-on-Wye, she liked to chat and was clearly bright, but seemed in no hurry to meet up. Conscious she wouldn't engage in IM sex he lost interest and so decided to focus on his online betting accounts. He had one with all the major brands. He took his gambling very seriously, monitoring every win and loss on spreadsheets, looking for trends and swings, anything that would make him more successful. The weekend had not been successful, not a single one of his ten bets or three accumulators had come in, and he had yet again worked his float to almost nothing and now needed to upload more money in order to place his bets this week.

He punched the return key and waited. He nodded his thanks as the screen showed the upload had been successful. William Hill had another £1,000 of his money and his float had been refilled. The losses this week meant this month probably wouldn't break even, but if he won big over the next few days then it could be limited. The quarter had been tough, a loss overall and £5,000 down, but tracking for the last twelve months looked even worse. In fact, if Peter was a nervous or anxious man then the last year would seem pretty scary. He'd already decided that he needed another poker game that should reset the balance of things.

His mind snapped back into the room with the irrepressible chirping of his iPhone. The name on the display simply read as "The Man". His cheeks filled with air and he blew it out slowly, casually he picked up the phone and said 'hello'.

The voice that greeted him lacked any formal pleasantry. Just clipped and precise, used to giving orders, to being listened to unconditionally and at no point during the thirty second conversation did it once consider if the listener was still there and still attentive. It knew he would be and it knew that failure to comply was not an option.

Peter nodded, his eyes closed his free hand pinching the bridge of his nose as he listened. He waited for the pause, the pause signified his moment to comply. "I understand," he said. The volume rose slightly and the voice reiterated its point more aggressively. "I understand."

Then there was silence. Peter remained in the same position for several seconds, as if waiting to be sure the voice had truly disconnected.

Wladimir looked at Valentyn, they held each other's gaze. The kitchen had been emptied of staff, they now loitered in the courtyard to the rear, patiently killing time until they would be allowed back in. Wladimir liked to discuss business amongst the sharp-edged shiny surfaces of his kitchen, it was at odds with the vibrant colours of the food it produced. Also, Valentyn, all good suit well groomed and pressed lines, found it moderately uncomfortable. Not that he had a great need to keep him on edge but the old man wanted to ensure the status quo be maintained. Valentyn sipped his coffee, not sure why the impromptu conference had been called.

"The inbound shipments, they have arrived?" the old man asked.

"Da." Valentyn replied with a curt nod.

"Everything as it should be, processing is in progress?"

"Da. Everything is as it should be with the shipment."

The old man nodded, he sipped his tea, Valentyn his coffee.

"How long before we will have all the documents and

details for the Librarian?"

"A few more days, there are a lot of people... we are all learning, it will be slow this time but faster next."

"Good and everything else is well... all running smoothly?"

Valentyn realised he needed to confess to a problem, be upfront but underplay the significance if he can. "We have small problems, here and there, nothing big."

"Tell?"

"The lawyer woman is still snooping... the investigator has been dealt with."

"But?"

Valentyn sighed, he kept a lot of the detail from the old man, partly to protect him in case of prosecution, but mostly because he didn't like to open the issues to public debate.

"Two soldiers are lost," he said finally.

Wladimir frowned and blew a short breath on to his tea. "How?"

"I am working on that."

"But the investigator will pry into our business no more?"

"Da," Valentyn offered assuredly.

"We need to be free of troubles, no mistakes Valentyn." The old man knew this was as severe a reprimand as he needed to give his enforcer, but one that he'd take to heart. "Can we cope without the soldiers?"

"Yes Uncle."

"The woman, is she under control too?"

"Yes Uncle."

Wladimir nodded. "The Librarian? He needs to learn to be respectful, my daughters have not made the situation clear enough."

"It is already organised Uncle."

"The fights... are they organised?" The old man hated boxing really, but understood it's underworld value.

"They are. Dimi fights on Wednesday, a man from Liverpool. They claim he is a champion."

Wladimir snorted, "Champion of what? Eating and drinking. The northerners are always fat and slow." Valentyn laughed at the comment; while not untrue the old man conveniently forgot that several Scottish fighters had caused mayhem in London in recent years.

"Dimi is ready and should win easily. Declan the Irishman and two others are handling bets for us."

"Good, keeping it small is smart."

"All the local gangs have been invited, they have been given the word on the Scouser... decent money is being put on him. The odds on Dimi are OK as a result. People will have fun and make money."

Wladimir nodded, he knew Valentyn could handle the fights easily enough, he'd fought in many in his time. "Keep my daughters away from it; you know how they get."

"They know to stay away Uncle."

"And the Gypsies?"

"Not coming... they know Dimi... their boy fights the fat bouncer next week, then we can have a 'final' between the winner of that and Dimi. It will be good for us to have the champion Uncle."

"It means nothing," sneered the old man. "Champion. HA! It's not like the old country Valentyn." The younger man said nothing, he knew better than to challenge the rose-tinted views his master occasionally had. Sure the violence and savagery in the UK didn't match home, but not much could. The men that fought in these unlicensed fights had to be respected and were as tough as they needed to be.

"You must also keep Yuri involved. He's getting things done, he needs to be involved more." Valentyn offered no response and, confident the message had been received, Wladimir waved his favourite soldier away. He rose from the stool and poured the remnants of his tea into the sink. As he passed Valentyn heading towards the swing door to the restaurant he rested a hand on his shoulder. "They can come in now."

Valentyn nodded and waited to hear the swing door bounce back and forth to indicate the old man had left the room. He frowned, gritted his teeth and swore under his breath. He took out his phone.

Eve Du Pisanie moved into the 5th floor of the multi-storey from the foul, piss-soaked stairwell. She shifted her black laptop bag from one shoulder to another: the weight of the bag had finally won the battle of attrition and she needed to change it over. The operation required her to put her shopping bags into the other hand and secure her small handbag before she could enact the transition. She failed to take into account the car keys clutched in her left hand, and as soon as she began the move of bags they clattered to the floor.

"Urrrghhhh," Eve groaned. She squatted down in the elegant and only manner that her long skirt allowed, she de-bagged realising that she would need to reorganise her load if she were to make it to the end of the row in comfort and without another stop. As she jostled the handbag into position she heard a sound, a scuff or scrape of a shoe on the concrete floor. It struck her as an odd sound and she peered around the quiet space looking for the source. She saw no one and heard nothing. Unconvinced and somewhat unnerved she looked more carefully, then she saw them. Two pairs of shoes and the accompanying legs could be clearly seen as their owners crouched behind a vehicle ten spaces ahead and only two from her own.

She froze, her mind raced and panic set it in, her breathing becoming shallow and a cold sheen of sweat formed on her back. She had reached the halfway point from the stairwell to her car and she had no idea if she should move forward or head back. She considered what they might be up to if they were not intent on mugging her... she came up with nothing. Maybe their selection wasn't random, maybe they were waiting for her specifically, after all the car park was popular and normally busy it would only be a matter of time before cars and people came by.

Eve reached into her purse and pulled out the small can of hairspray she always carried, then with a determined stance she rose to her feet, bags in place and walked to the row of cars opposite to her own. The feet shifted and shuffled behind the car, Eve tried to look like she hadn't seen them and had no idea anyone was hiding. She reached the end of the row and stood by a car that had been parked opposite her own and made as if to get in, the feet shuffled a little more then she heard steps. The soft slap of trainers on concrete gathered pace behind her; she dropped her bags and spun round to face the attacker.

The burst of hairspray hit the youth full in the face, he had no idea what hit him, but the burning sensation in his eyes immediately dropped him to the floor in writhing agony, Eve levelled a well-timed and evilly intended kick at his groin and made contact, ensuring the attacker wouldn't be getting up anytime soon.

Eve didn't admire her handiwork and raised the can once more, anticipating an attack from the second man any moment. Instead she saw the back of another short youth, hood up, disappearing over the centre railing and dropping to the lower level.

She heard a faint shout, "Better run bitch coz I'm gonna get some gangsta to hurt you."

Eve, shaking and unsteady on her feet looked down again, the fallen youth had crawled away from her and had begun a stumbling half run and tumble towards the stairwell. She gathered her bags and bolted for the perceived safety of her car, firing it up and managing to keep her composure to navigate the twists and turns and exit safely. The tears came freely and she thanked god she had only a few minutes to drive before getting home. She had no real idea who they were or why they wanted her. Whether paranoia or simple fear she felt it had meant to be more than just a mugging.

TUESDAY

Yuri sipped his coffee, then crossed his legs and tried his very best to appear like his idea of languid European chic. He slouched and would have lit a cigarette if the law allowed and if he actually smoked. He cast his eyes around the central concourse of Windsor Central station, now a myriad of designer shops, cafes and up-market stalls. Tourist heaven. He gazed from his table into the coffee shop hunting, for a 'yummy mummy' to admire, finding none his eyes moved to the neighbouring Cafe Rouge, a gaggle of women and babies clustered around two tables all chattering at once. "New mothers," he mumbled. Not Yuri's hunting ground, he had very specific tastes and types.

He smoothed down his blue suit jacket and flicked away some fluff that had gathered on his suit trouser. Belatedly, he decided to undo his suit jacket It became a complicated movement, and required the uncrossing of his legs and a bend of the back to ensure there was enough give to open the button. Once completed he cast his gaze around once more, hoping no one had seen the ungainly manoeuvre. Satisfied it had gone unnoticed he pulled out his iPhone and scrolled to his calendar; he needed to be sure who he was meeting today.

Janet, the lovely petite Janet, would be his guest today. They were only a week into their relationship. Yuri chuckled at the thought of calling it a relationship. He had met her via the internet, which is where he did all his hunting. She appeared perfect for his tastes, early forties, three children and over ten years of marriage teetering on collapse. She needed fun, excitement and a release from the daily grind. Yuri provided that service. They had swapped instant messages and then emails, it had happened, at least she assumed it did, at her pace and today finally, they would meet. In public, somewhere safe to reassure her. Yuri had led the digital conversations and Janet had willingly followed – it had taken a surprisingly short time for them to become suggestive, then implicit and finally lurid. Yuri had high expectations for this one.

Yuri double checked his site profile via his iPhone, he had learnt to keep his masquerades simple and close to the truth. The beauty of being accent free meant that he could eliminate the prejudices that came with being East European. The last thing he wanted to do was spook his targets into thinking he wanted a British wife. He used his dark complexion and non-Caucasian appearance to his benefit and had found that saying he was Corsican or Sicilian by birth worked best of all. A happy mix of the acceptable with the reasonably exotic, it dropped the knickers of the average bored housewife quicker than owning a Ferrari. So few people spoke another language in the UK that the ruse had worked without hitch at least ten times. The internet was indeed a wondrous thing.

Janet believed him to be a restaurant owner - close to the truth and it ensured his time was more plausibly available during the day. He elaborated a touch, stating he had shares in three restaurants in the area and that it was all part of a larger "entertainment" group. Yuri, like all good liars, knew to embellish but without creating a persona he couldn't afford to fake and also one that didn't make him seem too grand. Modesty worked in England. Janet had the bare bones of the story and now she had put up no objection, no argument to meeting. Yuri hoped she would look like her picture, too often they put an image from ten years ago, usually ten kilos lighter and before the second child, not that Yuri minded they would serve a purpose however they appeared.

He flicked through his account and the profiles of the people he had dated and fell upon the woman who used the avatar 'Marjorie Dawes' – she had been fun, nothing more.

He had boasted that he could get close to the Lawyer and while he knew no one, especially Valentyn, believed him, he knew better. Masha had shown some faith. She'd cornered him the previous afternoon and told him she needed some essential work doing for her. She had said he had to 'prove that he could walk the walk'. She wanted proof that the woman he talked about was indeed who he claimed and that he could get inside intelligence on the situation. Yuri had been sceptical, but his suspicions subsided when Masha demanded that he deal with only her and not Valentyn or her sister.

Yuri smiled at the memory. Anything that pissed off Valentyn, or better made him look a fool, was fine by him and he'd obviously be delighted to keep his extracurricular lady activities out of Zenovia's attention. No, Yuri had been delighted to be offered the chance to curry favour with the other daughter and ultimately Uncle. The last few weeks had presented him with options and opportunities, Yuri Sminsky had been waiting for a chance like this for a long time. He wouldn't waste it.

"Hello you.."The voice snapped him back to reality, "Janet... hi. Sit down."

She looked like her picture and a smile erupted across Yuri's face as he moved his eyes up and down her body. He didn't hide that he liked what he saw.

"Can I get you a coffee?"

She giggled a little and had a hungry, lustful look in her eye. "I haven't got much time..."

"Oh OK," he said.

"I live very close by... can we just er you know..."

Yuri smiled, "Sure, if that's what you want."

David watched the pub from across the street. Slough is an unpleasant town. No PR or urban regeneration project can mask the underlying truth. It is an ugly, dishevelled shit hole of a town full of the people and problems you'd expect in a place like that. Yes it has a huge trading estate and the biggest names in business reside there, but not one of the senior moneyed employees lives in Slough. The phone jockeys, the canteen workers, the factory floor monkeys might, but the rest live in Windsor, Ascot, Bray, Datchet or Wraysbury. The pubs reflect the clientele: barred windows, fake flowers in window boxes, huge adverts for SKY SPORTS LIVE and happy hour drinking, a cheap crappy ten pound gazebo straddles the huddled mass still clinging to a £7 a packet smoking habit – yet they'll all be the first to bemoan a cut in benefits.

No one likes Slough, not the poor sods who live in it nor the people that commute to it. Curious, thought David, that his brother, the personification of affluent middle class success and snobbery would walk from his almost sterile office in the town centre via the circus that is the Slough high street to reach the Hope and Anchor pub at the far end. David had to talk to him, try and clear the air to the point that they could at least be civil to one another and had arrived at the office without warning and had been lucky to see his brother striding out, he presumed, for lunch. David decided to follow, observe, before picking the moment to engage him.

Peter had entered the pub alone a few minutes before and David had dithered about following him in, he couldn't say why for sure, but intuition told him Peter would not be alone for long, so he waited and he watched. The barber shop next door caught his attention, it had a cluster of cheap polyester-clad teenage morons on undersized bikes outside it. They spat unconvincingly, adopted a wide-legged stance attempting to look 'hard' while listening to music on loud speaker via cheap mobile phones. It was the same act, in David's experience, that every rebellious youthful generation of teenagers had undertaken all around the world, just the clothes and music changed but the attitude remained one of naive bravado and boredom. Two lads went into and then came back out of the barber's a moment or so later – their skinhead haircuts remained unchanged but one now clutched a white envelope. The lads bigged it up, whatever they had achieved they seemed very proud of themselves.

David watched, amused by the scene that had taken place. Then he saw the two men, biggish, but overweight. Black leather coats over black t-shirts, necks adorned with gold chains, they looked hot and uncomfortable in the summer sun. Their short haircuts revealed the three layers of neck fat that always seemed to accompany men of a certain type. The two stopped outside the pub, looked across at the teens and shared some words. The yobs noticed being noticed and the bravado became muted, they adopted the pose of insolent indifference, guilt and fear spread like a rash through them. The shorter and fatter of the two men walked over, hands in pockets. He spoke briefly and harshly, though out of earshot, David recognised the mannerisms of a man stamping his status on an inferior. Moving faster than he looked capable of the man grabbed hold of one lad and shook him like a doll before pressing his block-like face hard into the lad's face. The boy's resistance faded and he meekly handed over the envelope and then pulled out some cash and handed that over too.

Once dropped back to the ground the boy scrabbled across the floor before he rose and scurried off. He and his mates moved off as quickly as the mini bikes, their low-slung trousers and the ever present need to look 'hard' would allow. David moved to his left a little to get a better view of the barber shop interior, he was sure that the two guys would enter it at any moment. They did.

David took the opportunity to move towards the pub, he crossed the road between parked cars and cast a glance into the barber's – the rag doll treatment was being doled out to the poorly tattooed owner, both men seemed to be giving their very best Grant Mitchell impression – no doubt one of them would be using the term 'you slag' at some point as well.

David had decided he'd seen enough of the local hoodlum floorshow and so strode into the pub, he cast a quick eye around the murky interior, and Peter had his back to him as he stood feeding money into a fruit machine. "What can I get you?" came the relatively servile question from the Glaswegian accented barman. David considered the pre-noon time and ordered a lime and soda water. The barman barely hid his contempt. David waited for the drink and sipped it to ensure it didn't spill and raised his foot to walk to his brother, but before it could be planted on the stained and depressingly old carpet the two leather clad hoodlums jostled into the bar. They had the air and arrogance of geezers and David's impending violence radar spiked for a moment. Without pause they moved through towards the fruit machine.

"Jocko the usual," the fatter one barked at the barman who didn't respond in either word or action.

"Edwards ya lanky streak of fucking piss." The taller man bellowed as a greeting towards David's brother. Peter didn't turn round. Not even when podgy paw slapped him with unnecessary force.

David moved to the right, a stained glass partition separated one area of the pub from the gambling section, he took up station there, he could listen and he could act. He assumed the two men were brothers, whomever was older proved impossible to determine, but David didn't really care. He couldn't hide his intrigue as to their relationship with Peter and how his brother would handle himself.

"Edwards... no hearty hallo or hug for your old mucker?"

Peter turned and smiled, "Hello Nick, hello Jason."

Nick, the shorter man smiled back, Jason stayed stony faced.

"So we get to chat face-to-face at last, been a while..."

"Has it?"

"It has, hasn't it Jase?"

"Yes Nick it has been a while, a month or so..."

"At least Jase, a month at least. Odd but I think it was the last time we played poker together, not seen you since then... been hiding son?"

Peter towered over both men, but he looked like a bowling pin compared to the two bowling balls stood in front of him. "Never, I'm here now aren't I, if I was hiding I'd be doing a pretty shit job of it."

Nick looked from Peter to Jason and back again. "Funny. I like you Peter always have, you play a good game of poker, bit up your arse on occasions, don't care for your politics but hey..." he gave a dramatic shrug. "Now rules are rules aren't they. You know all about rules in your work Pete, am I right?"

Peter tried to give himself a little room as the two men crowded him, "I do indeed know the rules gents."

"So," Nick cut him off, "if you know the rules then you

know that when you enter our games you have to settle all debts at the end of the night. Right? We can extend a little credit for our more regular players, but ya know only within reason."

Peter nodded again, a little scared but not displaying the full range of truly intimidated responses that the brother would usually expect. David stayed put and watched the reflection of the altercation in the grubby pub window.

"It's rude Pete to take my credit, lose my money and not pay me back...you've won a fair bit off me in the past, what goes around comes around. So, here we are..."

"Here we are..." said Peter.

Nick shook his head, "Peter I get the feeling that you're hearing me, but that you aint listening to me?"

Peter said nothing. Jason and Nick exchanged glances. Jason stepped forward and launched a short elbow powered punch. He never raised his fist, simply punched and pushed it forward, it landed just above Peter's beltline, and he drove it into his abdomen compacting his liver, a fighter's punch. Peter recoiled and doubled over, Nick caught his shoulders as he bent over in painful reaction and gently eased him back upright. David 'ooed' and winced a little at the impact, it was a good punch, unobtrusive but the pain and discomfort would linger for a while... a reminder.

"Do I have your full attention Peter?"

"Yes." he gasped.

"Good, so let's keep this simple, have you got my

money?

Peter gasped and groaned again, "Of course I have."

Nick glanced around the pub and a flicker of disappointment moved across his face as he realised that no one had taken a blind bit of notice. "Hand it to my brother then."

Peter raised his hand in a conciliatory gesture, the brothers leaned a little back waiting for Peter to produce the cash, the pause lasted a second or two longer than the brothers felt comfortable with and Jason adopted his best menacing expression. Peter realised that another blow was imminent and so raised both hands. "Jesus guys I don't have it on me, I'm not wandering the streets of Slough with ten grand on me... but I have it and will deliver it at the fight tomorrow night.

The brothers relaxed as they computed the information. "What fight?" they said lying very very badly. Peter looked at them and arched an eyebrow, "The smarmy shit that played on your poker game last month, Corsican or whatever, he said we'd get tickets for the fight, he took some details – I saw you cc'd in on the email boys."

In unison the brothers shoved their hands in their pockets and raised their chins pushing their heads up; each man producing a stunning triple ripple of neck fat. "Alright... we'll see you there, you will have the money sunshine or we will fuck you up."

"Right."

The brothers looked at him hard again and turned and

moved out through the pub, "Leave the drinks jocko, catch ya next time". As they marched through the door the barman looked up from the paper, surveyed the bar to confirm he'd not actually poured any drinks and muttered, "Aye lads and please do fuck off and die".

David sat with a smile on his lips, he really didn't know his brother, but he had been quietly impressed the lanky tart hadn't dropped to his knees and balled like a baby. He carried on watching in the mirror as Peter rubbed his side and allowed more of his discomfort to now show on his face. David took the chance to remain seated and hidden but to engage his brother. "So how much do you owe overall then?"

The disembodied voice took Peter by surprise and he had to look about him to confirm he hadn't imagined the voice. "When Mel and Kim show up playing the heavy over a debt it seems clear to me a man has a problem, wouldn't you say so?"

Peter still couldn't place the voice but at least he knew now where it was coming from, he moved in a wider arc than necessary to get a view into the window booth and as he made out the figure heaved a massive sigh of relief when he realised it was David.

"Oh it's you! Shit, you scared me!"

David raised his eyebrows, "More than the Mitchell brothers, wow!"

Before he realised what he had done Peter sat down opposite his brother and gave a little chuckle. "They are a little comical, but they are serious."

"Mmmm it seems it, I'll bet a ten grand debt to them is quite sizeable?"

"Nah... Chicken feed to them two."

"And what does it mean to you?"

Peter tensed up realising who he was with and how he really felt about him, more importantly it was the first time someone had discovered his gambling. "It's not serious, it's covered with this." He held up a betting slip.

David was no psychology or addiction expert but even he realised that relying on one bet to pay off another and saying it wasn't serious may be, in the least, a case of denial. David avoided looking at the slip, he eyed his brother, taking in more information than he had at the funeral, trying to look at the man and not his brother. He didn't like what he saw, drawn in cheeks, the faint purple ring of sleepless nights circled his eyes, his skin looked pallid as if he needed a good meal or burst of sunshine. On the face of it he was well turned out, suit, white shirt and no tie, but the devil is always in the detail; the suit hung off his shoulders, it looked baggy and shapeless, the detail and tailoring showed it had been a quality garment but it had been measured for a bigger, fitter and stronger version of the Peter that sat here today.

"It's none of my business how you live your life Peter, but I didn't figure you for the type to hang around with those two Muppets," David offered.

Peter shrugged and looked out the window, he avoided making eye contact. "I don't hang about with 'em, they're not mates. You don't get to judge me."

Daivd nodded. "So what are they?"

"I'm in a poker game, they run some of the nights... that's all."

The two men looked at each other then both looked away, equally eager to avoid the conversation that needed to happen but that neither had the stomach for right now. Peter sipped his beer and David ignored his drink. He had noticed how dirty and watermarked the old glass actually was. David sighed and made the first move.

"I'm sorry I was a bit harsh at the funeral...," he began, "I should have had a little more tact than that, just anxious to see mum, that's all." Peter just shrugged again. "Jacqui gave me a telling off. Said I needed to get over myself and pull my head out my arse and talk to you." David tossed the statement out, an opening gambit, something he hoped Peter might respond to. He got nothing back. "Mum said that you were taking the death hard... that you know; you and dad remained close." Still Peter said and did nothing by way of a reaction. "She would like us to try and be civil Peter, not really make up or best buddies or anything, but allow the family to be together sometimes..."

Peter, eyes fixed on the window, gave a small nod. "Ok," he mumbled. David couldn't be sure he heard his brother, but didn't ask him to repeat it. Instead he took pleasure in his very small triumph and went to sip his drink. He faltered as the sunlight illuminated the scum once more. Peter looked from the window and down towards the stained and cigarette charred banquette seating. "We weren't ya know," he mumbled.

David looked at him and this time needed clarification,

"Sorry?"

"Dad and I, we weren't close, not really."

David nodded, said nothing, hoping that he would open up.

"He was a miserable old sod."

David said nothing. Peter fixed his eyes on a dart imbedded in the ceiling and carried on. "Cold...really cold, I don't think he liked a single thing or person. Nothing. No one." Peter sighed at the memory. "The only thing he seemed to have any passion for, any real energy or commitment to, was hating or disliking things. "

David understood, he could feel the bitterness in his brother's voice, see the anguish faintly realised in the wrinkled lines around his eyes. David had spent a lot of time alone with his thoughts, first confined by walls then by regiment and always by memories and emotional baggage. He'd been angry with his father, sad for him, disillusioned, a myriad of confused and bungled feelings, but time moved on and anger was the one emotion that returned the least, he had outgrown hate. No, his father no longer played on his mind in the dark of night that position had been replaced by a different horror show. Peter seemed to be just coming to terms with it all, no matter what he did or achieved their father would not have shown pride, joy or love. David had deduced, alone in a cell many years ago that his father couldn't show what he didn't understand or hadn't felt himself.

"I'm not the best person to comment on Dad, he and I never saw the world the same way... anyway, I hadn't spoken to him for seventeen odd years," David said.

"No, it's peculiar isn't it, you dominated his existence before going to jail – all Jacqui and I heard from him was 'David this and David that... don't do that when you get to 16, I'll disown you... blah fucking blah'. Then he does, he actually disowns you..." Peter couldn't keep the sardonic tone from his voice, "I mean, Jesus, he never fucking let up. David is a disgrace, he has shamed the family... he spouted this stuff, not just once in a while, it was perpetual. Like a Sunday sermon."

David decided to look out of the window and avoid the look on his brother's face. "I just figured that once you were gone, disowned, that he would get over it and focus on Jacqui and me. Maybe even just take an interest in ME. I was wrong."

They sat in silence for moment, neither man moved. The bleeps, dings and flashes of the slot machine competed with the poorly piped radio and a warbling rendition of 'Paint it Black'. Peter moved first, he shifted his weight and turned his shoulders to face his brother for the first time. He pulled his slumped back upright and raised his chin as he engaged eye-contact. David returned it and the men very consciously sized each other up. David watched as Peter's eyes flexed and he imagined the cogs of his younger brother's brain turning in thought.

"You look old," Peter said.

"I am old," David replied.

"But you work out, you look pretty fit"

"I survive."

David watched as Peter's eyes again flexed as next

question seemed to be assessed.

"You do any boxing?"

"Some, in the Legion, during training; a bit in prison."

Peter nodded. "Jac's said you're a soldier."

"Was..."

"Retired?"

"Invalided out."

"Saw combat then?"

"Yeah."

"Shot?"

"Yep... but shrapnel is what forced me to leave."

"Nasty?"

"I s'pose."

Peter sipped his pint and looked at the ceiling. David watched and tried to deduce why his brother had mellowed without too much of a fight.

"I'll try David... but let's not get silly on this thing ok?"

"Ok."

"A lot of water under the bridge, whole fucking heap of resentment."

David nodded and conceded the small territorial gain.

"I followed dad's anti David sermon to the letter – figured he'd like me more if I did that. I worked out a long time ago that it had zero effect."

David went to say something but his brother put up his hand to stop him. "I've kinda got used to playing that role. It'll take me time to change. Civil I can manage."

David nodded, pleased that they had had a conversation at least. He looked at the shabby state of his brother and re-ran the encounter he had just witnessed in his head. Whatever his brother was mixed up in he'd developed the appearance of man under pressure.

"Peter, are you going to this fight tomorrow night?"

Peter tilted his head and looked back at his brother with a mock open palmed plea, as if to say, "C'mon, are you my Dad' look on his face.

"Just asking ok... I might wanna get in on the action."

"You like a bit of boxing?"

David raised an eyebrow, "I did a fair bit on bases or when on tours of duty. It's fighting, drinking and it's gambling. That's all we did."

Peter considered it for a moment, he appeared to weigh up his options, consider the consequences and benefits. "You any good at the fighting thing?"

"Yeah I was pretty good – you learn a lot in prison. A lot of ex-cons in the Legion too." David realised that the fight may be the slimmest of common interests they shared and his only route to some kind of permanent reconciliation.

"You can come along, but I can't guarantee you'll get in. It's a strict invite only basis. Taken me months to get an invite."

David shrugged, "Oh well... we'll see, money usually works out the problems." He saw Peter's eyes flex again. He saw a little light, a sparkle return to his eye.

"Where are you staying?"

"Mum's."

Peter allowed an exaggerated display of cognitive realisation play across his face. "Let's meet at the Vansitaart Arms pub, you remember where that is?"

"Sure," David answered noting the odd histrionics.

"About 8pm – best not tell Mum or Jacqui."

"I won't. I'll tell them I'm seeing you though, they'll like that."

David watched his brother as he got up to leave. "You be careful collecting your winnings, that's a lot of cash to carry around," he said.

"I always am David. Tomorrow... just come and watch and keep quiet ok. I know these people, some of them are serious. Know what I mean?"

David nodded. "I do."

Peter turned and walked out of the pub leaving David to ponder the sudden mellowing of his brother's mood, whatever the motivations he didn't fully trust it, but he was confident his brother had gotten involved in something he ultimately couldn't handle and if being around helped build bridges then it could only be for the best.

David stretched his back and it clicked and cracked in

the way that people who have violently abused their bodies know so well. He had shaved, and his clothes were freshly laundered, even his pants had been ironed. He couldn't stop his mother. He'd protested he would do it and that that she should rest, but she had waved him off and bustled into action oblivious to his protests. The iron had been too hot and there were the telltale signs of scorching on his black clothes. His Sergeant would have had fit about that.

He sat in a boardroom in a high-backed leather chair, he spun around through three-sixty degrees and felt ten years old again, so he did it again. The five empty chairs appeared to stare back their disapproval of his frivolity. David had no real concept of modern working life – he'd never had an office job, he'd used pcs and understood modern technology, he wasn't a hermit, but he just couldn't fathom or relate to what people would do in room like this. The impressive table, imposing chair and 'art' on the walls, he assumed, presented an accomplished and professional air. Eve's legal firm, if you believed the story being told by soft furnishings, appeared successful and intelligent.

The glass door twanged open and Eve entered, a laptop closed and tucked under her right arm and a mug of coffee grasped in her left hand, she bumped open the door with her hip and let it swing shut behind her. David watched, a little fascinated by what seemed an oft repeated manoeuvre, as Eve slipped into the chair opposite, free-wheeling for a moment before coming to a stop as she unloaded her cargo onto the table.

"Why do they call these boardrooms?" he asked.

Eve sipped her coffee, smiled and said, "A hangover from the halcyon days of business – power men and their power decisions."

"Do you have a board of directors?"

"Not as such – it's me and two partners. One silent. But we have a staff of twenty odd..."

David nodded, "So you need a big room?"

"It's expected."

They sat in silence for a moment. David calculated how their conversation would progress. Eve had protested she didn't want to talk about Thomas the old detective and what his death might mean. David had remained calm, merely pointing out that it was whatever the detective had been doing for her that had resulted in his death. David's involvement had been chance and no more. But the death reflected on his sister and he wanted to stay involved. She had conceded that and so here he sat. He eyed the laptop and assumed it to be an indicator that she would share some information.

He watched Eve push open the laptop and scroll through some documents, she shot him the odd glance and he noted she wasn't as comfortable as he with silences.

"Organised people smuggling..."

"Sorry?" he said, surprised she hadn't engaged eye contact before speaking.

"The detective, he had been part of a small team looking into people trafficking into the area. He had conducted our investigations in France for us... that's why we gave him the job of finding you. He knew the area."

David nodded, hoping Eve would fill in the details and excuse his lack of recent local knowledge. "Slough has seen a massive Eastern European migration, there is recession defying job surplus there, especially in the low paid areas. It means they came in droves to fill the void. Petty and organised crime came with them."

"Forgive me, but isn't EU migration entirely legal now?"

"It is. They aren't smuggled in, they are smuggled out of the UK and back to the continent."

David's confusion seemed no surprise to Eve. "We had the same incredulity when we found out, seems ridiculous right? But...when you look at it logically and with an entrepreneurial mindset you can see how it works."

David sensed a challenge, he narrowed his eyes and thought about it for a moment, now Eve didn't take her gaze off him. "Ok work with me," he said. "People want to get to the UK, the land of milk and honey bollocks, right?" Eve said nothing. "Those without connections or the money turn to villains, 'loan me the money or get me to England and I work for you' some shit like that, right? They are legalised slaves or whatever."

"Capitalism at its best; some can afford to pay but many can't. Keep going..." Eve did well to not express that she was a little bit impressed. "So," he continued, "they get shipped here, work, and pay some money back and when they cease to be of value they are smuggled out of the country... to what end?"

Eve turned the laptop around showed him a flowchart that now dominated the screen. He digested the content for a second and then looked up for the explanation.

"Thomas discovered the side-effect of legal migrant trafficking." She stressed the word 'legal'. "A lot of the poor souls that come in are useless and not fit to pay you back quickly. Old men and women, small children etc. Even working illegally and outside the minimum wage they are a poor investment for the villains. So they siphon off the 'viable talent', those capable of work in cash-based industries - building sites, kitchens, hotels, farming, whatever... we know they pull a lot of the young and vulnerable women into prostitution as well."

David nodded, "And that would leave the less able, the bungled and the botched, these are then shipped back out of the country, right?"

"Correct, but the firms that have arranged the transport of these people across to the UK don't want the hassle of doing it. Not least because if they return home they may affect future business, so they hire a 3rd party and they manage the repatriation process. Usually to a different country than the one they came from."

"This 'repatriation firm' charges a cost per head I assume?" David asked.

"Indeed, after all you can't afford to simply turn them loose on the street and potentially spoil a good scam."

"But why bring them over in the first place? Surely it's simpler to sort the wheat from the chaff at the start?"

"Maybe, but think of it from their point of view, they want to attract as much custom as possible, they can't rip people off close to home, word might get out. They shift so many bodies that there is profit in volume."

David smiled at the revelation, "So they pay a third party to take them off their hands, away from the UK operation and a long way from home. Neat. One presumes this third party makes money at both ends of the process?"

Eve shrugged and did a half nod, "That's what we figured, we tracked a shipment of people a few weeks back, it headed into France and another we are sure landed in Spain."

"So you investigator was in France looking for me, but the gang will have seen him over there a few times already. Maybe he got closer to their operation than he thought?"

"Sounds feasible..."

"What happens to the people next?"

"Once they are in the country they are farmed out to local gangs and simply sold on as sweatshop labour."

"Seriously? Sweatshops, here in Europe?"

"Oh yeah and it is very very big business already. With the arse falling out of the European economy, the need for cheap labour and operating outside the tax system has become the norm and not the exception," Eve said, taking another sip of coffee.

"How big?" he asked.

"First off we can't be sure how many trafficked legals come in and where they end up. But, thinking about the logistics, all distribution must be done via major hubs. We know Slough, Reading and Swindon are big employment areas in the South, so too Bedford, Luton and Leicester in the Midlands. These we believe are the major distribution hubs for the trafficking of legal migrants in the South. Leeds, Manchester and Sunderland for the North." David shook his head a little. Eve pressed on, "We think the true figure of migration to UK annually is about a million, with up to 70% of it coming via organised gangs. 10 to 15% of those shipped, we estimate, are then shipped back out of the country via this scheme."

David leant back and tried to do the numbers quickly, "So around 100,000 a year could be heading back over the channel?"

"That would be the top end of it sure." Eve smiled at him, "Horrible thought isn't it?"

"Yeah it is..."

"We estimate, and this is a stab-in-the-dark, that the UK gang is paid maybe £200 per head to ship out the undesirables and maybe about half again when they land back in Europe."

"Jesus."

Eve sipped her coffee and the pair thought for a moment.

"That's an estimate of a total value of £250 million – now we don't think that's all one gang, but that's the value of the business annually. We can't believe more than 2 or 3 organisations can be operating in the UK. At least not of any significant size anyway. There will only be one or two operating here in the South."

"Serious money."

"Yep, lowish overheads, little real risk, no one is

checking lorries leaving the UK and well the French... anyway, it's lucrative."

David stood up and turned his back on Eve for a moment. The business side of what they had discussed only partially masked the real issues and barbarity of what was taking place. Human trafficking, selection, slavery and cleansing. The gangs sorted good or profitable stock from bad, they kept their migrant work pool fresh and controlled. These people had European status and had a right to be here, to travel and work. There was no police or immigration official to bribe, no real risk. You simply get people into your debt, scare them half to death, control their documentation and control their life.

He had seen many horrific things in his life, had seen the lowest value anyone could put on human life. David wasn't naive nor a paragon of virtue, he couldn't be described as a saintly crusader that would ride in and the save the day. He remained a pragmatist, as shocking as it all was he focused on his loved ones. He'd been denied his family for too many years and now that he finally had them back he'd move heaven and earth to keep them safe.

"Rival gangs will want in on this, keeping control is going to be tough," he said. Eve nodded. "These are serious people, they found and killed your detective for snooping into their business, so they must know who you are!" David said.

"They do," she replied.

"They went to France to eliminate him and to scare you," he said.

Eve worked hard to maintain control and composure,

but her bottom lip quivered and as David turned to face her again, he caught a faint glimpse of it and for once her eyes didn't meet his. "Eve, what's up?"

"It worked David, I am scared." Her voice trembled a little, it could have been fear or embarrassment, so good was her attempted disguise of emotion. "I pretend it doesn't affect me that I know the police will protect me... but they do nothing, have done nothing." Tears began a slow descent down her cheeks.

"Police, they know all about this? Surely they are doing something – aren't they helping?"

"God no! All too much hassle, even when we showed them the letters and threats we have been getting. They simply don't want to believe us. They say our evidence is hearsay and circumstantial."

"Oh fucking hell Eve, have you been threatened directly?" David got up and moved towards her to try to comfort her. When he reached he failed to know what to do. And settled for a limp arm round her shoulder followed by a squeeze.

"I've had a chance to think about it David and I think I might need your help after all. I think I might need a bodyguard." David didn't blink and didn't show any reaction, as if a switch had gone on in his brain.

"Really? Me?"

"Yeah... I think they sent some men to scare me last night." Eve hadn't planned to tell him, but now with his arm around her and feeling his warmth and strength she couldn't help herself.

"What happened, Jesus, were you hurt?" he asked.

"I'm fine, just scared. I got one with my hairspray... it may have just been muggers. I'm feeling so paranoid. So scared." She pushed her head into his chest.

"Who else knows about all this, the inside knowledge on the gangs?" Head bowed she replied, "The full extent, the whole deal – other than us two, now, only your sister... sorry.

WEDNESDAY

Gregor and Oleg did not cut truly imposing figures; average height, average weight and a bit bland would be the best physical description someone could muster. Nothing in their appearance made them stand out from the crowd, a 'Crime Watch' identikit would simply show men, the wrong side of thirty-five, weathered features, solid frames but presentable in appearance. Clean shaven with short cropped haircuts, meant they looked like any small-town salesman with kids at home in the semi. That is unless you saw them with their shirts off. Then their ripped torsos' and body art would tell a very different story.

Oleg and Gregor came from the outlying suburbs of Kiev, they came from a soldier class of gangsters, their father's and grandfather's the same before them. From the neckline down they wore their gang heritage and allegiances on their skin. Gang and status tattoos adorned their bodies, fighting for attention with prison markings and the scars from a life of violence and crime. These men were soldiers, men with a simple credo, do or die trying.

They had been 'purchased', their gang subsumed into a larger more dominant one, their skills acknowledged and accommodated into the new regime. They volunteered for the UK posting, having been sold shares in the vision of the streets being paved with gold if you were a particular type of East European villain. They were here to serve The Uncle, to get rich and scare, maim or kill anyone they were told to.

The two tough men stood either side of a chair, a plain old 70's style school dining chair, they had that characteristic stance of a henchman, hands clasped in front of their groins, shoulders back. The chair and the men were located in a store room, boxes of vodka, and slabs of KP Nuts surrounded them. A suspiciously stained grey concrete slab floor looked up at them and a migraine inducing flickering strip light buzzed overhead. The only door was behind the men, the chair faced way from it and the chair's occupant only had a view of shadow shrouded brown boxes.

The man was a little unkempt, his trousers creased with over use and the shirt was part tucked in and part hanging out of his trousers. He shifted on the seat and pushed his hands into the chair and made to get up. With easy and controlled movements Gregor and Oleg rested a hand on his shoulders and pushed him back into his seat.

"Look chaps," the man said, the lilt of a well educated man under pressure coming through, "I appreciate the big fella wants a word but I need to go back to work…"

Oleg and Gregor said nothing and retained their dutiful pose.

"I mean you can't just pull a bloke off the street and march him into a storeroom like this... it isn't civilised."

He looked up and then from Oleg across to Gregor. They ignored him. He harrumphed a touch. "I'm quite important you know." He looked at the boxes and harrumphed a little more. He looked back up at his captors and got nothing in response. "I'll be missed, I shall... REALLY I will!" He said it with a little too much petulance in his voice. Oleg allowed himself a glance at Gregor, who allowed himself to glance back and they shared a small discrete smile.

"Oh come on, you drag me off the street and act in, well, frankly a rather aggressive manner... I presume for a reason? Are you going to tell me why I'm here?"

The man's voice was cut off by sound of the door slamming, it made him jump a little and sit a little more upright and rigid in his seat.

"You are here because I am not happy with you!" Valentyn's voice dominated the room, it filled every nook and cranny and bounced around the confined space reverberating around the stationary men. The man in the chair gulped.

"I pay you money. You do a job – I should be happy."

Oleg rested a hand on the now slightly shaking shoulder in the chair and steadied him.

"This is simple, right?"

The man said nothing and like a chastised school boy looked at his feet.

"ANSWER ME!" bellowed Valentyn.

The man mumbled a barely audible 'Yes'.

"But I pay you money, you don't do the job and so I am not happy." Valentyn bent down and pushed his face towards the man in the chair, so close the victim could taste his breath. He squinted a moment as his expression demanded the man in the chair look him in the eye.

"We agreed that you would process 100 units a week, correct?"

The man nodded.

"You did less than forty last week."

The man nodded.

"This is shit, right?"

The man did an odd half-shake and nod of his head.

"You wish to disagree?"

Oleg and Gregor shot each other an amused glance above their heads.

"It's just that, it takes time, some take longer to process and others are more complicated. I, er, underestimated the issues."

Valentyn did not look away; he didn't sneer or react in anyway. He just stared hard at the man. "What title did The Uncle give you?"

"Librarian..."

"Why does he call you this?"

The man shrugged. "I don't really know?" he simpered.

"You are the Librarian, you are the keeper of the

books. We all have a name, a role to play. These men are soldiers. I am the General."

The Librarian nodded. "So, would you like me to tell you their job," he nodded at Oleg and Gregor, "do I need to do that?"

"No."

"So... do I need to explain to you what it is I need?"

The Librarian shook his head, he didn't lack courage or physical strength, he knew when he left this horrid little room and made his way back into normal life that he'd curse his lack of bravery, his failure to stand up and have a go. Reality bites, no one likes pain, not really, few want to invite it and he was in too deep to simply fight his way out of it. This scenario was far removed from the playground bully demanding his bag of Quavers every day.

"You need to process more units, one hundred a week minimum for the remainder of the month. Then beginning next month it needs to be 500 units."

'Jesus' he muttered under his breath. "I'll try..." He stammered. "But we need to agree something, I need the paperwork in better condition."

Valentyn raised an eyebrow and moved back a little so as to more easily focus on the man's face, intimidation now over. "Talk to me."

"Well as I am sure you appreciate..." The Librarian began knowing full well that the self-styled General had no clue what he actually did. "I need to artificially create Social Security IDs and records for all of these people, they need to show dependents, addresses and the computerised records need to show that they have met all the criteria and they are eligible for the various benefits." Valentyn nodded his encouragement for him to get to the point. "I don't sit at a computer and type each one in by hand, that would be impossible and it would leave too big of an IT trail. I have a little script, a computer programme that extracts the required data from my files and imports them into the main central DSS computer system."

"This is faster correct...?"

"It is yes, also more or less undetectable - you see the programme reads my data and automatically allocates agreed safe addresses, registers them for certain benefits and it randomises who gets what level of entitlement, hopefully meaning we won't get too much of a pattern of new claimants. I also randomly exchange details of some old claimants with new so we can avoid everything seeming like a new claim and of course I alter the time periods to make it appear that a lot of the people I introduce have been in the system for months and years."

Valentyn nodded a little more thoughtfully, "All this is done by the computer programme...?"

"Correct."

"So what is making it all slow?"

"Well I just get handed the details of the people handed to me on paper, sometimes data is missing etc... well either way, and it's very very slow... I need to then manually enter all the data onto a spreadsheet so that I can upload it, let me show you." The Librarian ferreted into his baggy suit pocket and fished out a folded A4 sheet, he unfolded it and handed it to Valentyn, who looked over it like a disapproving father reviewing his son's homework.

"This is terrible," he offered.

"That's what I get every couple of days... it takes an age for me to sort it out. I said to the lady who delivers it...er, Masha is it? That it's making the process slow... but er, well... never mind. She didn't really listen, let's leave it at that."

Valentyn scraped a paw like hand across his face and drew in a deep breath. The sisters had assured him the data had been handed over exactly as the Librarian needed and that there were no problems. He pondered another issue, how had he not found out about the problems before? His soldiers should have updated him on this. "Tell me what she did?"

The Librarian winced a little, old school law of not telling tales stupidly playing havoc with his moral compass. He got over it quite quickly. "Well... she laughed at me. Told me I was a little man... then she, er, slapped me." This confession to his own physical weakness led to another bout of head-dropped shame. Valentyn patted him by way of assurance on the shoulder.

"You are a tall man, but a little man of courage. But one that works for me and has the right to respect, the right to do his job well if others are able to do theirs."

Valentyn rose to his full height, raised his chin and thought for a moment. Masha had been put in charge of the units upon arrival, she was supposed to ensure the information was good and up to date. He had seen with his own eyes that it had been shit.

"How would you like information, the best way, and quickest way to ensure the units are processed?"

"Well, ideally if you could use the Excel spreadsheet I gave you with all the fields and tabs on it, then if you could input all the data onto that, supply it to me on an encrypted USB stick..." Valentyn held his hand up to hush the man. His head was beginning to hurt.

"Oleg will give you safe email address to send the file to. I'll arrange for a USB stick, no problem. It will only ever have the week's data on it – send the same USB back with breakdowns and allocations. I need our accountant to verify the money being claimed into the bank accounts."

The Librarian nodded his consent and held out his hand for the list.

"No," Valentyn said, "this list stays with me, I'll get it and the rest of the week's units added to it. Send me spreadsheet before end of day... understand?"

He nodded. Valentyn then turned and walked out of the room. Oleg waited a beat or two and once certain that Valentyn had departed he spoke.

"You have iPhone?"

"Nokia Lumia... sorry," the Librarian responded.

"Ok, we do it old fashioned way, email is this..."

Oleg stared at the Librarian, who stared back confused. "You must write it down."

The Librarian nodded and tapped his breast pockets before reaching into one and producing a chewed blue ball-point pen.

Eve stared across the compact living room and watched David talk, argue and even plead with his sister. Jacqui had been less than welcoming, frosty even, to the idea that David might be able to help them, protect them. She went on the attack the moment he mentioned it, within thirty seconds her voice rose and she accused him of being the reason her investigator had died. They all knew it wasn't a rational thought, rather a deflection from the real truth that she and Eve had dispatched the man to find David, that David had been living a quiet life, alone and isolated from his family and whatever friends he had since the fabric of his life ended that horrific night all those years ago.

Jacqui's flat had a view of the famous castle across the river Thames, she could walk to the bars and restaurants of Eton in minutes and could be across the river into Windsor in a few more. The decor, furnishings and smell evoked the very ideal of a modern, controlled and successful single woman. Not one item of man clutter in evidence. The non-black TV sat in proportion to the room, the sofas had a plethora of intricately stitched, fabric-clad scatter cushions, scented candles and object d'art sat on clutter free surfaces. Amongst this shrine to feminine taste and success sat David, clad in his customary black cotton, looking powerful and the very epitome of manhood. He dominated the chair, a robust piece of furniture reduced to bit part player. A handsome, maturing, attractive man is what Eve could see. She had spent the intervening years wondering where he was, how he felt. It would be wrong to say she woke or went to sleep with him on her mind, she could go days, weeks and months without giving him a second thought. Out of sight is out of mind, but in moments of total aloneness she felt his presence, a shudder of realisation that David Edwards no longer participated in her life and that she missed him. Sometimes the feeling came when surrounded in a crowded room, she would hear the snatch of a conversation, a laugh or even see another man's smile and it would trigger a memory that in turn would haul her repressed emotions into reality, a nagging sense of regret and pain at his departure to the life that he had been forced to live. Eve had seen more of David than any of his family, she had been a regular visitor to his prison and David's absurd treatment at the hands of the law had been her inspiration to become a lawyer and try to make a difference. They had been girlfriend and boyfriend that fateful night, young lovers exploring the world, their emotions and each other. The system wrenched him away, branded him a menace and refused his bail and wrongly locked him up for murder. Her desperation to see him had driven her to send countless investigators on missions to find him; she needed to see him, to talk to him and hold him again.

Jacqui forced Eve to snap out of her thoughts by shouting her name, "EVE!"

"What?" she managed to reply without really knowing how the conversation had progressed. "Wake up...Why now? Why the sudden feeling that we need some protection?"

Eve shrugged, "The car park thing..."

"Oh please Eve, two chav twats bungle a mugging and now you feel scared?"

"Jacqui, for whatever reason, I just feel less safe... I can't explain it, maybe I have reached my tipping point?" she didn't sound convinced by her own argument.

"Tipping point... now? The latest bit of press made you feel more exposed did it? Drawn a bit too much attention to yourself have you?" Jacqui gave the barbed comment a potent dose of malicious hindsight.

"Come on Jacs that's not fair. I got really scared in the car park ok. I've admitted it may have nothing to do with the gangs and threats, but I can't help feeling the way I do, can I?"

Jacqui sat back down and folded her arms. Eve knew she wanted to argue and point out the silliness of her needing her gung-ho brother to protect her. They had been friends a long time and she knew that the eruption response would die down and reason would return. She cast her eye towards David, throughout the exchange he had remained placid, a fixed expression of compassion on his face allowing the words and accusations to wash over him. Now he spoke.

"I'll go if that's what you want Jacqui. I don't want to control anything, if I can help I will... that's all."

Jacqui looked across at him and smiled, "I know... it's just we've come so far, the idea of the press coverage is to make it too hard for them to touch us. The police should protect us, if not directly then simply by association."

Eve shared a glance with David, it lacked any degree of subtlety and Jacqui saw it immediately. "Oh for fuck's sake let's not get into another bout of Police bashing... please I don't need to hear that," Jacqui half-shouted.

"Jacqui, I'm trying here, I've been away a long time. Eve said she might want my help... as soon as she told me that you knew as much as her and were involved so deeply I... er…"

"You what? Thought you'd make up for last seventeen odd years and play big brother?"

David visibly winced and Eve shot Jacqui harsh look.

"Sorry…" he mumbled. "It's been a while, I'm struggling to know what to do, what to say. Hard as it may be to understand, you need to know that not a single day has passed since I was sent down that I haven't thought of you all. Every day I wanted to see you, be with you. I'm not good at explaining myself..," his voice trailed off and an awkward silence settled over the room. Eve stared at him, he'd shrunk into the chair and she became engulfed with pity for the poor soul that sat before her.

David had made Eve no promises on his release, she had assumed and hoped he would walk out of the gates of the prison into her arms and they could be together again. Hope, she learned that day, is unforgiving. He came out a different man, not broken but clearly damaged. His bitterness and anger should have been accepted but the turmoil and indifference she couldn't relate to. They spent the night together, a coming together at last, ten years after the last time and for one sordid night she tried to resurrect their love and to pull her David out of the man that had emerged from his cell. She saw him just a handful of times before he disappeared, each meeting more distant and closed off than the last.

Jacqui pushed herself off the sofa and edged towards

her brother, wrapping her arms around his cowed head and kissing with a gentle apology. "Sorry," she whispered into his head. He pushed his arms around her and locked together they swayed in the moment of reconciliation. Eve sidled out of the room and let them console each other, aware that the family had so much to grieve over, so much healing to do.

Five minutes later she heard her name being called from the living room.

"Eve?" Jacqui called.

"Yeah?"

"We heard the kettle boil... bring in some coffee would you. If we're gonna do this then we need to talk it through? You OK with that David?"

"Perfect."

Eve bundled the coffee things together onto a tray and went back into the room. She poured out three cups as David got more detail on the situation from his sister. He sat back and listened, thinking through each piece of information before finally leaning forward.

"So let me understand this," David said. "You have no admissible evidence or witnesses?" Jacqui shook her head and Eve did a half nod and shake.

"Which is it?"

Eve smoothed her skirt down, "Nothing we can use in court."

"This is why the Police aren't involved yet?"

Jacqui nodded, "I know it's wrong but look at it from

the police point of view this is people trafficking, but they aren't illegals. They have a right under EU law to be here. Sure the manner of their arrival is dubious and the conditions in which they work and live might be akin to Victorian mills, but unless they have formal complaints and hard evidence they simply aren't looking to find the problem, let alone resolve it."

"The witness? The one who won't testify, where is she now?"

"Reading," said Eve.

"She's at a kind of refuge, she's working and fixing her life up, she's terrified that speaking out will see her and her family back home get into more trouble, understandable really."

David nodded. "I'm trying to grasp why they felt so threatened by you and your investigation that they were prepared to kill a guy... seems over-the-top to me."

Eve raised her hand a little. "That would be my fault," she said. David smiled and waited for the explanation.

"I've been on the BBC London news a few times, helped with a Panorama documentary, you know 'expert lawyer fights for rights of the dispossessed', that kind of thing. Well about three months ago we exposed a series of brothels in Slough and shockingly to the wondrous middle classes, Windsor, as having trafficked and held women against their will."

Jacqui chimed in, "It ended up being a job we did with Thames Police and a few arrests were made, mainly low end pimps and prostitutes... that's when we discovered that very few were illegals and they divulged how they got here."

"That's where you found your witness, right?"

"Yeah, she gave us the most info and the Police couldn't really charge her with anything so released her to our care. The rest simply refused to say too much, but basically they were working to pay off their fare to the UK."

"The gang behind the brothels are naturally pissed off with you closing their business..." David added.

"Realistically, I think they were open again in different premises within a week. We proved an annoyance rather than a serious threat," Eve said.

"My point exactly. How did you go from an annoyance to enough of a threat to warrant killing a man?"

"The Slough Observer," Eve said.

"They did this follow up piece on Eve. 'Crusading local tackles organised crime.' They did it without consent, took our remarks out of context and cobbled together snatched interviews which exposed us as having uncovered a gang in the area that masterminded the traffic of these sex workers and other work gangs. Called her the 'New Wilberforce,'" Jacqui said.

"Then we got the note, followed by more a week later," Eve added.

"That's when we really knew we were onto something." Jacqui said it with a little steel and self-validation. She handed the photocopies of the notes to David.

'Stop investigating, you are pretty, stay out of this business and you will stay pretty,' he read aloud.

'We asked nicely, we won't ask nicely again. Stop'

'Stay safe. Stay pretty. Stay out of out our business. No more interviews. No more trouble.' He read aloud again, failing to stifle a small smile.

"Not terrifying stuff " Jacqui offered.

"Fairly serious stuff though," he held the notes up, "There not something the Police might take seriously on their own - but you carried on regardless?" he asked. Jacqui and Eve nodded but offered no further conversation. He got up and walked to the window and cast his gaze around the vista of playing fields, river and castle as quintessentially English as you could find. "Eve, you envisaged some kind of bodyguard thing... someone to stay close to the office and stay in the house with you at night?"

"I don't know," said Eve, "how does this usually work?"

"I was a soldier not a bodyguard. I did a bit of counter-assassination stuff but that didn't quite fall into this remit."

"It's more about Eve than me..." offered Jacqui.

"But if you can stay together, we could protect you both, plus safety in numbers, right?"

"Well Jacs you can move into my place, it's a town house on Alexander Road," Eve suggested and Jacqui shrugged.

"Is that near the Prince Arthur pub?" He asked and

Eve nodded.

"How secure is it?"

Eve considered the question, "It's alarmed with a private security firm response system. Deadlock windows and doors, pretty secure."

"I'll check it out... I'll move in too, be around in the evenings," David said. Jacqui raised her eyebrows at Eve who ignored her.

"We could hire some security guys to be at the house when you needed a break, maybe create a rota?" Eve added.

"Yeah – also let's have them cover the office as well. Create a proper security process for visitors and have them check car parks on a regular schedule," David said.

"I can sort that out; we have plenty of security contacts, "Jacqui added.

"It needs to be subtle, nothing overt. A single guy in the office and to travel with you if you go to meetings... make sure the office generally tightens up on visitors, that kind of thing," David added. Jacqui raised her hand in mock child-like fashion.

"Sir, one thing sir."

"Piss off Jacs," David said smiling, "what now?"

"I have a date tonight and I am in line for some action and I'm not missing out on that. Does this mean you have to chaperone me?" Jacqui objected.

"More info than really needed. Fine, so the protection is so essential that it can begin tomorrow, after your hot date." The sarcasm appeared lost on Jacqui.

David added, "Can you stay in tonight Eve? I have to go and do something with Peter tonight, but I won't be too late. Maybe we can go over to the pub and have a drink?"

Eve smiled. Jacqui smiled at Eve's smile and David looked at the pair of them. "What?" he said.

Peter fiddled with the buttons and closed his jacket, three seconds later he undid it. The herringbone jacket had become a staple of his wardrobe, technically too heavy for a summer day but Peter felt it leant an eccentric charm to his appearance. It had been a more expensive tailored purchase, made during an affluent winning streak and he associated it with good fortune, which he needed tonight. He'd had a chance to reflect on the week's events and all of sudden a dawning realisation had hit him: his long lost brother, muscles bulging and Milk Tray man wardrobe might be a bit of twat, but he did offer some tangible benefits when he considered his recent social descent into the murkier depths of Slough society.

No one in his gambling world knew Peter had a brother, he and David didn't look alike and David's appearance and demeanour would lend Peter a much needed steely edge, a more forcible presence in the business he had unfolding. Peter Edwards had always taken calculated risks and long before he saw his brother striding down Vansittart Road towards him he had determined that he'd be taking another tonight.

"I need to make a stop before we head over to the venue," he said to his brother by way of a greeting. David nodded, but looked longingly at the door to the pub before following his brother to his car, an Audi A6, the older model but in fine condition. David looked around at the Victorian terraced streets that surrounded him. He knew Peter had a flat near here but wasn't sure where. The area round the pub was one of the most affluent and sort after Windsor areas. It didn't surprise David that Peter had moved here.

Neither spoke as Peter sedately took the car over the relief road and into Slough. They cruised over the A4 and turned off into the maze of streets and smaller older industrial units that made up the Slough Trading Estate. Peter poked his arm across the car and said, "See that monstrosity of a building..." David looked at a funny block on large concrete stilts with an oddly decorated facade. "That's the one from the credits of 'The Office'.

David nodded. "Not seen it."

Peter thought about making a comment about being locked in cave for the last ten years but stopped himself. Instead he pulled the car into a parking space in front of a 'metal fabricators' or at least it used to be that. It's derelict and boarded window state indicated it had long since ceased being a legitimate business. "This is the stop. I need to collect those winnings. Didn't have time the other day." With that he pulled out the slip of paper he had at the pub, "Come in with me, these are colourful characters. Maybe place a bet on the fight tonight?" David frowned but obliged by getting out of the car and following his brother.

The front door had a heavy padlock and chain on it, Peter ignored it and moved along the side alley and round to the back of the single storey unit, his pace slowed and his step became a little more cautious as he rounded the corner, then he stopped dead. Ahead of him a tired old blue door barred the way, the door's frosted window took up the top third of the door and sat behind three iron bars, this proved an incidental detail as ninety percent of the door sat obscured behind 'Fuckin' Hell Mel'.

"Hallo FHM", Peter offered, his voice adopting that odd high pitched lilt that comes when confronted with an intimidating presence. Mel stood close to 6'8" and must have weighed a minimum of twenty-five stone, but he was fat, very very fat and rather like that great British strong man Glen Ross, he had proved his immense strength on numerous occasions, just don't ask him to run to the end of the road. Breaking heads was Mel's forte.

"Alright Geek, what's occurring?" Mel's nasally flat voice sounded constricted, an almost suffocated sound. David just observed, keeping his eye on the big fella and noting the general layout.

Peter stepped forward a little, "Got some business with the Irishman, lady luck smiled on me." Mel raised his eyebrows and without turning tapped his hand on the blue door. A second or two later it opened a crack, the metal safety chain still on.

"The Geek's here to collect," Mel said. The door slammed shut and for a moment it seemed as if that would be it. "He don't like big winners Geek, you know that."

Peter shrugged a 'what can you do!' back at him.

"Mind you, I aint seen you collect for a while..."

His revelation was terminated by the swinging open of

the door and a broad Irish brogue booming from the darkness within, "Fooking hell Melvin ya big shoite, shift yers arse, ya blocking all the light."

Mel shifted his bulk with the languid malaise of a dogsbody and the way in opened up. A dimly lit room greeted them, Peter nodded at David to follow him.

"Who's he?" Mel asked putting a slab of an arm across David's chest. David reacted subtly, pushing a little at the arm and forcing Mel to exert pressure back.

"He's with me," Peter said.

"Lovely, get a room maybe, but why does he want in?"

"Mel he might be a new customer, be nice?"

The disembodied Irish voice returned, "Mel let the fookers in will yers, it's just the Geek." Mel reluctantly did as asked, but kept his eyes locked on David, who stared right back.

The two brothers moved into the dim interior where the odour of mould and sweat dominated. The room comprised of two desks sitting perpendicular to each other to the left of the door, three old metal filing cabinets stood along the wall opposite, next to a slightly ajar internal door that lead to a corridor. In front of the desk sat a single mouse-chewed floral armchair. Perched on the edge of the right-hand desk sat a ruddy cheeked man in a cheap suit and no tie, his greying temples the last hair on his balding head. He didn't stand when they entered, he simply bellowed, "Geek, Jesus you don't look well man, eat some steak for fook's sake will ya. Liver and onions, my old father swore by it so he did."

Peter moved forward and still no hand of friendship greeted him. The door closed behind them and the light dimmed. Fucking Hell Mel had followed them in. Peter pulled out the betting slip and waved it with a smile, "I'm owed some wedge Declan," he said.

"Are yer now?" the Irishman replied, his smile lessening. "Show me the paper will yer." Peter did so and the bookie pursed his lips sucked some air through his teeth but happily for all refrained from actually tutting. "Dat's a big payout, a very big payout. A drink boys?" he offered them a bottle of Jameson's.

"It is indeed... not for me thanks." Peter said.

David shook his head and noticed the shadow change behind the door leading to the interior corridor. He squinted but saw nothing.

"I had a few big payouts on dis game, not many winning bets but dose dat did bet, won big." He looked at Peter as he said it.

"Are you trying to tell me something Declan?"

"Jees nuttin heavy, I'm a little shy at the moment I'm going to need to offer yer credit on dat bet, jez for a few days like."

Peter looked back towards Mel and then to his brother before settling his gaze on Declan once more. "I don't think so Declan. You owe me twelve large, you always pay out and you always collect. Today won't be any different."

Declan stood up and buttoned his jacket, "Don't be coming in heerz and be telling me what I will and won't be doing wid my money boy." The tone had changed and the room suddenly felt a little more desperate to David.

Peter held his hands up in placation, "Declan... I always pay you on time, have I shirked any debt with you? Have I?" He got no response. "Now we have done business for a long time and I know you have more than enough cash to pay me out and cover you're other bets."

Declan cut him off, "Don't tell me my business boy. I pay when I need to pay not when you want it, understand?" Peter shut his eyes and his shoulders slumped. "If I had a mind, maybeez I should talk to the Mason boys, cut you out the loop... dat's right boy I knowz what yers owes them."

Peter shivered slightly, "Fuck the Masons, why are you talking about my bets with the Masons?"

"People talk ya silly fooking piss ant... you iz borderline bad debt Geek. I keep my ear to the ground. It's why I'm still in business. And you aint been winning much lately." Declan spat the words out as if daring Peter to challenge them.

Peter looked around the room for some kind of support. Momentarily his eyes fell on his brother. He turned away before David could respond. "I need that money Declan," he said.

"I know you do Geek, but yer won't be paying the Mason's back with my money tonight... do yer understand what I'm saying to yers?

Peter searched for a response, his flitting eyes and downturned face giving away his inevitable contrition. David moved to just behind his brother. And spoke, "You owe him. You should pay him." He kept his hands at his side and his expression neutral.

Declan arched his eyebrows in surprise. "Geek! Have yers bought a little friend for moral support? Is dat what yers have done?"

"It's a basic principle of life. You owe, you pay," David said with a little more steel.

"Yers need to keep yer dog on a lead Peter, I doubt his bite is as bad as Mel's and I'd hate to see him get fooked."

Peter sensed some strength rise up in him, someone, his brother, was backing him up. "Declan you owe me twelve grand, I need it. Fuck the Masons. That's my business. I'm owed what I'm owed." Declan shrugged and moved back around his desk, "Fook off boys, yerz is boring the shoite outa me. Mel see dem out and break what you like on each fucker."

Mel didn't move fast. A man built for comfort but not speed. David set himself, swivelled on his left heel and before Mel had registered that he had spun to face him David launched the punch, swung up from the hip and up through the shoulder, half uppercut and half hook he put his entire body weight behind it, giving the punch more than he would normally, to compensate for the size of his foe. The sound of fist on flesh is distinctive and unpleasant. The gelatinous mass of Mel's gargantuan head absorbed the force of the punch, but David knew how to fight and drove his fist beyond the first impact and as he did so he felt the jaw separate, the teeth pop and the cheek bone fracture. The spray of blood that came from the mouth masked the sound of three teeth ricocheting off the wall and the snap to the right of the head coincided with a sagging of the knees and giant exhalation of air and pain by Mel. He teetered and then lurched to his right collapsing in a straight line fall; the impact caused the whole room to shake and for the desk tidy to bounce on the desk. Declan and Peter watched, mouths agape, mute and motionless, in awe of the pure physical destruction they had just witnessed. David didn't admire his handiwork he skipped over the prostrate giant and focused on the door to the corridor. He paused a beat and then levelled a straight kick to the doors right-hand side, it slammed violently inwards and the loud crack and thud of it connecting with an organic mass was confirmed when a loud scream emanated from behind.

David pushed behind the door, Peter and Declan didn't move, their astonishment broken only by David's return. He pushed ahead of him a big, but not Mel-sized, man forward on his knees, blood pouring from a hideously broken and bleeding nose. Once he had his man in the centre of the room he aimed a boot at his exposed arse and kicked him to the floor.

"Fucking hell..." Peter muttered.

"Sweet Jesus," joined in Declan, "did yers just kill Fooking Hell Mel with a single bastard punch?"

"He aint dead, now pay him what you owe him," David snapped back.

Declan looked at the pair of them in turn, he stuttered a little, befuddled by what he had witnessed. He pulled open a drawer and tugged out six bundles of notes. Then he turned and knelt at the safe on the floor behind the second desk and fiddled with the combination... he rose sharply brandishing a large hunting knife and thrusting it at the pair of them.

"Yers two bastards stay the fook away from me." He pushed the knife ahead of him, "Keep back, I'm taking my money from dis safe and walking out of dat door, get in my way and I'll stick the pair of yers." Peter backed away, but David moved forward blocking the Irishman's only means of escape.

"Go ahead and try?" He pointed to below his heart, "Aim here, quicker kill, guaranteed to incapacitate, no breast bone..."

"Fook yerself ya lunatic."

"Be smart. Give him his money. You owe it. You're a bookie you don't need the double whammy of the world knowing you're such a big cunt that you don't pay your debts and that your muscle is total shite."

"Fook it..."

"It's up to you... but I can and will take that knife off you and then shove it up your arse. Then I'll take the money anyway. You decide, pay up and survive reputation intact or play it cheap get a supersized arsehole."

Declan dropped the knife, it clattered onto the desk and he slunk into the far left corner, "Jezt don't kill me ok boys."

David urged Peter forward and mouthed 'money' at him. Peter pulled himself together stepped over bleeding lump on the floor and moved round the desk to the safe. He picked up the bundles and counted them. He gathered six more and added them to those on the desk. Peter levelled them into two bundles and wrapped two elastic bands around them and then tucked them to his inside breast pockets.

"Yers just taking what yer waz owed?"

"Yes Declan," Peter said. "I'm not a thief." Peter, his composure re-gathered, marched out of the door with the cocksure pride of the attacker and not the voyeur he had been.

Five minutes later, back in the car, Peter couldn't hide that he was still buzzing from the adrenalin rush he'd just had. David sat still and breathed deeply. "Fucking hell – one punch David? One fucking punch!" David said nothing. They drove through the industrial estate and headed towards Farnham Common before circling through a small patch of wasteland to arrive at an abandoned single-storey brick unit that nestled next to the railway line and stood in the shadow of a newly built and still empty office building.

"Did you know he might be reluctant to pay out?" David asked as they climbed out of the car.

Peter frowned, "He has a reputation.. he can be a bit that way, with some people."

"You figured I'd help..."

Peter froze a little, just a momentary pause that signalled he might be caught in a lie. "Not in the way you did, no. I figured he'd be less inclined to get physical with me if you were there, that was all."

David looked his brother up and down trying to find

the lie. He knew he'd been used and that Peter's newfound openness seemed to have nothing to do with brotherly reunion and more to do with practical necessity. He didn't really care, but understood that his brother was in a real mess. David needed to know how deep in the shit he had sunk.

"Tell me something about this fight tonight?"

"It's just a fight... some northern monkey, Scouser I think, is taking on a Russian or a Pole or someone East European. Stand up affair, basic 8oz gloved non-licence fight. Invited audience and big gamblers."

"Ok.." David said. He wanted to know more about the setup of the night ahead. "The East European fighter, is he mob handled?"

"No idea," Peter replied.

"But you got the invite from some guy at a poker game, a Corsican I think you said?"

"Did I? Yeah I think he's something like that. Yeah he got me the invite."

"Stands to reason that he and the fight organisers are connected then, same people?"

"Yeah maybe... does it make a difference?"

"Not especially, just like to know who my hosts are. It would be odd if the Euro guy wasn't part of a bigger thing." David noticed Peter trying to ignore the comment. For David the logic seemed simple, Jacqui and Eve had trouble with an East European gang and if a big East European is fighting in an unlicensed fight then the two things, if not directly related, could certainly have a link.

Either way, he'd find out more about the local gangland underworld tonight than he knew already.

"Declan..."

"What about him?" Peter asked.

"He'll have friends, connections."

Peter nodded.

"They'll be at this fight right? Would Declan be at the fight normally?"

Peter nodded again.

"Not concerned about that; given what we did?"

Peter shrugged, "It'll be fine..." he said, with little conviction.

"Hope you're right."

Peter seemed too relaxed about the situation and David wondered if he simply didn't understand the significance of what they had done. Declan would be connected for sure, there would have to be consequences for what they did. David knew that.

The old unit must have been an engineering works or similar, the oil-stained floor and oddly shaped patches of discoloration inferred that at one time large machines had occupied the space, drills and lathes maybe, supplied by the intricate array of rails and pulleys that remained overhead. Now it stood empty, barren of machinery and objects of industry. The walls bounced the sound around with confusing effect, while the small lead-lined glass windows appeared too fragile and insufficient to hold in the burble and excited hubbub that now filled the space.

Over two hundred people milled around the room, spread out in small clusters giving the appearance the area had been filled, but it was an illusion of modern social grace, the clusters occupied more space than they needed, a combination of false bonhomie and nervousness or wariness of others that kept people at a distance. The groups eyed each other with suspicion, conscious of the hierarchy and etiquette of such an event. The noise came from the talking, laughing and repeated slapping of each other on the back. The only area that remained clear of this behaviour stood to the far right about twenty feet from the walls, four iron sheets lay on the floor, covering maybe a twenty-five square foot space, one man stood in the centre of it, patrolling.

David surveyed the scene from the outside of the large faded and chipped red painted wooden sliding door. Peter had leaned forward to talk quietly into the ear of the taller of the two grey suit clad men minding the door, the conversation looked serious and formal. David listened hard and heard the familiar twang of the Russian language, if he had to level a guess he'd have said the speaker was a native of St. Petersburg. David tried to look nonchalant and unconcerned about the outcome of the conversation but the more he looked uninterested so the second of the doormen took notice of him. They caught each other in a glance, David decided to smile and nod his head in acknowledgement but the minder didn't return it, he stared for a moment then simply leant to his left, no turning or bending just leaning from the middle, never taking his eye off David. He spoke in a whisper and without hurry into his compatriot's ear and the stretch to reach his colleague revealed a small tattoo on the right of his neck, behind his ear. A small, five-pointed star with a burst of letters underneath. David understood immediately.

The French Foreign Legion is by its nature a melange of races and nationalities and the East European invasion of Western Europe is mirrored within it. Since the late 90s they had dominated the new recruits and they came from a diverse background, bringing interesting and scary service records, criminal records and back stories with them. David had served with, fought and made friends with enough of them to know the history of the tattoos and the branding of hard men around the world. The bouncer sported a mafia tattoo and the letters indicated time served. He'd need to see the shadings to know which branch of the crime world he heralded from, but David new the type. He focused back in on the two men, conscious that the tattooed one hadn't taken his eyes from him. Now his colleague joined in, he had to crouch a little to the whisper but neither man stood too tall, in fact they looked horribly average and unassuming. David knew this hid the truth; these men would be ripped, teak tough underneath their clothes and carrying an assortment of blades and other weapons.

Their interest in him struck David as odd, he had no noticeable facial scarring, prison or service tattoos to mark him out of the crowd but still they looked at him like he might be a threat, as if they had to weigh up his propensity to cause trouble and how they would handle it. Peter had to pull away once he realised the men now ignored him, he looked along their line of sight and saw that they were focused on his brother. He sighed and dropped his head a little.

"He's erm, er... my mate... visiting for a few days," Peter said. The two Russians ignored him, shared some whispered words and beckoned David over. A small crowd and queue had gathered behind them, but no one looked to push in or move past the four men. Clearly people knew what was expected. David moved forward and stood alongside his brother.

"Can I help?" he offered.

"He's... just visiting, he likes boxing. I thought... seeing as I'm an invited guest, well, that he could come along," Peter said.

The Russians stared a little more. The one with the tattoo asked, "You have ticket for him?"

"No..." said Peter, before David cut him off.

"I believe we can purchase them on the door, how much are they?" He pulled a roll of cash from his trouser pocket, "Fifty pounds, is that right?"

"You like fighting?" the taller Russian asked.

"I do."

"We don't know you. This is ticket only event, maybe you start fighting. We don't like trouble!"

David nodded his agreement. "I'm sure you can handle anything gentlemen. I just want to watch, maybe bet."

"Where you do your fighting?" the tattooed Russian asked.

"The army."

"British army?"

"The Legion."

The Russian smiled at hearing this and nodded his approval. "Which division?" he asked.

"Parachute Regiment, based in Calvi."

"My cousin is in Legion, infantry," He said proudly. He shared a final word with his colleague and then said, "Keep your money. Go in but be good soldier." David nodded his thanks and gently nudged and pushed Peter into the large building and the throng of noise.

Peter scanned the room and moved off towards the far corner where a makeshift bar had been set up, David tagged behind. Peter grabbed a can of lager and offered one to his brother who declined. Beer in hand, Peter mooched towards the back wall and looked across the room. "You see the guys from the pub?" he asked David.

"Coming in now," David said, nodding at the doorway. The two bald figures strutted into the room, their loud guffaws managing to rise above the cacophony. They stood for a moment a few yards in from the door, causing a minor obstruction to other guests, desperate to be recognised. No one in the room obliged, so they settled for the odd nod hello and moved into the crowd, hands thrust into leather coat pockets. "Let's go and see them and get the payment made," David said, looking at his brother.

"In a moment, let's make them sweat a little, force them to look for me a bit."

"Why?"

"Well, I'm pretty certain Declan will have spoken to these two at least, maybe others about what happened in his shop. Don't see any harm in my capitalising on that... do you?"

"Depends on how you define capitalise on it, doesn't it?" David said.

"You heard what Declan called me, 'Geek', not exactly respectful is it?"

"No... but then you're not a gun-toting eighteen-year-old gangbanger that watches too much TV, get over it. That said, I did wonder about that, why 'Geek'?"

Peter tried to ignore his brother's dig but the irritation it caused remained clear, "Oh it's because they all think I do stuff with computers, you know in IT... hence computer 'Geek'."

David nodded vaguely, failing to understand why anyone in the illegal fighting and gambling world would know or care what Peter did for a living. "Just remember it was me that floored fat boy, not you, your involvement is by association," David said.

"Whatever," Peter shrugged.

David looked hard at his brother and made some simple calculations. He'd hoped his intervention with Declan would help his brother, maybe even endear him a little in this new period of detente. He had the notion his brother might be involved in some silliness he couldn't handle and that his physical presence would offer him a way out, it appeared that Peter had the same the idea, but rather than support, Peter seemed to have assumed that in

David he had a fighting ally. Peter swigged from his can and nodded to the odd person, none seemed interested in carrying the nod into a conversation. The Mason brothers scanned the room, neck rolls bulging as their heads turned. The larger of the two, Jason, chatted into his phone as he looked out into the room. He spied David and paused, trying to place the face but couldn't, then he flicked his eyes across to Peter and the recognition flashed across his face like a toddler's joy at finding a sweet. He backhanded his brother on the chest and pointed Peter out to him. The two men adopted their attitude and bustled towards their prey.

Peter saw them coming a fraction later, he plopped his can of beer onto the window ledge behind him and tried to puff his chest out and stand strong. David took half a step backward and to the left. He quickly scanned the room and tried to locate the two doormen, both remained at the front door checking in the last of the guests; they'd be inside in a matter of minutes. His eyes settled on the far wall and a connecting door that stood near the steel sheets on the floor, another minder stood by the door and mirroring his place on the opposite wall another heavy stood near the bar. None of them huge, all of them serious and all of them exuded professionalism. Unlike the two monkeys that approached David and Peter now.

"Fuck me you turned up!" Nick the shorter of the two barked as he moved within non-shouting range. Peter gave him a half smile and nodded at Jason as well.

"Gents... I said I'd be here and I am. Expecting me to bail out?"

"Oh well you know, ten grand aint easy to find, we

figured..."

"You figured I'd not be able to get the money together, maybe fail to call in my own debts in time, that it?" Peter sounded more confident than he had in the pub, but David could see the tremor in his hands and hear the slight wobble in his voice. "Have a word with Declan did we? Talk him into holding out on me?"

The two bald brothers exchanged glances and shrugged, "Maybe," they said together. Peter shook his head in a rather trite show of disappointment.

"You two really don't want me to be part of the game tonight do you?"

"Fuck off office boy, hand over the wedge," Jason said as he looked hard at Peter with malice in his eyes. David still loitered unnoticed. Peter swallowed, pulled the bundles out of his pockets and held them close to his belly. Nick reached out and tugged them from his grasp, he flicked the bundles, rubbed the notes and then held each bundle to his nose and took a sniff.

"Nice" he said.

"Feeling all brave are we Peter, grown a pair have we?" Jason spat a little as he spoke. Peter held his ground and the man's eye. "Coz we spoke to Declan tonight and he aint very happy, very unhappy in fact. You've been fucking with things that you don't understand sunshine."

Peter tried a little laugh, "He owed me, I made sure he paid me," he stammered.

Nick stepped up alongside his brother and a sickly, wet-lipped gurn of a smile spread across his face. "You son, is proper fucked."

"Some bloke put Fuckin' 'ell Mel out of action. Destroyed the fucker we hear," Jason said. "Now I know you aint up to it, so I'm guessing the stacked fucker lingering behind you has the right hand responsible." David tried a hard man glare for the first time but neither of the bald brothers seemed to notice. "Mel aint likely to speak or drink without a straw for months let alone fight, you understanding me?"

Peter did. Peter now understood all too well. There was no point being an illegal bookie and having a monster like Mel on the payroll if he couldn't earn his keep. Mel worked the unlicensed fight circle, the Butterbean of the M4 corridor, and the winner of the fight tonight would fight the winner of a clash between FHM and some large Gypsy due to take place in a few days' time. That meant a lot of bets, a lot of serious money would be involved and David's right hand didn't just end Mel, it ended two big local fights. People would be pissed off.

"I know you understand... the big Russian aint a man you should annoy Peter. Play with fire and you will get fucking burned."

"I can handle the Russian don't you worry about me," Peter said.

"You can't handle your own cock," spat Nick. "If you have any sense you'd better get out of here, word's spreading that you're responsible and the Russian will hear about it soon enough." The two brothers moved back and finally turned away from them and moved into the thickening crowd of people. David's eyebrows arched at the revelations he had just heard. Peter had lied, he knew that the Russians were behind the fight and Peter had some acquaintance with them. David certainly wasn't a detective but the chance this Russian gang might be related to the Russians terrorising their sister and Eve couldn't be ignored. David didn't really believe in coincidences and the shit storm Peter had created might just be of use in solving his sister's problems, but for that to happen he'd have to play along, act the heavy for his brother and see how much he could find out.

Jacqui Edwards rolled over on her king-size bed and let out a growl like giggle, her eyes were closed and a truly satisfied smile spread across her face. She let out a deep sated sigh, "Oh shit I needed that," she enthused. The red flush of being freshly fucked still lingered on her cheeks, a light sheen of perspiration clad her body and she tingled from the inside out, a surge of pure delight pulsed through her with each beat of her heart. The duvet lay in a heap off to the side of the bed, Jacqui lay naked and happily unabashed with her left leg lying across the naked man that lay beside her. It didn't matter that he saw her naked now, any concerns she had over her body or whether her internet lothario would want her had long been banished. She had failed to play hard to get, coy became rampant desire and gentle flirtation warped into lip-licking desperation.

She rolled over onto her side and snuggled her head onto the exposed shoulder of her lover. Jacqui placed her right hand onto his chest caressed it and then gave it a tiny a kiss, "Thank you..." she said as her fingers moved over and lightly caressed his nipple.

"My pleasure," came the response. Jacqui jostled a little to get comfortable and swung her right leg over the man's body that remained doggedly still and impassive in response. Jacqui had never been one for impulsive or reckless behaviour, but a life dominated by a career that involved long unsociable working hours had forced her hand. Internet dating is a lottery, for every gem there are thousand turds and Jacqui had chatted, messaged or met with many of them. Internet dating is the slush pile of romance, you have to wade through the crap to find the best. She allotted suitors into metaphorical scenario baskets, and then acted accordingly on dates. She had three main categories, fun and frolics, sensible and sure and keepers.

There were subdivisions within each and occasionally some jumped from one category or another, but the fun and frolics tended to get the more slutty version of herself. The beauty of such a system meant she could have a regular stream of dinner dates with people that could at least read a menu that wasn't on a backlit board, have sex with a man that had vague knowledge of what a clitoris did and where to find it and lastly, if she needed to demonstrate to her mother or Eve that her life might be progressing more conventionally she had the odd one to take on a serious date.

Her Latin lover had proven a little different, he claimed to be of Sicilian descent, but couldn't speak Italian and had the lazy vowels and pseudo-intellectual pronunciation of the Thames Valley. Jacqui didn't much care, she knew he wasn't married and had even eaten in several of the restaurants he claimed to part-own. No, Yannik would never be a keeper but he had certainly been the best of her fun and frolics.

He had made her feel sexy, had looked at her with hungry eyes, a look that to Jacqui, at least, said, 'he wants sex and he wants it with me.' Their 'first meeting' had been in the ubiquitous 'safe public space'; the second date had been a few days later, lunch, followed by sex in a car, certainly erotic and passionate, if a little uncomfortable. Yannik had shown promise, however, and a physiological awareness and skill level that suggested more meetings would be fun. With each fuck (Jacqui hadn't managed to call it 'making love') getting a little better and richer in experience. Yannik had proven to be more than just an excellent and very considerate lover, no wham-bams and a lot of very personal consideration, he'd also been attentive, interested in her views and what she had to say. He had led conversations, pushed for her opinion and one of the delights of their pre and post sex engagements had been their conversations and Jacqui had found her time with Yannik to be more than just physically rewarding.

"You can smoke if you want." she said.

"Thanks... but not inside the house, it isn't nice."

Jacqui smiled to herself, he passed the test. She knew he'd be gasping pretty soon and unlike most men he hadn't yet looked at his watch or made some excuse to get away from the cuddle, he hadn't even mentioned something he needed to do.

"Do you want a coffee or something?"

"Can we stay like this for a while?" he replied.

"Mmmmmm sure we can," and she snuggled up once again. They lay in silence for a while and she listened to the steady beating of his heart and looked down his lean body to his now inert penis and she found herself lost in a delicious memory for a moment.

"So how are you Jacqui?" he asked, yanking her from the daydream.

"I feel great, don't you?"

"Not now fool... since the funeral?"

"Oh right," she let out a little giggle, "well you know it's just a case of carrying on isn't it. Being very English."

"I suppose it is, you weren't close you said?"

"Not really, he wasn't a pleasant man, very domineering, aggressive. He'd been an army man all of his life, not a good one mind you."

"How so?"

"Oh he got promoted, rose through the ranks but mostly because they had no one else and he'd been there the longest, nearly thirty years and all he managed was Major."

Yannik raised himself up a little, disturbing her position, but once he'd gotten comfortable again he encouraged her to settle onto his chest once more. "Did many attend the funeral?"

"Not really..." a tinge of sadness in her voice, "a few old timers and coffin dodgers from the pub and church, a couple from the golf club... we don't have many relatives, so it was pretty bare. Eve, my business partner came too."

"She is the lawyer, right?"

"Right, specialises in human rights. A proper crusader for the moral good."

"She is the one I have seen on TV right?"

"Yep, Eve helped the police to shut down some brothels; a lot of publicity came from that..." Jacqui's voice trailed off and her eyes letting a little of the sadness at the trouble that followed to show. Yannik sensed the change in her mood and squeezed a little with his hugging arm. "Anyway, you know all that."

"I do – but you work so hard, always doing something interesting... how's the latest project going?" he asked.

"Oh the server security stuff, yeah we have carried out a few audits and more should come. They are really dull and if the money wasn't so bloody appealing I'd lose them. Money talks though."

"It does, but I meant the project with Eve... the one about the migrants... have you made progress?"

"Oh you mean the 'worthy stuff', no wonga but lots of good will. Progress? We've narrowed it down to Slough being the main hub for processing the migrants and we have a good idea that some are kept to work and pay off their transport and some are shipped straight back out."

"It's fascinating... these people pay to be transported here and then are forced to work here, like slaves you say? Is it a big operation?" Yannik probed.

"We think several different gangs bring them in and another, master group, then organises and processes them once here, it's buying and selling people. But we think that there has to be more in it for the main gang... we just don't know what yet."

"So you are still investigating, still working on it?"

"Absolutely... it's too big to simply give up."

"But these are serious people, you said so, don't they scare you... they could hurt you?"

"Mmmmmm a little, but we have some protection now, we have someone serious too." said Jacqui.

"Really... interesting. Who?"

"Oh it doesn't matter; just Eve panics and wants to be safe rather than sorry. C'mon, let's get some wine?" Yannik made no move to get up, he watched Jacqui pull on a robe and amble towards the bathroom. He waited a breath before reaching down to his left looking for his phone that sat in his discarded jean's pocket.

The red wooden door had been pulled shut and the two Russians had slipped inside and split up to wander the room, the bar in the corner had descended into near chaos, several queues had also developed behind small clusters of men and large bundles of cash changed hands, some accompanied by a handshake others not. Slips of paper changed hands, some men were turned away from tables and others searched pockets for more notes. David took it all in, the noise and the chatter made the room, despite its size, feel close and oppressive. The heat outside and numbers inside had created a sultry taste to the air and people's brows showed the effects of the temperature rise. The talking had grown quicker and the noise louder, the impending sense of violence hovered everywhere. David felt the tension, saw the aggression and his mind recalled the beastings in basic training and some of his darker days in prison. The crowd had moved towards becoming a mob and soon they would be baying for their entertainment, demanding blood.

"Should be a good fight, the Scouser is supposed to be useful, a champion." Peter half-shouted the words into David's ear. "Big knockout record, had a few proper fights apparently," he continued.

"Right," said David, keen not to show his true experience and knowledge of the illegal fight scene. The countries might be different, but the principles remained the same. Rich men produced their trained pets and they fought, the crowd cheered and someone bled and bones were broken.

"Did you bet?" he asked.

"I did, nothing big, I don't bet big on the fighting... not confident it isn't fixed."

"So who's your money on?" David shouted.

"The big East European, Albert Dimitrenko... or ...Dimeiski or something... I saw him last year he beat the shit out some black guy from London. He's the home fighter gotta go with him," Peter replied. David nodded his agreement without conviction. He spotted the first of the doormen about thirty feet to his left by the back wall and David quickly scanned to his right and there thirty feet to his right stood the other doorman. He decided he should look behind him and the bar minder had moved forward and stood about ten feet behind them eyes trained on the pair of them. 'Fuck' thought David. Suddenly the situation had gone from serious to very heavy in the blink of an eye. He stared ahead but in his peripheral vision he saw the men on either side move closer and closer to them, the crowds of people between them parting without quarrel or recourse. David tensed, and balled his right hand into a fist, he widened his stance and began to calculate how he might extricate himself and concluded almost immediately that he had a chance if it was just him escaping, but that Peter would be a huge handicap. Accepting his fate didn't mean he could relax, pain might be coming and it's always better to be mentally prepared for it.

They reached them only seconds later, a pincer movement from three sides. Finally Peter woke up and realised what had happened, he wheeled around in a comic fashion and David had to curl his hand around his brother's bicep and squeeze it until he got his attention, "Steady Peter, relax." Peter opened his mouth to protest but the look in David's eye halted him.

The taller of the Russians stood close and spoke clearly, "Gentlemen, we hope you enjoy the fight. Please come with us, you have been invited to view it from the VIP area." He nodded towards the less cramped area on the other side of the steel sheets.

"Thank you," David said, "but we are comfortable here."

"It is a polite invitation, but it is not one you can refuse... you understand?"

Peter's face registered the appropriate level of fear, his eyes widened a little in panic and he stumbled and stammered, trying to summon up a response. The Russian cut off the need for him make any kind of reply.

"A gentleman will talk to you after fight, is better if you came with us now." He pushed his hand out to guide them to their right. David accepted it and moved off, dropping in behind the Russian to his right. Peter needed a gentle shove to fall into the line and despite the crowds they made it easily to the VIP area. They stepped between the wall and the significantly larger minder and moved along the narrow three foot wide strip of floor between the steel sheets and the wall. They made it to the corner and turned round and leant against the wall, their position giving them an unencumbered view across the sheets to the large baying mob beyond. They had been in place no more than thirty seconds when the red door slid, scrunched and screamed open. The heads in the room spun en masse to see the source of the noise. In walked five men; a bear of a man stripped from the waist up, wearing grey tracksuit bottoms and boxing shoes, flanked by two men on both sides, trotted into the room. He raised his gloved hands to the sounds of jeers and boos and the occasional, "Fuck off home" and "Wanker". His body lacked the definition of a true athlete but he had powerful shoulders and huge forearms and his body, back and shoulders had a hearty covering of sweat matted black hair. Certainly a more impressive hair growth than now remained on his head.

The crowd parted to make way for him, as they did so the screech and clunk of chains through pulleys began, the steel sheets on the floor began to lift and swing free from the ground, revealing the twenty-five foot square pit. A small section of the crowd, travelling scousers, began chanting and cheering, "TONEEE, TONEEE" as the bear reached the pit edge.

David looked in, the pit's floor sat about ten feet below the ledge where he stood, a rough concrete slab floor with dark stains, maybe oil, maybe blood, not easy to tell, a foot wide channel of ruts and old mortar lumps ran down the centre of the floor and up the walls on either end, evidence that two separate vehicle inspection pits had been knocked together. He considered the space, the fighting terrain, no one else would be in the pit but the fighters, gloves or not, this was a cage fight, no holds barred. It would be brutal. A deafening roar erupted around David and he looked up to see the side door had opened and in walked the other fighter, several inches shorter than the Scouser, but toned and muscular, and greased up ready for action. His entourage consisted of just an elderly man, maybe in his seventies, decked out in black linens. David liked his style. As the two fighters came together at the pit edge they eyeballed each other and the crowd whooped and hollered their idiotic approval. Random shouts and jeers emanated from the back of the room, helpful advice like "Fuckin' kill him Albert" or "he's big but he's slow".

David knew neither fighter would be hearing any of it, they'd just be focused on the task in hand. If they had fear or the gnawing realisation that they weren't up to the task then it would be revealed now. It's why fighters stare into the eyes of their opponent, searching for a weakness, some kind of indication their foe is more scared or more apprehensive than they are. Some fights are won before a punch is thrown, it's astonishing to see big hard men simply crumble at this moment. David had seen it, watched the ambition and anger simply wither to nothing right in front of him. David's focus on the fighters prevented him from seeing the man that followed through the door. He dwarfed both fighters, in height and stature, a stone carved face on mountainous shoulders, a serious man and a harder man than both fighters and all of the room, probably.

Valentyn looked across the pit and found who he had hoped to see. His Librarian,Peter, together with a man that he'd heard could fight. The destroyer of Fucking Hell Mel. He indicated to Oleg, putting his two fingers to his eyes and tracking onto the brothers. Oleg nodded his understanding.

"Is that the big Russian then?" David asked, clocking Valentyn for the first time.

"Yes," Peter said sheepishly, "his name is Valentyn."

"Where's the fella that invited you, the guy from the poker game?"

"Not here yet," said Peter, "Valentyn runs this the fights and hard stuff.."

"Fuck it Peter, the big fella is very interested in us. Why would he be so interested in us?"

Peter looked at his brother. "Nervous?"

"Shouldn't I be?" David said.

"But you're the big bad soldier boy... you can handle anyone right?" It sounded more sarcastic than Peter intended and David frowned at him.

"Don't be a twat Peter. Being beaten up and killed by the Russian mob in Slough isn't how I planned to finish the day."

"Don't worry about them, their bark is worse than their bite... later on, shut up and let me do the talking, OK?" Peter didn't look at his brother he focused on the two fighters descending the ladder and once on the pit floor their handlers laced on the puny looking boxing gloves.

David turned his attention to the fighters as well and murmured, Coz that has worked so well up to now hasn't it!

The chanting grew louder, the cheers became fanatical shouting, the last of the handlers scaled the ladder and from somewhere unseen a bell rang out and the two fighters moved forward to face each other, gloved hands held up around their faces. The two men circled, the bear pivoting on his back leg as the smaller man bustled around him, ducking and bobbing at the waist – feinting blows, looking for a way past, around the bear's long outstretched left arm. *'Don't waste energy,'* David thought looking at the Russian, *'let the big lump come to you, he'll get bored with the dance soon enough.'*

The bear moved forward with a surprising turn of foot speed and launched a right hook, the amateurish clubbing blow rebounded off the gloved hand of the Russian. From the position of defence the Russian threw his counter punch, a straight right, well delivered with a turn of the wrist landed flush on the bear's nose. It snapped his head back, the crowd cheered and the bear briefly gave ground before tucking up and moving after the smaller man once more.

The Russian saw an opening and stepped forward leading with a stiff left jab, he ducked under the clumsy defensive arm and landed a punch on the exposed jaw and followed up with a crisp clean straight right hand, a classic one two combination. The punch exploded onto the nose of the bear, the blood came immediately, trickling at first then a steady stream that gathered on his top lip and leaked over the mouth like barbaric lipstick. The crowd's roar became an ecstatic, blood thirsty orgy of sound with their fists clenched and arms pumping. Inadequate men living life through the violence and gore before them. David watched the Russian's movement, impressive footwork and good hand speed, he danced away from the bear once more, this time admiring the flow of blood he had caused. The bear shook his head and dabbed at the blood, he tried to smile it away. David looked hard into his face and saw all he needed to see.

"It will all be over inside another two minutes," he said to his brother.

The bear moved forward with renewed purpose, he thrust a slow left and swung a wide right, both missed, he followed it with left hook and then thrust his right arm out as the punch landed harmlessly on the Russian's gloves. Wrapping his arms around the Russian, the bear squeezed and lifted, letting out a guttural roar as he did so and hurled the smaller man at the wall. The Russian's back hit the rough concrete surface with a thud, but his hands remained high in defence. The bear swung a kick and it connected with the flesh around the Russian's middle causing him to bend sideways with the impact. Some boos and cries of 'cheat' broke through the cacophony of cheers. Looking to capitalise the bear threw a left uppercut, it curled up the middle of the guard and connected with the Russian's forehead, jolting him upright. That was followed by two half-hearted right hooks in quick succession which pushed the Russian sideways rather than really hurt him. The bear took a gasp of air and followed the Russian as he edged away along the far wall of the pit.

"You sure about that?" Peter replied.

The Russian launched an attack. The bear hadn't expected it and his arms still hung down as he recovered from his exertions of a moment ago. The Russian's lead right connected hard on his temple and the left upper cut connected solidly with his chin. The bear lurched forward, stung by the power and pace of the blow. He wrapped his long arms over the Russian's head and held on tight. With his head forced down by the weight of his opponent the Russian launched a flurry of short snapping punches into the bear's midriff, causing his left leg to rise up in pained reaction. Finally the Russian pushed the bigger man away with both hands and looked up to see a slow predictable right cross sail over his head. The Russian pivoted and swung a left hook, he turned his body and shoulder into it and the sweetly thrown blow connected with the unprotected ribs on the bear's right-hand side. The crunch wasn't audible, nor the whimper of pain it caused, but the reaction was plain to all, ribs had been cracked and the pain would be immense. The bear scuttled to his right, bent double at first before straightening and lowering his right arm to protect the vulnerable area. Like a wounded animal he circled away from the Russian who now composed himself and began to stalk his prey. He feinted a right and threw a swinging left, it clubbed the bear on the temple, then he feinted a right and threw the old one two, both landed flush on the nose. He stepped and back poked out a stinging left, then another and another, the punches peppering the bloody mask of the bear's face.

The sequence forced the bear to lift his left hand to defend his exposed jaw and the moment he did it the Russian cruelly attacked the exposed and damaged ribs, firing a double left hook into the body and lifting the bear on to his tip-toes, before switching the attack with a straight right and then a right uppercut. All landed with thudding ease and sickening effect.

The bear's legs buckled, he tucked his head into his hands and leant against the wall, swaying left to right trying to avoid blows that weren't being thrown. The Russian moved back to the centre of the pit and looked at the bloodied cowering mess in front of him.

"FIGHT" he bellowed, "FIGHT ME".

The crowd loved it and like bullies in a playground they began deriding the manliness of the Scouser, questioning his parentage and sexual orientation. Valentyn stepped forward and shouted into the pit, "YOU SEND US THIS USELESS SHIT TO FIGHT... WE WERE TOLD HE WAS A CHAMPION, HE'S AN OLD WOMAN!"

The bear uncurled his arms and cast an eye around the room above, he heard the calls now, the insults and jibes and as he swung his head to look for his handler a shower of gob and spit rained down on him. A big phlegmy blob landed squarely in his eye and as he daubed it away the Russian landed his sucker punch.

The right upper cut connected with the open-mouthed jaw of the bear and it snapped it shut with a crack, the left hook and the following right hook slammed onto each cheek, he was on his way down and out as the right landed but the second uppercut confirmed it, the head whiplashed back, the arms flopped to the side, a shower of blood decorated the wall behind and the once mighty bear crashed face first into the hard concrete floor ripping his eyebrow and cheek open in the process. It took less the three minutes from start to finish. The loudest roar of all came as the blood pooled around the bear's face and gathered in the mortar ruts and peaks in the centre of the pit.

The room emptied quicker than it had filled, the bookies' table had a third of the people waiting to collect winnings, people bumped each other and squeezed together to push through the door and out. It was only 9.00 p.m. and the night could still be described as young. Peter and David couldn't leave, their little corner of the room had only one viable exit, back along the wall and around the pit and one of the Russians blocked the path. They stood and waited, watched the masses vacate, looking on as the Scouse bear suffered smelling salts and his face being slapped until he revived. On shaky legs, still bleeding, he clambered up the ladder. A few loyal supporters remained, concerned and appreciative that he tried but the bitter taste of defeat and money lost still lingered on their faces. It seemed an age but finally the last of the guests had departed and the vast room seemed tranquil once more, only the hushed tones of the odd conversation could be made out. At the same time the guards left their posts and Peter and David mooched back into the space of the open room, carefully watched by the two door men but without any real concern that they would make a run for it. The big-stone-faced Russian, Valentyn, finished his conversation and dispatched two of the book-makers as he threw several large bundles of fifty pound notes into the bag of another lackey. He strolled over with an odd wry looking smile on his face and pointed at Peter.

"You... I turn around these days and you are always getting me in trouble." The finger waggled in a mock schoolteacher style telling off. Peter gave a nervous smile.

"Not planned, promise," he managed to reply. David watched the exchange carefully, trying to discern the relationship his brother had with this solid lump of a man.

"You love the fights, love to bet, remember business comes first always. Da, so the problem we discussed, is being resolved, thank you for your efforts on that," Valentyn said with a formal nod. "Now tell me about this man behind you?" He indicated to David. Peter turned and smiled, a reassuring 'see its ok' sort of grin.

"My brother David," Peter said, without any sense of pride.

"Brother... such secrets you keep. Maybe we should call you Hammer of Thor," he directed the comment straight at David. "There is a lot of power in those fists my friend." He held his own giant fist for emphasis, it resembled a bunch of bananas. "My friends tell me you were in the Legion?" The playful tone disappeared from his voice and instead a harder edge replaced it. David nodded his agreement and noticed that the two Russian doormen had moved in on the conversation. "The Legion is a serious place, full of bad people that go to some bad places. Do bad things..." Valentyn waited for a reaction, eyeing David's stature and demeanour.

"It is," David said.

"Are you a bad person David?"

"I'm on holiday. I came home for my father's funeral."

Valentyn raised an eyebrow and switched his gaze to Peter, he raised his shoulders and opened his palms in a 'why you don't tell me this' gesture. Peter did nothing. "So you are just a tourist, a civilian now?"

"Exactly. Just a civilian on holiday. I'll be going home again in a few days." The statement sounded odd to David, felt false, he had no home and he certainly had no desire to let this big lump know he'd been in France the week before. Valentyn nodded, "I like a guest who knows not to outstay his welcome," he said with pointed intent, "but you must not leave too quickly... you will need to stay for the next big fight."

Peter and David exchanged glances and at that moment the mood in the room changed. No other conversations echoed round the big space, it was silent but for them; just three Russians and the two English brothers.

"Business... my life is governed by business. I do a lot of business with different people. I am reliable and I make money and my business partners make money. You understand this Peter?" Peter nodded and looked less confident as he did so.

"These fights are a way of making friends, meeting new and old colleagues. It's good to put my champion against theirs. I like to win, winning is a good feeling." Valentyn's voice had risen a little, "A man like me has a lot of pressures, these events are fun for me, but they are still business. People attend fights, people bet and spend money. A lot of people make money, people respect that, people admire that and I, we, are proud that people like our events. Have a bad event and they might forget these things, maybe not work so hard or deliver so easily on deals. I would then have to work harder." Valentyn smoothed his jacket lapel, his brow sweat free despite the sticky heat of the room.

Valentyn put his hand on Peter's shoulder and gently guided him a few paces from his brother. The two doormen moved a little closer, to within striking distance of David. Divide and conquer. Valentyn spoke as if just to Peter but ensured all could hear. "You gamble too much Peter, you mix with bad people, the Masons are morons, don't play poker with morons. You lose a lot and if you play with the Masons you will lose more than you can win." Peter's head had bowed a little and he looked fragile next to the mountainous Russian. "If you have problems with that stupid Irish bookmaker fucker then you speak to me Peter. You tell him that you owe the money to me; you watch how quickly he pays up and shits his pants. You need to remember who your real friends are Peter."

David flexed a little, he could feel his muscles tensing, his heart rate rising and a surge of adrenalin pulsed through his body.

"Peter, you should not let your brother fight with people like Declan and FHM. You are civilians, workers of the world. Such places are not for you, when you do things like that you make me nervous. You work with me, I need you to do things and if you do things like this then other people might want to take revenge and then where would that leave me?"

Peter gulped a little, "Declan won't want to come after me..."

"No Declan won't do a thing because I have told him that if he does I will remove his kidney and cook in front of him, then make him eat it." No hint of humour in his voice. "He hates offal Peter. Remember Declan is an arsehole, but a useful arsehole in a limited way. You have made him less useful and forced me to work harder, I don't like that Peter."

Peter nodded his understanding.

"You are smart Peter. You know I am very unhappy."

Peter nodded.

"And because I am unhappy you are going to help me... right?"

Peter nodded again.

"Good, I knew you'd understand. Mel was due to fight at one of my events, he was to fight a Gypsy," Valentyn said. "Now he cannot fight the Gypsy. These Gypsies are important people to me and I do not like them to be unhappy." Valentyn bent a little and leant forward towards Peter, turning both their backs away from David and putting a few more yards between them and just out of earshot. "You will stay with me, work with my people... stay where you can be no trouble. You understand?" Valentyn had proved throughout his life to be resourceful and to take advantage of adverse situations, now he had such a chance. "You owe me Peter." he said again, a little more venom in his voice. Peter visibly gulped. "So this is how it is going to be... you will stay with me, with the family, for a few days, work to make the administration more efficient, make the system work, Da?"

"I have work... people," Peter foolishly interrupted.

Valentyn didn't pause a beat, "Make me happy. You can call in to work and be sick. It will just be for a few days."

David watched the exchange closely, he could sense the fear the anxiousness in his brother, his shoulders had hunched and then his head dropped, he looked like a small boy in fear of a cane-wielding Headmaster. He hadn't heard the last few moments of conversation, but David could work out the gist of the situation; his brother had more than a monetary debt to these people and unlike the Mason brothers, these guys really scared him.

Valentyn beckoned over Oleg, who left David's side and walked across to the big Russian, words were exchanged and he nodded resolutely at his boss. Once the exchange was completed Oleg moved forward and waited a second. Peter, head still bowed, moved to join him and without a glance backwards he followed the Russian towards the side door. David watched, he said nothing and he raised no objection.

Valentyn watched the two men go and then turned his attention to David. He smiled at him. It strove to be a welcoming and engaging gesture but it simply looked sinister. David greeted it with gritted teeth and a frown. He stood upright and pushed his shoulders back while clasping his hands in front of himself. He knew he had no position of power here and it was time to take his lumps, verbal or otherwise.

"Soldier... your brother has agreed with me."

"You surprise me..."

Valentyn forced a small smile. "He understand how important the work is he does for me, he needs to have no outside distractions," Valentyn said, squaring up and facing David from a few feet away challenging him to contradict his edict. David said nothing and did less.

"Your brother tells me that you are happy to help us, to help him."

"Did he?"

"He said you'd understand the problems you had caused."

"Problems I have caused?"

"Fucking Hell Mel! He cannot fight the Gypsy in the next fight."

"Well unless the Gypsy is a paraplegic then that's probably lucky for Mel.

"Maybe," Valentyn said.

"Your man who fought tonight... he'd have beaten fat Mel even quicker than he did that big lump tonight."

Valentyn nodded, "You think my man is a good fighter?"

"He's young and fit, throws his punches well... not great hand speed, but good enough for this type of fight."

Valentyn nodded again. "So you understand and you will help your brother, you will help me?"

"Do I have a choice?"

Valentyn shook his head.

"Then I will."

Valentyn smiled. "Do you need to train, do you need time?"

"Not really – I'm not going to get much fitter or learn much in a few days."

"So you fight a lot?"

"No, what's your point?"

"It is good to go to gym, spar, train to get proper ready."

"Is that what you want? See me fight first."

Valentyn shrugged.

"Let's not dance around this fella. Do you need me to try to win or do I need to take a dive?" Valentyn smiled, he liked the tough little man in front of him. He had been a soldier, he showed no fear, but he loved his family, he'd do what he could to keep his brother safe and that made him useful, as long as he was kept on a short leash.

"You need to fight for real, but win or lose, is fine with me. You are not my fighter..."

"You want to know where to bet, right?"

Valentyn nodded, "You can bet too."

David shrugged. "Ok. If I win or lose you let Peter go, right?"

"Right, he is not a prisoner. Win or lose I won't hurt

Peter."

"Or me..."

"Certainly not. You do job, you go."

"When is the fight?"

"Same day, next week... this is ok?"

"Sooner the better. Where?"

"It is up to the Gypsies, no one will know for sure until the day, but it will be close by." Valentyn smiled again. "You want to know who you are fighting?"

"It doesn't matter."

"He is very good, very tough. A Gypsy champion. From a line of Gypsy champions."

"He'll bleed like any man." A shiver of pleasure at the thought of it being a Gypsy ran through David. "Who's taking bets?"

"Declan of course... you wish to bet on the fight?"

"I like sure things," David said.

THURSDAY

Yuri sat across from Zenovia in one of the Cossack Dacha's velveteen-clad booths. Neither had spoken for a while. Zenovia's furrowed brow gave away the fact that she had been wrestling with his latest revelations and might be struggling to comprehend their significance. For his part Yuri waited, he had grown used to seeing her do this, she would eventually work it through and come up with the questions and even some answers that might help. He took in the surroundings and looked at the fake dome ceiling, the room looked tired and in places shabby. The room needed updating, redecorating at least, but the old man hankered for tradition and he knew no changes would happen soon.

"This is interesting..." Zenovia finally managed to say. "Real interesting." She didn't look up and the furrows didn't recede. Yuri opened his unobserved eyes wider and blew the exasperation gently from his cheeks. He had not yet reported back to Masha on his special mission and findings; wanting to maintain his special relationship with Zenovia first and foremost.

"I have not told Valentyn this news yet... but I will need to tell him soon."

"Thanks." She offered and said nothing more. Yuri knew he had begun to walk a tightrope between the sisters and Valentyn - he had to be very careful. Valentyn more or less knew how he came about his information and Masha did for certain, but Zenovia didn't have a clue and he needed to keep his philandering under wraps for now. Her tantrums had the capacity to be lethal and legendary so Yuri erred on the side of caution.

"Valentyn has tried to scare the lawyer woman away, it hasn't worked. Something has happened to the two soldiers in France, either way it has been costly and Valentyn has failed to make the problem go away," he said, looking hard at Zenovia.

"Yes Yuri – I get all that, Ta for repeating it to me but

just a bit slower," a hint of sarcasm in her voice. "What I'm trying to work out is the significance of it all."

Yuri fell back against the cushioned booth, taken unaware by the barbed retort and now not sure what it was that she could be mulling over. Zenovia finally leant back and nodded to herself. "What?" he asked.

"Secrets and lies, they do for everyone eventually Yuri." As she said it his brow furrowed with confusion. "Valentyn would'av always had to deal directly with the lawyer woman sooner or all later. Father has also pushed for Valentyn to speed up the process of dealing with the merchandise and so has already taken the Librarian to task. They got some new system and are trialling over the next few days to make it quicker. Masha has fucked that up so badly that Valentyn has lost faif' in her."

Yuri nodded, he knew that Zenovia's role was one of supply. She had been working with the trafficking gangs to bring the merchandise into the country, hide them and to move them around the sorting facility. In truth this easier element of the process had gone smoothly but yet the old man's faith in his youngest daughter remained low. Yuri understood the rivalry between the sisters, he had much the same with Valentyn. The old man relied on both men to keep his daughters side of the business running well. The sisters hardly spoke and didn't involve each other in their plans, Yuri had long exploited this rivalry but if Masha and Valentyn made the new system work then Wladimir would fail to acknowledge Valentyn's failure.

"Will the system work?" he asked.

"It should do, it'll make it quicker and cleaner, more

automated so Masha will hav' a chance of delivering the numbers Papa expects. The Librarian is now apparently under the sole control of Valentyn. Have you met him?"

Yuri hesitated but managed to shake his head. Masha, no doubt with Valentyn's guidance, had kept the Librarian's identity a secret; the fewer people that knew him the better. Whenever the old man had met with him, Yuri had been dismissed as surplus to requirements. "I have no idea who he is, but this lawyer woman is dangerous, she and her partner understand the business and will keep investigating... the more they appear on the TV and in newspapers the more likely our little slaves will find out about them and maybe get brave and try to tell all. She must be eliminated."

Zenovia nodded her agreement, "Yep. But it's all in the timing. I fink you should report back to Valentyn that the lawyer and her investigators are wary – mebbe even scared. Mebbe tell him that they are temporarily stopping. That way, Valentyn will focus on the big shipments and forget about them, assuming he's done enough to deal with the problem."

"Dangerous game... for me," Yuri offered.

"It is, but you stay close to ya sources, keep track of what these women are doing and when the time is right we can step in with decisive information and stop them directly."

"... And your father will think Valentyn has failed and we have saved the day. Very good, I like the plan."

Zenovia smiled a little, "The secret is to undermine Valentyn and Masha. You need to stress to Papa your worried over security, avoid actual details an' facts, and be vague but concerned. Don't criticise Valentyn directly Yuri – be smart. Be concerned only for the business. Right?"

Yuri nodded as if he knew it all already.

"We'll force Valentyn to deny any problems exist... the stronger his denials the better for us when we reveal the real size of the problem. It's important to sow seeds of doubt with my father early on, he remembers everyf'ing."

"And what about the protection?" he asked.

"They have ex-police working for them, maybe it's like a bodyguard or something. Serious to her is not serious to us. "

"True but we need to be careful, we shouldn't trust the job to the normal soldiers. Valentyn would find out." Yuri added.

Zenovia nodded her agreement. "I gotta visit the Gypsies... talk about the speed of the shipments, maybe they could help?"

"They hate Valentyn at the moment, so they might be good friends to have," Yuri offered. Zenovia looked at him with raised eyebrows... as if asking for him to explain. "Oh the big fight last night, Valentyn's man won easily and should have been up against the winner of some Gypsy fighter and a bouncer guy that are due to fight next week. Turns out the Gypsy is fighting some new guy and no one knows anything about him. Some bookies won't take bets, it's causing a stink."

"Useful ta know... how'd you find all this out?"

"I had a big poker game lined up last night, Valentyn

cancelled it without warning, but many of the players were at the fight, they were all talking about it. You want me to find out more?"

"Mebbe, it might not be important... but let's see what the Gypsies think, they love their fighters and prefer to avoid chance. Mebbe we can help them ... if they're up for helping us. Find out what you can about the new fighter."

"So the house is secure?" Eve had watched David as he had made the tour of the property, she noted his attention to detail, his focus and was glad that he would take a personal stake in her protection. David had been methodical, starting from outside the house and assessing its strengths and weaknesses, then he'd moved indoors. He went from room to room, stopped, surveyed, assessed, noted details and moved on. Finally he sat down at her unnecessarily large rustic pine kitchen table and made copious notes. Now though, the notes finished, a steaming cup of coffee being ignored on the table in front of him David seemed lost, transfixed by an alternate dimension and nothing Eve could say seemed to connect.

"Earth calling David, DAVID!" she finally called out, a half shout, more exasperation than anger. David's attention switched and he pivoted on the chair and faced her.

"Sorry... Miles away for a second."

"Light years more like, Jesus. Do you zone out like that a lot?"

"Er yeah, maybe... Not sure."

"You're not sure, how can that be?"

"I live and travel alone, don't have too many people talking to me. Nobody takes too much interest in me."

Eve found that hard to believe and reasoned that David avoided people and conversation and his drifting into his own little world was simply a defence mechanism given the strict disciplined nature of his life. "So is it secure... the house?" she asked again, determined to get a sensible answer.

"It's ok. If anyone wanted to get at you then they would have to force their way in – that would be very noisy and very obvious."

"So they could still get in?"

"Nothing is 100% secure, there is always a way in, it's a question of how hard it is to do...effort versus reward. Coupled with a protecting presence in the house they won't come for you here. Your home is safe." He said it with a dead pan expression on his face.

"Promise?" she said.

"Promise. But be sensible and when you're here I'll be here, but keep your wits about you ok?"

"Sure, I best not open the door to strangers then..." Eve said attempting to inject some much-needed humour into the room.

"Best not," he mumbled back. Eve looked at him hard again, it seemed obvious that something was troubling him and occupying his thoughts and she wondered if it had anything to do the poor night's sleep she knew he'd had. Three times she awoke to the muffled screams and shouts coming from David's room. She recognised them as night terrors, that horrid half-way between nightmares and being awake. She also knew he'd risen at five and sat in the leather chair in the front room until she mooched into the kitchen two hours later.

"David... is something bothering you?"

"Yes," he said, matter-of-factly. The response was so un-British it took her by surprise. She waited for some kind explanation but he offered nothing more.

"David, would you like to talk about it?"

"No, not really."

Eve understood he'd had a tough week, a tough life even, but for the first time she too had become frightened by the situation they were in. The police offered little help or protection and the more she and Jacqui had investigated, the further from the help of the law they seemed to get. Her PR status as the crusading moralising hero did wonders for the balance sheet, but never had she seriously considered it would endanger her. She'd finally managed to sit with the man she had loved and stood by for so many years and hated not being able to simply hold him, talk to him and be with him.

"Please try and talk to me David. I've wanted to talk to you for so long..." She stopped mid-sentence, aware she shouldn't burden him with her emotional baggage.

"It's been a strange week Eve. My life has turned upside down and I'm struggling to understand where I fit in, where you all fit in with my life... it's kinda easier if I just take a role and do it," he said.

Eve nodded, appreciating the sentiment and his need to be defined as something he could be comfortable with. She didn't like it mind you.

"Eve, what does Peter do, his job, what is it?" he asked.

"I'm not sure," Eve said, furrowing her brow and actually trying to think it through. "Computers or something, maybe accounting?"

"Jacqui said that too. Peter denied he did either. How can no one know? I mean he isn't an accountant... you'd know if he were and to be an accountant he'd have taken exams, had to study. He works for the council right?"

"Aaaah now that I do know, he works at the County Council offices, but not for the council. Your father lectured me on it when I introduced Peter to someone at the company's golf day."

"How does that work?"

"Peter works for some kind of government quango – he works with several County Councils at the same time, some sort of centralised control... you know Old Big Government nanny state bollocks," she said.

"Doing what?"

"Well he seemed pretty good at it, always has a fair bit of cash on him, and drives that big Audi and lives in a pretty plush flat in Windsor. I do know he got some kind of promotion about eighteen months back... no idea to what though. He keeps himself to himself David, more and more recently."

"Do you know what he was up to before the promotion?"

"Yeah, sorry, he headed up the team that implemented the new benefits and housing computer software across various Thames Valley councils." Eve threw away the detail as if it had no interest or value, the way people do when they don't understand it.

"Mmmmm so a bit to do with computers, IT then... the 'Geek'," David muttered. Eve's eyes followed David's as they searched the room. "But he left that job a while back?"

"Yes. The software got put in or loaded... whatever and so he was moved upwards, he was very proud of his completing it on time. His new job meant he stayed local but doing what exactly I have no idea." David was staring into space, a vacant expression hung on his face as if he had heard nothing Eve just said. "David, who is 'The Geek?'"

"Oh err a friend of Peter, it's a nickname for him."

"Nice. You met his friends? That's more than Jacqui and I have managed in the last few years. I didn't think he had any."

David looked at her, a small smile grew in the corners of his mouth but never erupting into a grin.

"Eve; when did Peter get into poker and gambling?" Eve stared at him as if he had just sworn.

"Peter? Gamble? Never as far as I know, your dad hated it didn't he? I remember he wouldn't even have a bet on the Grand National. Is Peter a gambler now?" She and David held their gaze for a long moment, longer than necessary or comfortable. It had an unspoken meaning and the intensity unnerved Eve forcing her to break away first.

"It's about value. If you are of value then you are useful. Cease to be valuable and you cease to be useful." He said it as much to himself as to Eve.

"Thank you brother Jung... can you tell me what any of this has to do with the security of the house, my safety? Why is Peter so important?" Eve expected some kind of answer or response but David gave her nothing. "Peter, sweet Jesus, he's hardly been around this year. I know he played the doting son at the funeral but honestly he rarely sees your mum, never sees Jacqui other than at the odd family get together... he's become a bigger cock than you can really imagine."

David nodded his partial agreement.

"It's as if he acted like he had no family at all," David muttered.

Eve snapped her fingers several times at David. "Snap out of it, you keep drifting in and out of the conversation, what is it?"

David smiled at having being caught, he spent so much time alone with his thoughts that certain social skills hadn't fully returned. Keeping focused on conversations being a primary issue. "Sorry, force of habit... just mulling Peter over in my mind. Mum wants us to try and get along, be civil at least. I just find him a quandary."

Eve smiled, "Oh and you're mister open and candid are you?"

David shrugged, caught in an uncomfortable comparison so he changed the topic of conversation. "So the security guys are in place at the office?"

"They are." Eve didn't challenge the shift in direction.

"You and Jacqui will share car journeys where you can and she knows the alarm codes and how to lock all windows and doors?"

"She does."

"I'll stay here every evening and or accompany you if you head out."

"Correct."

"Jacs is fighting that bit isn't she?"

"She is," Eve replied. "She thinks she can take care of herself... the old police training and frank refusal to be a damsel in distress."

"Is that what you are, are damsel in distress."

"No I'm a damsel in THIS dress!" She wafted her skirt as she made the joke.

"That is the worst joke I have ever heard."

"You should get out more."

David half-smiled. "No excuses anymore. That's true."

Eve's face showed her own frustration with her insensitive remark, but she knew that to try and make up for it would be to only dig the hole deeper. So, with no more jokes and the security audit over the pair stood in the living room and shared a moment awkward silence.

"Should I drive you back to the office?" he asked.

"Nah... I'm done for the day, it's lovely out and I'm not

in the mood."

David swallowed and he let his nervousness show, "What had you got planned?"

"Nothing much, thought maybe I'd spend some time with my new house guest, if he's keen?" David smiled at the way she said it, a cheeky grin on her face.

"That would be cool," he mumbled back.

Eve looked at him and raised her eyebrows, "So... what would you like to do?"

"Erm not sure, what is there?"

"Well let's assume the cinema is out, it's been years since you've been here, anything you want to see, catch up on?" She grabbed hold of his hand as she said it, hoping he'd look her full in the eye. He shied away.

"I er, well... It might seem a little odd..." he stumbled.

"Spit it out David."

"The Great Park... I'd kinda love to walk up to the Copper Horse statue, take in the view... maybe cruise via the spinney near the school. Revisit a few old teenage haunts."

Eve shut her eyes for a second not wanting the disappointment to show in her eyes. "We can do that, let's drive up to Saville Gardens and walk in from there."

"Thank you."

FRIDAY

Valentyn removed his perfectly tailored suit jacket and

put it onto a fold-away hanger. He searched the shabby gym for a suitable place to hang it up. He settled for a hook on the back of the door that led into a small office off the main room. Theoretically the main tennis court sized space had been converted into a gym, but all that had happened was the insertion of a raised boxing ring at the far end, then an array of free-weights, bench presses and stretch mats filled the room along with heavy bags and speed balls that hung from the ceiling. This was a fighter's gym, bleak, cold and uninviting. Not that Valentyn used it; he trained alone and at home. A suit looked out of place and the removal of the jacket to reveal a crease-free, starched and seemingly ice-white shirt allowed him to relax a little.

Masha admired the big man's physique from a far. She had few valid reasons to come to the gym, but she liked her visits and hoped she'd see men training, but week days at mid-morning saw the place devoid of fighters. Valentyn moved slowly down the room, picking his way through the dumbbells and weights. He reached a heavy bag and, like any man, couldn't resist putting his hands up and throwing a left then a right and a little bob and weave for good measure. Masha fumbled along behind, staying close to the mirrored far wall, unsure why the mirrors were there but unwilling to reveal her ignorance.

"The Gypsies are still unhappy about the fighter being switched," he said at last. "They don't like surprises." Masha knew this already but in the family business the Gypsies fell under her sister's jurisdiction and so she had avoided any contact with them so far. "We need the Gypsies on our side. The shipments will be coming in much faster and we need it to go smoothly." He still hadn't turned to face her and Masha while agreeing with hearty nods failed to give a verbal response.

"I know you are there Masha, I can here you breathing."

"I'm here Valentyn."

"Then you agree that it is important to keep them happy, to keep an eye on them?"

"I do, yes."

"Why Masha? Tell me why we must keep an eye on them?"

Masha looked at her feet and then around the room, like a schoolgirl trying to work out a maths question when singled out in class. Then she spoke, "We rely on the Gypsies to hide some of our new units prior to processing, they could cause a lot of trouble if they wanted to... so they should always be kept close and made to feel important."

"Correct and what else specifically."

"My sister is in charge of import and export logistics... but shouldn't be trusted, we must be clear on what the Gypsies know and understand to be sure the operation remains in our control, not hers and Yuri's."

He turned to face her and smiled as sincere a smile as he could muster. "Correct again. Whenever there is a link in the chain that you don't wholly control Masha you never trust it. You watch it and you try to control it from afar. Did you see the numbers this morning?" Valentyn had the numbers and so Masha should have had them too, it had been part of the new administration set up. The process had been more automated, the Librarian had been true to his word and once his proposals had been instigated then, as if by magic, the system began to work more quickly.

"I did see the numbers yes. We have processed nearly one thousand units this week already."

Valentyn nodded again, relieved she knew that much at least, he doubted she had interrogated the numbers, bothered to look or even could understand the bigger significance they held. "It is good and we should have nearly five thousand done in a month. But... the numbers showed me a new concern." He waited to see if the girl had any notion and was about to speak again when Masha beat him to it.

"The supply of units into the warehouse has begun to slowdown, or can't keep up with the pace we now process them. The Gypsies aren't shipping them from the containment units to us for processing quickly enough, maybe they are too disorganised."

Valentyn did a fine job of hiding is surprise at her response and managed to add, "...or maybe they wish to hold out for more money?"

Masha nodded and smiled at the big man, "The Gypsies were useful when we needed to set this system up but they might become a liability moving forward?"

"Da. They might." Her insight surprised Valentyn for sure, and her analysis of the situation had been so spot on. This was a rare if not new phenomenon in his relationship with her and he couldn't hide all the shock and surprise from his face.

"You were never happy about using the Gypsies were you?" She asked, feeling smug at having proven to Valentyn that there was a little more to her than he had assumed.

He shook his head, "No... they're always trouble, there is no trust outside their community. When the numbers get really big they won't be organised or professional enough - we need to remove them from the process." Valentyn had argued this point with Masha's father, Wladimir, on many occasions. The Gypsies were the cheap and convenient option when the numbers were low and the risk small. As the operation grew he had worked hard to convince the old man to remove them from the supply chain. The key as always was to get the units into the country and hidden safely, keep them scared and on edge, then move them through the administration and benefits claims process before shipping them out across the country or abroad. Valentyn, and now Masha, knew that total control would be the only way.

"How do we remove the Gypsies? We cannot go to war with them?" Masha said it like a statement but lacked the knowledge to be certain if they could or not. Valentyn moved across the gym and battered a speed ball as he moved alongside her. He waited for it to stop swinging.

"We could but it would be painful and constant. They are like vermin and have family connections everywhere. We hit them here and then we'll be attacked in Reading, Birmingham, everywhere. No, fighting them is not the answer, they love their money and they love to gamble." He looked across to the ring and the end of the room, "We need to appeal to their sporting nature... they do honour a deal and a debt. Force can come later; their people won't come back at us if they fail to meet a deal."

Valentyn thought he had it all covered and at that moment a small, but essential, piece of the jigsaw bumbled into the gym area. "Yuri!" he said. "Welcome, glad you could come."

Yuri had on an old pair of grey tracksuit bottoms and a black vest, it showed off his biceps. The over-trained, all-for-show biceps of the typical modern gym monkey. "You said to meet you here... who am I to disagree?" he said. Valentyn ignored the barbed comment and beckoned him down to join them.

"I am pleased with what you have done for me Yuri, you have helped a lot with the Lawyer woman situation. It's good to know the problem might have gone away. I wanted to thank you." Valentyn towered over Yuri and he draped an ape-like arm over the smaller man's shoulders. "You also missed the fight this week, Dimi was quite excellent, destroyed the fat man with fast punches."

Yuri bobbed his head in a non-committal way. He had heard the stories of the fight and seen a video of it on someone's phone. He'd had money on Dimitrenko to win, the odds had been lousy though, so he'd gone for a finish inside three minutes where the odds had been better. He had won well.

"I know you like to work out and are interested in the boxing," he squeezed Yuri's bulging bicep, "so I arranged for you to train with Dimi." Yuri looked up surprised and delighted at the gesture, yet still suspicious of it. "Masha, I think Dimi will be in the changing room, would you be so good as to see if he is ready to show Yuri a thing or two?" Masha smiled and nodded her consent, while scuttling off out of the gym towards the changing room entrance. Yuri extricated himself from the arm and moved towards the heavy bags. He bypassed the biggest one that Valentyn had hit and moved to the lighter one at the end of the line and just like the bigger man he too put his hands up and ducked and weaved before throwing and an inexpert left right combination into the bag.

"Turn the wrist over Yuri, palm down and wrist locked in a line with the forearm," he said. Yuri tried to ignore him and winced privately at how much the punch had jarred his arm.

"Thanks for this," he managed to say with half-hearted but genuine feeling. He was spared further scrutiny with the return of Masha and Dimi, who hunched under a hoody with his hands shoved into his pockets. The fighter ambled across the gym like a surly teenager. Valentyn decided he needed to make a point.

"Aaaah Dimi so good of you to come, I consider it a personal favour that you are willing to spend time teaching my colleague Yuri some of your skills." Dimi didn't need to be warned again, he caught the look in the big man's eye and knew better than to question his authority or physical ability. He still vividly remembered Valentyn stripping off and climbing into the ring with him to test whether he was ready for paid fights.

"Da Valentyn," his accent thick and nasal. "Yuri, good to meet you. We go to mirrors... show me your punches." With that the two men moved away from Valentyn.

"Have fun boys," he called after them. Masha watched as they began shadow boxing, with Dimi improving Yuri's stance and basic balance. She beckoned Valentyn to her and she edged closer to the boxing ring.

"Why did you bring him here?"

"I have my reasons," he said.

"Share them please Valentyn." Her voice had a small hint of authority, the whine had dropped and purpose had replaced it.

"He's away from your father and from Zenovia for a while... also he needs to see something here today, needs to witness it first-hand."

"Why?"

"Yuri is a rat... he says and does nothing that doesn't suit him, I trust nothing he says to me. I know that whatever he sees today will be told to whomever can hurt me or make me look foolish the most." He dismissed any further conversation by moving around the ring to the corner where two fighters awaited his attention.

David checked the address again. He had the right place, he looked up the street and back down again. Behind him sat the headquarters for O2. The building ahead had no sign up, no kind of indication it contained a gym. 'Members only' he mused. He checked the message again, he didn't like mobile phones but the one the Russians handed him seemed simple enough. It made calls and you could text. Not much else, they had sent him a message that was short if not sweet. *"Come to Bucks Ave. Slough. Unit 139. We need to see you fight."*

They hadn't seemed worried before, maybe something had changed. He couldn't refuse the invitation nor did he want to. He took in the surroundings again noting how this back street of the trading estate must represent what the whole place must have looked like in its early days. Small single storey buildings that housed small industrial, mechanical and engineering businesses. Now they were dwarfed by the colossal corporate monoliths on the other side of the road, these little building were now forgotten and unseen by the majority of Slough visitors. David felt isolated and hidden despite the vast glass and steel structures that dominated the immediate area. An unwelcome contrast to his day with Eve.

He and Eve, the previous day, had walked through the neat suburban streets of South Windsor and worked their way to the edges of the Windsor Great Park. From there they had weaved a path through herds of deer and wonderfully majestic old oaks to the tree lined 'long walk' that connected the famous Windsor Castle with the impressive hilltop Copper Horse statue. They had chatted about nothing in particular, she had updated him on the movements and lives of people he might remember. He hadn't been very interested, but as she spoke it gave him an excuse to look at her. David had noted the slight resignation and wistful look on her face as she mentioned various marriages and births that had occurred to mutual friends. The walk back been part hand-in-hand but David had no idea how to move it on. Scared of pushing too fast too soon, aware that the passing of time had been different for him but that Eve hadn't achieved the personal milestones she had just recounted and that he might be to blame. Now he stood with the ugly view of these squat buildings and the nagging sense that he'd be acting violently once again. He shook his head with frustration. He should have kissed her. He should have said something. All he did was recount the security arrangements

Now Eve was being protected by the office security Jacqui had sorted for her and Eve and when the text came he'd welcomed the chance to work out how Peter was involved with the Russian and if it confirmed his suspicions of a link to Eve's investigations. He had no idea what Peter had or hadn't told them, he doubted Peter had even mentioned his family much, clearly they hadn't made the link from Jacqui to Peter. He didn't socialise with her and they had limited personal contact, also their focus had been on Eve, she had been all over the TV and the detective had been working for her and under her instructions when he travelled to France. Either way David knew being close to these guys would lead to more information and he just hoped he could handle what they had laid on for him.

He pushed open the aluminium framed door and walked into the small entrance hall, he recognised one of the Russian doormen, Oleg, who pointed to a panelled door but said nothing. David pushed through and discovered a somewhat ramshackle changing area... he looked around and saw no showers, the compact room had no windows and an odour of stale sweat and Vaseline lingered. It brought back memories and had an oddly comforting effect on him. He dropped his small black backpack on the bench, removed his linen shirt and pulled on a black t-shirt. He dropped his linen trousers over his black trainers and tugged on a black pair of black combat style shorts – the only ones he owned. He hung it all up on a broken peg and moved back towards the door. Oleg waited for him and guided him into the gym.

Two men worked a smaller heavy bag on his left, David recognised the man holding the bag as the fighter from the other night but not the man pounding it with amateurish zeal. The other doorman from the fight bench pressed weights near a window, long slow reps, a toning and not a strength workout he noted. Then at the end of the room he saw Valentyn, the towering Russian stood in suit trousers and shirt and dwarfed the two fighters in the ring. He lectured them a little, speaking in Russian. The two fighters, reasonably big men in their own right, came together in arm and headlocks and wrestled and jostled around the ring for a few seconds before Valentyn yelled them to a halt.

David stopped about ten feet from the ring and sized the Russian up. The big man had excellent balance, he moved well, with a grace and ease that belied his gargantuan size. The two men in the ring, by comparison, looked heavy legged, cumbersome by comparison. The fighting and wrestling carried on for more than a minute, throughout Valentyn talked and moved and circled the ring, finally he called out and the men stopped and trooped back to a corner and leant on the top rope breathing heavily. Then Valentyn noticed him.

"Ah David, thank you for coming."

David nodded.

"You are ready for a work out?" he asked.

"Message said you wanted to see me box... let's box."

Valentyn noted the lack of cordiality. "Don't be in such a big hurry. There has been some bother about you fighting, the Gypsies don't know you, they know Fucking Hell Mel... I have had to manipulate the odds to favour them. Valentyn let his voice rise and spoke with unnecessary enunciated clarity. He wanted to be sure the room heard what he had to say.

David nodded again. "So you wanna see what I got... See how much to lay on me or on the Gypsy to cover the bookies' loss, right?"

Valentyn grinned and leant on the top rope and looked down at David, "Something like that, yes." David swung his arms in a windmill fashion and then stretched his neck from right to left. Once done he walked round to the right of the ring and hopped onto the apron, laying his un-gloved hands on the top rope he vaulted over in one easy fluid motion. He landed, bounced on his toes, threw a few loose punches and ended with a Mui Thai round house kick. Valentyn took mental note. "You," he said, pointing at the fatter of the earlier combatants, "go get three sets of gloves, 8oz and some head guards as well." The man didn't blink he just obeyed. David looked out of the ring and saw a plain and podgy woman looking up into the ring with an unhealthy enthusiasm. Usually David would wink and smile with ladies at a fight but he thought better of it. She might smile back.

"You know kick-boxing?" Valentyn turned and asked David.

"Some."

"Karate, Ju-Jitsu... Judo?"

"Some."

"How come so many, you learn in the army?"

"In the Legion and from fellow soldiers..."

"You have a fighting system you prefer?" Valentyn squared himself up.

"I like Capoeira for fitness... but prefer SAMBO for fighting."

"Sport or Freestyle version?"

"Oh I don't compete. I just use the combat version."

David watched as Valentyn took stock of him once more. David knew he couldn't be classed as an expert in any one martial art, he had no belts or grades but had such a good all round grasp of unarmed combat that if he dedicated himself he knew could. No, David had perfected something more sinister and more practical. Ten years in prison and the life he'd spent in the Legion taught him more than any one system of combat could. He had the fighting instinct of a pack dog, hit and run. Do it fast, do it with meaning and get away quickly. Hit before the opponent knows you want to hit them. Pick your spot beforehand, calculate and determine weakness over opportunity versus incapacitation. Do it all before the opponent even realises he's going to be hit. Keep it like a street fight. Real life doesn't often include gentleman morality.

David now studied Valentyn studying him. David had already guessed that the big man had been militarily trained, he looked an athletic forty-five plus. Seriously powerful but poised and controlled. He assumed the big man had trained in SAMBO, all Russian soldiers had the basics but somehow Valentyn looked like he excelled. A combination of many cultural influences SAMBO is an amalgamation of Eastern martial arts, street fighting and Russian traditional wrestling, with so many East-Europeans in the Legion it had become the defacto martial art.

Most practitioners had a preferred strike method, feet or hands, some preferred to take the opponent to ground early. David sized up the Russian, he'd prefer hand and elbow strikes and to take his man to the floor where his bulk and strength would be a huge asset. That strength was his weakness, a naturally smaller fighter, David preferred to stay away from the floor, be more fluid and use kicks to keep his distance, utilising high speed-strikes to prevent nasty choke holds or arm-bars. David appreciated that Valentyn knew all of this too and both men realised that each of them was doing exactly the same thing.

The chunky fighter hefted himself into the ring bringing the little exchange to an end. "Give one set to him" Valentyn pointed at the other fighter standing in the far corner. Valentyn grabbed a set of gloves and handed them to David.

"Wraps?" David asked.

"You care if we wrap hands?"

David shook his head. "Not really."

He'd guessed the poor sap in the corner would be his test and had done his groundwork already. He stood around 6ft 3", heavy through the waist and big muscle mass on his shoulders and arms, another big-arm freak.

"Rules..." Valentyn bellowed. "Three minutes straight boxing and nothing else. I say stop you stop. Understand?"

Both men nodded.

"Don't hold back..." With that Valentyn moved back and left the space for the men to fight.

David moved to the centre of the ring and took up a classic boxer puncher stance, knees slightly bent, weight balanced and up on the balls of his feet, able to pivot forward, back and side to side on the spot or skip away in any direction. Boxing had been something he learnt in prison. Being terrified everyday proves to be a massive incentive, he'd gotten fit and muscled within months and as a genuine murderer in the eyes of prisoners he had an automatic level of respect, but he knew it wouldn't last forever. The boxing programme had been his lifeline, a way to prove he had the guts and the power without needing to fight on the landings. After ten years he had become a well-schooled cruiserweight, 14 stone of tough competent boxer. Now after eight years in the Legion he had been taught how to kill with his bare hands and had done so on several occasions... he entered this little scuffle with a deserved amount of confidence.

David focused on keeping light footed, but as soon as required he could lower his weight and leverage tremendous power. He tucked his chin down a little and kept his hands at chin height. His opponent had little real balance and limited coordination. In truth, David presumed he'd charge, hoping power and intimidation would work... he did just that, two stumbling steps forward, telegraphing his right hand lead. David stood his ground, raised himself with a flex of the knees and threw his own right hand, trusting speed and accuracy over raw power, he connected flush. As the punch landed he shifted his weight forward and punched through the target as if trying to reach the back of the man's head.

The effect was instantaneous.

His opponent's eyes rolled over white, the forward momentum stopped, his leg faltered and gave way, followed by the ragdoll style collapse of his body. He hit the canvas with a resounding thud, legs and arms all askew. David skipped to his right and circled the fallen man.

"Jesus," he heard from outside the ring, the man that had been pounding the heavy bag stared at him. "One punch?" Valenytn said. "One punch and you take out one of my best fighters?"

"Maybe he was tired from all the cuddling you had him doing when I arrived?" David answered back, hoping that was him done and he could go.

"He is a respected fighter on the circuit, never knocked out in one punch..." Valentyn shook his head a little surprised and annoyed but yet a smile on his face. "One fucking punch..."

"He had no respect." David said.

"What?" Masha asked from outside the ring.

Valentyn answered the question for David, "He charged at him, threw a right hand lead, a slow first punch, he had no defence and no respect that David might be able to fight back."

"And he threw a perfect right hand counter," yelled Yuri from the side. "Wow that was sweet as... is he OK

Valentyn?"

"Shut up Yuri... this is no good, I need to see you fight, box... Dimi get up here and put these gloves on." Yuri's trainer paused a beat then without a word he walked to the right but didn't look David in the eye once. Yuri charged to his kit bag that he had left on the floor by the gym door.

Valentyn grabbed the foot of the prostrate man in the ring and pulled him away, the chunky fighter did the rest to remove him from the ring as the felled man began to come round.

Dimi had the spare gloves on fast and had whipped off his hoody. David remembered the toned and athletic physique, he knew he could fight a bit, had pretty good hand speed, but David figured he'd just watched him level a former opponent and one that young Dimi had never knocked out before. David knew that tended to have a psychological effect on fighters. Yuri moved towards the ring with his phone stuck out in front of him, recording the action.

David shook his arms out once more and moved to the centre of the ring, Dimi circled, conscious of the power he had witnessed. David didn't chase or cut the ring off or pressure Dimi in any way. He just watched and waited.

"Dimi fight him don't jog round him," yelled Valentyn.

"He can come to me," Dimi shouted back.

David waited and watched, the pressure for the Russian to engage would be too much. No judges, no score cards, you can't win an unlicensed fight on points. He'd have to come forward at some point.

"Hey Valentyn," David called out, "you sure you want your hero to fight me now... aint he supposed to fight the winner of me and the Gypsy. I don't wanna hurt him."

Valentyn gave a short laugh at the insult, "DIMI, do you hear that... do you hear what he thinks? FIGHT him or do you want to fight ME!" yelled Valentyn and with that the young Russian became more aggressive, urged on by some despicable incentive. He threw a double jab, both fell short, then a left to the body and right to the head, blocked by David. He darted in quicker this time and closed the gap, he connected to David's midriff with a left then a right and tried a left hook to the head. David had his right up in defence and glanced the blow away. David watched as he moved back with a jump and his hands low. Then he waited again.

Dimi skipped about for a minute, his legs and lungs would have a gentle burn now and would need a few seconds break – David knew he'd try one more attack. In came Dimi, a straight left to the body, a lunging soft punch, David let it land and covered up again as the follow-up straight right bounced off his guard. David stepped forward just as Dimi began his backward skip away, David threw his left hook. Faster than Dimi could punch and quicker than expected, it landed high on his temple while he was still moving back. His legs wobbled on landing, balance gone he fell into the ropes and bounced back into the ring interior. David threw a hard left hook to the body and caught the Russian flush on the rib cage, he then followed it with an uppercut and it tore through the high handed guard and connected with the Russian's chin, Dimi's head rocked and he lurched to one side to get away. David dropped his hands and turned and followed. Dimi let out a big gasp and gulped in air. About now the bell should sound for the end of the round... no bells here. David feinted a left and Dimi sagged back and covered up, but no punches came.

David paused, let Dimi right himself and peek out from behind his high guard, then he let his punches go. A double jab, right hook, left to the body, then he stepped back and let Dimi throw a soft counter jab, ducked underneath and fired a straight left at the Russian's heart and another left to the body. He swayed back and threw the overhand right, a sharp snapping punch connected with Dimi's jaw and slammed his head sideways. He stayed upright but hurt. David took two steps back and caught his own breath, it had been a while since he had been in the ring and he realised he'd been holding his breath. Foolish. He took in some air through his nose and looked at what faced him. Dimi had felt the power and speed of the punches and had been hurt, but he shook it off, raised his hands and came forward once more.

Three minutes later David stepped away from Dimi, who had slumped to the floor under another quick fire barrage. He had slumped to one knee and more than six minutes of continuous boxing had exhausted him. No one counted and Valentyn made no attempt to pick his man up; the only sound in the gym his laboured breathing. Dimi dabbed at his bloody nose, the swelling under his right eye had come up alarmingly quickly.

"He doesn't need to be hit anymore," David said.

"Niet. He gets up then we carry on," Valentyn replied.

"No. No we won't," David said emphatically pulling at

a glove's Velcro strap with his teeth to emphasise his point. "He's done and if I hit him too much more he'll be done for good."

"I decide if the fight is over," bellowed the giant Russian clambering on to the ring apron and vaulting the top rope. David wasted no time in reacting to the threat; he dropped swiftly to a crouch and back swept his right leg in a fast arc, it connected behind the advancing Valentyn's calf and his momentum carried him into the air and then flat onto his back with a crash. David sprang to his feet and stood over his fallen foe, his foot pressed under the big man's chin, pinning Valentyn to the ring floor.

No one moved, everyone just stared. David realised what he'd done and the situation he'd created. He looked down at the big man to gauge his reaction. Valentyn's anger turned to embarrassment with untimely haste. He forced a smile and looked up at him, a resigned look in his eye. David deduced that whatever anger had been in him a few moments ago had now dissipated. He pulled away his foot, flashed a forced grin and held out his hand, Valentyn took it and in a combined effort he hauled himself to his feet.

"You are fast, very fast."

"Sorry about that..." David said. "You came at me looking like you meant business, instinct took over."

"It's fine... I understand. You are right too. Dimi can fight another day, no need for him to be hurt more. Dimi go and change I'll talk with you later." The beaten fighter rose and clambered from the ring.

Yuri tracked his iPhone with the moving figures,

filming the exit as he had the whole fight. He trotted away out through the door. Valentyn noticed and smiled. Then nodded with exaggerated force towards the exit and the remaining, but now shocked and motionless, men in the gym also headed for the door without a word. David watched them leave as he tugged the last glove off his hand and then wiped his brow with the hem of his sweat-drenched t-shirt.

"My brother?" David asked.

"He is well, working hard," Valentyn replied as he moved to the ring apron and clambered over the top rope and down onto the gym floor. David didn't follow, he just leant on the top rope and carried on talking.

"Doing what exactly?"

Valentyn turned and looked back at David, Masha moved to his side and stood a little closer than David thought necessary. He doubted she was his girlfriend. "What can my brother seriously be doing to further your illegitimate business interests?"

"You assume he's doing something illegal?" Masha asked.

"Er yes...the unlicensed boxing, ex-soldier bodyguards and general criminal theme to everything makes me assume you aren't exactly legit." He still wondered who she was, she spoke with confidence, as if part of the inner circle.

Masha smiled and shrugged but said nothing more, Valentyn didn't add anything either. David wanted to draw them out and find some kind of connection to Eve and her crusade.

"I'm just here on holiday, I don't live in the UK, it's a different place from the one I left... but I have seen the news, read the articles. East Europeans don't have a great reputation... especially here in Slough." He threw it out there like a bated hook and hoped for a nibble.

"Don't believe everything you read, we are not all evil," Masha responded, an unemotional tone to her voice. "I have lived here all my life... I am as English as you." David smiled at the comeback.

"I've no doubt, but the influx of workers from the old eastern bloc hasn't been universally welcomed, you use a lot of Russian born labour... Valentyn, the other guy back there and Dimi... these aren't local boys, you're not adding to local economy are you?"

"Business is business, we do use local people sometimes. They are often lazy, don't work as hard as foreign workers."

"And they cost less..." David jumped in. Masha held herself back from making a quick response, a limiting hand on the shoulder from Valentyn helped.

"We pay our employees fairly. The local papers and TV have had a long running mission to undermine the Russian and Polish community here, they tell stories... shut down our businesses for a while, but they have no proof because we don't do anything wrong. The police have given up now."

"But not the press, the article a week or so ago... that said Russian gangs in Slough were trafficking people for the sex trade... is that what you do?" David gambled on a direct attack, he hadn't used Eve's name or indeed implicated anything specifically, but he wanted some indication they trafficked people. Valentyn stepped forward and partially blocked Masha, he made it clear she shouldn't speak anymore.

"So many questions, why do you care?" Valentyn reintroduced the steel to his voice. David stood up straight and rested his hands rather than his elbows on the top rope. He had scored a point over Valentyn, but he doubted the big man would be so easy to deal with in a true one on one fight. He needed to trade off, offer something personal about him and try to finesse a slip out of the big man.

"I'm no saint... you can see from today that I don't live my life by the same rules as Peter. I have more in common with you and your world than you can imagine." In part this was true, David had fought alongside Russian mafia exiles and had been fighting numerous gangs and militia forces in the world. "You want me to fight the Gypsy... I'm doing that. I'm doing it so you release my brother, nothing more complicated than that. You gave me your word and I gave you mine. I have to trust that you will do as you say you will."

Valentyn nodded. "I will keep my word... and after today I will happily bet that you will beat the Gypsy. I'll even offer you a share of the winnings, but our business is our business. Not you, not the lawyer woman on TV or the papers or police can tell me to stop doing what we do... so after the fight I give you your brother back, he's even being paid for his time... He should able to square some of his debts with the idiots he has on his back too. We are not animals David. We are in business."

David pondered momentarily why the two had to be mutually exclusive. The revelation was in. This was the gang that Eve was crusading against and he'd seen no hint of competition, no mention of other players in the arena. They ran Slough, they controlled the traffic in and out and they had David and they had Eve in their sights. They hadn't connected David's link to Eve, why would they? Jacqui had been more low-key and a periphery figure in all this but she too remained in the firing line. These operations weren't small-time and Peter had more involvement than just gambling debts, they needed him, he was valuable to them and not just once but for some time now and maybe moving forward.

"Can you find your own way out?" Valentyn interrupted his rapid train of thought, "We need to be somewhere else."

David simply nodded and said 'sure'.

"Oleg will contact you again about the fight venue. Stay healthy little man."

"Valentyn!" David called after the big Russian, who turned slowly and waited. "Understand something about me... I can fight, I'm good at it, lucky that way I suppose. But I don't start fights, never have."

"Your point is?" Valentyn asked.

"I don't start them... but I do finish them."

Valentyn smiled. Short leash he thought.

"I understand."

"I have your word, you have mine... that needs to be enough."

"It will be."

Valentyn turned and walked away, Masha trotting by his side, without looking at her he spoke clearly and firmly, "You need to call your sister... now!"

Yuri had wasted no time in leaving the gym and heading back to the restaurant to show Zenovia the video he had made on his phone. While he delighted in the section that showed Valentyn's humiliation she focused much more on the way the new fighter had destroyed Dimi's spirit and ability to fight. Zenovia knew the young fighter had tremendous stamina but the resistance seemed to have been sucked out of him. The meeting with the Gypsies had been arranged the day before, but now she had something a lot more useful to share with them. She pressed Yuri into being the driver and two soldiers had been hand-picked from the ranks. Whatever Zenovia planned to say or do today, she wouldn't discuss it with Valentyn.

Yuri had expected to meet the Gypsies in a caravan, he had modified his expectations from a wooden hand-painted thing pulled by a horse, but he had hoped it would at least be some kind of mobile living area. Instead he sat on an upturned bottle crate behind two bumper-to-bumper parked Toyota Hilux 4x4's. The layby had recently been fitted with various anti-caravan defences to ensure the grassed area couldn't be parked on and bollards ensured vehicles of a limited size could access the lay-by itself and the collection of tired recycling bins at the far end. Yuri had never engaged too much in Gypsy politics, he didn't care much for their rants on land access and the closing of 'free space' for them to park. His understanding had been built, like many, on what brief interactions he had personally had and the general negative press the groups received. Nothing had been positive and stereotypes seemed to be reinforced at every turn. Freak show fly-on-the-wall documentaries hadn't helped matters either.

Zenovia held court and the two Gypsy men sitting opposite her on old moulded plastic school chairs listened to every word intently.

The men were in their late fifties, unshaven with an assortment of badly done tattoos running up each forearm. The greyer haired of the two sported a fine mullet and a swallow tattoo fluttered above the neckline of his yellow Ralph Lauren Polo shirt. Yuri knew his name, Mike. The man to his left, more portly and minus the mullet but with an unkempt black shrub of hair in his head was his brother, Patrick. Both men had fat, calloused hands and the vague appearance of being unwashed, whether they were actually dirty or not Yuri didn't know, they just looked that way. While these charming figures engaged Zenovia in conversation two baseball hat and tracky-bottom clad hangers-on loitered behind, staring at their opposite numbers, Valentyn's impeccably attired soldiers. They had been here fifteen minutes already and Yuri had been pushed out to one side, where he lingered on his crate while he waited to be invited to a pow-wow he'd rather avoid.

"So ya understand gents, for now, keep the units coming slowly... don't speed it up. No additional units will come to you until we clear the backlog as well. Got it?"

Patrick nodded with a sense of disinterest. "We can't shift more people through, even if we wanted to," he said. His accent somewhere between Irish and yokel Ipswich. "Yerz got to appreciate that we control a lot of camps but not enough to hide that many people."

Mike nodded his agreement, "It's grand that yerz happy with the service so far... but remember we can't house people indefinite like. If yerz want us to slow down the numbers we ship to the warehouse then you need to slow the number we got coming in. There aint much of an overflow facility. Ya know what I mean?" Mike's accent was less guttural than his brother's and he had the sense of a man that had become conscious of how the world viewed him.

"Plus you need to keep the big feckin' freak off our back. I don't need him at all!" Patrick added, with undisguised anger.

Zenovia nodded. Valentyn had always said they lacked the organisation to meet future demands and he was right, he'd demonstrated his irritation to them personally. Zenovia remained more practical; they were part of the process and part of her plans and would need to be kept on side. Money talked before and it would again, that and the possibility of payback to Valentyn would keep the deal sweet.

"I get ya frustrations. Jesus I even share some of them. Keep the flow of units to the warehouse as slow as ya' can for this week. I promise we'll then arrange a mass transit out, at our cost, next week."

The two men swapped a glance and then Patrick asked, "Why would yerz want to do a mass transit, that's gonna be nearly five towsand people in one go... that'd be tough to manage. You'd clean us out completely; we'd still be getting our money right even if we had nothing to look after... you know til the next load arrive?"

"You would." Zenovia had to be careful, she needed enough room to make Valentyn look incompetent but not to grind the process to a halt and while the gypsises had no long term future she needed to throw them a bone of compensation.

"Valentyn promised ya how many units?"

"You fuckin' know that love," Mike barked. "Up to a towsand a week, containment for forty-eight hours and then shipment to the warehouse. Twenty quid a head. Adult or child. No more than five hundred in anyone shipment, we've made plans based on that deal." Mike emphasised the point by clearing his sinuses and spitting onto the floor.

"Boys – go and wait by the car please." She waved her two soldiers away. "Yuri bring the crate here, sit by me." The three men did as she asked and Mike and Patrick tilted their heads to acknowledge Yuri. "I'm not blind fellas. I know that Valentyn has been abusive, aggressive about ya operation," she continued, "I don't see it the same way... and as ya know it's my father that runs the family, Valentyn is, well merely a soldier."

"Just a soldier is he? Well he's scary big fucker I'll give

him that," spat Mike.

"Yeah dat big man has fucked us over and frankly I don't trust the fecker." Patrick made no attempt to hide his contempt.

"Yeah well the big fecker has exceeded his authority when negotiating this deal with you, there won't be that many units coming through to you. I'm sorry but that's how it is. You've seen the papers recently? There's heat on what we are doing right now."

"You talking about the lawyer, the Du Pisanie bint?" Mike asked

"Yeah... that's her."

"Right fuckin' busybody that one... did a whole thing on women's rights and so-called abuse to wives and kiddies and such like in the traveller community, right load of old bollocks... every fucker taught we waz like some kinda animals. Pain in the arse moral crusader that one."

Patrick chimed in, "Between her and the cunts at Channel 4 we've been made to look like a right bunch of arseholes."

"Right fit though, the lawyer bird, you would wouldn't you..." Mike joked.

"Sweet Jesus yes, I'd do her proper job." Both men laughed heartily and Zenovia joined in with a nervous and a somewhat too enthusiastic giggle.

"Ya know her then; that'll help...Valentyn had been supposed to be dealing with her. Ya know making her less interested in our business and, well, he's fucked it... again."

"Lady, yer talking way to much for someone weez know is right fucking dirty. Is ya dancing round sumink? Coz this aint Strictly Fucking Come Dancing, get ta the point. Me and him want to go to the pub," Patrick said.

"Alright. From now on the shipments will only be five hundred units a week... half what was promised by Valentyn... but we'll pay you double for them units for the next month."

Mike scratched his bristled chin, "Then we go back to the normal pricing right?" Mike asked and Zenovia nodded. Mike shook his head, "It's not right ya know... it's a shite way to do business. First the fight bollocks up and now this."

"I get ya... but I have something ya might like to see, something that you'll enjoy and might help you with the fight this week. Yuri show them." Yuri produced his iPhone 6 with a proud flourish, opened the video up and handed it to the unimpressed pair. He winced a little as the sweaty fingers left marks on the screen. The two Gypsies watched the video with increasing interest and just the occasional passing expletive. The two tracksuit-monkeys began to stoop over and watch too. "Good right hand," "fast hands" and similar phrases emanated from the small group. The video stopped and the men looked at each and nodded their appreciation and admiration for what they saw.

"That fella having the shite kicked out of him... that's the boy who fought last week against the fat scouser aint it?" Mike asked.

"It is," said Yuri.

"That's big Valerie falling on his arse at the end aint it?" Patrick chortled.

"Funny as fuck that... good epic fail for YouTube that one," Mike added.

Yuri smiled but couldn't really hide his lack of enthusiasm for the conversation.

"And we should assume that the tough fucker doing the beating, that's the guy that did for Fucking Hell Mel with one punch," Patrick said.

"It is."

"Hmmmmmmm," mused Patrick, "so my boy Aiden will be battling with him next week. He's fast, real fast. Your Russian fella hardly landed a punch, what's this new fecker's history?"

"Ex-army, English, no previous on the circuit. We thought you would appreciate the inside knowledge."

"We do... not sure of yerz motives mind you. Might change the nature of the fight. Think we'll go bare-knuckle for this one... this fucker up for that?" Mike said it with a smile on his face.

"It won't be a problem. You are to be accommodated for the inconvenience caused. Whatever you demand of Valentyn he'll agree too."

Mike chuckled, "Mebbe we should ask if Aiden can use a fucking gun!"

Patrick stared at him, "What the fuck is dat supposed a mean?"

Mike shrugged a panicked look, "Jesus Paddy, I meant

it as a joke... nottin else."

Patrick conceded, "Alright then, don't be makin' out my lad is some kinda pussy dat's all!" The two brothers shared a moment of macho posturing and then turned back to face matters at hand. Yuri swallowed hard and Zenovia pushed on eager to seal a deal.

"So it's a deal. We'd like to ask you to do anuvver job for us as well. I gotta run but Yuri here has the details. And I guess ya understand to keep this discussion between us for now. Right? After the fight, next week maybe, all will become a lot clearer. Cheers gents, nice doing business wiv ya." Zenovia offered no handshake and no one seemed interested in receiving one. The two Gypsies just waved a silent cheerio. They all waited until the big BMW roared into life and had pulled away.

"Can you email me the video of the fighter?"

"Sure," said Yuri. "This additional job... we are prepared to pay a one-off fee for. £25,000."

Patrick and Mike whistled. "Serious dosh pretty boy, spill the details."

"The lawyer woman, Du Pisanie, we need her removed and dealt with."

"As in DEALT with?" asked Mike. Yuri Nodded.

"We'd like it public... she needs to be found and we'd like it brutal."

Patrick and Mike stood up and took a few steps away from him and conferred. Neither raised their voice or showed any particular emotion. After thirty seconds they appeared to reach a consensus and pulled in one of the minders. He listened, slightly bent so that Patrick could whisper without Yuri overhearing and then nodded his consent as well. Patrick and Mike returned to their seats.

"Deal. She's quite a local face mind, gets tougher to da job."

"I'm sure you'll manage somehow."

"When do you want it done by?" Mike said.

"Soon. I'll send you the details, her address and so on, when I send you the video." With that Yuri stood up and pulled the brown envelope from the hiding place tucked down his trousers under his jacket. He tossed the money to them.

"Payment in advance?"

"That's all of it too. I trust you will do as you say."

"You sure about doing that pretty boy?"

"Of course... if you don't then Uncle will murder every traveller man, women and child he finds for one hundred miles around, maybe the mothers too." Yuri kept his face as still as possible. The two Gypsies looked at him and let out wry smiles.

"He could fucking try too... that's the second big talk threat you Ruskies have made to us... it's getting a bit boring like," Mike said.

"You have heard the stories about us. Never doubt it. Oh one thing, I saw the fight video live... I also saw your boy fight last year. My advice... make a side bet on the new guy. Valentyn will lay down ten grand on his man on fight night... you're going to need to do the same to save face. A smart man would cover his bets."

Yuri did up his jacket and walked away. He had to walk until out of sight before he could call a cab. Zenovia had left no car.

SUNDAY

David busied himself in the kitchen. He wiped surfaces with a cloth and then re-aligned the jars of herbs and spices in the rack. He ordered them alphabetically and ensured the labels all faced forward. He'd done the same to the jars and spreads in the fridge. Sundays are funny days for those that live alone. It's a quintessentially family day, they had always been that way when he was younger too, maybe not happy laugh-filled experiences but at least he had someone to share them with back then. In recent years he hardly computed a Sunday from a Saturday. Eve had taken herself away to make some calls and catch up on paperwork, he had the run of the house and had been left with nothing to focus on and only his memories for company. His mother had pushed for a family lunch, a Sunday roast but Jacqui had winced at the thought and while part of him craved it, David had also felt uncomfortable at the idea. He hadn't rationalised why, but put it down to having too much too soon. He felt as if he were trying his family back on for size and it wasn't comfortable just yet.

No one had mentioned Peter, but he knew of course his brother wouldn't be able to join them even if the family feast had happened. The idea fizzled out as quickly as it had been mentioned. Undaunted, his mother demanded a

Saturday afternoon stroll with her son and now twenty-four hours later David wondered if the whole thing had been a carefully choreographed plot to help him determine his future.

She took him down to Home Park to walk along the river and around the old Rugby Club. He'd played there as a boy and though it was now summer and closed up he could still get a sense of the place, its smells and the noises that remain so universal in team sports. David's mother had taken the skill of talking but saying nothing and made it a fine art, she probed but never questioned too hard, enquired without pushing or offending. She'd wanted to buy him new clothes, something colourful and it took considerable patience to dissuade her from the notion that he had become a man only a whisper away from a tramp like existence.

"I wash, I clean my clothes Mum, I don't sleep in caves... well not all the time," He said as they sat down at a table at Cafe Rouge. He'd been assured that both Jacqui and Eve would stay in the Windsor house together until he returned, it meant he could relax a little.

"So you have slept in caves then?" she asked, a little incredulous.

"That was a joke, honest. Sometimes... if I fancy it then I hike across from place to place. I then pick up a small tent and might camp out for a few days."

"Really?"

"People forget how huge France and Spain are... a lot of empty and wild space. I love it, I can live off the land if I need to. Travel or stay put, its fun."

"It's not for me, but you don't seem to have done too bad on it," she replied. They sipped their coffee and tea respectively, David casting glances around the constant flow of tourists and shoppers and his mother doing that old English woman's habit of looking into the distance with an expression of disdain on her face.

"I know it's silly for me to expect you to think of here as home."

"It would be yes..."

"But don't you want a home? Settle and build a home life."

"Like normal people..." he added for her.

His mother blushed at how he had read her thoughts and simply nodded her agreement.

"Not now, not yet. I might. I'm living like this because I want to, I like it. It's freedom." He said it as if it were matter of fact, assuming that the listener would understand and not argue.

"What about those that love you?" she said.

David breathed in heavily and considered his response, "Love is not geographically limited, and they'll love me no matter where I am."

"Not all love is the same..."

David thought for a moment and wondered what she meant, then feeling like a fool he understood it and tried to distance himself from the question.

"Well no one is in that category right now."

"Aren't they?" she said. "I knew you'd been wounded but no one told me you'd gone blind," his mother said.

David held his palms up and furrowed his brow in confusion.

"She has waited a long time already. I doubt she can wait much longer. Blimey I doubt she is even sure of how she feels, what she feels for you anymore. Spare her a thought if you can."

David nodded.

"I know men pretend to be simple creatures and assume women are complicated. Silly media gibberish. Everyone is simple and complex all at the same time David."

David shrugged.

"You and she are an unfinished element in both your lives... it needs resolution. It's not a debatable point. You're back here so that you can either re-open doors or firmly close them. You're not alone in needing to do that. You understand me don't you?"

David did. A mother's frankness can be charming but often it is a blunt tool for a wake-up-call. He knew he'd been suppressing his Eve emotions under the confused state-of-mind his return had created with his family. Eve, the wonderful divine Eve, could she love him still? Did he love her? His mother had said nothing more on the subject and underlined his sense of child-like idiocy by forcing him to have a '99 Flake from the ice cream kiosk by the river.

All night he thought about what she had said and how he would broach the subject. Eve had finally removed the burden first thing Sunday morning, insisting on a light evening meal, just the two of them. David had then pottered and tidied for two hours straight, his mind in a total state of flux. Jacqui had been out all day, having moved to the back bedroom as requested, but had a girly get together and another hot date with her Latin lothario. Once she had found out about Eve's planned dinner she kept shouting, "Gooseberry alert, Gooseberry alert," so had stated categorically that she would be home late.

While David implored her to think safety first, Jacqui would have nothing of it and had flounced out. In truth David had other misgivings, he hadn't seen or spent any real time with his sister since she was in her teens, and he had hoped his coming back might have led to a decent reconciliation and the chance for them to get to know each other properly. Instead he'd had emotional attacks, accusations and a pretty ambivalent reaction. The Eve situation puzzled David, his emotional development had been stunted by prison and the Legion, he knew that all too well and his romantic vocabulary hadn't ever moved beyond the primary level; that said even if he wanted to verbalise his feelings for Eve he'd have to decipher what those feelings were.

David folded the tea-towels and then moved to the front rooms and checked the locks on the windows once more, the front door had been bolted and made secure, the back garden had no rear access accept through other people's properties and David couldn't see that happening. He glanced through from the dining room into the knocked through adjoining kitchen, his eyes scanned all the way to the folding glass doors at the end and the garden beyond. A vibrant red cedar deck started where the redwood interior floor ended and on it he saw the already partially laid table for dinner. His heart skipped at the thought of the meal ahead and warm smile played across his lips. The sound of footsteps on the stairs pulled him back to reality and Eve glided off the stairs through the kitchen and out to the table. She surveyed David's attempts and then sauntered back into the kitchen. She collected all the elements she needed to complete the job and hummed a tune he didn't recognise as she finished the collection. Once at the table she began the precise process of deconstructing all he had done and setting out the table as she preferred it.

David watched, partially obscured by the living room door. Her hair lay at full length, it collapsed like a dark wave onto her tanned shoulders, her ankle length summer dress tied behind her neck, slender arms bear with a perfect arc of naked back on show. David loved looking at her, a beauty he'd found no comparison for anywhere in the world. She had been beautiful when he left and she was stunning now.

David turned his head away and took in a gulp of air, his head sank to his chest and he rested his arms on the door frame. Herein lay the problem. With Eve and all her wonderfulness came memories, the root cause of the flashbacks and all his horrors. He'd seen enough military doctors and shrinks to understand that he'd spent every day since his release from prison running, sprinting away from the issues that haunted him. He'd delayed talking to her but he couldn't hold it off anymore, as soon as the issue with the Russians resolved itself he'd leave again and he'd return but never for good. Asperger style emotions didn't make him blind, he knew this stunning woman wanted him, loved him. Before returning he'd hoped for nothing more than a simple case of closure, that when they finally talked about their lives and how they felt that she would realise there was nothing in David she wanted, that he couldn't be the man she needed, she could move on and forget him. He could then just leave her to her happy life. Mission accomplished. Whatever feelings they had could be worked through the system and discarded so they could get on with their lives.

Now he knew differently, the simple act of laying a table, seeing her and being with her made him realise what he ached for, needed and desperately wanted. He conceded to his fear and ran the cold tap and took a long drag from a glass of water. He had debated long and hard whether to bring any of it up, to talk any of it through with her. She needed to know, had to understand and appreciate how his addled brain worked. He wished when he touched her and kissed her that all of it would float away, dissolve into meaningless memories but they wouldn't.

For David, to be with Eve meant he had to re-live that night, confront one of his many demons and relive the night he killed a man for the first time.

The evening was young, the weather barmy and the sunset still several hours away. Windsor on a Sunday night isn't buzzing. The bar had only twenty customers in total. Jacqui sipped a cocktail and looked across at her hot date, he'd checked his phone again, the fourth time in the last half hour, add to the two phone calls he had made and the one that he had received, from a woman no less, and Jacqui could tell she was not his number one priority. She adopted the pursed-lipped shoulders back pose of the slighted. In order for it to be effective he needed to see it and Yannick had failed to look up from his phone in a while. So she drank some more, the cocktail finished she waved at the waiter and pointed for him to bring number three.

Eve served the salad with elegant movements and an expertise with salad tongs that David admired, she nestled the neat pile of leaves next to the roasted chicken breast on his plate. He smiled gratefully, the smell was wonderful.

"Is this Rocket?" he said, pointing out a leaf with his knife.

"It is, you don't know Rocket?" she mocked back.

"I know of it, just not had it yet... not been exposed to such delicate culinary delights to be honest." David could feel her look him up and down, he daren't look up, unsure if her face would show pity, surprise or an abject look of horror at his ignorance. Instead he carved a hunk of chicken off and shoved it into his mouth. They ate in silence for a few minutes, occasionally gulping wine as the evening summer sun warmed them.

"This is a good wine," he said, "not French though, too bouncy... is it new world, South American?"

Impressed, Eve took another sip and looked through

the glass at the straw-coloured liquid, "Very good it's Argentinean actually."

"Sauvignon Blanc, somewhere at altitude, Mendoza probably, but one of the smaller Vineyards." He hoped he was impressing her.

"Oooh you are good, it's a Tomero... did you read the label?"

"No I did not, if two summers working in French vineyards doesn't give you a fundamental understanding of wine nothing will. I also drink a fair bit of it."

"That's where he found you isn't it... at a vineyard?" She asked the question as she ate, attempting to be nonchalant but inquisitive.

"Yeah that's right, my second summer at the place... well I say that, but I only did the harvest the year before. It's good fun."

Eve chewed, David drank and the silence returned. He could tell she had a thousand questions and wanted him to tell her every detail about everywhere he had been. To chronologically catalogue his life for her, especially since he left the Legion.

"I like having no home, no roots. Just travelling around, staying as long as I want to or need to. The internet keeps you connected to the world, if you need to be."

"And in the winter?" she asked, a motherly tone to her voice.

"I'm not a tramp Eve... I don't live in the forest, off the land or something weird like that. Last winter I spent in

Nice and Portofino... an old Legion colleague owns a bar in Nice and his family own several restaurants and cafes in Portofino. The bar needed a doorman come barman and when that slowed right down I did some driving and fixed up their properties. Nothing major but it paid some pocket money."

"But where do you live?"

"Oh you'd be amazed how friendly and helpful the human race is, floors or settees when you first arrive. Everyone knows someone in these sort of towns who has a room to spare or holiday let that is empty. I barter for them... you know, let me stay free for a month and I will decorate the whole property... that kind of thing. People tend to like me, I'm lucky."

Eve shrugged and made that same face that David had seen in others so often, those trapped or immersed in the corporate way seemed in anguish at the prospect of uncertainty, it terrified them, where he revelled in it. "Surely there is no future in that, I mean don't you worry about getting old and having something safe... or a family?"

"I'm open to offers, truly I am. Someone shows me a better life or the kind of security and stability you mean, I might take it, I'm in no hurry Eve. I have some living to catch up on. Some living of my design and my choosing." She was about to say something else and held back, she knew his life history and hopefully understood his need for freedom.

"Are you happy though?"

He hadn't expected that question and it took him a

moment to comprehend the enormity of its meaning. A sigh escaped before he could speak, "Am I happy? No, not really Eve. Am I incrementally happier than before... yes! You could say I'm happier..."

"How?"

"Well just track my life. I remember being happy that summer, you and me seeing each other for the first time, the parties going to the pub... then 'it' happened." David paused and Eve took a breath in as the memories overran her conscience. "Then there was immense unhappiness that got mixed with a lot of hate, a lot of fear and no small dose of anger. Prison has that effect."

"I can imagine..."

"No disrespect Eve...I don't think you can. You helped overturn the evidence. I'll never know how to thank you for that, getting the charge down to manslaughter. So... happier than before but not happy...still quite a lot of anger."

Eve smiled but it was half-hearted and painful to see David recounting his life in varying degrees of unhappiness, David didn't have emotional baggage in the conventional sense it was more akin to a Pickfords removal lorry.

"I understand now that I ran away to the Legion. I can't be sure but I rather think that I hoped it would kill me."

"Is that physically or metaphorically... killed?"

David let out a smile, "Oh in hindsight the latter. At the time I think. I would have settled for the former.

Death and me have had an odd relationship for quite some time. I don't fear it, don't look forward to it, it's simply something I've had to know all about."

"You don't mean just your own death but the killing of others, don't you?"

David could sense the question had led Eve to the very limits of what she wanted to know David had done.

"Yes... Yes I do."

"I'm sorry I've been busy, look no calls and no messages for twenty minutes now, don't be angry with me baby." Jacqui looked into Yannick's eyes and despite her reservations and desire to pour the fourth cocktail over his head she couldn't tear herself away from him. He did seem to have an odd job, she knew he lied periodically but then who the fuck cared. She had no intention of marrying the guy and he was handsome, charming mostly, and staggeringly good in bed. She hadn't felt as alive and wanted for years.

"I forgive you... but keep the phone off," she slurred.

"I will, it's all about you now, I promise." He leant forward and they managed a clumsy kiss before she dropped her head down to kiss his neck. Unseen Yannick checked his watch.

"I have missed a dinner date with my brother for you Mister."

Yannick made the 'oh really' face and tried to look like he cared.

"My long lost brother... back from the dead." she mumbled, "I've been a bit mean to him, it's not his fault Peter is such a twat or Dad for that matter." Yannick's face changed to one of confusion... he pushed her more upright and moved the cocktail a little further away.

"You have two brothers?" he asked.

"Yeah Peter and David."

"Peter I know of, he's the accountant you don't really like... who is David?"

Jacqui laughed in that drunken way when your face can't show the emotion you really feel. "I don't know, seriously I don't know him. Not seen him since I was a teenager. Ostracised from the family, a jail-bird."

Yannick steadied her once more and held her gaze, making her focus; the cocktails were catching up with her fast, "Tell me about him?"

"David... well he killed a man in a pub fight when he was like eighteen, nasty business, got stitched up with a murder charge. A load of bollocks about it being a pre-mediated attack coz the guy had been rude to his girlfriend... a load of bollocks. Right?"

"Sure..." Yannick said.

"No seriously, all bollocks, they had witnesses from the pub saying stuff that wasn't true... it was a bunch of pikey travellers sticking together. David went down for murder."

"So he's just come out of prison?"

"Naaaah, don't be soft, this was years ago. He did ten years... then he disappeared, hated my dad, went and joined the French Foreign Legion. Can you believe that the Foreign Legion."

"Wow," Yannick muttered, a curious expression of concern on his face, "you don't meet many people that have been in there."

"No, a proper hard nut now apparently, anyway big brother is our protection our saviour..." she slurred the words with pride then let out another cackle of laughter. Yannick supported her and made an apologetic face to the couple sat next to them at the table.

"He's the protection you mentioned, I get it now. Baby, do you have a picture of your brother?"

"Aaah sweet you wanna see my family... yeah my Mum made me take a family shot of all of us, let me get it it's on my phone." she fumbled in her bag and produced a BlackBerry. She navigated through the features and pulled up the picture. Yannick took it and studied it hard for a minute.

"The tall streak... that's Peter my boring brother. The solid lump with the short hair, is David... look at me, the rose between two thorns!"

"You are lovely!" He threw the remark at her as if out of necessity and studied the faces of both men. He knew them. He'd met one a long time ago when playing poker and the other just a few days before. He looked at Jacqui and shook his head seeing them all together the family resemblance was plain to see. "Your tall brother looks familiar. I think I have met him?"

Jacqui laughed, "Peter? Really?"

"Yes... I played poker with him... but he doesn't have the same name as you?"

"Na, his surname is Edwards. When I started on my own I wanted a different name to my police identity, I use my mum's maiden name, Evards. I told you that already, silly."

He looked blankly at her, unable to recall if that were true. He cursed himself inside his mind and mentally joined the dots of information. A bold and clearer picture painted itself. He needed to check one final thing, "Your other brother has an interesting face... he's dressed in black, does he always dress like that?"

Jacqui scrunched up her face in a quizzical search for a fact, "Yeah, ya know what he's not worn anything else since he came over from France."

Yannick propped her up again and flashed her his brilliant smile, "How would you like to come and stay at my place tonight?"

She smiled, having never been invited back before and nodded with a cheeky grin. "Let's go, we can get some food on the way."

"Mmmm whatever you say."

"I have gone over and over that night in my head. I must have relived it a million times. Why did we go there? Why did I react? I can't fathom it. I've given up trying to. It happened." David said.

"You didn't do anything wrong... they were arseholes, the guy took a swing at me... if he had connected the trial and the case would have been different."

"I hit him so hard Eve. No hesitation, no fear. No warning." David looked down at his feet. "I knew for maybe a minute or so before I threw the punch that I was going to. I had made up mind I was going to punch him."

"Really?"

"Inside, outside the pub. Either way I'd had enough of his mouth."

"When he went for me that was the final straw..?"

"Yeah and the opportunity, he never saw it coming."

They sat motionless for a moment each absorbing the detail and information they had shared. "It wasn't murder David, you didn't plan to kill him, you reacted and the outcome was accidental." It seemed more a justification for herself than for David and he looked her over but she didn't make eye contact.

"I know Eve... the difference I am referring to is not a legal one. I didn't murder him. I killed him. I made conscious and tangible decisions that were violent and aggressive. They resulted in me killing him."

Now she looked at him, her eyes a little distant and her expression blank. "I did it Eve... I spent time in prison for a crime I committed. He didn't fall and bang his head, it wasn't accidental or unlucky. I drove the man's jaw-bone into his brain."

Eve tried to look away to tear herself away from the ugly truth was confronting her.

"Every time I shut my eyes I see his face. I see him before and after the punch. He haunts me, he terrorises my every darkened moment." Eve said nothing and couldn't look him in the eye. "When I look in the mirror I see what I am."

He left it like a question, a challenge, a gauntlet thrown down to Eve, the woman who had loved him, campaigned for him and even built her life's work around the concept of helping the fallen and the dispossessed. She took the challenge.

"David... you are a victim too, an innocent man caught in a moment. A moment you couldn't repeat if you tried. Whether we use the word kill, murder, manslaughter, semantics won't change the fact that you didn't intend fatal harm."

"None of that matters. Eve... you know you hear new fathers say to people that they can't explain the overwhelming change in themselves, their protective primeval instincts that kick in when they hold their defenceless child for the first time? They say you're never the same again. Your view of life is different. Taking a life is the same effect, but with anguish and despair in place of joy and hope. I hope you never experience the hideous feeling of taking a life... but all I can say is that it changes you beyond comprehension and it forces you to take journeys through the rabbit holes of your subconscious and it isn't pleasant. No matter how long it takes or how torturous... when you come out the other side you can only ever come to terms with one thing; 'I KILLED'. The accepting of that is how you move on."

Eve wanted to speak but the words didn't come, she

wanted to console him, to argue, maybe point out that the person's soul mattered more than their actions, but she couldn't trust she really believed that.

"I am a killer."

"David, please..." the tears came before the breathless heaving of her chest and the crumpling of her shoulders.

"I'm a killer. I don't like it. I can't change it. The stench of it will never leave me, like bloodstains on my hands that I can't wash away... it's part of me, and I'm sorry."

Eve finally lost her reservations and the emotion boiled over, she fell forward out of her chair and barged the table from her path and grabbed at him. A desperate lunge and need to hold him. She wrapped her arms around him and buried her face into his neck before pulling back and peppering his face and head with kisses. He didn't respond just rested his hands on her back, steadying her as she continued with her passionate assault. She slowed and then gathered his head in her hands, cupping his handsome rugged face and she pushed her lips hard onto his and kissed with as much strength as she had.

"I don't care David, I never did. I know you..." she poked a finger into his chest. "I know what's in here, I have seen that man. What you did doesn't make you evil or bad... you've been in prison and through wars and Jesus Christ knows what horrors and hells you have witnessed." She shook her head, eyes closed, almost exorcising her imaginations from her mind's eye. "One day you'll tell me things if you want to... I'm here for you, I need to be here for you. I need to hold you and know you are alright and that to help you understand the world hasn't forgotten

David Edwards. That he matters and is loved and wanted... you've paid your penance and more."

David's eyes sought out hers and when they found each other they locked onto each other, he saw the spark and fire dancing there and felt the full force of her resolve and passion. At that moment he adored her, loved and wanted her like he had never wanted anything in his life. His hand worked its way around her neck and he pulled her towards him, she put up no resistance and their lips met and they kissed each other. A deep wonderful kiss the kind that made the world stand still, just for a moment.

Yuri needed to take stock, to think through his next move and to ensure they would turn out as they needed to. Yuri knew he was ambitious, he accepted he had to be ruthless to achieve certain aims and he knew his place in the current order of things. He poured himself a glass of half-decent whisky and took a slug, it had been quite an effort to subdue the bloody woman. She had accepted more drink happily and despite his adding the crushed sleeping tablets it seemed an age before she finally stopped trying to remove his trousers and demanding sex.

The cocktail and wine mix had ensured that Jacqui Edwards or Evards, whatever her true name is, didn't understand the implications of going downstairs rather than up. To her the man she knew as Yannick had simply converted his basement into a bedroom. In truth she had been taken into a small anti-room off the main basement. Yuri's games and TV room occupied the larger space but the smaller room contained a double futon, red walls, adjustable lighting and a projector. His cinema room had been mostly soundproofed, had no windows and with a padlock it could be locked from the outside. Yuri presumed she'd sleep it off until mid-morning, she'd wake to find herself naked and cable tied face down on the futon. As a make shift prison it worked rather well.

Jacqui's mobile phone sat on the table, he'd already had a good look through the pictures and the contacts list. Without doubt her long lost brother was the insanely tough boxer from the gym, the man that would fight the Gypsies. What had come as more of a shock was the picture of her other brother, the tall geeky gambler that had played on several of his poker nights. Valentyn had the tall brother hostage and was forcing the cooperation of the soldier, that was an open secret in the gang but Yuri knew no boxing fight would keep the Gypsies quiet they wanted Valentyn's blood. He mused over the new information and drank another slug of his whisky. He had made contact with Jacqui on his own initiative, her name had been mentioned with the lawyer and he used the web to find her. It took less than ten minutes to find her twitter and Facebook profiles and she had exercised some control of her privacy settings, he knew everything about her he needed to know in just a few minutes. It had been so easy she let anyone see her timeline and in it she openly discussed internet dating. Finding her profile and organising a chat and a meet had been meat and drink to Yuri after that.

Valentyn didn't have a clue about any of it, he never used social media had never been on Facebook and Yuri played it all to his advantage. He let Valentyn continue with his limp fear tactics towards the lawyer, Yuri just waited until Masha, the family, noticed his worth and asked him for help. That's when he had given deliberately erroneous information to Valentyn so as to further undermine him with the Uncle. No, Yuri deduced, Valentyn really didn't have control of things, he presented the image of being ice cool and all knowing, but he had seriously fucked up this time. He and Zenovia didn't need to create any bigger problems to expose him, his failure to keep the Gypsies in line would be seen as a betrayal all on its own. The final nail in Valentyn's coffin would come at the big fight.

He just needed to be patient, he now had all the aces, the Gypsies would deal with the lawyer and Valentyn's failures would be exposed, while Yuri would be toasted by both sisters and their father. He took another slug of the drink and drained the glass, proud of his deductions and the career development it would mean. Siding with Zenovia had worked in the short term but his brief unison with Masha would now be key. Whichever sister succeeded their father he felt confident they would be easily manipulated from afar.

One thing he had to determine was the timing of the fight. He needed that to happen before the soldier missed his sister and the lawyer got suspicious. The sooner the fight ended the sooner the lawyer could be removed and the shorter the time he had to play kidnapper. He toasted his empty glass to his genius and sat down to send and a text to his new Gypsy allies. Then he dialled Zenovia.

Zenovia tapped the mobile phone against her teeth and

contemplated what she had just heard. She sat a little more upright in the bed and pulled the duvet up to cover the gentle rolls of fat below her breasts. She cast an eye on the sweaty slumbering mass next to her and raised her long-nailed hand and brought it down hard on the naked hairy buttock with a resounding 'thwack'. The mass stirred. "Gerr'up, get dressed and fuck off downstairs," she barked. The body hefted itself out of bed, gathered the discarded clothes and bumbled out of the door, shutting it behind him.

She pressed the speed-dial on her phone and waited for the answer. The voice on the end sounded eager and in need of entertaining. Zenovia sighed and pressed on.

"F'ings have changed," she said. "Yeah, the Gypsies are lined up, they know whatta do... stop worrying, just listen, please." Zenovia waited until calm had returned and she began again. "We've a new asset... we got the lawyer's business partner, it don't matter how... because it don't. We hav' her and she's safe. We've the leverage to make the lawyer woman stop and the Gypsies are on our side, we need to use them wisely. If we can make Valentyn look like a fool and rescue the business then we'll force Papa's hand... the time is now!"

MONDAY

Wladimir sipped his tea and turned the page of his newspaper. He'd read several different titles in his life in England and recently settled back to reading The Times. The smaller format appealed to him and it felt like a high-class tabloid. The paper sat sprawled across the large round table what was once the cabaret and dance floor. As he aged he found that some days he liked to feel the majesty of the dome above him.

He checked his watch, Valentyn would not be in to give him a morning briefing, he'd made do with a short update from his daughter Masha. He'd been impressed by her grasp of the figures and the details she knew about the admin process. Not that he wanted show it. He didn't care for all the details but liked the end results and for a brief moment he felt something akin to pride in her. He now waited for Zenovia to appear and no doubt babble at him and demand something or other. He hoped Yuri would be on hand to translate her youthful drivel and to carry out the remedial action he had no doubt would be required. As always with his youngest daughter, he heard her coming long before she entered the room.

He put his elbows onto the table and rested his chin on his hands, he flicked his eyes to the mirror ahead of him. He could see all that went on in his restaurant from here while affecting an air of indifference. Zenovia came through the reception hall doorway, jabbering and half-shouting into her mobile phone. Two men followed her... they took him by surprise he couldn't quite place them. His daughters usually had just one soldier in attendance, a novice or new recruit from the homeland. Valentyn had found that as the job wasn't a glamorous one none of his seasoned troops wanted to do it, so it was best to hand it to the ones who knew no better. Zenovia finished her call and gathered the men close, they were attentive, deferential and nodded their consent as each instruction was given. Neither man paused, they went off to conclude whatever instructions they had been given. More to the point the instructions had been given in English as well.

He watched from the mirror as his daughter briefly checked her profile in the mirrored door to the ladies bathroom and then smoothed down her white shirt which sat over a pair of dark grey trousers. Wladimir realised that for the first time in as long as he could remember he didn't hate what his daughter looked like. She walked over to him, if not with confidence then certainly with more assurance than usual.

"Papa!" she greeted him from behind. He feigned interest and grunted, pretending to be engrossed in his newspaper. "Papa!" she tried again, "I have the updates and one or two things to discuss with you?" He looked up into the mirror and saw her smiling at him he gave her a curt grin and folded his paper shut before turning to face her. No seat was offered and she didn't ask for one.

"Tell me something I don't know," he said.

Zenovia cast her eyes over the table and saw he had the morning's data, "I see ya have the numbers, they're alright, good, getting better but we still have some headaches to resolve."

He nodded for her to continue to enlighten him.

"The movement from phase one storage to admin and then out again is a little slow Papa... this is due to some short-sighted planning when we set the process up..."

Wladimir ignored the barbed comment, a clear dig at Valentyn and to some extent himself, but not completely untrue.

"OK, tell me more," he said.

"The Gypsies are slow to push units out and don't have the capacity to store enough at once... I met the Gypsies yesterday and they always talk about problems and hold ups... they're going to be loadsa trouble in the long run."

"You want to remove them from the system?"

"Not in the short term... but in the long term yeah."

"What does Valentyn think?" he asked.

"Well he finks they can cope... but his new system puts too much pressure on 'em and they are the hold up to the admin process at the moment... he has more faith in them than me but kinda agrees that a change might be needed." She said it with an even tone, no blame or emotion attached. Just business.

"How many units will leave the country next week?"

"Nearly five thousand... it's hard to be completely accurate but it should see the end of the backlog and mean we're bang on ready for the big deliveries every week." She said it knowing that her confidence was based on the Gypsies performance, which she had already guaranteed to be seriously below par.

"Good. Valentyn assured me there would be no problems... I am pleased to see my team doing so well."

"Thank you Papa. There is one bit I wanted to talk to you about though."

"Go on..."

"The newspapers and the coverage from the lawyer woman..."

"Valentyn has this under control," Wladimir waved his hand at the situation with a dismissive arrogance.

"We are certain?" She used '*we*' and not '*you*' with deliberate effect.

"Valentyn assured me last week that they are running scared and that the investigations have stopped... they might come back but for now all is well."

"Ok Papa!" She said it in a near whisper and with just the right amount of disappointment to get his fuller attention.

"WHAT! Please don't play games if you have something to say... say it."

"I don't wanna to tell tales, but it's an important time for the business... we need to be sure there are no problems..."

"Speak child or I will get angry..."

"Don't be cross now Papa... the information I hav' came to me because the person had concerns that it might not be being passed on... they're so very loyal to you and the family Papa..." She couldn't complete her defence statement, her father cut her off.

"Yuri... right?"

"Yeah Papa... as you know he's had the inside knowledge on this and has been Valentyn's source... well he says they're scared, for sure, but not running scared... in fact they hav' new protection. Serious new protection and hav' been moving forward not holding back. Doing more investigations and looking for more witnesses..."

Wladimir said nothing, he fumed a little but held his full emotions in check. He didn't like his best General derided but he couldn't ignore the accusation that he had been lied to. Masha had told him about the cancelled fight and how the Gypsies were unhappy with re-arrangements, it was all bad business and all directly controlled by Valentyn. This added fuel to the fire that his favourite might be spread too thinly.

"What do you suggest daughter?"

"We need to be careful is all. Eyes open, not be too relaxed that's all. I have asked Yuri to monitor it more closely and he's got two men to help him. If they get too close then we can act more decisively. I wanna to be careful."

He nodded his consent. "Yuri should keep us informed daily on this... the moment we think they are doing more TV or reports in the paper or have new witnesses and they are talking then we have to shut it down immediately."

"I'll make sure Papa." She rested her hand on his shoulder for a moment, but ensured she didn't linger too long and then turned and bustled out the door. Wladimir looked at his paper, went to sip his tea, then stopped short realising it was now cold.

David slept better than he had ever slept. A sound slumber that even army revelry would have had trouble rousing him from. The three hours of lovemaking, kissing, talking and holding would have helped exhaust the most hyperactive, but for once David's mind couldn't drift to the dark places and the demons remained hidden in its darker recesses. He had woken early, the force of habit overcoming all, but he'd just lain in bed, Eve's head on his shoulder and his arm around her, for a long time. Finally when she stirred there had been no awkwardness no strangeness, just love and tenderness in their embrace. Showers and breakfast came and went in something of a blur and it wasn't until Eve mentioned work that David even considered Jacqui.

He checked her room and the bed hadn't been slept in, he called her mobile from Eve's landline and only got voicemail. Finally his concern growing he asked Eve about her boyfriend.

"Oh some restaurant owner or something... not actually met him, why?"

"She hasn't been home, I was worried that's all."

"Silly sod... she's fine, I got a message around midnight, said she was a bit drunk but going to stay the night with her Latin lover?"

"She wrote that in a text?"

"Well almost... there were a few typos and she always calls him that. She'd better hope he never reads her messages, she's a bit graphic." David put his hands up to stop her revealing any more.

"Ok enough... I'll catch her at the office later today. What are you up to? Wanna spend some time with me?"

She leant forward and kissed his face, "that would undeniably be wonderful but duty calls. We have some folks that need to be interviewed over in Uxbridge, apparently they escaped some compound where they were being held after being smuggled in. They had all their documentation, money and valuables stolen and were treated like prisoners... they're singing like canaries, can't have any close dependents back home so I need to see how much they know and what they will potentially testify to!"

"Fine... Go to it my crusading angel..." He smiled but the disappointment showed in his face.

"Sorry... our little lie in, magnificent though it was, has left me a little short of time. I'll be finished by seven tonight promise... dinner again?" She had a little wicked smile on her face.

"Same dessert?" he asked.

"Better..." she replied kissing him on the cheek, grabbing her briefcase and charging for the door. "I'll be taking two investigators with me to the meeting today... I'll be safe!" she hollered back, before slamming the door closed.

Alone, coffee in hand, David remembered he had a mobile phone, and he remembered his brother. The brief oasis from other people's issues, problems and shit ended. He went in search of the phone and found it in a pile of clothes from the day before and he flicked it on... there was a message.

The fight is today. We will collect you at 2.00pm at Windsor Riverside station'

Jacqui lay in agony. Waking to find herself naked, bound face-down on a futon at both ankle and wrist, with the thumping head of a Hades-style hangover, it's debatable whether the physical pain hit her marginally before the all engulfing emotion of fear. She hadn't been hurt or otherwise abused, but an overpowering feeling of being shit-scared had enveloped her. She tried to reassure herself that no actual bodily damage was a positive. With that realisation she couldn't shake the overriding sense that she was in a great deal of trouble. The room had no windows and while a series of overhead spotlights were on they had clearly been dimmed. She tried to remain calm and thought back to her police training. She told herself not to panic and to avoid wriggling and writhing to get free. That only led to more pain. Instead she concluded she needed to relieve the cramping and avoid any rapid movements that would cause the short sharp pain of her bindings cutting into her skin.

Once she had reached a modicum of comfort she assessed her makeshift cell, she deduced it had to be temporary. There was no toilet facility and keeping people naked would always be a short-term option. If it were only temporary then it meant her stay would be a short one. She worked hard not to think about the consequences of that and decided she had been kept alive for a reason and no matter what reason, however vile, being alive meant an opportunity to escape.

Jacqui had no external indication of the time of day nor how long she had been lying unattended so she just waited, occupying her mind with an array of assumptions and decisions she would make when specific collisions of consequences occurred. The main and repetitive theme seemed to be based around a combination of freeing one limb and causing irreparable damage to her captor. She had finally determined that if Yannick was her captor, which appeared likely then he would surely attempt to rape her, and if he did she would be ready. She decided she would treat the whole episode as some bizarre sexual fetish, play along as best as her stomach could take and offer a blow job. Then she would bite his cock off.

Her reasoning being that he would be incapacitated enough to not harm her further and she would have time and opportunity to escape. Happy she at least had a plan, Jacqui determined she had to wait and occupy herself with pondering why Yannick had done this. Her pondering didn't last long, having not heard a significant sound since she had woken up Jacqui could now hear doors slamming and the sound of footsteps above her. At some point more than one person used some stairs. Then for a few minutes it went quiet. Then she heard a door slam just a few metres away and the heavy sound and vibration of footsteps again, she had assumed she was in a basement and the sounds that now reached her seemed only to confirm it. The rattle of a lock and the fumbling of the door to the room guaranteed she would see her captor, a twist and a writhe later and she had positioned her head to face the door. The door swung open and the face Jacqui expected to see failed to materialise.

The dumpy and frankly ugly face that greeted her shocked her, whoever she was she clearly had no clue that Jacqui would be naked and trussed up like a prize turkey. A shocked hand went to her mouth and she turned and yelled out of the room.

"Yuri... why's she naked?" Jacqui listened hard but only heard the dulcet tones of a Thames valley accent. A disembodied voice, a voice Jacqui recognised, answered back.

"I thought she'd be less likely to escape... you know, feel more vulnerable naked." Yannick was the voice she heard and in a matter of a millisecond Jacqui connected the dots. Her Yannick, real name Yuri. Russian not Sicilian, no doubt he had been working for the gang she and Eve had under investigation. Jacqui couldn't rein in her impulse reaction, "You little shit!" Jacqui yelled towards the door. "You lying little shitting arsehole twat face!" she bellowed again. The dumpy woman turned to face her, a quizzical expression on her face.

"Yuri, she isn't happy with you is she?"

With that Yuri poked his face round the doorframe and saw the sight for himself. He baulked at the scene that greeted him and resigned himself to accepting that the naked element of the imprisonment had been excessive.

"Yuri... are you fucking her for real?"

Yuri nodded with a 'what can ya do' style shrug.

"Why?" she asked.

"Why not..."

"You think this woman is beautiful?"

Yuri frowned, "Beautiful... No... but she's good fun, she's good in bed."

Jacqui rolled her eyes and flopped her head onto the futon trying to block the conversation from her mind.

"How else would she trust me... you tell me how I'd get the information you and your sister needed." He raised his eyebrows at her as if demanding some kind of intellectual argument. Masha just shrugged.

"You make her cum?"

"Of course...many times, she always had more to say after wine and cock!"

Jacqui bellowed, "ENOUGH... I am here you know. I can hear you... and you keeping that cock isn't guaranteed!"

Yuri went to say something but pursed his lips and held it back. Masha shook her head at Yuri with almost parental disappointment. "Did my sister know that you were shagging her for the information?" He didn't answer and just shrugged again. "It matters ya know... she thinks you were getting the info from one of your many informers... she'll be jealous," she added finally.

Yuri's face contorted into one of surprised confusion, "you know about it Masha... about me and Zenovia?" he said, hoping for something other than the truth.

"That you fuck my sister? Yuri the whole bloody business knows you do, they know that you do what she tells you to do as well!" Masha added the comment with a touch more sarcasm than strictly matched the number that actually knew about it. Jacqui decided to interject.

"Excuse me... Masha is it? And whoever you are... Yannick, Yuri cock knob? But is there a chance I could be untied please, I can't feel my hands..." Jacqui watched as the dumpy woman, who seemed to be in some kind of control produced a hand-gun and pointed it at her.

"Yuri take off the ankle straps, at least she can turn

over then." Jacqui couldn't see the faint look of distaste come over Masha's face. Yuri did as asked and Jacqui twisted the hand straps allowing her to flip over and sit, legs outstretched with her feet crossed.

"Thank you... now if you could either untie me or at least get me some kind of bucket."

The two captors stared and Jacqui and asked in unison, "Why?"

"Because, geniuses, I'm busting for a piss and this looks like a nice futon." She didn't really need to go that badly but the more she tried to keep them engaged the more likely she would be to find some method of escape. She saw Masha smile and tug something from a black bag on the floor.

"Listen lady, Yuri is going to get your clothes and you can dress in the toilet over there. Don't try and be a hero ok?" Jacqui nodded. "I'm not going to kill you... I need you alive for now, but I will shoot your fucking foot off. Understand?" Jacqui nodded again, the mention of pissing had actually raised the issue further up her immediate physical requirement agenda.

"Yuri, use these handcuffs, one on her right wrist and once in the toilet cuff her to the radiator?"

He nodded, then stopped, "It's under floor heating... there is no radiator," he said.

Masha rolled her eyes... "Men," she said, looking at Jacqui as if there might some kind of sisterly affirmation. "Find a pipe or tap or something then..." Yuri nodded again and gathered up Jacqui's clothes and tossed them in the toilet across from the main room. Then he scooted into the room with Jacqui.

"Soon you'll be moved. You'll wear a hood. If you behave you won't be hurt. If you misbehave we will hurt you very badly." Jacqui noted the steel and unemotional blankness of the woman's eyes. She had no doubt she meant what she said. "And if you misbehave a second time we'll kill Peter too."

Jacqui stopped dead when she heard her brother's name.

"Where are we going?" David asked for the second time. The Russian driver once again made no comment and didn't even appear to have registered the sound of the lone man in the back of the gun-metal Range Rover. The conspicuous beast of a vehicle had picked David up outside the Windsor Riverside station, stopping in a truly inconvenient spot and sounding its horn until David appeared. Twenty minutes later and after a short but circuitous tour of the Slough trading estate, the car now sat in a jam due to a traffic light failure at unattended road works near the building where they filmed The Office. David recognised the area as soon as he saw the building and when the car sneaked off a side road he noticed that it had stopped outside the same derelict looking industrial unit that he and Peter visited just a few days before. David wondered if FHM had been wired together and been put back on duty.

The car idled for another five minutes until finally two bodies strolled around the corner. Valentyn and Oleg wore crisp, beautifully tailored black suits, white shirts and no ties, more boy band rejects than hard men at an unlicensed fight. David didn't care, he wanted to get the charade over with as soon as possible. Valentyn sauntered to the open back door and swung his huge bulk onto the seat next to David, the car rocked and then listed a little with the additional weight.

"You are ready?" Valentyn asked.

"I am," David replied.

"I have placed bet on your success... the odds are good."

"Really what are they?"

"2/1... which is reasonable...I can double my money. Declan agreed to secure £25,000 for me." Valentyn said it like a father to a son, expecting thanks for the faith.

"What odds for the Gypsy?"

"Now 3/1, a lot of money came down on him yesterday. He was bigger odds than that but he has become more popular... the good opening odds helped that. You want to bet?"

David nodded, always happy to take advantage of any opportunity to earn money easily and cheaply. He pulled out his modest bundle and handed it to Valentyn.

"Two grand on me please."

The big Russian opened the door and barked a command in Russian at Oleg, who took the bundle and hurried into the shabby building. Valentyn looked his man up and down and David felt uncomfortable under his gaze.

"The rules have changed... the Gypsies have decided to make it a more basic affair." David looked across the back seat at the Russian. "It's now mitts only, no gloves. Extreme fighting. Last man standing..." the Russian finished.

"Right... they didn't fancy a boxing match against me?"

"It seems so... sensible on their part yes?"

"No not really. Boxing is my weakest discipline. Anything goes?"

"No choke holds and no submissions. Everything else is fair game." The Russian said it like a statement but David could sense he sought reassurance.

"Fine, better for me."

With that Oleg returned and handed a pink slip to Valentyn, before barking rapid questions at the driver. The driver replied with a degree of impatience as Oleg clambered into the front passenger seat. The car, with just the four of them, pulled away and David felt obliged to ask one more time. "Where are we going?"

No one replied until they were out of the trading estate and trundling through Northern Slough on Oatlands Drive. They emerged from the shambolic mess of poorly maintained homes onto the Wexham Road and then turning East on the A4 briefly before disappearing into the mire of the Langley Estate. The big car eased through the non-descript streets and the houses and general residential decor improved they finally exited suburbia via the Iver village road. Valentyn looked at his watch and then over to David.

"Slough is beautiful..." he said.

"Not a word I would use."

"A town of infinite opportunity." Valentyn smiled as he said it.

"Where are we going?" he asked again.

"They wanted us to go to one of their Gypsy sites... we said no to this. I don't like to go into such places." His face inadvertently expressed physical distaste at the thought. "We are meeting them in a tunnel..."

David nodded and then furrowed his brow as he fully realised what had been said, "A tunnel...?" He looked from Valentyn to the driver and then back again. No one replied.

David tried to get his bearings as the car swung round bends and across junctions, he recalled a pub name or shop at a turn or deviation and tried to place where he was. He closed his eyes and conjured an aerial view of the area in his mind. He'd been away too long for it to be detailed, but significant landmarks and major roads remained unchanged. The Iver road from Langley ran west to east, parallel to the M4, when they zigzagged and turned left through the village they came out onto another minor road but which also ran alongside a major motorway. David noted the relative shift of the sun's position and he knew he'd ended up heading north and the big road to his right had to be the M25. He opened his eyes and looked for a road sign to the next location, he just saw the names Uxbridge and the M40 before the car slowed... the driver leant forward in that customary way someone does when looking for a hidden turning. He saw what he wanted and pulled the car off to the right into a gateway for a long abandoned water pumping works. They were between two villages now and as about as remote as you could be in this part of England. The pump works had long been abandoned, every window had been smashed and a high security fence surrounded it. The fence looked strong and well maintained but the gate sat open and seemed to have no attendee. David made mental notes once more.

The Range Rover eased its way round the right-hand side of the building, passing between the main building and the smaller, more derelict out-buildings. The security fence that surrounded the old compound pushed left towards a line of trees that ran along the adjacent canal. Now out of sight of the road they could see that an entire panel of the rear fence had been cut away and they could exit the compound and drive onto what looked like a legitimate but rarely used farm track. The track ran for about five hundred metres towards the looming presence of the motorway embankment before it disappeared into a dark gaping hole in its side.

As they approached the tunnel entrance, vehicle headlights flashed three times from deep within it. The driver slowed to a crawl and nosed the car into the tunnel, as everyone's eyes became accustomed to the light they saw the car that flashed them, it was a rust bucket of a Volvo estate parked along the left-hand wall, with enough space for two vehicles to pass it side by side.

Oleg buzzed down his window and a man in the vehicle issued a simple direction in a half Irish brogue, "Follow dis tunnel round to yerz left, when yerz cum out park on der right hand side between der trees."

David counted the men in the car... two. The car could, and no doubt would, easily block the exit from the tunnel. He frowned and cast a glance around the Russians, no one showed any similar concern.

"Did you approve this place without seeing it first?" he asked.

"No... we have done some deals here in the past... it is unseen from the road and a good secret place to meet." Valentyn said it with casual indifference.

"Ideal place for a deal where you don't want the buyers to leave on their own terms." David replied.

The tunnel twisted slightly to the left, just enough so that you couldn't see the exit if standing at one end. They emerged into a small field, large Oak and Birch trees formed a spinney like perimeter and their branches almost shrouded the whole area in a lush green leaf canopy. David spun on his seat to take in the entire vista, heavy shrubs and undergrowth grew around the tunnel entrance up the motorway embankment. Two white Transit vans and a battered Toyota Hilux sat parked to the left, a mob of ten or so men lingered around and between them. Another cluster of battered and mud-splattered cars and 4x4's sat in the far corner near to some kind of animal shelter. Another small group of dishevelled mongrel looking men mingled around them.

They pulled the car in where they had been told to and they climbed out. David did another perimeter scan, the motorway and tunnel hemmed them in on one side and behind the perimeter of trees stood more fields and woods and not much else, David searched for signs of a second entrance, the tunnel and this tiny bit of field on the other side of the motorway looked like it had been one of those bizarre planning headaches for the motorway construction team, with the owner refusing to sell all his land and forcing them to ensure he had the same access, hence the tunnel. The mob of men all turned and watched as they got out of the vehicle, the hot weather meant everyone should have been in shirts alone, but everyone seemed to be in jackets. Guns, mused David, a lot of hidden guns.

The uneasy sense that this event would get messy and nasty washed over David. He understood the Gypsy mentality and their devious sense of communal spirit better than most, they had helped stitch him up for a murder sentence all those years ago. They looked after their own. He'd been only too happy to fight a pikey for money, payback always felt good. Something troubled him though, if they had bet a lot of money on their boy then they expected something significant to happen here today and as he cast his eye around the crowd something stood out... everyone was a Gypsy, the fight would take place in daylight with no invited guests.

Valentyn moved forward, the short cropped tufty grass made his leather shoes and suited attire appear ludicrous as well as inappropriate. David hung back as a mullet-sporting man in a thin leather jacket moved forward to greet him. They exchanged words and it all appeared convivial, but David watched what happened behind the Gypsy and how everyone else behaved. Then he noticed it. In the far right corner a tumble down lean-to, a stable of sorts, stood maybe twenty feet in front of the fence. The angle deceived the eye and a casual glance made you think the stable butted against the fence. In fact the fence bowed outwards giving a wide corridor of space behind the stable. He looked beyond the perimeter at the longer grass leading away from the shelter, it had been flattened in a set of parallel lines, tyre tracks. David mused on it for no more than a second, concluding that the fence panels could be moved, providing an alternative access in and out of the field behind it for those in the know. His nervousness went up another level.

Valentyn came back towards them shaking his head and smiling as much to himself as for their benefit. "These fucking people," he said.

David kept his eyes on the lean-to, convinced it would be hiding something important. At about twenty feet long and ten feet deep, a number of the back boards had slipped and the resulting gaps allowed light to filter through; David could see through them to the fields beyond. It happened once, then again and then once more, several of the gaps of light became blocked, meaning something or someone pacing back and forth behind the lean-to. David assumed it would be his opponent, but that proved untrue when the middle of the three white vans rocked and creaked on its suspension before the rusted rear doors sprang open and a man stripped to the waist stepped out. David gave him a cursory glance, about six foot-four, square shoulders, powerful arms but a toned and not over-muscled body. David sensed strong legs under the black tracksuit trousers, older but more of an athlete than he had expected.

"Ok.. rules much like we discussed, their fighter wants to use mitts, you happy with that?" Valentyn said.

David nodded, "Check his and check mine in front of

them; make sure there isn't anything funny with them," he said.

"Sure... also no rounds, no time limit... just last man standing."

David nodded again, but his attention diverted back to the lean-to. Whoever the wanderer was he'd moved to the far end nearest the trees. David could see the figure through the largest gap in the dilapidated carpentry. He squinted and recognised the face, he tried to place it. His thoughts were broken for a second as Valentyn and a representative from the Gypsies fiddled with the silly red mitts he'd been forced to wear. As the man attempted to twist David's hands palm up he pulled them free, "Fuck off... are we gonna fight or fuck each other?"

Valentyn let out a deep throated chuckle and helped to shoo the irritant away. David pushed his focus back to the lean-to and the man. It clicked, the synapses did their thing and his brain retrieved the memory. He had seen the figure at the big Russian's gym.

"Remember no choke holds, no submissions..." Valentyn repeated.

"It won't get to that anyway. How many men you got here today?" David asked.

Valentyn looked puzzled for a moment then said, "Me, Oleg and the driver."

"No one else... no one here before us, waiting with the Gypsies?"

"No... we only had this place confirmed when we were all together at the bookies. Why?" David felt another wave of unease, alarm bells went off in his head and he knew the set-up stank. Something else had to be occurring, the fight had all the trappings of being nothing but a cover. He felt sure of it and his life experience had taught David to listen to his instincts.

"No reason... Valentyn are you and your guys carrying?"

The big Russian eyed him and a wary look came over his face, "Always."

"Good. Something serious?"

"Yarygin PYA... and in the car we have something heavier, why?"

"Might be just me, but I don't like the all Gypsy crowd... no external witnesses. I get a sense that things might end up getting a little bit silly here today... what do you call heavy?" David wanted to know because while the Yarygin is an adequate short recoil semi-automatic weapon, it would struggle over the distances in the field and no matter how good these guys were. He doubted they would hit much from more than thirty yards.

"It's new, Chinese, the QBZ-95... modified for NATO ammunition."

David held back his surprise. He had heard great things about the rifle but few had been seen outside of China unless being carried by the People's army. A lightweight and highly controllable weapon, it was ideal for the scenario they faced.

"How many do you have?"

"Just one... you worry too much, these Gypsies make

too much money from us to do anything silly. All will be fine... beat this guy and let me buy you a drink...Ok?"

"Sure... but humour me, get the driver to turn the car around, leave the engine running and have the rifle loaded and ready by his side... just to be safe."

Valentyn chuckled and shrugged, "Sure..." and then barked a few words in Russian to the driver, he took a moment to fully realise the command, but did it without question.

"Show me where we are fighting?" David said to Valentyn. Oleg let his boss and David take the lead, he moved towards the entrance of the tunnel where David surveyed the dry and dusty ground. Dry and heavily rutted, where the ground had once been muddy and driven on, he looked into the tunnel and noticed that as you went further inside the ground got softer and damper and certainly more slippery.

"Let's get this over with," David finally said.

Valentyn moved forward and stopped when he noticed the Gypsy.

"Who the fuck is this?" he bellowed.

"Oh dat... this is Ferdy. He's fighting today." Patrick chuckled.

"He's not who is meant to be here... where is the other one?"

Mike shouted back, "Well we figured you'd changed your man so we might do the same. This is Ferdy Feathers? Yerz heard of him?"

Valentyn shook his head in disgust and turned to David and looked to him to answer the question. David shrugged and shook his head.

"Should I have heard of him?" David said, to no one in particular.

Valentyn moved towards him and spoke in a hushed tone, "He's been a professional. A good one. An English champion I think. Retired... he is supposed to be the best bare-knuckle fighter in England."

David frowned. "You had someone loose to him before?"

Valentyn nodded.

David sized the man up again. "This aint no prize-fight."

"We can cancel... call it off," Valentyn said.

"No you can't. Whatever else happens today, this fight is gonna happen."

Valentyn, looked around at the field and Gypsies and he realised why David had been so cautious. "I'm sorry soldier. I had no idea about this."

"I believe you..." David said with genuine understanding. "Go check the mitts. I'll put on a show no matter what." Valentyn put his arm on David's shoulder and squeezed. He spun round and walked towards the Gypsy fighter. "I'm pissed off... the fight goes ahead. Champion or otherwise your man better fight by the rules."

"Whatever you say Valerie."

Valentyn checked over the mitts and nodded his approval, the mob of men scattered and encircled the tunnel entrance, and just a couple remained with the vehicles, David looked across but couldn't see the figure behind the lean-to anymore. Now just he and his opponent stood in the shadow of the tunnel roof, a semi-circle of men watching the twenty square feet of fighting space.

Patrick, the mulleted leader of the Gypsies, hushed the general hubbub of the crowd and then addressed them as if a major ring announcer. "Gentlemen, you know the rules... let's have a fuckin' hard and dirty fight and may the best traveller win." A small roar of approval and laughter went up from the small crowd.

David strolled to the centre ground, hands relaxed at his side and nodded to his opponent, who bounced up on his toes, hands held high. "Alright?" he said.

The Gypsy lowered his guard a moment and replied, "Fuck off yer twat and get on with der foiti'n."

"Small crowd... not many wanna see ya lose," David said, his arms still relaxed by his side.

"Yeah... sommit like that," the Gypsy said back, "don't have too many fans of your own though... just ya few Russian girlfriends."

"Nice... gay jokes from a no doubt habitual wife-beater."

"Feck off. I'm a fucking champion, what are you?" the Gypsy hollered back.

"I'm a proven and convicted Gypsy killer."

The Gypsy froze for a fraction of a second. David noted the dip in confidence and added another barb to his assault on his opponent's ego.

"Remember big man - I'm being paid to do this... 'Smack up a pikey,' they said. 'Easy money,' I said. No fucker here is gonna enjoy this. Coz people don't like watching cruelty to a dumb animal. You're just business. Live or die, you don't fucking matter to me."

David held his ground and watched as the bigger man tried to ignore the words and pump his confidence back up. The Gypsy circled him. "No matter what happens here midget man... you and your lady friends are proper fucked either way." The Gypsy said it without thinking and the moment the words came out of his mouth all of David's thoughts and fears manifested themselves into a new sense of reality. He wasn't meant to make it away from the fight. No one was. The more he looked around the more he thought that the Russian boys were as dead as he was. The fight was a distraction. Eve and Jacqui were the targets.

The Gypsy sensed the loss of focus and launched an attack, he swung a trained and fast haymaker right hand which would have hit if David hadn't skipped away to his left. David snapped a left jab to the body as he moved back into the fray, the Gypsy failed to measure the speed and absorbed the punch with his stomach.

"Come on Ferdy... get hold of him, fuck him up," came a disembodied shout from the crowd. David wanted to keep the crowd subdued and off-guard so he bounced forward, firing a quick left hand as a feint, then he ducked down and swung in two sharp hard body punches. They connected. The Gypsy bent at the impact and threw a counter left hook which partially landed on David's ear. Both men levelled themselves and Ferdy swung a crude lead punch but it found only thin-air. David had long pulled back and resumed his easy fluid circling. The Gypsy clenched his teeth and bustled forward, cautious but aggressive, first a left then a straight right. Faster than David expected but easily blocked, he went for a grab at David's neck as they closed together; David saw it coming and dipped his head and thrust forward, smacking the top of his head into the face of the advancing man. The crowd saw the butt and booed in a pantomime show of irritation.

The impact caused instant damage, the exposed teeth dug into David's crown ripping the flesh before being bent out of shape causing a flow of blood into the Gypsy's mouth. The crowd roared its approval of the cut but abated as they saw their man spit a mouthful of blood and phlegm onto the floor. The Gypsy twirled around and let fly with a barrage of hateful and angry punches. No easy exit meant David covered up, arms and hands clamped around his head. Punches rained down on him with violent force. He rocked and wobbled from side to side but nothing hit him clean. As the torrent abated David took a chance and side stepped away from the Gypsy. David got his bearings and saw the Gypsy breathe a little harder.

David struck quickly. Took one step forward and launch a Mua Thai style front kick which connected with the Gypsy's midriff, stopping him dead in his tracks. David swung in a left punch to the head, connecting with the jaw and as the hands moved to cover the head he pushed his hands over the back of the Gypsy's giant head and grabbed hold. He found leverage and launched his knee up through the arm guard. His knee found the forehead and sent the bigger man reeling backwards but not down. Surprised the big man stayed upright, David was a little slow to follow up and as he moved in throwing a right hand punch, a big overhand left counter-punch from the Gypsy reached him first. The hammer-like blow exploded onto David's temple and his eyebrow ripped open in a ribbon of blood.

David staggered and stumbled backwards. The crowd barked their approval like a pack of dogs. Their blood was up and their lust for violence was peaking. David shook his head and tried to clear the blur the blow had caused. Another big blow like that and he'd be down. Once that happened he knew it would all be over for him. He shook his head again and managed to focus a little more.

The Gypsy charged and lunged with a long straight left and right punch, David moved inside them and fired a short arm right hand to the Gypsy's chest, aiming for the heart. He landed the punch but missed with a follow up right-hook. David skipped to his left again and moved away from the bigger man who rubbed at his chest. David noted that the big man was following and not trying to cut his movement off... David circled a little more before stopping and planting his feet. The Gypsy failed to react fast enough and walked on – right into a fast left- right combination that landed flush on his face. He absorbed both punches and launched another swinging left and right. David pulled back from the first but the second caught him hard on the neck. Not a clean blow but enough to send him careering to his right again. The crowd screamed their approval once more.

David took a deep breath and tried to bring his heart

rate down. He was tired, and if that were the case for him then his opponent had to be nearly exhausted. The Gypsy's sheer size and weight meant that even half blows were having a debilitating effect on David. He needed to land three blows for every one of the Gypsy's in order to have the same effect. Fast and furious, he decided. That was all he could do.

David moved to the centre of the fighting circle. Fair play, he knew he wouldn't have to go looking for the Gypsy who trundled towards David. He faked a left-right combination. The Gypsy slowed and as his arms instinctively went to cover his head David settled and spun, launching a back-kick into the pit of the man's stomach. As his victim bent double he attempted another knee to the head. This time the Gypsy saw it coming and blocked it by grabbing David around the waist and heaving him into the air as he squeezed for all he was worth.

Pain ripped through David's torso like a knife wound. He arched his back and struggled for breath as the pressure on his ribcage increased. He acted without rational thought and brought his fist down hard on the exposed rear of the giant's neck, the first blow had little effect the second caused the Gypsy to sag at the knees. David saw his chance and flung his body weight over Ferdy's head and the two men teetered a moment before the Gypsy crashed backwards onto the tunnel floor. The force launched David clear of the Gypsy's grasp and David rolled forward and jumped to his feet. Ferdy was slower and David turned and fired three hard straight punches to head before skipping backwards away from a defensive swing.

The two men eyed each other across the fighting space, both back on their feet. Each man bleeding and in pain. David, less fatigued than his opponent who seemed on the edge of total exhaustion, shook out his arms and put his hands up once more, ready for action. Ferdy smiled across at him, rose from his slight slump, arched his back and roared into the tunnel as beat his hands on his chest. It was the endgame. David knew it. The big man couldn't take much more and he'd do something desperate to win. So he waited and watched.

"Come on Ferdy... the lil bastard is fooked," Patrick yelled from the light at the side.

Mike joined in, "Yerz a champion man, break the fecker's head open."

Ferdy ran a hand across his mouth and pushed the steady flow of blood from his nose across his face. He looked at the crowd, seeking inspiration. They cheered and ranted and the volume of noise rose once more in the tunnel. Ferdy charged.

The big man swung amateurish kicks at David and lunged with a front kick. David stepped into it, eschewing evasion for a more direct form of defence. He caught the leg with his right hand and held it firm. Teetering on one standing leg the Gypsy couldn't reach David with his wild, flailing swings. David, leg in hand, began to circle, forcing him to hop around like a shoeless fool on hot coals. As they began their second circuit the crowd began show their annoyance and boo the action.

"We came to see a fight not a fucking audition for Strictly Come Dancing," one rotund spectator shouted.

"Hit the bastard would ya" came another.

David could sense the Gypsy was close to collapse, his breathing had become erratic and a look of bewildered discomfort covered his blood-stained face. He halted the merry-go-round and raised his left hand. The Gypsy tried to rush his hands to cover the exposed knee but David proved too fast, driving his fist in from the side onto the exposed joint. The sharp agonising pain caused the big man to yelp out-loud and as soon as David dropped the leg he crumpled to the floor.

David admired the man's pain threshold and ability to take punishment as he rose to his feet, but now knew he had a non-functioning right leg and a very tired and cramping left one. The cocky athlete that started the fight had been reduced to a big man swinging inaccurate blows from a distance. It would only be a matter of time before the fight ended, David could pick and choose how.

Patrick urged his man forward and while the spirit may have been willing the body couldn't respond.

"Come on Champ get at him would ya..."

David moved forward and threw a left hand and a right hand hard into the Gypsy's face, his head thudded back each time and as he slumped backwards onto his arse the blood began trickling down from cuts above both eyes. David, back to the tunnel, stopped moving and looked out across the field. The men around the Gypsy cars weren't there anymore. He couldn't tell if they had joined the crowd or not. He flicked his eyes to the Range Rover, the Russian driver wasn't in the vehicle. David scanned the crowd and couldn't see him anywhere.

Patrick and a crowd member hauled their fighter to his feet and pushed him limping back into combat. David dodged two more powerful but wild swings, skipped behind him and landed two crisp punches on the Gypsy's kidneys that sent the fighter staggering further into the darkness of the tunnel and down into the mud once more. David turned away from him and walked back towards the crowd.

"Well Valentino," Patrick called across to Valentyn, "seems your boy is a bit too good for my fella..." Valentyn ignored the jibe at his name and smiled. "How about we make it a little fairer?"

Before Valentyn could speak or move a shotgun appeared under his chin, Oleg felt one in his back and on instinct he raised his hands. Both men could do nothing as their guns and knives were removed from under their jackets. Valentyn shot David a steely eyed look of apology, but it contained no trace of fear.

"This is very bad mistake," he said to no one in particular.

David watched helplessly as the small crowd began guffawing.

"Don't be thinking the driver with tha' big fuckin' gun is gonna ride to da rescue... that little shit is pig food already." The Gypsy leader held out his hand and a large aluminium baseball bat landed in it courtesy of a flunky. Without breaking stride he marched over to the big Russian and swung the bat with full force into his midriff, doubling him over and catapulting him backwards several feet and leaving him convulsing on the floor in agony.

David made no move forward, his turn would come for sure, he had to hold his ground and wait. Maybe they only wanted the Russians. Either way trying to run now was pointless. He had to stay calm and wait for an opportunity. Instead he looked at Patrick who had near hysterical laughter at watching the big Russian fall to the floor.

"Oh that felt good Valerie... it really did, shall I stand you back up so that I can do it again... I tink I will." He motioned to the crowd and several moved forward and hoisted the big Russian back to his feet. "Not the big fucking I AM now are yerz? Don't worry handsome," he shouted at David, "we won't take long with this... just some fun like." The crowd held Valentyn's arms out wide and Patrick swung a right-handed punch into his midriff. Two others joined in and reigned punches onto the exposed body before fatigue got the better of them and Valentyn's limp bodyweight became too much for the others to hold upright.

"Nice gun..." Patrick held up the Russian's pistol. "Fully loaded. Expected some kind of trouble then did ya big fella? Well I'll bet you weren't expecting this now were ya?" Patrick spat down on the fallen man and one of his followers followed suit laughing as they did so.

"This is howz ya put the shits up someone, traveller style. Ya don't fuck about with 'messages' ya get the bastard thing done. Seems yerz people don't think ya can get the job done any more... need some traveller bollocks to finish ya shit for you." The venom and aggression poured out of him making the veins in his neck throb. "Ya fucking com to our home and play lord and fecking master... think yerz somekind of fucking superman." Patrick slammed a kick at the prostrate Russian. "Well they aint here to help yer are they... don't have much love for you do dey?"

David edged closer so he could clearly hear what was being said, hoping to reach a narrow gap in the enclave of Gypsies.

"Fuck us around with ringer fucking fighters... costing me money, disrespect me... we had a deal. My boy woulda creamed the fat fuck you had lined up first and we'd have a nice mega fight at the horse fayre. Twat!" he bellowed.

Nudged by one of the mob, Patrick looked up at the advancing David he poked the bat at him and yelled, "Stay the fuck still you... deadliest man in the west you might be but I'll cut your balls off and feed them to that whore lawyer of yerz."

David halted, the mention of Eve suddenly making him immobile and a wave of nausea and fear engulfed him. "Yeah I know all about you and her... lover boy, playing house together... got a real family business going on there. Well that silly slag has put too many noses out of joint." Patrick turned and included the near prostrate Valentyn into the diatribe, "Couldn't deal with her could ya... well we have and unless I am very much mistaken in the next hour she should be feeling the full proper fucking force of a travelling man."

David launched himself at Patrick, rage, vengeance and death written all over his face. David focused on one thing only, getting his hands on Patrick; but he never reached him. Without warning, pain erupted all over his body; his legs went into spasm and his body shook violently. He landed on the floor and rolled over to locate the source of his agony. His attacker held a long black rod about three feet long. David recognised the beaten fighter immediately and then, as the rod made contact with his leg once more, he realised he had felt the full force of a cattle prod.

"Oooh hoooo, that bit of news really pissed him off boys... look at him. Sweet fuck it hurts that though don't it. Ferdy, get him in the fucking balls will ya!" And with that Patrick did a little dance and let out another belly laugh. "Maybe that Russian fella will let me have a go on yerz sister.. ya know seeing as I'm missing out on the fit lawyer."

David screamed a guttural noise of hatred but lost sight of the Gypsy leader as the cattle prod landed again. The pain shot through him as though molten glass had been injected into his blood. He curled into a tight ball and tried to block out the pain. No matter how much it hurt he knew he had to stay conscious, stay alive and get to Eve's house quickly.

"Enough with the fun lads... bring that Russian prick over here." The as yet unhurt Oleg, gun to the back of the head, was marched into the tunnel. The Volvo from the entrance had backed towards them with its boot open. Oleg stared into the back of the beaten up old Volvo estate and saw the back seats had been lowered and the boot was clad in black plastic. He swore in Russian and shut his eyes. The bullet passed through his brain and as he slumped to the floor a strong boot in the back ensured he tumbled head first into the boot. Two of the travellers hoisted his feet up and folded them into the car.

David struggled to break free, but the fighter dropped a knee onto his head and applied all his weight pinning him to the floor. "Do we do this one next?" he shouted across to Patrick.

"Na... keep him there, let's finish this sack o'shite and we a can all have some fun with that prick... make a new video. Hard ass? My arse." Patrick motioned to the five men gathered round Valentyn and they hoisted the big fella up onto his feet, a small almost pathetic moan coming from him as he hit upright. Patrick raised and swung the bat again, but this time Valentyn reacted, he launched his giant arms upwards from his moribund stance and with immense inhuman power shrugged off the over-confident, half-hearted lifters and using both hands he caught the bat in mid-flight. He wrenched it from Patrick's grasp, dropping to one knee as he did so. Several flailing arms swept punches over his head and then he twirled the bat quickly above his head with maximum force. He connected, once, twice and a third time with arms, chins and hands, scattering the crowd around him. He lurched to his feet with a roar and took a more determined aim. The madness and rage that erupted had an unnerving effect and the bullies in the crowd began to scatter. Valentyn picked out one aggressor, a fat man in a blue anorak and shoved the bat at the man, not a swing but an aggressive lunge that saw the rounded bat-end punch into the man's stomach, doubling him over and levelling him. Valentyn pirouetted and swung a big right hand at one more Gypsy who had come on the attack, connecting with his jaw, the sickening crunch of broken bone accompanying the sound of him collapsing to the floor.

All eyes looked towards the rampaging Russian. David

took his chance, he put his hands under the knee of his assailant and with all his strength he pushed and twisted up. The fighter had no idea it was coming, his attention still fixed on the Russian. David shunted him up into the air and grabbed at the cattle prod, twisting and wrenching it from his grasp as he fell backwards. David sprang to his feet with the agility of a gymnast and slammed the Cattle prod into the Gypsy fighters face, he leant into it, using his body weight to push the cattle prod pins into the man. Trapping him against the floor as the massive burst of current pulsed through his head.

David spun to face the other attackers near the car, but they hadn't seen him their eyes focused on the Russian who now had hold of another of the Gypsy mob and appeared to be trying to strangle the life out of him. The field had descended into chaos and had been filled with fleeing men, all attempting to get back into their vehicles and out of the secret entrance. The guard from the entrance of the tunnel ran to join Patrick who had been levelled by Valentyn's first arching swing. He picked up the dropped pistol and aimed it at the Russians back. David scanned and assessed the distance and merits of what he had decided to do. He took one step forward and then javelin style he launched the cattle prod at the kneeling would be shooter. It struck, electrode first on the side of the temple, a residual shock and the force of the prod knocked him to his left the gun firing harmlessly into the ground.

The shot screamed out through the tunnel with a deafening roar and echoed painfully around the concrete lined tunnel. Everyone froze in shock at the sound of the shot, some men then patted themselves to be sure they hadn't been hit, others dived for the floor and thrust their hands over their heads. The former soldiers reacted fastest. David began to run for the tunnel but two Gypsies had begun gathering shotguns from the old Volvo. He did a fast one-eighty turn and sprinted back towards the field as Patrick got unsteadily to his feet, pistol in hand. David charged, he didn't break stride and levelled the man with a full force rugby tackle, his shoulder hitting the exposed right hand part of the rib cage and Patrick flew through the air with the gun dropping from his grasp. David ensured his full body weight landed on him slamming his elbow into the man's cheek for good measure.

Valentyn, consumed by rage charged for the Range Rover. His half limping run got him to the car just in time to see two of the fleeing Gypsies that had garnered some courage level their shotguns at him. Diving for cover in the foot well the shotgun blasts peppered the car shattering the windscreen. From his prone position Valentyn still managed to start the engine and it roared into life. Half sitting at the wheel he careered the vehicle into the field. David scooped up the dropped pistol and utilised the distraction to dive into a forward roll up onto the embankment on the left, crawling into the bushes and shrubbery for cover; he dropped onto his belly and waited.

"We gotta to act now." Zenovia's voice had the hushed urgency that came with people who were scared but exhilarated. She listened to the response on the other end of the phone and shut her eyes willing for the patience to deal with the call.. She paced around her bedroom with the same air of impatient petulance she had developed at thirteen when she didn't get what she wanted.

"It's too late for that now... you agreed to this. It's happened a little quicker than expected but if we don't take advantage of it then we aint never gonna get another chance." Her voice came out with more control than she felt and regardless of whether she wanted to be part of the changing events now in motion, she knew she had to ride the wave of change until its conclusion.

"It's felt good to be taken seriously, to show how we can manage... I'm going to do this and if you wanna be part of it then you have to commit. Can you do that?" The reply, while swift lacked conviction and Zenovia felt the need to express herself with more clarity, "Valentyn is outa the way. His main soldiers are being dealt with, the lawyer bitch is dead... and the librarian is under lock and key...we can control him now. We hold the power to the organisation, the future is the people trafficking. Money talks and we control the serious money."

Silence greeted her last outburst. Zenovia waited, she needed her sister to stay strong and stick to the plan. A short garbled reply finally brought about a smile on Zenovia's face. "Don't worry about Yuri... he finks he's smart, finks because we fuck and I let him do those fings to me that he's in charge. He'll do anything for me... or at least he'll do anything for me if he thinks he'll reach the top of the family."

Masha's reply made Zenovia smile. "At last... you're thinking straight. Yeah if we can use him once more then kill him too, it would make life a lot simpler."

The Range Rover charged forward at the two men in the field as they tried to re-load. David saw Valentyn sitting at the wheel, his face marked with the scars of flying glass, tug hard at the steering wheel, the car skidded sideways towards the men sending them scurrying in opposite directions. Valentyn steered the car for the only exit he knew, as he rounded on the tunnel entrance he floored it. David heard the gun shots, two loud blasts and then the sickening sound of moving metal hitting a solid surface and then colliding with more metal. Finally all he heard was the whine of an engine running and a vehicle going nowhere.

David waited a beat or two and looked around the field. He saw five men down, either dead or unconscious. Two others were in the tunnel, he had no idea if they were alive or dead. Two more Gypsies climbed to their feet in the field and went over to the semi-conscious Patrick. One vehicle, the old Toyota Hilux, had already left, with who knows who in it and David could see two more Gypsies running towards the lean-to stable. David calculated these had to be the last men standing. He had made a decision, not a hard decisions to make, just unpleasant to implement. These men would have killed him, that much he knew for certain, and they had friends that were off to hurt Jacqui and Eve. They had vehicles; he needed to move fast and he doubted he could thumb a lift on the M25 that ran above him.

In a film David would pick off the two men with his pistol and be left alone with Patrick, he'd deliver some strong vengeful line and then end the conversation with a clean kill, an expert shot to the head or maybe the gut to leave the man to die an agonising and painful death from his wounds. David didn't have the time, he rose to one knee and took aim. The first bullet hit the fatter Gypsy through the neck, spraying blood over the shocked remaining hairy one. The second bullet hit him below the heart but it entered through the ribcage, hitting a lot of bone and soft tissue and with less than twenty yards to travel it made a horrid bowling ball size mess on exit. The third bullet fired hit the slow rising Patrick in the groin, entering the body somewhere between scrotum and bellybutton, it had a tougher time working its way through the pelvis and spine, but to its credit the Russian pistol lived up to its trademark 'one-shot-stop' reputation.

David waited to ensure the screams had the familiar ring of those of a dying man, then he bolted from his cover towards the remaining white van the Gypsies had left behind. He snatched a look inside the open rear door and confirmed he didn't have any unwanted passengers. He slammed the doors shut and ran to the driver's side, lucky to find the keys still in the ignition, he gunned the engine and careered the old charabanc around the lean-to and followed the levelled grass tracks out of the field.

Zenovia came striding into the Dacha's kitchen and looked around, she found Yuri sitting on the stool outside the walk-in freezer. She looked him up and down and could see he had the glazed expression of the shocked and scared; his eyes focused on nothing in particular and somehow he seemed distant. Her eyes rolled in exasperation, she needed him focused and together if the plans she had made could succeed.

"Yuri..." she called.

He didn't reply or even lift his head.

"Yuri, wha' happened at the fight, did the Gypsies do as expected?"

He turned and looked at her, "They are horrible people," he muttered. Zenovia sighed and hoped he hadn't had an attack of conscience. She waited to see if he'd say anymore and when he didn't she spoke with a little more authority.

"Is Valentyn taken care of, his fighter too? Are they outta the way? Can we move forward?"

"Much more..." he said.

"Much more... what ya talking about?" she said more than a little perplexed by his attitude and behaviour.

"They are dead... they set them up and ambushed them. They are dead."

Zenovia tried to stifle a smile. "You sure?"

"Yes... I left once they had killed Oleg and the driver. Valentyn had been beaten to death with a baseball bat." Yuri stifled a retch and shook his head at the memory. Masha contemplated the grisly demise, but without the lurid memories, brushed it off. Valentyn being killed by the Gypsies would alter things, they should have simply taken him hostage, that had been her plan. She could then have negotiated his release and shown her father how much the business needed her and how incompetent

Valentyn had been. Instead she would have to move quickly to make this new occurrence work in her favour.

"How'd this happen?"

"I promised them double money if they dealt with Valentyn at the fight, the same way as they dealt with the lawyer woman..." he muttered.

"Why'd you do that!" a degree of genuine shock on her face.

"I er... thought it best to get the Gypsies to do it... no one trusts the Gypsies right? We say they double-crossed Valentyn. There is no way Uncle will carry on working with them... he'll destroy them and with no Valentyn on hand he'll turn to us to take over. Right?"

Zenovia looked at him and wondered if he could actually be that stupid. Her father would of course crush the Gypsies but he'd torture any and all to find out why they had double-crossed and killed his favourite General. What's more he'd send for mercenaries from the old country to come and deal with it. There would be a massacre and she would be even further from power.

"Oh Yuri... stop f'inking for ya'self!" If being around her father had taught her one useful thing, it was that nothing is so bad that it can't be seen as an opportunity.

Yuri looked at her and said, "What can we do?"

"My father won't turn to us, not for this... he'll get Russians to help, he'll look to the old country to solve this. We won't be expected to handle a war. If Valentyn stayed alive then we'd control it, but his death is war..." She left the reasoning to sink in.

"What can we do?" he asked again. "Your father won't surrender power!" he said.

"No he won't but without Valentyn we can take power... by force," she said.

"You mean you would kill your father?" he said, shocked and peering at her to see if she had been joking.

"Why not? It's all that remains between me and complete control."

Yuri couldn't quite believe his ears, the logic made sense but the calm and calculating way she said it put him on edge.

"You'd kill your own father"

"Me? No Yuri... I can't be seen to be part of this, no I need to be seen to hav' an alibi... the old country needs to know there was no internal struggle. I will be with my sister. Nah the only person who can do this is you."

"Me? Kill Uncle? I couldn't..." he stammered and almost fell off his stool.

She clasped her hands around his cheeks, "F'ink Yuri... you can get close, ya trusted. Also everyone assumes you are at the fight... you hav' an alibi."

He shook his head vigorously.

"But f'ink... we can blame the Gypsies. They killed Valentyn and the others at the fight, they tried to kill you too – you escaped. Clever boy"

Yuri nodded and joined in, "Then they killed Uncle... they will get all the blame and we get the business."

She smiled at him. "It's the only way we can get the money!" She whispered the final words, her voice sowing the seeds of sedition in the weak mind of a greedy man.

The old van had never seen a service or any real love, but she worked. With no map and no real idea of where he needed to go in order to get back to Windsor, David reverted to his mental map. As soon as he found a tarmac road he would need to turn right. He had the M25 behind him and the M4 to his right, he should be fine. Sweat poured off his brow and his knuckles had turned white with anger as he gripped the steering wheel. The gash above his eye had already congealed and begun to dry out. He ignored the pain and his grubby state and gritted his teeth, swerving the van around a shabby looking stable, scattering a mangy Shetland pony and unimpressed donkey. Finally he saw a tarmac road, the gate hung open from the last fleeing Gypsies

High hedges prevented him from getting a view but as the road swung away to the right he saw the tops of lorries on the M25 away on his right. Being parallel to the great London orbital motorway gave him a sense of where he was. Lakes sprawled to his left and now approaching fast before him he saw the familiar gleam of aluminium clad industrial units. He punched on the brakes and skidded to a halt. Most of the units appeared derelict or abandoned, a sign of the times. A smattering of work vans and rep type saloons sat outside some of the larger units, the estate looked like a forgotten corner of commerce.

David took in low deep breaths and slowed his heart rate, he focused his mind, centred himself and in a matter of moments he felt his arms relax and his body become a little less tense. Calm again he opened his eyes and looked for a road sign, a fast route out, and he glimpsed a large grey oblong perched about five hundred yards away. He nudged the accelerator and the van limped towards it. The oblong sign showed a layout plan of the Court Park Industrial Estate, complete with an amateurish graffiti tag. The exit lay straight ahead with the signs for Iver and Slough underneath. He sped up slightly, needing to remain in control if he planned to be of help to Eve and Jacqui. Patrick had boasted they had them both and they were going to kill them. He had no idea where Jacqui or was or meant to be. He had no idea if Eve had made it home.

He fought the urge to power the van forward as tears began to form in his eyes and his lips quivered. He knew crying wouldn't help anyone, that he needed to control his emotions and fall back on his training, but something made it impossible for him to stop. It had taken him seventeen years to truly find Eve, to find himself. If something had happened to her now, if he hadn't protected her, he'd never be able to forget or recover from that.

David caught a glimpse of himself in the mirror. He looked a sight. Blood and mud mingled over his head and face and he had the damp sweaty hue of man just returned from physical exercise. He'd need to attend to his appearance to avoid suspicion. He guided the old van into the village of Colnbrook, keen to avoid the major roads and lots of traffic lights. The road wound its way through the village of Wraysbury and he opened the van up, pushing it to over seventy between the villages, overtaking cyclists and the odd car with convincing white van man enthusiasm; to drive any slower would draw unwanted attention and be unrealistic. He gunned the van over the double mini-roundabout in the centre of Datchet, giving any half-hearted drivers no time to get in his way and made it across the level-crossing in time to see the barriers drop and a train roar past.

David exhaled at the near miss and pushed on towards the junction, eager to get past the dithering driver of a clapped out Citroen Visa ahead. He pressed hard on the horn as the old woman in the car let another gargantuan gap pass by without pulling out. It had no effect. After what seemed an eternity the little car finally trundled out and swept the opposite way to which it had been indicating. David swore out of the window and floored the accelerator, slewing the cumbersome van across the road as it trundled toward Windsor.

He had one option – head to Eve's house. She was due to meet him there and it would be the only place she didn't have protection during the day. He hoped he was right and that he could get there in time.

As the van passed through Windsor David kept his wits about him, he eased it round the one-way system and then up St. Leonard's road and pulled the van off into the church car park a few hundred yards from Eve's house. He breathed deeply, his arrival would be unseen, he had no idea who or what he'd find at the house, and he just hoped he'd got there in time. Mind focused, he jumped out of the van and set off with long confident half-run strides down the suburban street.

David had been able to think in the van; to rationalise the events and try and work out what had been going on.

Valentyn had been double crossed, no doubt in his mind. He had been certain that the dark-haired guy in the field was the same man from the gym. If he had been there without Valentyn knowing then someone in the Russian's organisation had decided to clean house. That included Jacqui and Eve. When David realised all this his heart began pumping faster and the fear gripped his stomach like a vice. Jacqui and Eve meant nothing to them, they were a threat, a hindrance that needed removing. Peter however, had value and some defined use and had a degree of safety as a result. These people had set him up to die, it didn't take a huge leap of the imagination to work out what they planned for the two women.

Eve's front door stood ajar. How long had it been like that he wondered, no neighbour checking, no one caring. Her car sat out front and no one walked by, not a soul stirred and David remembered it was a weekday, only the affluent and working lived in streets like this, tall Edwardian villas and three storey Victorian town houses loomed over the narrow street, what cars remained were executive and large. He doubted anyone was home for ten houses either side of Eve's. He had the benefit of surprise, no trap would be set for him, and they would assume he was dead; murdered as planned.

He could afford to be bold, he needed to be quick. He ran across the street between the parked cars, up the four steps and through into the hallway. He landed with a soft grace and dropped to one knee. Then he listened. Silence replied. He cast an eye around and saw footprints, boot prints had caked the hall carpet in dry mud, some led to the empty kitchen, the majority lead up the stairs. His eyes followed them, he saw the upturned table on the landing and a small pot plant crashed on the carpet, the remnants of its roots trodden into the carpet.

He shut his eyes and banished away the imaginations of his mind's eye and leapt three stairs at a time to the landing. The pot plant detritus led along the landing, the picture on the left wall hung wonky and the rug had been kicked up. David saw the blood, a smear no more than an inch long and a finger wide shone out from the magnolia painted walls near the entrance to Eve's bedroom. Muddy finger prints clung to the door frame. A splash of blood on the carpet in the entrance to the room.

David knew what he would find.

Hope surged through him, maybe he would be wrong.

Maybe no one would be inside the room.

David placed his feet with deliberate care, as if hoping to avoid waking anyone sleeping inside, he kept his hands off surfaces and edged into the room.

Eve lay on the bed.

Her beautiful hair a tumbled matted mess over her face. Her arms lay twisted above her head as if compelled to by some invisible force.

The elegant summer business suit ripped and stretched. Torn and battered but still clinging to her limp frame.

The blood lay in a deep crimson pool around her waist and groin. One shoe clung defiantly to her foot.

The knife jutted out from her like a barbaric flagpole. No life, no sound came from her.

David dropped to his knees and sobbed. Violent

uncontrolled gulps of emotion poured out of him, his chest heaved and shoulders bounced as he tried to contain the pain and anguish. David curled into a ball on his knees on the floor and buried his head into his arms. Shutting out the world, hiding his face from the grim reality of his life.

It took him another few minutes to stop convulsing. He tried to focus and centre himself. He needed to think and needed to work out what to do next. He rose to his feet and looked at the scene on the bed one more time, no matter how revolting and despicable he never wanted to forget it. For the first time he saw the daubing on the head board. Finger painted writing scrawled the message he had heard at the fight. *'proper fukked'*. David drank it in like fuel, a black mask of hatred and violence descended over his face, his eyes turned ice cold and his jaw tightened.

The Cossack Dacha didn't do lunch. A strictly evening only venue, it suited the atmosphere of the place; a dark almost seedy space that longed for a more elegant but equally immodest age. Yuri delighted in the fact that for most of his working day he could mooch around the big dining room without the worry of clientele. Being at the beck and call of the old man used to be an active and full time job. Endless meetings and showing respect to the London families ensured Yuri learnt his trade and stayed at the heart of the business. Did the old man respect him? He doubted it. He hadn't seen him genuinely respect or value anyone other than Valentyn. Yuri had never been certain that a lot of that was't borne from fear as much as appreciation.

No, the old man valued people for their contribution but only if their use could be measured in £'s and not emotional value. He clung to the values of the Russian clans and kept his daughters close, but offered them no hope for the longer term, Yuri had no idea what the family would be once the old man died. The Russians knew it made a healthy profit and a series of distant cousins could be easily rounded up in the motherland to be parachuted in to run the business when the old man croaked. Yuri knew blood would always be considered more valuable than loyalty, without the sisters he'd never rise to the top. He had figured he'd taken a bold move in telling Zenovia that he'd set up Valentyn and taken Jacqui Edwards hostage. That she had then told her sister shocked him. He had assumed they hated each other, but when the opportunity came they again proved blood mattered more than loyalty. If you want to write your future, then you need to make hard decisions and be prepared to act on them. Yuri had nowhere to turn, his fate rested in the hands of two fat girls and a horde of Gypsies.

The knife had a long serrated blade, maybe thirty centimetres long. It had been sharpened to a point beyond the necessary and Yuri had it fastened to the inside of his sports coat, easily pulled away but hidden enough from a casual glance. He pushed into the dining room and looked for the old man; his heart jumped a little when the space at the usual booth sat empty. He spun his head round and surveyed the room. Wladimir stood in the middle of the dance floor staring up at the glass dome above his head. He would have heard the door swing but still he didn't move, staring intently at the glass above.

Yuri edged closer, put a hand into his jacket and closed

it on the handle of the knife. Sweat formed on his brow and he took a deep breath as he stepped onto the polished maple floor.

"Has Boris come in yet?" the old man asked, without looking at Yuri.

"No." he answered, confident that the head waiter wouldn't be coming in for at least another hour.

"This dome is filthy..." he jutted his thumb up towards the light. "The bulb still hasn't been changed either. Did you not tell them to get it sorted out?"

Yuri took a deep breath and stepped a little closer. "I did Uncle."

"Then why for the love of god is it still shit? Yuri, deal with these things more quickly. I don't want to mention them more than once." He pushed his hand at Yuri with a dismissive waft of contempt. "This place is going to the shits," he muttered, turning his back fully on the younger man, still failing to look at him.

Yuri tightened his grip on the handle and pulled the giant blade from its hiding place and stalked another yard closer. His heart thumped and he worried that if maybe the old man could hear it. His brow had the familiar sheen of the terrified on it and with each step he took his legs became heavier. Yuri had seen plenty of pain and death being inflicted, he had even partaken occasionally, but he had never killed. He had fired guns at people and seen them fall, but he had never been a soldier, never a cold blooded killer. Now with the old man at his mercy he faltered, he had to summon up the will; a quick stab would end the old man's reign and usher in a new dawn and his daughters would take power and would need Yuri to run the business. The knife came out of his jacket and the light briefly caught on the sharp metal blade. Another step closer. The old man's head jerked up and cocked his ear to listen. The sound of a door banging and pots clanging drifted into the room from the kitchen. Yuri ignored it, the old man didn't.

"Who the fuck is making so much noise." The old man looked at his watch, "Chef is never early... maybe one of those damn idiot porters." As he chuckled, Wladimir turned to share the joke with his aide and right-hand man.

Yuri froze, the old man's face had a smile on it, then his eyes found the knife and Yuri watched the reactions play across his old features in a matter of a second. He assessed his comrade's stance and the weapon and without hesitation he bellowed..."ASSASSIN"

With the word barely complete and the sound ringing in his ears Yuri lunged forward. His technique unskilled and the aim poor, the knife moved forward as the old man tried to evade. Age dulls all reactions and while still fit the old man couldn't move fast enough, he waved his hands at the knife but couldn't move his hips and body away. Yuri over reached and finally the knife made contact and as he did so he pushed forward hoping to make it a one stab attack. When he opened his eyes to survey the damage he didn't see what he had expected or hoped to. But he heard the scream, a guttural howl of pain and fear resounded around the room. Yuri's giant knife had punched clean through the old man's left palm, the blade rammed through to the handle. Yuri tried to pull it back out, but the serrated blade snagged on the myriad of bones.

Another scream and a spray of blood erupted into the room. Yuri tugged again but only succeeded in tearing into the hand further and hauling the agonised Wladimir closer to him. Clutching his left wrist with his right hand the old man collapsed to his knees, eyes fixed on the blade and blood coursing down his arm.

Yuri twisted the blade put his foot on the old man's chest and heaved again. This time the flesh yielded to the metal and the blade tore through the hand severing the last two fingers as it came free. He staggered back with the effort and had to steady himself once more. The old man collapsed to the floor, he had lost all form of vocal control and had simply begun to omit an animal roar, as much with anger as pain. Yuri raised the knife and shut his left eye, taking aim, he marked his desired point of entry on the exposed throat with the blade descending he pulled up. A new and different human roar joined that of the mutilated Wladimir. A sound so violent that Yuri spun his head to see what had made it.

A human made the noise, a giant human with a close cropped haircut and a hideous open wound running from his hairline to chin and across his left eye. Yuri backed away. Valentyn moved with a laboured shuffle. His right leg was rigid at the knee and as he emerged into the light the full extent of his injuries became apparent. Valentyn's shirt had been died red with his and other's blood. Glass fragments were embedded in his forearms and now caught in the multiple restaurant lights in a macabre glitterball effect.

He dragged his right leg like a weight behind him and the fingers on his left hand protruded and jutted in a grotesque broken finger puppet show. But Yuri saw the violence, anger and hate in his face and he heard the words he yelled as he came towards him, to defend his master and to kill him. *"DIE, DIE, DIE."*

Yuri lost what little nerve he had and flung the knife in a wild panicked arc. Thrown with no skill, the unbalanced hardware twisted and swirled in the air and slapped hard into the chest of the charging Valentyn. Valentyn reacted as any human would, he flailed his arms up to his face to deflect the knife, he misjudged his path to Yuri and tumbled to the floor as the knife hit him. The strength then seemed to desert him and Valentyn collapsed into a bloody scarred heap, the giant knife lying ineffective at his side. Yuri's self-preservation instincts told him to flee. Fighting and killing both men, even a wounded and exhausted Valentyn, hadn't been what he signed up for.

He ran.

David lifted his head from his hands. He refused to look at the bed again. He moved out of the room, careful not to put his hands on anything, and went downstairs. One concern dominated all others now, that of his sister Jacqui. He moved from room to room, she clearly hadn't slept in her bed, hadn't been home when the attackers came. The relief at not finding her body in the house, meant nothing and that she could still be in danger if not already dead.

David didn't want to linger in the house, he wiped as many surfaces as he remembered touching, his fingerprints would still be on record and he didn't need to have to explain his role in all of this. As he wiped around the kettle his eyes strayed to Eve's cork notice board. It had the bills and post-its you'd expect and one or two photos of Eve and her friends. One amateurish print showed Jacqui and a man, his mind raced to recall who it was and what Eve had said. The picture was one of those self-taken smart-phone efforts, grainy and blurred with Jacqui's arm in the bottom corner. The man in the picture had his hand over part of his face but Jacqui wore a beam of a smile. It was a good photo of her, capturing her spirit, he understood why she'd liked it. Eve had said the man was Jacqui's Latin lothario, the man who had put a smile on her face. David looked at the face, half hidden, obscured and the realisation dawned on him. He knew the man, had seen him twice before. It was the man from the gym, the man from behind the stables at the fight. He had been the man Jacqui saw last night.

David held the mobile phone in his hand. He still hated the things, but conceded they had their uses. He had just called 999 reporting two crimes. First he outlined the 'gang' murders at the tunnel and then the assassination of Eve Du Pisanie. He used those exact words, he needed the police to come with a clear idea of the situation fully formed, and their natural assumption would be that all of it would be gang related. That's the nature of the police, they only investigate what doesn't already add up. The call could easily be traced back to the phone and he intended to make sure it would be found by the police at the next major crime scene he planned to create.

David had no idea where to find the Russians but he

knew exactly who to go to get the information needed.

Fucking Hell Mel stood in front of the door of the old industrial unit and David couldn't be sure if the dumb look of terror on his face stemmed from the chance David might hit him again or that Mel thought he shouldn't have been alive. David didn't care what Mel thought he strode forward and the big man stumbled aside without a murmur.

Four minutes later David strode back out carrying an orange plastic bag. FHM looked from the bag to the door and then back to David. He moved towards the door but the stare from David halted him.

"Listen up fat boy. You're hopefully smarter than you look. I don't exist, right? You aint seen me, not now, not ever. When the arsehole in there wakes up I suggest you both shut up shop and get out of Dodge for a while." Mel offered no reaction, "Mel, nod if you understand?" He did. "Good boy. No one else will come collecting on that fight today." The relief on Mel's face seemed total when he heard the news. "Is that Declan's Jag parked on the corner?"

Mel nodded.

"He said I could borrow it." Mel rooted in his pockets and pulled out a set of car keys, he tossed them over and mumbled something, David tried to understand and when Mel repeated the garbled statement through gritted teeth he got it.

"Yeah I beat the Gypsy...I beat them all."

Blood Ties

Blood seemed to cover everything. It had stopped pumping with the force it had done but it still oozed and gathered in pools on the floor around Wladimir. The polished maple floor had been coated, smeared with a thick dark red viscose coating that had been spread around like an overturned can of red paint.

The old man sat holding his now wrapped hand. The once pristine white napkins, stained and heavy with blood, had stemmed the flow and he now focused on staying conscious. He had turned a deathly shade of white and his lips appeared grey. Shock had taken the bite away from the pain but with each passing moment he appeared a little closer to death. Valentyn had summoned the last of his great strength and hauled his master to a sitting position. He pulled napkins and table clothes from the dining tables and wrapped the old man's wounds as best he could. Then he sank to a reclining position next to him. His great body finally obeying the laws of nature; the pain hitting him and exhaustion felling him at last. Yuri's knife no longer littered the floor, Valentyn scooped it up and hid it beneath him.

Masha and Zenovia arrived together. They trundled through the kitchen doors into the vast dining area and screamed in unison. Hands coming to their mouth in shock, repulsed, at the sight of the blood. The stood motionless as if afraid of blood and tentative about moving towards and aiding the fallen men for fear of contamination. Neither woman offered any real comfort or assistance. Valentyn turned to face them in the slow deliberate manner of a man in pain.

"A doctor. Where is the doctor for your father…"

Valentyn demanded. "Find a bandage or something better to stem the blood."

The sisters seemed caught in a trance, they huddled out of earshot and talked at rapid speed. They wore frantic expressions and gestured with a wild frenzy. Their conversation could have lasted until both men had passed out or died, but Valentyn had other ideas.

"Women for god's sake stopping nattering. Your father is dying."

The two of them stepped out of the shadows and circled onto the floor. The big man had lost a lot of blood, his body had been abused, assaulted and maimed but his energy, his inherent sense of duty refused to die.

"How long for the Doctor?" he blustered.

"He's coming... he was on the golf course," Masha said quickly.

"Too long. Call the ambulance. Just tell them he had an accident in the kitchen!"

Wladimir shook his head with a feeble wobble and in a hoarse whisper he mouthed, "No."

Masha nodded her agreement. "No. We have to keep this quiet. There is too much at stake. No officials until we know what has happened."

"Fine," Valentyn snorted, "but get Uncle something sweet... a Coke, something like that, he needs it for the shock."

"Sure..." Zenovia said, but neither woman moved. "Wha' happened?"

Valentyn let out a growl of agony and spat on the floor in disgust.

"That traitor Yuri. he must have set me up with the Gypsies and when he thought I was dead he came back here and tried to kill your father."

The old man stirred and looked at his daughters, "Bastard" he muttered. The two women looked at each other and cast a knowing glance then a nod of approval to each other.

"After I spoke wiv' the Gypsies last week Papa, Yuri stayed on a bit... he said he had to discuss some Poker business wiv' em?" Zenovia said it with a slight simper in her voice.

Masha then chimed in as well, "He's been very difficult for a while Father, not taking orders and causing trouble for Valentyn."

"Bastard," the old man managed to mumble again. Valentyn looked at his leader and saw a man slowly fading away, his head swung back to the less than concerned daughters.

"Yuri's always been arsehole, nothing new this week."

"He was good friends with the Gypsies, made loadsa money from his gambling and poker... he was pissed that you upset 'em over the fights." Zenovia said it without the simper, reserving that for when addressing her father.

"HA! So because of that he double crosses all of us. Never! He doesn't have the balls." Valentyn did his best to stare down Zenovia, attempting to warn her with his eyes that he would tell her father of her inappropriate behaviour if he had too.

"Yuri's hated you for a long time Valentyn... you showed zero respect, not ever," she bit back.

"Respect is for those that deserve it. Yuri offers no respect. He only wanted the big prize, never prepared for the hard work needed to get it."

"What happened with the Gypsies Valentyn? They are supposed to be our partners?" Masha moved into the conversation deflecting attention away from her sister. Her father turned his sweat covered head and looked at his daughters.

"You never trust Gypsies... you use them, they can be good for some jobs but never trust them. They serve themselves. Always." His speech had the laboured breathless quality of a man close to unconsciousness.

"Maybe Papa but we have worked with them for over a year... no problems. They make a lot of money from us. Valentyn - well be honest, you made no secret of your desire to get rid of them. Cut them out. Everyone knows it." She avoided Valentyn's gaze and focused on her father. "What happened at the fight?" she said. Valentyn looked from one sister to another, they stood closer together than he had seen before, the usual hostility and spite didn't crackle between them.

"I took the soldier to the fight, they set the rules, the place... it was an ambush."

"You didn't spot the ambush?" she asked, an accusatory tone in her voice.

Valentyn shook his head and thought back to how

nervous the soldier had been, the questions he asked and realised he had been over confident.

"As you said... these people were our partners, why should I suspect them of doing something like this?"

"Like what. Tell us..."

"Twenty men, lots of guns... while the fight was going on they killed our driver, attacked the soldier with electric rods... they executed Oleg." Valentyn's voice dropped at the admission.

"You are our General Valentyn... you protect the family, what if our Father had been taken to the fight? Masha made no attempt to hide her accusatory tone.

"You walked int'a a trap. Fuckin' hell when do the Gypsies only take a few blokes to a fight? It's always hundreds, a big event." Zenovia added with a hint of disdain.

"Two men died in France hunting the Lawyer's investigator, the Lawyer woman keeps appearing on TV and in the papers... you say it's under control. But is it?" Masha continued.

"Doctor..." the words came with a pitiful moan and Wladimir sagged a little further and looked closer to death.

"He's coming papa," Masha said, with the first hint of compassion since they had entered the dining room. "Valentyn we have been concerned about your running of the business for some time, you took too much on, too much responsibility and didn't share the burden with us." Masha indicated her and her sister, "We could have helped; maybe focused better on things."

Valentyn coughed, part in derision. He pulled himself onto one knee, the pain evident on his face and the effort to rise to his feet clear in the strain and tensing of his muscles, but he made it upright and teetered a little once at full height. The sisters didn't move, not a step backward, no sense of giving ground.

"I see what this is... the beloved daughters seek power, the family wants a coup. Goodbye to the Tsar hail his Princesses," he sneered.

"Say what you will Valentyn but you have failed and Papa knows it." Masha looked him in the eye. "You kept the Librarian secret from all of us, we know you have him under lock and key making the new shipment process work. We know you sent his brother out to fight the Gypsies. So you saved your fight and reputation but you were wrong about the Gypsies, they hated you. You got lazy you didn't bother to investigate did you?"

"What are you talking about?"

"Your new pet soldier," Zenovia joined in, "your secret weapon. Turns out he's the Librarian's bruvver. Shocked? Well I bet you never knew that they had a sister too." She said it with a smile, a smile that came with knowledge of seeing the images from Jacqui's phone and Yuri's insider information. Valentyn joined the dots in his head and said nothing.

"Jacqui Evards, she's the boss of the investigating firm, the one that works closely with the Lawyer. You don't know her by her real name - Edwards. Yuri told you he had her under surveillance right? Well she has two brothers. The soldier is one and the Librarian, Peter

Edwards is the other."

Wladimir stirred at what he had heard, through a dry mouth he whispered, "Is this true Valentyn?" The big man nodded and fully understood what a fool he had been.

"How did you fail to notice the connections?" Masha asked.

Valentyn remained silent.

Zenovia wanted to rub it in and ram home their advantage. "Ya failed to keep control of Yuri and ya refused to use his 'street intelligence' – too arrogant!"

Valentyn looked at her with an expression of frustrated contempt. Nothing he could say now would make a difference nor explain his personal failings.

"How did you fail to find out more about the Librarian's family connections? We own our people. That's how we do business." Masha drove the point home, tag teaming with her sister and enjoying it a little too much.

"And then ya allowed a trained killer to come into our organisation wiv-out checking on him." Zenovia sounded more triumphant than her sister.

Masha turned to her sister to deliver the summing up, "so Yuri has double-crossed us, he wanted to seize power by using the Gypsies as his muscle. They kill you and the soldier, Yuri then kills our father... maybe us. Either way the plan is for the Gypsies to get the blame. Yuri runs the family and controls the trafficking and has the brother and sister locked up. A neat plan." Masha added a sense of inevitable resignation to her voice, she appeared more measured and mature than ever before.

"He failed though didn't he? I protected your father." Valentyn found his voice when the notion he'd failed as soldier was mentioned.

"Valentyn... get real. It aint enough, not with all them mistakes. D'ya realise how close you came to messing up the whole trafficking deal?" Zenovia said.

He nodded. "The Gypsies said they would deal with the Lawyer, did they?" he said.

"Probably."

Valentyn stayed quiet but turned to his only salvation. Wladimir had his eyes on his favourite soldier and a sad look came over his face. He gently shook his head. "You always protected me... have always been there. But you can't be General anymore. You understand."

Valentyn did. Honour and respect. He had shown much of the former but little of the latter and he had made mistakes. He had never wanted to deal with the lawyer woman, believing she would simply disappear in her own time. And the Librarian, he never bothered to check on such a sad and lonely man, never realised he actually had a life. Valentyn had controlled his gambling and ensured he lost and owed money making him dependent on the Russians for his livelihood. He would need to fall on his sword. Stand down. He was out of the business and would leave in disgrace.

"My daughters... you will run the business from now on. They are in charge," the old man added. "Find Yuri..."

Masha bustled forward towards her father and kissed him on the forehead and stroked his ashen face before mopping his brow a little. "Zenny... please see about the Doctor" she shouted at her sister, who didn't hesitate and left the room at a run.

"When you escaped the Gypsies... did you kill all of them?" she asked Valentyn.

"Some." He said.

"So there are some still alive?"

"There are millions of Gypsies..." he said wearily.

"The ones at the fight... are they all dead?"

"The ones that matter. I think so, yes"

"You killed them all?"

"No"

"So who killed the others?"

Valentyn chuckled, "The soldier."

"He was good. As good as you thought, how many did he kill before they got him?"

Valentyn let out a smile, "They didn't get him. He didn't die."

David parked the Jag up on the curb on double yellow lines, maybe a hundred yards from the alley that led to the rear entrance of the Cossack Dacha. A place he knew little about, he'd never eaten there, in fact he knew no one that had eaten there and the place had been a town enigma ever since he could remember. How had it stayed open and survived people had asked? Now he knew.

He wiped a rag from the Jag's boot over all the inside surfaces that he may have touched. He did the same to the outside doors. He had checked his face and general appearance in the house. The blood had come off easily enough and his shirt hid the scorch marks from the cattle prod. All in black, his hair at least styled, if not smart he looked presentable. He placed the hand gun he'd taken from the Gypsies and put it inside a small cardboard box he found in the back seat. With that tucked under his arm he moved away from the van and toward the alleyway. As he suspected, at the end of the alleyway amid a cluster of commercial kitchen detritus, a man stood smoking a cigarette near a back door.

He looked up at David and didn't acknowledge him until David had almost reached him.

"Delivery," David said. The man nodded and pushed away from the door, he turned without looking at the package and unlocked the door, David waited until the door had been pulled open, then he moved. He stamped his foot down hard on to the back of the man's knee, the snapping sound precipitated the man's lurch forward and tumble to the floor. David didn't admire his work he merely extended the same leg into a side kick that connected with the back of the falling man's head. His neck had broken before he hit the floor, landing neatly inside the open door. David stepped in and pulled the body into the corridor and closed the door behind him.

The gun sat tucked into his waistband, out of sight; David walked with a confident pace down the corridor, he rounded a corner and passed an empty office, plain and without adornment. David had a plan, of sorts, he needed to find the location of his sister, that was priority one, setting her free. Then he would seek revenge. He hadn't thought about the moral implications of his actions; that would come later. He had enough demons a few more wouldn't hurt him. Self-defence had been justified long ago and though vengeance created a whole new inner emotional conflict David had enough ammunition to deal with it.

The kitchen had no one in it, but he could hear voices coming from beyond some double doors, he assumed it was the entrance to the dining room. He moved towards them and took the chance to look through the glass porthole at the top of the door. Two women and two men, he recognised Valentyn immediately. "Tough bastard," he said to himself. He'd been proud of his own escape but would have bet his house on the giant Russian dying in that tunnel. He listened hard but couldn't make out specific words. He looked for another route out of the kitchen, only one door marked 'Balcony' suggested it might work. He skipped over to it and nudged it open, it led to an enclosed wide spiral staircase, he looked up and saw nothing, so eased his way around the bottom steps, gun at the ready.

He stayed low, exiting the staircase by opening the door as little as possible. The balcony was nothing more than a narrow gallery looking down onto the main dining area of the restaurant. Several tables for two butted up close to the handrail but it looked as if the space had rarely been used in recent times. David edged to the rail, crouched low and scrambled round the balcony so that he could see the faces of the people below. He saw the brutalised old man and the two strange looking women talking to him; his mind buzzed at the recognition of the short fat one, she had been in the gym, part of the ruling class of the organisation.

The familiar figure of Valentyn, exhausted, bruised and bleeding sat on the floor beside the old man; the big man looked defeated. The gun loaded and ready felt heavy but familiar in his hand, he closed his eyes and thought for a moment. Take Valentyn down first but what if he is the only one who knows where Jacqui is... Peter too? He needed to listen, then he heard something interesting. Yuri had gone missing, he too would have to be found.

Masha looked Valentyn up and down, yes this big man could be stupid and complacent but he had proved his toughness time and again. Today had been no different, he had been forced into a scenario that no normal man could survive or even consider beating and yet he had. She and her sister had underestimated him and overestimated Yuri's capabilities. Now there had been a man that seemed to be his equal, the soldier, the fighter that had taken Valentyn down with ease in the gym had escaped the Gypsies as well. This man knew they held his brother and it would take no time for him to realise that his sister had been taken prisoner too. Masha knew such men and he would be coming for them and he would come hard.

"I don't believe it." Valentyn's voice snapped Masha out of her thoughts.

"What?"

"Yuri... he would not have thought up this on his own, he isn't brave enough." Valentyn looked at the old man and then back to Masha, "Why are you so friendly with your sister all of a sudden?"

"You forget your place Valentyn. I run this family now. The business is mine."

"Sure... what do I know."

"Where is the Librarian? At the warehouse?"

"Yes, he's locked away in the office upstairs, the one without windows. I planned to let him go today. I promised the soldier," said Valentyn.

"Hmmm, his job is done, the new system works, the back log is clear?"

"Yeah. He can do the job remotely again, as planned. He can be useful in the real world."

"His brother... what do we do about him?"

"Nothing. He'll come for us, just wait and see."

Masha said nothing.

"I haven't seen someone like him, at least not here in England," Valentyn said.

"Are you scared of him Valentyn?" The mocking tone Valentyn might have expected didn't materialise in her tone of voice. Masha had a real concern that her soldiers might not be able to handle David.

"Scared? No. Concerned? Of course. Where is his sister... he will be more easily manipulated by what happens to her."

"Yuri moved her here this morning, she is in the cellar. Why?"

"Having her here is an invitation for the soldier... you should keep him away from here, never let the enemy behind the gates. Make contact with him as soon as possible. Negotiate on your terms," he said.

"Thank you we can handle him," Masha said.

"No you can't."

Masha stared at him looking for some kind of comfort. "What will you do now Valentyn?"

"I don't know. There is nothing for me here now."

He looked down at the old man, his head had lolled to the left and he had lost consciousness and seemed to be losing his fight. "He won't survive this... you and your sister have killed him," he said with a tired sigh, no real emotion, just a weary sense that the inevitable would happen.

"You can't stay in Windsor, in the South even... you know that."

"I know." Valentyn looked set to say more but stopped when Zenovia bustled in.

"The doctor will be here in a few minutes. He said we must keep the hand raised and a tourniquet at the forearm must be very tight." Valentyn waited for one of the women to do it, they didn't. So he bent down and applied the doctor's advice.

"Zenny... we should move the woman, What's her name?"

"JACQUI!!!"

The shout came from above and echoed around the

room. The women's heads twisted and they spun their bodies around seeking out the source of the sound, they stared up at the dome as if the voice had been from god itself. Valentyn checked for his gun, he had none, just the giant knife. Zenovia pulled a small semi-automatic pistol from her trouser pocket with the confidence of a rank amateur and pointed it widely towards the gallery as she did so. Masha opened her mouth to yell at her to stop being silly but gunshots drowned out her cry.

The first shot hit the gun itself, sending it spiralling in the air and forcing Zenovia to jump in alarm. The second shot followed in no more than a second and the bullet ripped through her left thigh, a small neat entry and then an explosion of blood, flesh and bone as the bullet's exit wound created a melon-sized hole in the back of her leg. The leg jarred backwards as if attached to a rope pulled with phenomenal force. Zenovia collapsed in agony, her screams violent but silent. Masha stood in shock, a fixed stare of disbelief on her face. Valentyn lay across the limp body of the old man and covered his head, waiting for the inevitable shot that would rip through his side. He heard the next shot and he knew that if hadn't felt it then it wasn't aimed at him. He dared to look up, Masha's body had already begun its arm flailing fight to the floor, a bloody mess engulfing the left shoulder of her white shirt. She hit the floor with a sickening thump her head bouncing back down on the hard floor, no screams, no sound at all. As the shot echoed and the vibrating sound lessened Valentyn looked up and saw the shooter. David Danjou skipped over the gallery railing and lowered himself down the supporting pillar with the ease of a gymnast. His feet hit the floor and the gun was ready to fire before Valentyn could attack.

David surveyed the carnage, happy with his shot selection and accuracy. His old Sergeant would be proud, three shots, three hits and imminent threat neutralised. He kept his gun trained on Valentyn. The big Russian had scrambled to his feet and stood in front of the old man's body, a defiant shield.

"Good shooting," Valentyn offered.

"Thanks," David said, looking at the sisters. Both lay unconscious, Zenovia would be dead in minutes, her femoral artery ruptured and the wound pumping yet more blood onto the maple dance floor. He stepped carefully, keen to avoid any more evidence getting on to his clothes and scooped up Zenovia's gun.

"Why didn't shoot me you?" Valentyn asked with surprise.

"Deal with the imminent threat first."

Valentyn shrugged his shoulders in confusion.

"Take out the gun first... then the fat one, she's a relative and the new boss."

"You have been listening?"

David nodded and pointed to the gallery, "I heard enough."

Valentyn nodded, "So you don't see me as a threat?"

David laughed, "Any man that can come out of the shit at the tunnel is a man to be respected." He offered laconic salute and Valentyn nodded his appreciation.

"You and I have some history, we also share a common enemy." He cast his eye on the women. "They set you up as much this prick Yuri..."

"Maybe so."

"Is the old guy dying?" David asked.

"He'll be dead in a few minutes for sure... they never called a doctor. They wanted him dead, their own father. There is no honour anymore." The two men shared a moment of common experience and said nothing.

"No guards here either... just one man on the back door. He had no protection," David said. Valentyn nodded, the sisters had planned it well.

"I need to find my sister and get my brother. I can't be killing Russians and Gypsies all day... I can get my sister from the cellar no problem, but where is my brother, Peter? What's this warehouse?"

Valentyn smiled, "Why should I tell you?"

"It's over big man. No one can hide this much death and mayhem. The whole racket, the trafficking, the whores, the gangs – it's done. You're done. Let me take my family out of this. I did everything you asked, so has Peter."

"Respect. Family and Honour. All that men like you and I have is our word." Valentyn muttered. "The warehouse is on the Dedworth Road. Fairacres Estate. Unit 7."

"Guards, people?"

"Lots... it's why no one is here! I can call, tell them to

let him go. I can do it now. I promised you he could go." David looked at Valentyn and went for it, he needed to avoid fighting more men and would prefer his brother to be gone by the time police arrived. He tossed him the very phone Valentyn had given him. He made the call and barked orders in Russian. "It's done."

"Now, this Yuri?"

Valentyn sneered. "Yuri Sminsky. He lives in Slough. No 44 Queen's Road. Please kill him for me."

"After I kill him for me, I will. He must have been part of Eve's death. He was at the fight and had to be working with them."

"Eve... oh the lawyer woman. You two were together?"

"Sort of. It's complicated... but I loved her."

Valentyn said nothing. He stared at the soldier looking for the malice which now drove his revenge. He saw only sadness and emptiness that Valentyn knew too well.

"Can I ask you a question?" Valentyn said.

"Be quick."

Where did you live before you came back here?"

"France, Saint-Innocence."

"Saint-Innocence... really?"

David stared down at the Russian as the cogs of his brain turned once more. No one is innocent and no one escapes. "You sent the men to kill the investigator didn't you?"

Valentyn nodded. "I did. We thought he was in France

investigating our French operation." Valentyn knew as well as David what this meant. He was the man in charge of dealing with Eve. The man responsible.

"It was you. You killed her." He said nothing more. Valentyn gave a resigned nod.

David raised Zenovia's gun and fired.

Jacqui held the teacup in that familiar cradled grasp of the shocked. It tasted good and she enjoyed sipping the hot liquid. The summer sun shone high above and her ordeal appeared to be over. David had been more than attentive and she really had to sit him down and tell him with real zeal that she hadn't been hurt or molested in any fashion.

David had relented and once they had found their way back to their mother's house in Datchet he had flopped in to the armchair and cried. She left him alone, ushering her mother's concerns away, realising he needed the space and time alone. The Edwards clan hadn't as a rule been good at public displays of emotions and seeing her powerful and heroic brother, his arms clasped around his chest, weeping like a child had disturbed her. The news about Eve had a numbing effect on her too, she knew Eve would have been in trouble once she had been taken and she wished she had listened to David's warnings. She could never shake the belief that this kind of thing only happened on TV and that they were safe, the real world of police and law would protect them in the end.

She sipped more of the tea and felt the sun's warming rays. The patio door slid open with an un-lubricated squeak and David came out. He had changed from one set of black clothes into a new clean set and held a plastic shopping bag with what looked like his discarded ones in his hand. He strolled towards her, chin up and all traces of his crying gone.

"I need to burn these," he said, holding up the bag.

"Mum has a bonfire thingy at the bottom of the garden... she's down there now. You can burn it with the garden rubbish."

He nodded.

"Getting rid of the evidence?" She asked.

"Yeah, seems prudent. I'm not sure what they have of me on file anymore."

David had done what he could at Eve's house and had followed a similar line in the Cossack Dacha. You can't confuse the forensics, but you can alter how they look at the scene. "I tried to cover my tracks at the Russian place," he said. Jacqui nodded, realising that he needed the understanding of forensics to confirm he'd done ok.

"Run the scenario for me," she said.

He gave her the overview of the shooting and then finished it with, "Once Valentyn had been dispatched I used his gun and put a bullet into the old man's chest and another into the fat one, Masha."

"Wanting that to look like the murder weapon?"

He nodded, "Then I put the tall girl's gun back into her

hand and fired a shot towards the ceiling and then the back wall."

"Making sure she had gun residue on her hand."

"Yeah. I did the same with Valentyn, I put my gun in his hand for the ceiling shot."

"If they look hard at it all then they'll find the angles are wrong I'm sure. But with the tunnel and Eve... they'll have enough to link a story together."

"I used Valentyn's hand to dial 999 on the mobile, effected my best Russian accent. I put it on the floor by the big Russian's feet too. It kinda adds up."

Jacqui nodded and tried to comprehend how she would deal with the mess and investigation that would surely follow. Carrying Eve's work on had been something she had decided already.

"We need to talk about Eve..." She faltered, not sure if she wanted to.

David paused. He blinked hard as if recalling images in his mind and then dropped his eyes to the floor and breathed in deeply. "Sometime. Soon... but not now. Ok."

Jacqui studied his face, the blank expression that stared back had a ghost like quality to it. She imagined a veneer that merely rested over a tumult and angst and barely understood emotion. She knew she should leave him alone, not push any further, but she wanted to know.

"Did you love her? I always knew she loved you, the old David at least."

The face didn't move, the voice little more than a

whisper. Almost pleading but refusing to crack. "Not now hey Jacs."

Jacqui went to speak but stopped herself. The powerful man before her was on the edge of an emotional void and despite it being her brother she realised that she didn't know him. Had no frame of reference for how he'd react or what he needed. She reached a hand out to rest it on his shoulder, to offer some comfort in contact but before she reached he spoke.

"Did you call Peter?"

"Yeah. He's out too, they let him go and he's destroying his hard drives as we speak".

The question had broken awkward moment of silence and pushed them into a matter of facts. Jacqui felt relieved and carried it on. "I can't believe how deep he was in. I mean he was the brain behind the whole benefits scam... he had designed the computer programmes that milked the benefits system. Clever stuff really."

"He has a gambling habit and a lifestyle envy thing. Don't beat him up for that just yet. Hate him for being spineless and letting you and Eve walk headlong into a shitstorm. But not for being a weak character. That's just being human."

"What now?"

"The police will talk to you... remind them you reported the Russian threats and the death of your investigator. Once they sort out the mess at the tunnel and the restaurant they'll figure some kind of gang war between Russians and Gypsies took place and Eve was caught in the crossfire."

"They'll look into it more than that..."

"Maybe but it all ties together ... sort of... it makes a kinda sense. You were threatened and they did nothing. You told the world this trafficking was happening and they did nothing. The PR storm alone will freak them out."

"You don't have a lot of faith in the police do you?"

"Do you? I don't have an overpowering faith that they want to do the right thing and that getting the right man, every time, is a priority. Too many examples stitch ups and insider deals for me."

Jacqui didn't try to fight the logic, David had too much history and too much of an axe to grind with authority in the UK for it to be worthwhile.

"You were never kidnapped, never involved. No one really knows about me. I never came home for my father's funeral. There is no record of David Edwards entering the country. You know nothing of my whereabouts or my new identity."

"You leaving today?"

"I think so. I have one more visit to make and then I'm gone."

"For good?"

"Who knows... but we can write, I can call, we'll see each other Jacs. It's not like before."

"We can Tweet and Skype..." She saw the blank look on his face, "I'll explain another time. You're going after Yuri aren't you?"

"Well I'll check his house out, but he's done a runner that much seems certain. He's the only one that ties all of us to the situation. "

"I'd be happier with him out of the way that's for sure. I think I'll stay here with mum for a while as well..." Jacqui said.

"Do you want me to take you back to your place pick a few things up?"

"Please...I'm coming with you to Yuri's as well. No arguments. I need to know he's gone or... dealt with...OK?

David nodded, realising she needed to see this through to its end as much as he did. She had lost Eve too.

"He's definitely been to the house." Jacqui said it as she and David climbed the final steps to her top floor flat, she never used the lift. Given his bashed and abused state David wished she had, just this once.

"How can you be sure, we only looked in the windows?" He asked as she pushed open her front door.

"It's where he kept me, I recognised the place. They didn't blindfold me til we got to the front door. The dresser in the hall, its drawers were left open, stuff scattered across the kitchen worktops. The guy was meticulous about appearance and neatness, his house was pristine when I was in it. He's done a quick pack and bolted."

"Once a policewoman always a policewoman hey?"

"Stands to reason, grab a passport, some money and run. He knows either the Russians, the Gypsies or the police will be all over the place within a few hours anyway."

The pair of them made their way into the open-plan lounge diner of Jacqui's flat. David eyed the comfy looking sofa and slumped into it and shut his eyes. "Any idea where he would have gone sis?"

Jacqui moved towards the kitchen, "None. He wasn't who I thought he was, but judging by what you said he has..." It took a moment for David to register the silence and break mid-sentence. He opened his eyes and looked towards the kitchen door.

"Jacqui? Jacs... you ok?"

A voice came from the kitchen, edgy, shrill and laced with fear.

"No soldier boy she isn't ok."

David made an effort to rise but was cut short.

"Stay the fuck on the sofa." the voice barked. A noise of shoes scraping across a tiled floor came from the kitchen and then eventually two figures emerged into the lounge. Jacqui had one arm pulled behind her back and a kitchen carving knife at her throat. Yuri held the knife tightly, his knuckles glowing white, held her close to him and edged to the door.

"Stay sitting. I'm not stupid enough to fight you."

"Yeah you are," David said.

"I'm outta here, not looking back, half the Gypsies of

southern England and any Russian within five hundred miles will want me dead. I'll just add you to the list."

"So why haven't you run yet?"

Yuri shifted his weight and the knife blade pressed into the flesh, Jacqui winced as it made a mark. "I need cash... my savings aren't quite enough."

"Money you want us to give you money?"

"Not her... just you. Declan proved more chatty than Mel. I know you cleaned him out. You must have over a hundred grand soldier boy. I want it," he snarled

"Un-fucking-believable. Even now it's about money with you." David spat the words.

"Shut up or li'l sis gets a new fucking mouth ten inches wide across her throat." The knife blade made skin on Jacqui's throat turn white under the pressure. "Where is it?"

"It's in a bag, a black holdall in her car. Down in the car park."

"Go get it and bring it here."

"No. Not happening. Not now, not ever."

Jacqui winced again and simpered and then pleaded, "David please.".

"Jacqui think of your training, think how you were told to handle this..."

Jacqui's face showed anger first and then a slow realisation as she understood and a little fire sparked in her eyes. Yuri looked at David and tightened his grip on the knife, then he barked, "I'm not messing about. I'll cut her... get the money."

"You won't cut her. If you do you'll have to deal with me... and that means death fella. You prepared to trade your life for hers?"

"Fuck off you won't let her be hurt." Spittle fell from his mouth as he talked.

"I lost my dad and the love of my life this week... I'll handle it. Let's just wait until you get tired. Then we'll see what happens." David rose to his feet and stood six feet in front of the pair of them.

"You're fucking crazy. Stay back!"

David went onto the balls of his feet and flexed at the knee and nodded at his sister. Jacqui didn't hesitate, she raised her foot and stamped it down, scraping along Yuri's shin and landing hard on his foot with extreme force.

Yuri yelped and as he did so Jacqui flung her right elbow back into Yuri's gut as hard as she could. As he recoiled from the impact his hand and the knife came away from her throat. Jacqui ducked down to one knee and as she did so David's powerful right foot shot above her, the

kick missed her by centimetres and connected with Yuri's chest, the impact sudden and powerful. Yuri flew backwards and hit the wall, the knife tumbling to the floor as he did so. Yuri's limp body rebounded off the wall and David smashed his fist into his temple sending the body lurching sideways in an unconscious heap.

Jacqui rose and hugged her brother and they squeezed each other as hard as they could. She kissed his cheek and started to cry. David held onto her as she sobbed and took her full weight in his arms as she lost control. As her sobs subsided she still clung on hard, and when the tears dried up she still didn't want to let go.

Epilogue

Yuri Sminsky regained consciousness. He had been sat upright, his arms gaffer taped behind him, his legs bound with the same stuff at his knees and ankles. He'd been left naked, a white A4 sheet of paper stapled to his chest. It read:

"This is the man who double-crossed you at the motorway massacre. Compliments of the winner."

When his vision cleared and he could focus he saw some caravans and a scrubby lane. In front of him a large crowd had gathered. Women, children and men stared stony-faced back at him. A round pug-nosed face, with just five teeth left in the mouth spoke, "Oh hello young fella, glad yuse is back wit us... you and me and few'o us big fellas back there is gonna have a little chat. Ya get me?"

The Eurostar heading for France, for home? David considered the concept of home and knew it didn't register in his life. Paris would be a start-point, but he considered his options. He hadn't been to Spain for several years, he liked the food and the people didn't intrude. Maybe he'd head out to the Atlantic coast, away from the Brit tourists but still by the sea. He had money now and he should let it work for him.

He thought about Valentyn and the years both of them had wasted serving ungrateful masters, his mind drifted onto his brother and the confirmation of what he always knew, no, blood isn't always thicker than water. Jacqui, she loved him unconditionally and always would. He'd come running if ever she needed him and she'd do the same for him.

He tried not to think about Eve. He wanted to avoid the thoughts that dwelled on what might have been, what he had missed and the life that could have been. He wanted to stay awake and never sleep again because with it came the faces and ghosts of his life. At first he had tried to fight them, embrace the menace they represented confident he could handle anything his subconscious could throw at him. He was wrong. The demons rose each night to taunt him into making amends, to pay his penance. He knew there could be no escape, it was hopeless, and he would have to live with them for the rest of his days.

With each sleep the demons arrived and with each sleep he understood that he had to look into the very face of hell. Forever, a penitent man.

The End

Acknowledgments

This book once again owes its successful completion thanks to the support, time, advice and input of others. Too many to mention them all by name. Special editorial thanks go to Liz and Jon and Rob for candid suggestions, feedback and reading endless manuscripts. Huge thanks to Ed for the cover design and support.

To Kay and family for the love and encouragement to keep on going and getting it done.

Thank you all.

Printed in Great Britain
by Amazon.co.uk, Ltd.,
Marston Gate.